ENGLISH MUSIC

Lond: print: for M.ris Dor.t Euans. Cum priuilegio. Are to be sould by G
Cowe print in Sowtheb

ENGLISH MUSIC

Peter Ackroyd

Alfred A. Knopf
New York
1992

cp. 1

Illustration Acknowledgements

Frontispiece, 158, 384: British Library; 26: © The Frick Collection,
New York; 72, 248: Mary Evans Picture Library; 200: detail of
Still Life with a Volume of Wither's Emblems by Edward Collier, Tate
Gallery, London; 302: British Museum; 348: Wiltshire Archaeological
and Natural History Society.

Manufactured in the United States of America

FIRST AMERICAN TRADE EDITION

Acknowledgements

The first inspiration for this novel came from the Victorian medium, Daniel Home, and the short account of his son in *Incidents of My Life*. Any other relation to people living or dead, real or imaginary, is entirely coincidental.

The scholarly reader will soon realize that I have appropriated passages from Thomas Browne, Thomas Malory, William Hogarth, Thomas Morley, Lewis Carroll, Samuel Johnson, Daniel Defoe and many other English writers; the alert reader will understand why I have done so.

'... he who can interpret what has been seen is a greater prophet than he who has simply seen it.'

St Augustine, *De Genesi ad Litteram*

'Invention, strictly speaking, is little more than a new combination of those images which have been previously gathered and deposited in the memory: nothing can come of nothing.'

Joshua Reynolds, Discourse II

ENGLISH MUSIC

ONE

Y ES. I HAVE RETURNED to the past. I have made that
journey. 'You can't go back,' you said when I told you
of my intention. 'Those days are long gone.' But, as I explained at the time, that is not necessarily true. One day is
changed into another, yet nothing is lost.

So the old hall was there when I went back. The site of my
earliest years, the site of the Chemical Theatre, remained just
as it was and, when I looked up at the outline of its dark slate
roof against that autumn sky in 1992, I did not know whether
I was an old man still or whether I had become a child again.
Of course the surface of things had changed: seventy years
before, the City Road was a blackened thoroughfare of small
shops and factories. I remember how the old hall itself had
stood beside the Bee-Hive Boot Works and a shop which sold
fancy goods like calico and trimming: now there was a car-
rental showroom and a Superdrug chain-store, although I
believe that I could make out the shape of the forgotten
buildings. On the other side of the hall there had been a
dairy, and the family who owned it kept a cow in the back-
yard; they also sold soap and candles which, it was rumoured,
were melted down from its predecessor. On that same spot,
when I went back, there was a Spar supermarket. Yet something remained the same. How can I put it? The situation of
the buildings, the disposition of everything, was familiar to
me. When I went back . . . how far should that be?

The hall had been constructed in 1892: I knew this because
the numbers had been scratched into the brickwork just below
the roof and, whenever I glanced towards them, the date
itself used to fill me with foreboding. I never understood why,
although now I do. It was a typical London building of the
late Victorian period, but on a scale appropriate to the narrow

streets and small houses that had spread across this area of Hackney near the City Road. Close by was Bunhill Fields, the final home of William Blake and John Bunyan, and the hall itself was supposed to have been built on the site of a Dissenters' chapel which had been destroyed during the East End riots of 1887. Some of the older people remembered that time, when an attack upon the new Anglo-Catholic churches in the area had turned into a general assault upon all religious establishments. The chapel was eventually rebuilt as a community hall run by the Board of Guardians, but by the time of my childhood, in the Twenties, it had become a hall of miscellaneous purposes. It had become a meeting place. And the placard outside read, simply, CLEMENT HARCOMBE. MEDIUM AND HEALER. He was my father.

'Welcome to the Chemical Theatre. Where all the spirits of your past come in dumb show before you.' So my father always began, in those days, but I did not recall his words until many years later. He repeated them just before he died, and I wrote them down soon after in order to express the true nature of the man. It may seem strange that an entire personality can be sealed within a few words, but it is so. For him they had all the resonance of a notable, even a dangerous, past against which he still measured himself; but at the time they meant nothing to me and, in those moments before his death when he spoke them again, I turned my head away. Had I done so many years before? Had I turned my head away when, as a child, I stood beside him on the stage of the Chemical Theatre?

I still remember the odour of the hall itself – or, rather, I am taken back to the period of my infancy whenever I once again smell dust, or paint, or the not unwelcome scent of human decay. My father held my hand tightly after we had stepped on to the wooden stage, in the glare of the gaslights, as if I were about to fall or run away; he used to press me closely against his side, grip my shoulder, or, most frequently, place his hand upon my head. When we stood together there, it must have seemed that I had literally grown out of him, sprung forth from the palm of his outstretched hand. He released me only when he crossed the stage and sat in front of a small upright piano: he always played at the beginning of each performance. No, it was not a performance. Not then. It was, in truth, a ceremony. A ritual.

My father prided himself on being an artist, and that in more than one sense, but he was not an expert player of music. He knew several hymns, and now whenever I hear 'Jerusalem' the swelling voices take me back to that time when the frail notes of the old piano echoed around the hall; I can feel once again the dark brick of the building tainting the space around me, and I experience the sense of physical oppression which invaded me before each evening's meeting. My father played too slowly, as if he were not really convinced that the notes followed one another, but there were times when he had the strength or the confidence to improvise: he would reach a sudden crescendo, or devise a sequence of notes which exhibited a richer pattern and which seemed to spring from some buried memory of music he may once have heard. But he was not a good pianist. While he played I walked over and stood beside him; I can still recall putting my fingers across the small holes left in the side of the piano by the wood-worm burrowing their way out towards the air. As soon as he had finished, he stood up, put his hand upon my head once more, and led me towards the centre of the stage: this was a practice from which we rarely, if ever, deviated. He had a thin gold ring upon the second finger of his right hand, and it used to press down upon my scalp as we stood there together. After a few moments he recited the familiar words: 'Welcome to the Chemical Theatre. Where all the spirits of your past come in dumb show before you.'

I could never estimate the size of the audience: it was a small hall, and only held some seventy or eighty, but there always seemed too many bodies crowded together, too many expectant faces. The people sat upon low benches, the wood worn and shiny with over-use; many of them examined their hands with apparent curiosity or looked down at the cracked green tiles beneath the seats. They rarely looked at my father, but more especially, as I sensed, they would not look at me. It was as if they pitied me. They were arranged in rows in front of the stage, although it was not a real theatrical stage but a rectangular platform raised about two feet from the ground. There were a few small square windows down each side of the hall, and three rows of gas-lamps illuminated the interior. In the winter months the hall was brilliantly lit and all I could see of the outside world were patches of blackness, but in the summer the hall remained unilluminated as a gradual grey twilight filtered through the windows during the course of the meeting; perhaps it was the twilight which I most feared. Now, in my memory, this period of my life seems to recede for ever, because I know of nothing that happened before it – only the slow passage of the seasons that encircled my life as my father and I stood together in silence upon the stage.

He still held me, but he passed his other hand across his face. He said nothing for a while and, as a result, created one of his more powerful effects – the playing of music and then the silence, in that transition creating a tension which only he could break. I see now that it was his way of acquiring power over them. Could it be possible that the music would never start again? Could this silence last for ever? 'There is someone here,' he would suddenly begin. 'Someone has come here. Who needs guidance.' My father always spoke in a deep voice, with a strong emphasis upon each phrase; perhaps he played the piano before each performance in order to internalize its music, because his own voice was ordinarily light and unemphatic. I do not know. 'Yes. Someone has come to us tonight.' At this point he would hold on to me more tightly than before, almost bearing me down into the ground, and then usually with quavering finger he would point out one among those before us. It did not seem curious to me at the time, but often I found that I had been looking at the person whom he then singled out. There were even times when I felt compelled to point in precisely the same direction, but my father always managed to anticipate me.

Yet what was it that had arrested my attention? What had I seen when, with my father's hand upon my head, I looked out at the men and women sitting on the wooden benches in front of me? There were occasions when they were made up only of outlines, of serpentine lines, that were so sharply distinguished from the light that the people seemed to be bound by thin wires which trembled in the confined air. Then it seemed that all their colour and movement were being forcibly held within these lines – as if they were the painted models of a cardboard theatre suddenly suffused with life. But there were occasions when I saw something else. I saw phantoms. My recollection of these things is now so distant and so dispossessed that it might be the memory of some other person and yet, even as I write this, I watch the scene again; each man and woman had an outline still, but it was larger than the material body and consisted of a silver contour which seemed to vibrate before me. Yet this was the strangest thing: these phantoms issued from the human body, but in almost every case they were bent over towards the ground as if they were sighing. On occasions one would lean backwards, towards the being from which it had come, and it was then I saw that it was about twelve or thirteen inches taller than its material habitation. There was a world of energy lingering upon the earth, and I believe that this was what my father saw when he touched me. I cannot recall being alarmed, or even particularly surprised, by my vision; no doubt a child of eleven or twelve can accept all manner of strangeness before ordinary existence closes around him.

Sometimes my father held me up towards the people, as high as he could reach, until I was parallel with the row of gaslights above the stage; if I turned to look down at his face through the glare, I could see his eyes tightly closed and the sweat breaking out upon his forehead. Sometimes, too, he would step down from the platform, holding me in his arms, and carry me across to the person at whom he had just pointed. Yes, I am being borne upwards, my hands around a stranger's neck. I can see light all around me even as I inhale the scent of stale face-powder and feel the pressure of my father's gold ring in my back. I had my arms around the neck of an old woman, and then I said 'Daniel'.

Daniel. It was the name of her only child, dead many years before in the Boer War. My father put me down and carefully led the old woman on to the platform; I took her hand also, for in uttering the name of her son I had laid claim upon her. I stayed beside her while my father disengaged himself for a moment, in order to turn down all the lights except those immediately above the platform. It was the winter of the year, as I remember, and the rest of the hall was quite dark. Now I stood behind her, my father in front: he had placed his hands upon her, but all the time he was observing me. Daniel. He took her shoulders and, in the deep emphatic voice which was so much a part of the ritual, he began to talk to her. 'Daniel,' he said. 'No need to worry. No need to worry.' I was staring at the row of gas-jets above her head; the flames were swaying slightly, no doubt caught in one of the draughts which circulated within the hall. 'Daniel knows about the pain in your side. Your left side. It will pass.' I turned my head and glanced out into the darkness around me: for a moment I thought I could see the phantoms, bending forward and staring down upon the ground. It was seeing, and not seeing. 'Happy now. Very happy. Daniel says it is nothing. Go away soon.' The old woman was shaking as I held her, and I knew that she was crying.

'Daniel,' the old woman said, as she raised her head towards my father. 'My dear.'

'He is happy. He remembers Blackie. Is that right? Blackie. Playing with her when she was a kitten. Is that it? World without end. Happy now. As you will be.'

And that was all. My father removed his hands from her shoulders and took two steps backwards. Now it was time to play my part. I took her arm, as I had been trained to do, and stood silently until my father had turned up the other lights; the phantoms had gone and while everyone blinked, or coughed, or shifted on the benches, I led the woman back to her own seat, where she remained, weeping, with her head bowed. My father was walking nervously around the platform, waiting for me to return to him.

In this period his powers were at their height and, as a result, the hall was often full. In London there have always been groups of people fascinated by the kind of work upon which my father was engaged, and it was not long before his reputation created a modest following. There were also others who came out of curiosity and so it was, on this winter evening, he stood before seventy or eighty of them: young men and women who had entered the hall separately and sat quietly at the back, middle-aged couples who chatted before the meeting began, old people who generally sat at the front and watched everything with eager eyes. Yet among these there were some less easy to define; they carried themselves with an air of both defiance and anxiety, as if they no more belonged in this place than anywhere else. How old did I say I was at this time? Was it eleven or twelve? And yet even then I believe I knew that these were people who had somehow failed in life – and there were times, yes, even then, when I realized with horror that I might one day occupy the same small space upon the margin.

In those days almost everyone was drably, if punctiliously, dressed – the women in shapeless hats with long coats buttoned up to the neck, the men in bowlers and double-breasted overcoats, with three-piece suits, starched collars and narrow ties. My father and I always wore the same clothes, too. I had a peaked cap, stiff collar and a short grey jacket which was known as a 'bum-freezer'. He was carefully dressed and for the performances wore the same black three-piece suit with a watch-chain strung across the double-breasted waist-coat. He was a young man then, still in his early thirties, and yet in his dark suit he might have been of any age. He touched the chain of his watch, even now as the meeting continued, but he never once looked at the watch-face itself. Never once. The old woman, whose dead child was called Daniel, had gone out into the night; before she left the hall she had put some coins in the empty McVitie and Price biscuit tin which my father always placed beside the door. He watched her leave and then he turned to me, once more taking my hand before he addressed those who remained. They were very quiet. 'Some of you know me. But I am not important. Clement Harcombe is not important. Our friend has just left, taking with her awakened impressions of Daniel. I simply opened the door for her.' All the time he spoke he kept my hand firmly clenched in his own. 'When you go out from this place tonight, you will see the light from the hall pierce the darkness as you cross the threshold. That is all I have done: I have opened the door, and allowed the light to pass through.'

This was a time when death was in the air. Six or seven years had passed since the end of the Great War but, on looking back at it now, it seems to me to have been still a period of privation and mournfulness; it was as if all those deaths had cast a long shadow forward. Whether this is a reflection of the true circumstances of the time, or simply of my own condition as a child, I cannot say. But when I recall the dark coats and hats, the pale faces, the smell of Weights cigarettes; when I remember the monotony and anxiety which seemed so much part of the lives of all those whom my father knew; when I see once again my father standing before them in his three-piece suit – then it is with some conviction that I can describe this as a world dominated by the dead. By the spirits of the past. 'Come towards me now,' he said. He always employed the same words. 'Open the door. Let the light shine through and ease your journey. Come and be healed.'

There must have been occasions when no one came forward, but now I can only remember the times when one or two people rose from the wooden benches and nervously approached us on the platform. It might be an old woman with rheumatism, a young man with continuing headaches, or an older man with severe pains in his chest – when they came up, my father instructed me to step down, take them by the hand and lead them towards him as he waited for them with arms outstretched. My memory of this bears now the aspects of a dream for, as far as I can recall, I could always feel their pain when I first held them. It was not that I suffered it (that would have been too great a burden to endure), but rather that, in some moment of perception, I understood the contours of their sickness; it was as if a light had suddenly been switched on within an unfamiliar room. But there were others who seemed to carry images of the past within themselves. As I touched them I could see a dead father, or grandfather, or ghost further back, rising up and looking at me. All was vouchsafed in a moment, and then it was gone.

The faces of those people have gone now, too – all except four or five whom, as this story will show, I had good reason to remember. One face in particular comes back to me, from that same evening when my father heard the voice of Daniel. There was a young man who had often come to the meetings, and who always sat at the back of the hall in as inconspicuous a position as possible. He was one of those who came simply to be near my father, and he kept his eyes fixed on him throughout the evening. I noticed that he had a pronounced nervous mannerism, for at regular intervals the left side of his mouth would curve upwards and he would twist his head and neck in the same spasmodic movement; yet, when my father played the piano at the beginning of each performance, the music seemed to calm him and his seizures passed away. I am sure that my father recognized him well enough, but he never seemed to look at him and never once mentioned his presence to me. It was as if he liked to keep people silently in their places.

But on this particular evening he rose from the bench, and for the first time came forward when my father invited the audience to 'come and be healed'. It was with something like affection that I hurried down the aisle to take him and, as I touched his arm, I felt the power of his injury – the force of the hurt which propelled him into his strange nervous convulsions. At the same moment he looked at me in a curiously shy way, as if he knew how much I had discovered of him. Then I led him towards the stage. 'Yes,' my father was saying. 'Come forward. Come this way.' I guided him on to the raised wooden platform and I stood behind him as my father placed his hands upon his shoulders; it was the same posture always, the supplicant between us while my father remained within sight of the audience. Now he looked past the young man and stared into my face as he asked the familiar question: 'Tell me what has brought you here. How can I –' He always stopped at this moment, although he pitched his voice so that the whole hall reverberated with his words.

'It's my mouth.' He leaned forward and whispered to my father. 'It jumps up and down.'

My father said nothing. He was still looking towards me as he passed his hands three times over the young man's face, head and neck. 'Take it away.' His voice had grown even louder now, but he was still looking at me. 'Take it away.'

The young man made a sudden movement backwards, and he might have fallen if I had not been there to support him; then I felt him shuddering in my arms until he grew calm. I knew that it had gone. I knew that my father had cured him and that the nervous agitation had left him at last. He turned around to look when I took my hands away from his back; he was standing upright now, but he had so bewildered an expression upon his face that it was as if the sudden liberation had frightened rather than consoled him. After a few moments I led him towards his seat; he did not want to let go of my hand, however, but stood clutching it before he sat down once again. My father was always exhausted after the performance of the healing, and he spoke in a slower and quieter voice as I stood with the young man at the back of the hall. Both of us were listening intently as he talked of the spirits which worked through him; he held out his palms towards the upper air in order to locate the source of their power. Then the young man smiled at me and sat down.

I never properly understood what my father meant by the spirits of the past or the spirits of the dead; in a sense such things meant nothing to me, for I believed that all the power which my father described was literally emanating from him. I did not necessarily stand in awe of him as a result, because I had grown up with that knowledge: he was my father, and it was only natural that he should be pre-eminent. So much is accepted in childhood that the young inhabit a thousand worlds, brighter or more terrible than the one in which we all think we live. I considered myself at the time to be merely the child of a wonderful man; it was always a source of pride to me that I was allowed by him to participate in the events here related, and nothing which occurred in the old hall seemed to me to be strange or mystifying. It had become so much a part of my life that I conceived it to be part of life itself. Did I believe that I might inherit the powers which my father demonstrated? No, not then. I saw myself always as his assistant for, when I looked out over the people assembled here, I knew that I wanted to be of his world and not of theirs.

The meeting came to an end very quietly. My father played no more music but raised his hand in a gesture of farewell as the audience slowly walked out into the night. He was exhausted, as I have said, but when they had all gone, his weariness left him and his energy seemed to be redoubled. 'Bovril prevents that sinking feeling, Timothy,' he said, patting me on the head. 'And so do I!' He went first to the biscuit tin by the door in which all the contributions were placed; he never looked inside it but simply emptied its contents into a Gladstone bag he carried with him. Then he

walked quickly back to the stage and gently closed the lid of
the piano before smoothing it with his hand; he hurried
around the hall, extinguishing the lights one by one, while I
trailed after him in the gathering darkness. He never discussed
the incidents of the evening, but preferred to question me on
what even then I considered to be trivial matters. 'Tim.
Timothy. Did you polish your shoes before you came out?'

'Yes, dad.'

'And that's another thing. You should never call me dad.
Not here.' He was just locking the door of the hall as we spoke.
'You should learn to call me father. It has more of a ring to it.'

'Yes, father. More of a ring to it.' I knew that this was a
habit he detested – my repeating what he had just said. But I
could not help it. I never could help it. He merely looked at
me, however, before bending down to brush the dust of the
hall from the turn-ups of his dark trousers. I could *not* help it
and I said again, 'A ring to it.'

'Timothy! There are plenty of new words. Don't use up the
old ones.'

'Tell me one then, dad. Father.'

'Palimpsest. Look it up when we get home.'

We first had to return the key of the hall to the caretaker.
He lived in Tabernacle Close, just a few hundred yards away,
and of those journeys now I most vividly recall the soft light
of the infrequent street-lamps as well as the strange sense of
desolation which accompanied me in this London evening
time; it was as if I knew that I would be walking down such
streets all of my life. The house of the caretaker smelled of
pepper and, when his wife opened the door, my father and I
took a step back. 'Mrs Franklin,' he said. 'The key.'

She had a strange, scared expression but she was always
smiling. And when my father said, 'The key,' she laughed;
she had a wonderful laugh. Then she looked down at me and
brushed my cheeks with her hands. She glanced at my father
for a moment, and then at the dark London sky. 'There's
always a key,' she said, before she closed the door.

It was time for my father and me to return home, so he took my hand and we made our way back to Hackney Square. It was here that we lived in lodgings, on the ground floor of a house overlooking the ragged patch of grass and pebbles which comprised the 'garden' of the square itself. It was a quiet place, and set in such a maze of streets that it was almost undiscoverable except by those who actually inhabited it; it was part of a faded and dilapidated area, but on looking back I suspect that its very remoteness, its air of being withdrawn from the busy life of Kingsland Road or Brick Lane, made it appear more derelict than in fact it was. It seemed to be hiding from the world, and in its loneliness had succumbed to internal decay. But my father loved it. He loved to inhale the odour of old stone and of brick blackened by coal dust, although to me it resembled nothing so much as the smell of damp cardboard. He was fascinated by the crumbling dissolution, whereas even at that age I detested it – detested it, perhaps, because it seemed to encroach upon my sense of my own self and even on occasions to supplant it.

'Let's get lost,' he sometimes said on these journeys towards home. By which he meant that we would approach Hackney Square from a different direction to the usual one, and that we would make our way through what were to me less familiar streets and alleys. 'Do you want to get lost, Tim?' There were occasions when we passed the burial ground of Bunhill Fields and approached Hackney Square from the south through Old Nichol Street and Hand Alley; there were occasions when we would approach it from the north, by way of St Agnes Well and Bowling Green Walk; and often we would walk up Brick Lane before coming upon the church at Shoreditch, which, to my childish gaze, was a monstrous and bewildering sight. I recognized most of the area, but sometimes I was truly lost and held on to my father's hand with determination; I suppose that he always knew his way, although there were occasions when the apparently endless sequence of passageways and courtyards and squares gave me the impression that we were walking quickly in order to stay in the same place.

The fearfulness of a child is a strange thing. It need not be attached to an immediate cause at all, for there was nothing in these narrow streets of London to frighten me, and I suspect that I was possessed by some general dread of being abandoned. The damp light, the vistas of old brick houses, the cracked pavements, the small front gardens and all the smells of urban life embodied for me the idea of solitariness itself. So it was that I held on to my father's hand, and from time to time looked up at his bright face. 'There it is,' he might say as we passed Bunhill Fields. 'Can you see the monument to John Bunyan? And there beside it is the grave of William Blake. Our friend, Mr Blake, saw angels. The invisible world, Timothy. The invisible world.'

He mentioned such things, as far as I can now recall, in so ingenuous a manner that it was impossible to know precisely what feelings they evoked in him. But he was quite different when we walked along Brick Lane. 'Look,' he would say. 'Just look at the squalor here. Look how people are forced to live. It is terrible, Timothy. Unendurable. There's nothing like poverty to turn you around.' I did not understand what he meant by that. To turn you upside down, so that all the comfort and security of ordinary life seemed transitory or uncertain? Or to turn you around, from the invisible world to that more immediate one which contained suffering and desolation? Certainly there were many people in those years who endured great want and hardship; and I am sure, now, that some of them came to my father's meetings in order to find solace in the prospect of a life after this one. 'No one should have to live like this,' he would say, pointing to the open entrances of the tenements which lined the streets just beyond Brick Lane. 'It degrades people. It torments them. It turns life into a valley of pain, Timothy. The valley of the shadow of death.' His words frightened me, and in fact I came to understand how closely in those days the prospect of destitution shadowed ordinary life – how much despair lingered just beyond the area which my father and I inhabited. But then his mood changed, and he started whistling as we drew closer to Hackney Square. 'Don't be too sad,' he said, looking down at me and noticing my expression for the first time. 'Pack up your troubles in your old kit-bag.'

So, having disposed satisfactorily of both the visible and the invisible worlds, we finally returned home from our 'lost' expedition. Yet this was the curious thing: whenever we approached Hackney Square from a new direction, or from an unknown congeries of streets, the appearance of the square itself seemed to be subtly altered. Our lodgings had also changed since, on our return from unfamiliar streets, they became more remote; our three small rooms, so precious to me as a haven, might as well have been occupied by strangers. If we approached it by a route which was half familiar, it would take me a shorter time to feel once again at ease there. Then, in turn, as a result of these sensations, I began to experience some idea of my own growth and change.

But to go back to that night, the night he had said 'palimpsest' to me. My father had taken my hand after giving the key of the old hall to the caretaker's wife, and together we began our journey to Hackney Square. It was a November evening, but it was unseasonably mild and we lingered along the route homeward; we were not 'lost', for my father seemed too tired or distracted, but there was no urgency in our walk. 'Do you know what I'm going to do next?' he suddenly asked me. He was looking all around, at the darkened shops and dimly lit houses, even as he spoke to me. 'Do you, Timothy?'

'No, dad.'

'Father. I'm going to recite a poem to you.' He stopped in the middle of the pavement and put one hand out into the air. 'When April with his showers sweet –' He stopped, unable to remember the next words. 'Etcetera. Etcetera. Etcetera. Then do folk long to go on pilgrimages. That's what we are, Timmy. Pilgrims.'

He was still standing with his arm outstretched and, although there was no one close to us, I was embarrassed.

'Come on, dad. Let's go.' I put my head into the small of his back and tried to push him in the direction of our home.

He turned around to laugh at me, but then he became very still. 'Hush,' he whispered. 'Come here a second.' I walked around him and raised my head, as he pretended to straighten my peaked cap. 'I think,' he said, 'that someone is following us. I saw him in the light.'

'Where?'

'Don't look! Don't look!'

We walked on even more slowly than before; the streets were much darker then than they are now, and the pavement was only illuminated within the circle of each gas-lamp before disappearing into the night again. Whenever we reached an area of light, my father nonchalantly gazed at an advertisement or peered into a shop window while all the time keeping a close watch on someone behind us. For some reason he wanted to be seen by our pursuer. 'Pears Soap,' he said. 'For a matchless complexion. He *is* following, Timothy.' To me it seemed a terrible threat; but to my father it was no more than an elaborate game since, instead of going in a straight direction towards our lodgings, he encircled Hackney Square three times. He was about to go around a fourth time, while I walked beside him as a more and more unwilling accomplice, when he suddenly stopped. 'Quick,' he whispered. 'Keep up with me!' We ran back along the pavement and had gone no more than twenty or thirty feet when we both saw a silhouette just ducking around the corner of a small brick-maker's yard at one end of the square. We turned the corner, too, and almost bumped into our pursuer. 'Well here we are,' my father said in his most affable voice. 'I know you. I know you very well.'

I also knew him: it was the young man whose nervous spasms he had cured that night.

'You do know me, sir. You helped me.' He was wearing an old-fashioned gaberdine overcoat, which, as he spoke, he began to unbutton. 'You cured the mouth,' he added. 'I wanted to thank you, but I didn't know how –'

My father grabbed his shoulders with both hands, just as he had done in the hall itself. 'What is your name, my old friend?'

'Clay.'

'First name?'

'Stanley, sir.'

'Well, Stanley Clay. There is no reason to thank me.' Once more he had adopted the rhythmic cadence of the voice he used during the meeting. 'Is there someone you think of? Someone you loved?'

'Someone dead?'

'If you like.'

'There was my father –'

'Then thank your father. There is a presence around you. I felt it in the hall.'

'But does that mean . . .?' The young man seemed suddenly uneasy. 'Does that mean he is always watching me?'

'Everyone is watched,' my father said. 'Everyone is watching everyone else.' He had said this very quickly, as if he were not at all sure what he meant by it, but then the cadence returned. 'This is where we live, Stanley Clay. This is our home.'

'The earth, you mean?'

'No. Where *we* live.' My father drew me towards him. 'Hackney Square.'

He took my hand once more and we started walking towards our lodgings, but to my surprise Stanley Clay had decided to accompany us. 'Mr Harcombe,' he said in the same quiet, earnest way, 'is there anything I can do for you? I'm a good workman.' When I looked at him at that moment, I sensed that he would never be anything other than what he then was – poor, disturbed, lonely. All the stages of his life seemed to pass before me, as I watched him trembling in the darkness. How can I explain this now, even to myself? In the evenings my father would sometimes read to me passages from *The Pilgrim's Progress*, and I remember once looking over his shoulder at the illustration of that pilgrim with a book in his hand and a great burden upon his back. *That* is what I saw. Where others may have noticed only the wanderer himself, I recognized the book and the burden which he carried with him everywhere.

Stanley Clay was still talking eagerly to my father; it was clear that he felt himself to owe a great debt to him, and that he had been brought up to believe that all debts ought somehow to be repaid. We were standing by the gate to the house in which we lived; there was a small 'front garden' beside us, although it was no more than a patch of soil out of which some sunflowers grew in late summer. I loved those sunflowers. I love them still in memory, although then they were for me inextricably associated with my father and my father's life. When he talked of the other world, I thought of them turning their visages towards the sky. When he talked of the light, I thought of the radiance which seemed to issue from them. They were taller than me then, and when I stood among them it was as if they were protecting me. They were my guardians.

'A piano tuner!' my father was saying. 'That's a fine profession. Tuning the music of the spheres. That's what you do, Stanley Clay. Tell us, Timothy, what does Shakespeare say on the subject?' When we were in the presence of other people he always spoke to me as if I were an adult. I looked up at the sky, and for an instant saw the heavens as a vast building in which we were privileged to dwell. 'Untune that string,' I said, 'and hark what discord follows.' I did not remember ever reading those lines, but I knew them.

'I could do something with that piano in the hall,' Stanley Clay was saying. 'I could take a look at it. Tune it up a bit.'

My father did not immediately reply but put his hands on the young man's shoulders. 'So we will meet again.' This was his usual way: he never liked to request or even formally accept a favour. He simply assumed that, mysteriously, it would be done. I sensed that he wanted now to go inside, so I opened the gate and walked down the small path ahead of him. 'My son is very impatient,' he explained to Stanley Clay and then, with an obvious gesture of farewell, he followed me. 'Do you think,' he said as soon as the front door was closed, 'that he's properly cured?'

I did not understand why he had put the question to me – it was he who had healed him, after all – but I knew how to answer. 'Yes,' I said. 'He is cured.'

That evening was the same as other evenings. My father never allowed us to eat before the meeting. When he stood in the small hall and conversed with the spirits of the dead, or healed the sick, he needed to remain alert – empty in every sense, while he waited to be filled with the presence of others and the sound of other voices. It never seemed to me unfair that I stayed without food as well: I, who was so much a part of him, was only too eager to share his self-restraint. Of course we were always very hungry on our return and we would go at once into our small kitchen, which was really no more than a scullery with a Belfast sink, a water boiler and a greasy gas-cooker. 'Have you got a penny for the gas?' he would often ask me, as he scanned the wooden shelf for the constituents of a meal. And, if I close my eyes, I can still see the old household goods rising up in front of me. The bottle of White's Lemonade. The yellow tin of Colman's Mustard. The green box of Tip-Top Tea. Dark bottles of Whitbread Stout. Oxo. Bournville Cocoa. Nestlé Milk. It is strange how those perishable objects, so easily discarded, should be the ones I remember most vividly.

My father would take down anything he needed with a flourish, as if he were a conjurer about to make the object disappear. Indeed he did perform such tricks for my benefit; an egg would vanish only to re-emerge from my ear a few moments later, or a spoon would be found in one of my pockets just after I had searched for it there. Our meals were simple enough but, although my father never had much money, I cannot recall any sense of privation in my childhood.

This was largely because of the enthusiasm which he brought to everything, even shopping or cooking, and the most commonplace food was for me lent an aura of enchantment. Our meals might include pease pudding, with a farthing's worth of pork crackling on the top; bloaters were a favourite dish, although I had a particular preference for the cow-heels which the butcher's boy would leave on one side for me to collect on Thursday afternoons. Saturday was special, too, because in the evening the shrimp man came on his rounds. He pushed a van through the streets and each week I would run out, shouting, to stop him. We ate the shiny shrimps with bread and watercress, a meal which was always followed by rice with a dollop of strawberry jam in the middle. I can see it now, and taste it – and wish to be a child again.

When our supper was prepared we would take it into the small front room as if we were carrying the spoils of some tremendous victory; this room was also my father's bedroom, although it rarely bore that aspect for me. There were rugs on the floor, with an assortment of caricatures, engravings of buildings, and maps of old London hanging on the walls: I thought of them as wonderful works of art. There was scarcely any bare space at all, and here I felt quite protected as I sat on the old brown sofa which at night became my father's bed. It was placed beneath the window and, when I kneeled on its cushions, I could see the mottled green of Hackney Square. The sunflowers grew just beyond the window, too, and in early autumn they were so tall that they cast a shadow into the room and upon my face as I stared up at them.

We had three rooms altogether: my father's room itself, the kitchen which looked out upon a bedraggled back garden and, between them, my own narrow room. In fact it was really no more than a grandiose cupboard; it had no windows but it contained a bookcase as well as a small bed and, to me, it was the epitome of luxury. I would say now that it was a room without a history, but at the time I was conscious only of its peacefulness and silence. The bare yellow walls looked down upon me, and I was at rest. Perhaps that is because the other parts of the house were quite different: we had to share a toilet and bathroom with the families who lived above us, and whenever I ventured up the stairs I was always invaded by an unaccountable fearfulness. Perhaps too many other people had trod the same path. Too many other people had lived here.

There was a strangeness about my father's room, also, but for me it was the strangeness of enchantment; there were times when I found him quite mysterious, and something of that mystery had entered what he liked to call his 'cabinet of curiosities'. It was here, then, that we brought our supper after the meeting. There was a small wooden table which we would place in front of the sofa and, with the curtains open to let in the night, we would sit and eat. Sometimes my father was too preoccupied to say anything at all; I never knew or even guessed why this should be so, although now I do. But on most occasions he would be animated and even light-hearted. The respite from his work seemed positively to liberate him – not that he ever referred to the meetings themselves and, as far as I can recall, he rarely talked about himself. Instead we discussed what he used to call 'English music', by which he meant not only music itself but also English history, English literature and English painting. With him one subject always led to another and he would break off from a discussion of William Byrd or Henry Purcell in order to tell me about Tennyson and Browning; he would turn from the work of Samuel Johnson to the painting of Thomas Gainsborough, from pavans and galliards to odes and sonnets, from the London of Daniel Defoe to the London of Charles Dickens. And in my imagination, as he talked, all these things comprised one world which I believed to be still living – even in this small room where we sat. It was a presence around both of us, no less significant than the phantom images which I sometimes glimpsed in the old hall. He had taken on the task of educating me, as I discovered later, and so there was a method in everything he said. But at the time it seemed to me that only he knew of such things, and that somehow the knowledge of the past (indeed the past itself) came from within his own self; it was almost as if it were a secret between us, a secret inheritance.

I was accustomed to these late hours, but there were nights when my father, no doubt in a fit of parental guiltiness, sent me earlier to bed; I would hear him playing some music on the gramophone, while I brushed my teeth in the kitchen-sink. Then I hurried into my own room, put on my pyjamas, which were always neatly folded on top of the bookcase, and waited impatiently for 'the reading'. I was always in bed by the time my father came in to me, and I would pretend to be asleep until he 'woke' me by blowing softly on the back of my neck. Then he took a book down from its shelf, and began.

We had a large collection, and I can still remember the creased spines of the volumes in the bookcase. *Great Expectations* with its dark blue cover and gilt lettering; *The Adventures of Sherlock Holmes* and *The Memoirs of Sherlock Holmes* in a thick red volume, the very shape of which was for me a source of pleasure and relief; *Robinson Crusoe* and *A Journal of the Plague Year* in narrow green volumes and paper so thin that I could see the print on the other side before the page was turned. My father also possessed a collection of Elizabethan songs, a large volume which lay on its side beneath *The Engravings of William Hogarth*: sometimes I would take them both from the shelf and open them out upon the floor. I did not read them, or really even look at them; I simply rested my head on their pages, which were to me more comforting than any pillow. These were all books which my father had purchased over the years, which he read and read over again, but there were also volumes which he had bought with the specific purpose of educating me. There was a history of British painting as well as an anthology of English poetry and a six-volume set, which my father had once carried home triumphantly from a market stall on Ludgate Hill, entitled *The Beauties of English Drama*.

But on the top shelf were what my father called the 'special' books, by which he meant the books which he was reading to me at the time. I cannot now remember all of them, but I do recall how on these particular winter nights he had begun *The Pilgrim's Progress* and *Alice in Wonderland*, reading them alternately in case I became too bored with the adventures of Alice or too fearful over the hazards of Pilgrim. I realized that *The Pilgrim's Progress* was the more ancient book, not because I had any knowledge of the author but because the name of my grandfather, Josiah Harcombe, was inscribed upon its stained and yellowing fly-leaf. My father said that it had 'come down' and, whenever he employed that phrase, I had an image of the book itself with its black cover and the raised letters of its title floating down from some part of the sky until it landed softly at my father's feet. He used to read it to me on three nights of the week, the other nights being given up to *Alice in Wonderland*, and, although I cannot claim that it was my favourite among his books, I recall the sensation of intense pleasure which I felt when he turned the familiar pages to find the spot at which he had previously left off. By now I would have snuggled down beneath the faded blue eiderdown which covered my bed; my father would bring up a wooden chair and, sitting beside me, he would begin in a low and melodious voice which was much like the one he employed at the meetings.

There were occasions when the narrative so interested me, however, that I would sit up in the bed and peer over my father's shoulder at the pictures which illustrated the text. Of Alice's adventures, for example, I still recall the menacing face of the Duchess who nursed a crying child while a cook stirred the pot beside her: I always assumed that the baby was about to be boiled and eaten, and that the expression on the Duchess's face was one of hunger. I remember, also, the image of Alice climbing on to the mantelpiece and starting to fade into the looking-glass above it; I never cared for her, in any case, since she resembled an old woman simply dressed up as a child. Then there was the drawing of the Red Queen flying through the air with Alice being carried along behind her: and, when I saw this, I felt afraid.

There was only one illustration in our edition of *The Pilgrim's Progress* but I never tired of gazing at it since, as I think I mentioned before, it became for me a true image of life. It was of a man carrying a book in his hand, and a burden upon his back; he had turned to look at the distant vista of a city, and he had an expression of horror upon his face. There was such dread and loneliness in this image that it threatened to engulf me but now, when I picture it to myself, it is so associated with the condition of my childhood that I cannot help but recall it with nostalgia. Is it possible to be nostalgic about old fears?

And what kind of fear was it that afflicted me then, as I listened to my father reading from the old books? I hear the sound of his voice again, I see the book resting upon his knees and his glasses slipping from the bridge of his nose. All these things return and I am once more curled up within my bed, gazing at the cracked plaster of the ceiling, and, sometimes, as he reads, falling asleep.

TWO

A ND AS HE SLEPT, HE must have dreamed a dream. He was standing on a vast plain, but in the distance he could clearly see a small house which (so it seemed to Timothy) had chimneys in the shape of words: words like *raven* and *writing* with the 'r' and the 'w' fixed to the roof while the 'n' and 'g' pointed upwards towards the sky as the smoke billowed from them. 'But how,' he thought, 'can smoke come out of words?'

He saw someone running towards him from the house; it was so large a plain that it would have taken hours to reach him, if there had been such a thing as Time in his dream, but in a very short while indeed he recognized the figure of a young girl in a slightly flounced white dress. She had long hair which streamed out behind her in the wind and, as she ran, she called out, 'Life, life, eternal life! How shall I grapple with the misery that I must meet with in eternity!'

'Why,' Timothy said to himself as he watched her hurry past him and flee into a dark wood, 'that's Alice!' He thought he had glimpsed the faintest possible sneer on her face but he had no time to consider this, for now, from the same direction, hurried a tall, swarthy man with a burden on his back and a book in his hand. 'And there's Christian!' The man was muttering to himself as he passed Timothy. 'Oh dear! Oh dear! I shall be too late! Won't He be savage if I'm too late! Oh my book and burden, how late it's getting!' And he, too, began to run towards the nearby wood; even when he stumbled and dropped his book, he did not stop to retrieve it but continued in his headlong career.

'Please, sir,' Timothy shouted, picking up the book from the dry plain and hastening after him, 'You've lost your –' But Christian was already gone between the trees and was nowhere to be seen. Timothy opened the volume, but the curious thing was that, although the words seemed to be in English, he could understand none of them. They ran on from line to line in the familiar way but, as soon as he tried to look closely at a sentence in order to make sense of it, the words always swarmed to the margins of the page and left a white space at which he stared in bewilderment. 'Well,' he thought, 'this is quite a peculiar thing.'

'*You* may call it peculiar if you like,' a voice said behind him. 'But I've seen peculiar things, compared with which that would be as sensible as a thesaurus.' Timothy turned around in alarm, to find two men standing behind him, identically dressed in frock-coats and stove-pipe hats. 'Before you ask, as all boys *do* ask, I am Obstinate. And this is Pliable. Or is it the other way around?'

The boy stared at them for a moment. 'I remember you,' he said. 'You're in *The Pilgrim's Progress.*'

'I wouldn't swear to that,' Pliable replied (for it was he who had been talking all the time). 'I wouldn't swear to that unless it was written down.'

'But it is written down. It's a story. I've read you in a story.'

Pliable looked away, as if he were trying to hide some momentary distress. 'You may call it a story, if you like. But to us it is – oh what *is* it exactly? Evangelist was explaining it just the other day.'

He turned to Obstinate for assistance, but Timothy broke in excitedly. 'I never knew that stories could come true, but here I am in the middle of one! Do you think a book could be written about me?'

'It would have to be a very strange one, since you're hardly a character at all,' Pliable muttered. 'It would have to be an allegory, or a vision, or some such thing.'

'Is that the Book that can never die?' his companion asked him hesitantly.

'I don't know. Doesn't everything die?'

'Not according to Alice.' Obstinate put his hand out to the

boy. 'Don't worry. Don't listen to him. You may turn out to be a character, after all. Goodbye.'

Obstinate and Pliable turned on their heels and walked briskly away, leaving Timothy with the book still in his hand. 'This is the most provoking thing,' he said, 'to be left alone in a story and not even know who you are meant to be. I wish dad were here. He would know exactly what to do.'

'I shouldn't say dead if I were you. I should say farther.' The boy saw a head appear in the air – not a pleasant head, but a ragged and bloody object. It looked to Timothy as if it had been ripped from someone's body, and he stepped backward in alarm. 'I should go farther, if I were you.' The mouth opened and from it issued a scream which spread across the plain; then the forehead and the ears started to disappear, the nose and cheeks and eyes grew vaporous until only the open mouth remained. And then the mouth vanished, too, leaving only the scream behind.

'Yes. I should go farther,' Timothy spoke very loudly in order to drown out the scream. 'If I am in a story, I might as well go on just to see what happens next.' So he walked over the plain towards the dark wood but, however fast or far he travelled, the wood always remained at the same distance from him. Yet the curious thing was that the landscape itself continually changed: one minute he was on the vast plain and, at the next, he was crossing a river; he was climbing over a wicket-gate and then without warning he found himself in a valley, walking along the narrow track of a dried stream. Until he saw ahead of him an old woman, standing very straight, with a crown upon her head. 'Why,' he said, 'it's the Red Queen!' In truth he had always been frightened by the drawings he had seen of her, but now she looked so dolefully at the steep sides of the valley that he quite took pity on her. She was reciting some words in the air, and an echo of her voice reverberated all around.

'Is it a longing for the dead?' she called out.

'Longing dead,' came the echo.

'What dies in the morning?'

'Dies mourning.'

'But the absurdity of staying?'

'Absurdity staying.'

Timothy stood silently in front of her, but she seemed not to have noticed him. 'This is monstrous,' she was saying. 'What *is* the point of an echo that only answers back? Off with its head!'

'It's dead.'

'I shall scream!'

'Ice cream.'

The Red Queen sat down suddenly upon a large rock and, with a shudder, covered her ears with her hands: she was now so bowed down that Timothy was afraid that her crown might fall into the rubble beside her feet. He was about to walk past very quietly when she looked up at him. 'I don't suppose,' she said, 'that you've met a real queen before. It's a terrible sight, isn't it? Even here.'

'I don't know where "here" is. Not exactly.'

'In the Valley of the Shadow of Death, of course. Where there are hobgoblins, satyrs and dragons of the pit; where there is a continual howling and yelling, as of a people under unutterable misery who sit bound in affliction and irons. And over this valley hang the discouraging clouds of confusion, and death with wings outspread. At least that's what the White Queen told me the other day.' Even as she mentioned the White Queen, she seemed much enlivened. 'Although, if you ask me, she makes up a great deal just to impress people. It's very sad, really. And what,' she said, finally turning to Timothy, '*what* are *you*?'

'What am I?' Timothy was so confused by the sudden question that he hardly knew the sound of his own voice. 'I'm a child . . .'

'Oh don't bother me with that nonsense.'

'I didn't mean –'

'What is the use of a child that doesn't mean anything?

Children always mean something. That is why they are so disagreeable.' The Red Queen seemed entirely to have forgotten her earlier lamentations, and was in a thoroughly good humour. 'Now let's have a proper game and start all over again. What are you?'

'I . . .' Timothy was now so bewildered, and so frightened by all the noises around him in the Valley of the Shadow of Death, that he had forgotten his own name.

'I is a very strange name for a child. I suppose it might stand for Isoecho which, as you know, means *I saw echoes*. Or Isadora. Are you an Isadora? Speak up, brush your shoes, ignore the howling of the people in affliction, and tell me.'

'I was just about to say,' Timothy added, 'that I can't remember my name.'

This did not surprise the Red Queen at all. 'Well,' she replied, 'look it up. You have the book. Look it up.' Indeed Timothy was still carrying the volume which Christian had dropped in his headlong flight. 'You know what they say, don't you?' the Red Queen added as Timothy now took it from under his arm and opened it. 'Verily, it was made by Him that cannot lie.'

Timothy looked down at the page only to realize that all the words were now inside out, or backwards, or somehow different. 'I'm afraid I can't read this,' he said.

'Of course you can't read it. It's a looking-glass book. You're only meant to hold it and *look* as if you've read it. That is the meaning of criticism.' At this Timothy, suddenly feeling himself to be in so alien and lonely a place, so lost from his old life, burst into tears. 'I wish you wouldn't cry real tears,' she said in disgust. 'They're quite useless here, you know. They just smudge everything.' But now the Red Queen recollected her own earlier affliction and sent up a series of doleful cries which echoed around the Valley of the Shadow of Death. Then she crouched down beside Timothy and once again grew confidential. 'I must walk without the sun,' she told him. 'Darkness must cover the path of my feet, and I must hear the noise of doleful creatures because of my sinful state. That's what it's all about.'

Timothy rose and, trying to control his tears, pretended to look down the valley. 'But what am *I* doing here?' he asked of no one in particular. 'And how can I find out who I am?'

'You could ask Christian, although he should be in Wonderland by now. You *might* try Alice, of course, but she was last seen in the City of Destruction and is probably in a very poor temper. Oh look, here they are now.'

Timothy turned to see Christian and Alice running, hand in hand, towards him. 'Make way!' Alice was screaming. 'Make way!' Then Christian called out, 'Come on!' and grabbed Timothy's hand: without having time to say farewell to the Red Queen, the boy found himself running alongside his two new companions. Christian held his hand ever more tightly and, as the wind rushed past them, he shouted in Timothy's ear, 'Faster! Faster! If we want to reach the end of the story, we must run twice as fast as this!' Then Alice began to sing in a very high voice indeed:

> ''Tis true, it was long ere I began
> To seek to live for ever:
> But now I run fast as I can,
> 'Tis better late than never.'

They ran and ran until they were clear of the valley and found themselves climbing steadily upwards. 'Where am I going?' Christian suddenly asked Timothy. At the same moment Alice also turned to address the boy: 'Whither must I fly? To be here is a fearful thing.'

He was now so out of breath that he could say nothing in reply but gradually, holding them both tightly by the hand and slowing down his own pace, he managed to reduce them to a trot, to a walk, to a crawl, until finally they stopped altogether. They were on the summit of a hill, from which the landscape seemed to stretch for miles and miles into the distance. Timothy looked out upon mountains and valleys, with plains and marshes beyond; he could see castles and hills, palaces and rivers, towns with narrow paths between them, woods, fields, dark cities shrouded in smoke, springs and grottoes, decaying buildings and bright new dwellings, crowds of people wandering across a plain as well as solitary human figures bowed towards the ground, children at play, animals grazing in meadows, churches and cemeteries, lakes and trees, all tumbled together. Then for a moment he thought he saw Hackney Square, with a young man asleep beneath a tree. 'That may have been my father,' he said out loud. 'Before I was even thought of.'

Christian screwed up his eyes, seeming to recognize certain areas of this landscape and not others. 'All these different views are terribly confusing, don't you think?' He put his hand upon Timothy's shoulder. 'They are meant to be divided between books, you know. One view is quite enough for one book.'

'Brooks. Not books.' Alice turned sharply to Timothy, as if it were he who had spoken. 'Divided between *brooks*. In any case, we might as well enjoy it now that we're here. It's called aesthetic distance.' She took a tortoise-shell comb from the pocket of her white dress, and began slowly and sleepily to pull it through her long bright hair as she sang:

> 'Wouldst thou be in a dream, and yet not sleep?
> Or wouldst thou in a moment laugh and weep?
> Wouldst thou lose thy self, and catch no harm?
> And find thy self again without a charm?'

And then Christian took up the song:

> 'Lay it where childhood's dreams are twined
> In memory's mystic band,
> Like Pilgrim's withered wreath of flowers
> Plucked in a far-off land.'

'It's the oddest sensation,' Timothy thought to himself – for in this place even the most secret thoughts emerged in the form of sentences – 'it is the *oddest* sensation, but I believe that there are two different sorts of things mixed up here. Two stories.'

'They are both dreams, if that's what you mean.' Timothy looked around in alarm: Alice and Christian had vanished and in their place stood a large White Rabbit. 'And, as we say here,' the Rabbit continued, smoothing his whiskers with one paw, 'you must believe steadfastly concerning things that are invisible.'

'What was it you said?' Timothy had been so perturbed by the sudden absence of his companions, and so bewildered by the spectacle of a Rabbit some six inches taller than himself, that he had not heard the words of the strange creature.

'I didn't say anything about *what* it was. I was trying to tell you *that* it was.'

'I didn't mean –'

'Oh well if there's no meaning, it saves a world of conversation. Surely the Red Queen explained that to you pages and pages ago.'

'Pages?'

'If you ask another question, I am going straight down that hole.' The Rabbit pointed dramatically towards a small opening in the turf. 'Yes, her pages. A Queen must have pages. Just as a book must have royalties.'

'I'm sorry to ask so many questions.' Timothy was now thoroughly confused and embarrassed. 'But I really don't understand a word you have said since you arrived.'

The White Rabbit smiled, took a watch out of his waistcoat pocket, and began reciting to it:

> 'Things that seem to be hid in words obscure,
> Do but the Godly mind the more allure;
> But if thou shalt cast all away as vain,
> I know not but it will make me dream again.'

The Rabbit put his watch back in his pocket. 'I was in danger of losing Time then,' he said confidentially. 'That's why I had to sing to him. If he decides to stay, you see, Time will answer all of your questions. Why is a boy like his father?' he asked very suddenly.

'I don't know. At least I think –'

'That's the kind of easy question Time will answer straight away. Did you say there were two stories here?' The Rabbit had a disconcerting habit of changing the topics of conversation at random, and Timothy merely nodded. 'Well as far as I am aware, Time knows only the one story. His story. Come on, we'll miss the race.'

The Rabbit hurried down the hill, with Timothy following close behind. He had an opportunity to look around, however, and he noticed at once how peculiarly grimy this landscape had become; the rocks were striated with dark lines and passages, while the ground beneath his feet was mottled with purple patches. He peered a little closer at the earth as he passed, all the time keeping the White Rabbit within sight, and to his surprise he found that it was made out of words crushed up and compacted together. But there was no time to consider these things properly for, now that he had reached the bottom of the hill, he found himself taking part in a competition. He was in the middle of a course, around which several contestants were running while others merely stood in a variety of striking attitudes. They might have been statues. 'Figures of speech,' the White Rabbit explained as they walked over to one of them. 'There's Amplification. And there's Apostrophe. Bathos is just the other side. Don't they all look grand? I wouldn't be surprised if they were related to one another.'

The race itself seemed to be hardly a race at all, since none of the contestants paid the least attention to one another but wandered back and forth across the track, stopped, started again, sat down, or fell asleep. One young man limped off the course altogether, and the White Rabbit clapped him enthusiastically. 'There goes a Broken Rhyme,' he explained to Timothy. 'He was tripped by a Tumbling Verse. Oh look, here's Empathy and Sympathy!' Two twins, dressed alike in green T-shirts, were jogging along the track and holding out their arms to an imaginary audience. But then the Rabbit began to tremble, and Timothy could distinctly hear the chattering of tiny teeth. 'I knew it!' he whispered furiously. 'I knew there would be trouble!' With trembling paw he pointed towards two knights in bright silver armour, who were dragging behind them a corpse in gaily coloured clothes of scarlet and blue and pink.

'Who has been hurt?' Timothy asked.

'Not hurt exactly. That's a Dead Metaphor. That's what he is. He's just been killed by the Heroic Couplet.' The White Rabbit was clearly distressed at the sight. 'They are not meant to do anything like that. Not here. They should be placed in a Stock Response and have Particles thrown at them. Heroic Couplet! More like Mock Heroic.' The Rabbit had lost his fear and had now grown quite indignant. 'There is no order here at all, you see. No order.' His words grew paler in the distance as he hurried away, leaving the boy alone once more.

'I suppose,' Timothy thought as he watched the contestants roll on the ground, or kick each other, or move the winning tape, 'that there is no order here because there is no meaning. But how can you decide to have a meaning in the first place? And who decides what meaning you should have? Can you just make it up as you go along? It is all very queer. Very queer indeed.'

'And the meaning of that is,' said a voice beside him, 'excuse my interruption, won't you?' Timothy looked around to find a very tall man bending down so that his face was close to his own. 'My name is Giant Despair. How do you do?' He put out a white, bony hand, which Timothy shook reluctantly. 'Excuse me for interrupting, but the meaning of *that* is Christian and Alice. They went towards the town called Uncertain. That way, actually.' Giant Despair lifted one of his white fingers and pointed towards the setting sun.

Timothy still had the book which Christian had dropped and now, hugging it tightly in anticipation of once more seeing his friends, he ran off in the direction suggested to him by Giant Despair. He had not travelled very far, however, before he heard sounds of crying and squealing; he hurried ahead and, much to his surprise, found Alice up to her waist in a foul black swamp. She waved one arm towards the boy, and he could see the mud slipping and sliding across her dress.

'Help me!' she cried. 'For Christ's sake help me! I am in the Slough of Despond.' He ran over as she cried out, even louder, 'To be here is a fearful thing!' Timothy carefully put down Christian's book upon the bank beside the Slough, and then leaned towards her as far as he could; he put out both hands for her to grasp, with an effort she reached them, the tips of their fingers just met (what a strange pleasure this was for the boy), and then he was able to take her hands in his own. He strained backwards, all the time raising her from the mire, until there was a sound just like that of water running out of a bath and Alice was freed. She struggled on to the hard ground, and lay there panting for breath. Her bright hair was begrimed with mud, her clothes were daubed with scum and dirt, and she began to weep bitterly. 'Just look at my lovely white dress,' she said. 'It's ruined. Shit!'

'Where is Christian?' Timothy asked her very quietly. 'Did he leave you behind?'

'I don't know. And I don't care.' The little girl was now in a thoroughly bad temper. 'The last time I saw him, he was trying to squeeze his tears into a bottle. Holy water, he called it. Don't ask *me* why.'

Timothy did not care for the foul smell emanating from the Slough, but he was now too frightened of Alice even to suggest that they leave this place. 'Where would you like to go next?' he asked her hesitantly after a few moments.

'I don't know. I'm quite seriously thinking of going into another story. I'm absolutely sick of this one. I don't suppose you have any ideas, do you?'

Timothy remembered all the evenings he had spent with his father, and all the stories which had been read aloud to him, and he felt at peace. 'Can you really go from one story to the next?' he asked her, just as she was bending over to remove clumps of mud from her dress.

'Of course I can. Don't ask such ridiculous questions. I can go wherever I like. I can even,' she added, straightening up with a sigh, 'I can even go backwards if I wish. Back to the beginning.'

'The beginning? The beginning of what?'

Alice was just about to answer him when they both heard the confused sound of cries very close to them. They rushed forward and found Christian struggling in a pool of water. 'I can't swim,' he called out to them. 'And these waters are rising. Help me!'

Alice watched him struggling for a few seconds, with something like a smile upon her face. 'This is the only water for miles and miles around,' she said, 'and you manage to fall into it.'

'I didn't fall. It crept up upon me unawares. You see,' he added, 'these are my tears. I'm drowning in my own tears.'

Timothy dived into the pool, which was not in truth very wide or very deep; the water was curiously warm and he could taste its salt in his mouth. How pleasant it would be to float here, he thought, and to forget everything that has happened to me this day: is that what Alice meant about going back to the beginning?

But now she interrupted his reverie. 'I hope you don't suppose that those are real tears,' she told him. 'Christian does everything by design.'

And at this moment, as Timothy swam towards him, the pilgrim put his fingers in his ears and began to call out to the sky, 'Woe is me!', 'I am undone', 'I curse the time!' and so forth.

'He hasn't got any sorrow, you know,' Alice went on, quite unconcerned. 'It's all his fancy. He just likes the sound of his own voice. He likes the words. If there were no words, he wouldn't feel a thing.'

Then, as Timothy put his arms around him, Christian cried out, 'They that sow in Tears shall reap in Joy!' before being hauled by the boy on to the dry ground. 'Well,' he said as he wrung out the sleeves of his dark jacket, 'I think I made my point very well.' Good-humouredly he took Timothy's arm and began walking with him just as if they had never broken off from their original journey. 'I could tell you all my adventures, if you like, beginning from this morning,' he said to him. 'The adventures first, of course, and then the commentary. Commentaries take such a dreadful time.' They walked on together arm in arm while Alice trailed behind them, kicking out sullenly at the twigs and small stones which lay on the path beside her. Timothy had only minutes before been walking towards the setting sun but now, curiously enough, the air began to grow warmer, the flowers larger and more vivid, the grass softer and deeper. 'If I am not very much mistaken,' Christian explained to Timothy, 'we are now entering enchanted ground. Something important is bound to happen.' And as they walked further within this charmed place Christian repeated 'Important'. Then he added 'Unimportant' as if it had just occurred to him, and quite soon he was uttering both words alternately. 'Unimportant. Important. Unimportant. Important. Unimportant. Important.'

Alice, who was still sulking some paces behind them, began to declaim in turn, 'I mean what I say. I say what I mean. I mean what I say. I say what I mean.'

The air of this place was very sweet and, as they chanted in unison, Timothy started to feel drowsy. 'Words must have some meaning after all,' he said to himself. 'I will explain it to them later, but I really ought to have a little sleep now.' He left Christian's side and crept into the shade of an old lime tree; it threw an inviting shadow just across the path, and he lay down among the roots which curled over the ground.

'Words must have some meaning because they come from the Book of the Law,' he said in that delicious state of fatigue just before slumber. 'Was it Alice who told me about it? That's what we're searching for. That's our pilgrimage.' Then he fell fast asleep.

When at last he woke up, night had descended upon this enchanted place. A great mist and darkness were all around and, although he sensed that Alice and Christian were somewhere close to him, he could see nothing. Wherefore he was forced to feel for them by words: 'Hope,' he shouted into the air, and that word had all the clarity of a white ball thrown in a trajectory through the night. After a short pause other words emerged out of the obscurity. 'Sentence,' Christian replied, and then Alice cried out, 'Ending.' It was as if they were talking in their sleep, their words governed neither by faith nor reason. So when Christian called, 'I will seek it again,' Alice took up his cry with, 'A wood without a name'; then Timothy suddenly joined in the game and shouted, 'It is always the same.' It was still so dark that they could not see each other, but their words had found them out.

Now Christian struck a light, and all at once they found themselves in a circle around a broken pillar; they had been much closer to each other than they knew, and they were so embarrassed by their proximity that they stared very hard at the pillar in front of them. For upon it, in the faltering light of Christian's candle, they saw words inscribed in an unusual hand. Some had been worn away, some seemed only half formed, and although Christian traced each letter with his finger he could hardly puzzle out the meaning. Alice was far cleverer. 'Of course,' she exclaimed in delight, 'these are verses!' And she proceeded to read what had been etched upon the stone:

> 'This pillar is like paint upon a flower,
> Like words in flight with aerial power,
> Its quest for shape surpassing altogether
> The tangled clouds of human weather.

'Why,' she said, breaking off in disgust, 'this is nonsense verse. It has no meaning whatsoever.'

'Carry on with your reading,' Christian told her solemnly. 'I may pick out its truth.'

So Alice continued with:

> 'All Nature in a state of rage
> Because the word is unassuaged.
> How can the pilgrim plot or plan
> When verse around him does not scan?

'There is more,' Alice added.

> 'How can I rhyme *story* with *pain*
> When harmony must be maintained?
> What is the point of making sense,
> Alice, when it is all at my expense?

> 'I suppose it's time for the refrain,
> For the refrain.

'How can it possibly know my name,' Alice inquired rather crossly, 'when I have never spoken to it at all?'

'You never speak to Poetry,' Christian replied. 'Poetry has to speak to you. Look.' He pointed to the base of the pillar, where Timothy could see the words glowing in the light of the candle:

> Christian is quite right, you know,
> I may be fast, I might be slow,
> But on almost all occasions
> I make up my own quotations.

'I never heard such nonsense in my life,' Alice said. 'Poetry must take the consequences of its own behaviour, just like everybody else. If not – why, there would be nothing. Nothing to hold on to.' She leaned against the pillar at this point, only to tumble on to the ground, since it had already begun to disappear; the outline of it lingered, but after a few moments only a few words were left suspended in the air until they also glimmered and disappeared. They vanished all the faster now that the darkness began to lift, and the mist to clear, and in the gathering light Timothy helped Alice to her feet. He was by now quite bewildered, and she only discomposed him further by suddenly bursting into tears. 'Why do they do it?' she sobbed. 'Why do words do it?'

'Be careful.' Christian was gazing thoughtfully at the space into which the verses had disappeared. 'You know what happened when I cried.'

'I am not you. I am I. Although I might as well be anyone in this place, for all the attention I get.'

Timothy walked away from his two companions; he stood in the shadow of the old lime tree and kicked the dust with his foot. 'I am determined,' he said to the tree, 'I am determined to find some meaning in all of this. If only I could find the right way to begin –'

'I believe I may be able to help you there.'

The boy turned around to find himself being addressed by a young man in a very large top hat with a sign, IN THIS STYLE, 10/6, stuck in its brim. 'Why,' he exclaimed, 'it's the Mad Hatter!'

'It is very provoking,' the man replied, '*very* provoking when one is called that. Especially when it is shouted at one like a Hindu curse! I am the Interpreter and, according to the rules, now I have to take you to my house and explain everything that has happened to you.' Timothy looked around anxiously for Alice and Christian since, in truth, he was unwilling to go anywhere without them. 'They can come too,' the Mad Hatter added wearily. 'As long as they know the way.'

This seemed a peculiar request, since it was he who took the lead and guided them towards a little house; they had not walked very far before Timothy realized that they were back upon the plain which he had seen at the beginning of his dream. 'Can it be true,' the boy thought, 'that I have come all this way only to return to the place where I started?'

'Hush!' The Mad Hatter raised a finger to his lips. 'No idle thoughts. Not in here.' Whereupon he pushed open the door to the little house, which they had reached very suddenly, and ushered them all inside. He stood watching them for a moment, before carefully locking the door. 'This is the time,' he said, 'when I will show you that which will be profitable to you. I can explain all the books that ever were invented, and a good many that haven't been invented just yet.' He lit a candle, and beckoned them into an adjacent room which was hung with many pictures. 'I call this,' he said, 'my significant room.' In the flickering light of the candle it seemed to Timothy for a moment that the paintings which surrounded him had suddenly come alive. 'Here,' said the Mad Hatter, pointing to a canvas which depicted great crowds in movement, 'here is Vanity Fair.' Then he placed the candle up against a landscape, which showed three travellers in a dark wood. 'Here are The Good Companions. And over here is a portrait which,' he added modestly, 'I executed myself. Is that the right word, by the way? Executed? It is called The House of the Interpreter. Which is exactly where you are now. This is my house. How do you do?' He put down the candle, and solemnly shook each of them by the hand.

Alice was not amused, however. 'You told us you were going to explain what had happened,' she said. 'But there is nothing here about *me*. Nothing at all.'

'Oh, there will be.' The Mad Hatter seemed to be enjoying her display of bad manners.

'That is by far the most confusing thing that I ever heard!'

He took her by the arm, but she rudely shook him off. 'Temper!' he replied in high good spirits. 'Little girls who cannot keep their tempers will find that their tempers keep them.' Alice at once burst into tears, and at the sight of them the Mad Hatter stepped back in horror. 'Oh no. Oh dear me no,' he muttered. He was clearly frightened. 'Alice, dear. Dearest Alice. If you will only stop crying I promise to explain everything. Wouldn't that be nice, dear?' She shook her head and continued crying. 'There will be something in it for you, just wait and see.' At this point Alice wiped her eyes and smiled. 'Let me show you my beautiful garden, dearest girl. Just through this door.'

He pointed towards the hearth in the room and, when Timothy looked more closely at it, he realized to his surprise that there was indeed a door inside the fireplace which had the words OPEN ME inscribed upon it. 'I wonder,' Timothy thought, 'if we will have to go through fire to enter the garden?' But the Mad Hatter took a golden key from his bookcase and, marshalling the others behind him, bowed his head and entered the fireplace. The door opened easily: each went through in turn, and Alice, Christian and Timothy found themselves to be in a wonderful garden with beds of bright flowers, and gravel walks, and cool fountains, stretching to the very horizon. Then Timothy noticed a very odd thing: the bright flowers were all of the wrong colour. The roses were blue or grey; the daffodils were green with orange stalks; the violets were silver or gold; and the chrysanthemums were all striped in red and black.

'Behold the flowers,' the Mad Hatter was now saying, 'diverse in stature and quality, in smell and virtue. Also look where the Gardener has set them, there they stand, and quarrel not with one another. In this you may see a metaphor.'

It was Christian who heard it first. 'There is some vibration in the air,' he said. 'Like the approach of thunder.'

'Not thunder,' the young man replied, 'but a natural explanation. Walk with me this way, and all will be revealed to you.'

So, with him as their guide, the three companions followed a spiral path which took them down a gently curving slope until, beneath the shade of a great oak with silver leaves and golden branches, they saw a collection of musical instruments. 'Look upon this,' Christian said to them. 'A viol, a lute and a recorder huddled promiscuously together. And here is the sackbut which makes such doleful music that it sounds like thunder.'

The Mad Hatter touched his arm. 'That is known here as the Ground of Music.'

But as Timothy gazed upon these instruments, he grew puzzled: for although no one was playing upon them, and although their strings were still, sounds began to rise from them and fill the air of the garden with melodious notes. Then, curiouser and curiouser, the music itself was turned into song:

> 'Turn about and touch these strings
> Which rare English music bring;
> Music which ends as it begins
> And contains truth within its ring.'

It was not until he had finished that Timothy realized that it was actually he who had been singing this; he did not understand how he had begun, but he had the strangest feeling that he had been singing for a long time. Perhaps the sweet air of this place had sent him into a profound sleep but, then, how could he have sung as he slept? 'It sounded very pretty,' he said to the Mad Hatter, who was standing beside him, 'and it seemed to fill my head with ideas. Only I don't exactly know what they were.'

'That's precisely as I expected,' he replied. 'Just so.

Now that the music had ceased, Alice was becoming angrier and angrier. 'It's no good pretending you had anything to do with it,' she said to the Hatter. She came up to Timothy and pinched his arm very hard. 'The music isn't his invention, you goose. He knows no more about it than you do. Which I presume is *very* little indeed.'

'I never said it was mine,' the Mad Hatter replied. 'You are a curious child, putting words in other people's mouths when they never wanted to be there in the first place. You must always find out from words where they want to go before you use them.'

Alice ignored this homily. 'I don't believe there was any music at all,' she said. 'I believe you made it all up.'

'You don't know much, do you? *He* made it up. It is his

music, after all.' To Timothy's astonishment, he saw that the Hatter was pointing at him. 'He's dreaming now. And what do you think he's dreaming about?'

'Nobody can guess that,' Alice replied crossly.

'Why, about *you*! And if he left off dreaming about you, where do you suppose you would be?'

'Where I am now, you ridiculous creature.'

'Not you! You would be nowhere. Why, you're only a sort of a thing in his dream!'

Timothy had no time to reflect upon this curious statement, because Christian came up to him and with a smile murmured, 'Eternity! Eternity! Oh life! Oh life!' Then he added, 'Will you, won't you, will you, won't you, will you join the dance?'

The four of them clasped hands and began dancing in a circle around the oak tree while the Mad Hatter, in a high clear voice, began to chant:

> 'Ever drifting down the stream –
> Lingering in the golden gleam –
> Life, what is it but a dream?'

To which Alice replied in the same high chant, just as if they were children playing a game:

> 'Now, Reader, I have told my dream to thee;
> See if thou canst interpret it to me.
> But if thou still cast all away as vain,
> I know not but 'twill make me dream again.'

And Christian, in turn:

> 'For us, our toilsome days are now quite ended.
> But you, now Art and Life are strangely blended,
> What of your own life . . .'

It was at this point that Christian's voice began to fade away; he, and Alice, and the Mad Hatter went through the garden singing, but Timothy could not understand what they said.

He was alone once more and, when he looked down, he saw Christian's book on the ground just beyond the shadow of the oak tree; he picked it up but, when he opened the volume, the words retreated and left only a white space behind. 'This is how it all began,' he said. Yet everything between, all that had happened to him, seemed to be so frail, so insubstantial, so easily lost. He might as well never have lived at all. 'All the people here were so lonely,' he added. 'They acted like that because they were afraid.' And indeed there had been a terrible sorrow dispersed among them; there had been nothing ahead of them and, somehow, nothing behind them. The music remained, however. He heard it again, as a continuous presence beneath scenes which he could now hardly recall. Perhaps there were some who never heard the music, and for them there would be nothing to remember. But there was something now which would always hold Timothy in its embrace.

So he awoke and, behold, it was a Dream. His father was beside him; he had fallen asleep with his arm around his son, and the book from which he had been reading had dropped to the floor.

THREE

'PALIMPSEST,' MY FATHER SAID, AT breakfast on the following morning.

'What, dad?' I was still lost in the traces of my dream, and the word seemed to be coming from some far distance. It was as if deep clouds were rolling above me, obscuring the pale vision of the sky.

'Did you look it up in the dictionary?'

'Oh no.' I did not, at that moment, ever want to look into another book. 'I forgot.'

'Is there something the matter, Timmy?'

'No. What should be the matter?'

'I'll show you what the matter is. When I catch you.' He stuck a half-eaten piece of bread and jam in his mouth, like some grotesque tongue, and then rose from his chair with his arms outstretched. It was an old game with us but one that I secretly dreaded, because now he began to chase me around the room, into the kitchen, into my own room, always two or three paces behind me. I would be laughing but I was also afraid, and when eventually he caught me I curled myself into a little ball until he let me go. 'Well, you should look it up,' he said, calmly finishing the rest of his bread and jam while I stood panting before him.

Our breakfast was a late meal, although I never realized it at the time. I knew very little about the lives of other people, of other children, because I had always been brought up by my father. Ever since I could remember, he had been beside me; I could no more imagine life without him than I could imagine life without myself. My mother had died when I was very young – that was all he had ever told me about her. Perhaps it was strange that he, who spent so much time communing with the dead, never mentioned her; but it did

48

not seem so peculiar then. Certainly she remained a powerful if unmentioned presence in both our lives. There was a photograph of her in my father's room – I can still recall the heavy silver frame which surrounded it, so bulky and ornate a border for this frail image of a young woman. There were times when, in my childish fancy, I thought that the frame had killed her. She was sitting on the grass, her legs tucked beneath her, wearing a long dress of some flowered material; it was a park, I think, and there were two or three trees lightly defined behind her on the sepia print. The outline of her hair was blurred, which led me to believe that there was a slight breeze blowing; she was glancing away to her right with a serious look upon her face. Her companion must have told her to keep very still, or perhaps it was an instinctive expression – simply the way she looked at the world. Her name was Cecilia. I always knew this, although I cannot recall that my father ever mentioned it. I discovered, much later, that she had died while giving birth to me; his silence was a way of defending me against some knowledge of my self.

So we lived alone, my father and I. Why he chose not to send me to the elementary school in the area, with all the unhappy consequences which followed, is no longer a mystery to me. At the time he made our life together seem like some vast and stupendous secret, and yet no one could have been more proud of me in front of his friends or even chance acquaintances: 'Timothy Harcombe,' he used to say, 'knows everything.'

'Dad –'

'Oh yes, he does. Excuse the interruption. Timothy Harcombe can tell you about literature and history and music. All things visible and invisible. Isn't that right, Tim?'

'No, dad. How can I know what's invisible?'

In truth I had no special knowledge, and whatever information I possessed came directly from my father. I have already explained, I think, how in the evenings we would discuss

what he called 'English music', but our daily routine was of a
more orderly and practical kind. He was a patient and as-
siduous teacher for, if he remained constant to anything in his
life, it was to my education. After our late breakfast he would
clear the plates from the table, put out his books, and then
begin. A page of English history. A page of science. A page of
Shakespeare. How far away those days seem to me now. Yet
once again I see my father before me, bent over a book, his
dark hair falling into his eyes, his finger moving from line to
line as he recites the lesson; and now he is looking up at me
with that bright glance of his, and I return his look. Those
distant days.

There were times when he could not look at me, however,
when he became too depressed or disconsolate to continue
with my lesson. He would put down the volume and stare out
of the window at Hackney Square, sometimes sighing, sometimes rubbing his eyes. I never understood the source of his
mood, but I never failed to share it; I, too, became miserable
or uncertain and stared out of the window with him. But my
father's depression never lasted for very long, and there were
many occasions when I could almost see his spirits rising
within him. 'It's raining cats and dogs,' he would say, looking
mournfully out of the window. 'I wonder, Tim, where that
phrase comes from? Cats and dogs. I can't see any pet falling
from the sky, can you?'

He was already looking more cheerful, and glanced at me
as he spoke. 'And that's another thing, Timmy. A red letter
day. Have you ever seen a red letter? I certainly haven't.'
This cheerfulness was a tribute to my father's temperament,
which might otherwise have crumbled under the difficulty of
our circumstances, but at the time I suspected that he masked
his own depression simply to relieve mine. In this, as in so
many other things, I was to prove mistaken.

There was always the Harcombe Circle to keep my father
amused. That was our phrase for it – the Circle comprising
all the acquaintances who had over the years become attached

to him. I do not think that he had any friends of his own making. He never sought out companions, or made any particular gesture to interest or attract anyone. Instead he seemed to collect people by accident, as it were, particularly those who had seen him at his work and who had come passionately to believe in him. I suppose that I was one of their number: I was one of the Harcombe Circle, which included Margaret Collins, Matthew Lucas, Jasper Burden, Gloria Patterson and then, eventually, Stanley Clay who had followed my father home on that winter evening. Names now, only names which I write down, names of those who must have died long ago. I cannot dwell on the fact that I am now the only one to remember those evenings which we spent together in Hackney Square. Evenings when my father would lecture them, provoke them, teach them, prompt them, lead them forward into a world which they hardly knew to exist. Those were occasions of warmth and light now grown cold, as time has spun them further and further apart. And I am left here with only the names.

My favourite was Margaret Collins. We often saw her in Hackney Square since, after the lessons of the day were completed, my father and I would walk outside for a few minutes. She lived only a few streets away and, since she worked as a cleaner for some offices near Whitechapel, she used to return home in our direction. There were times when my father seemed literally to fall over her. 'Tim,' he said on one occasion, 'remember this. There is always a reason for a hedge.' He put out his hand and plucked a dark green leaf from one which bordered the small front gardens lying off the square. 'A hedge can protect you, Timmy. Protect you against the wind of the world. Oh goodness me, it's Margaret!' He had stumbled upon her, for the very good reason that she was extremely small.

'I was just having a think,' she said. 'I shan't be stopping, thank you very much.' She was about four feet in height, shorter even than I was, and now she took my hands for a moment as if she were about to dance with me. 'I've got to scrub my steps,' she added. 'Pumice and chalk. Pumice and chalk.' She was then in her late fifties but she had a determinedly brisk and cheerful manner, which no doubt had been acquired to conceal all the pain she must once have suffered. Somehow I sensed even then that she had made a definite decision not to be cowed by her own smallness—not to retreat into some private world of shyness and isolation. I am sure, too, that my father helped her in this resolve, and this principally because he never seemed to notice her lack of height. It did not occur to me then that he rarely seemed to notice anything about other people.

'Come into our parlour, Margaret,' he said. 'Take the weight off your feet.'

'There isn't much weight to take off,' she replied. 'I'm a very light creature, you see. We light people just float around.' In fact she began to skip along the path: I opened the door for her, she slipped past me into my father's room, and immediately flung herself into an old brown armchair. Her legs dangled some inches from the ground and she was scarcely bigger than some of the cushions placed at the back of it, but she seemed quite at home.

My father was still talking when he followed her into the room. 'Now, tell me, Margaret, what you were thinking about when we met you? Thinking of me?' She nodded, pleased at his sagacity. 'And of course at the same time I was thinking of you. And Timothy here now, well he was thinking of both of us!' I did not bother to contradict him, and indeed at that moment perhaps I even believed him. 'Imagine all those thoughts, Margaret, twisting and turning in the air.' She looked about her, and then looked at me. 'They brought us together this afternoon. The three of us united in a common bond, created by the power of the invisible over the visible. Doesn't that give you a sense of belonging?' My father did not so much talk to her as narrate, or lecture. It was always his way with the members of the Harcombe Circle. 'You see,

Margaret, nothing in the world happens by accident. How could such a wonderful thing as the world be ruled by chance? If you look carefully enough, there is always a pattern. The ripples on the surface of a pool creep out slowly to the margin. We are on the margin, Margaret. We are on the margin.' Margaret merely nodded since, like the rest of the Harcombe Circle, she was too overawed by my father to do anything other than listen to him expounding his faith. The fact that he was neither famous nor rich from his work never seemed to occur to them, as it never occurred to me, at that time. No doubt they considered such matters to be of no importance.

For had he not cured them? Margaret had come to him five years before, when he pursued his work in Kentish Town, and he managed, as she put it, 'to straighten my bad back'. She did not mean that he had literally made it straight, since she was still slightly hunched as a result of her cleaning work, but he had removed the pain from which she used to suffer. I was on the platform beside him at the time, as she never tired of telling me, although for some reason I did not remember the occasion. I simply took it for granted that I was always with my father. I stood beside him now as Margaret clambered down from the brown armchair: my father had completed his remarks for the afternoon, and she prepared to leave at once with her usual briskness and decision.

'Tonight,' was all she said.

'Yes. Tonight.'

So Margaret was in the hall that evening, together with two other members of the Harcombe Circle, Matthew Lucas and Jasper Burden. They nodded and smiled at me before we began, but they made no sign to my father; they did not want to disturb or distract him while he was preparing for the rigours of that evening's work. He seemed more assured and elevated during the meeting, however, precisely because he had seen them (while pretending not to do so); he always felt more hopeful in the presence of those who believed and trusted in him, just as he was often woefully put out by a group of sceptical or merely inattentive spectators. I shared these moods, and no doubt the silent harmony rising up from our familiar companions helped me that night to see more clearly the full extent of my father's powers. One incident even now remains within my memory. I was holding on to the arms of an old man who had been contacted by his grandmother, dead for more than fifty years. I knew at once that something was happening – I could even hear words being formed in my head – when suddenly the man grew very warm. His body became so hot that it seemed to me that his clothes were being scorched, and in alarm I took my hands away from him. My father looked at me in bewilderment as soon as I did so, and it was clear to me that he had recognized no change in the old man; he sensed only that a link had been broken when I involuntarily stepped backwards. At that precise moment the man turned and stared at me. 'It is you,' he whispered in a voice which might have been that of his grand-mother, so odd it sounded, 'it is you!' No doubt he was blaming me for the disturbance I had created; but I shall never forget the sudden heat of his body or the strange, deep look which he gave me when he turned around.

At the end of the meeting my father, who seemed to have hardly noticed the incident, was very tired. The Harcombe Circle were waiting for him outside the hall, but he did not return their greeting. 'Timothy will take you home,' he said. 'I have to return the key.'

It was our custom on some evenings to invite the Circle back to Hackney Square, but on this occasion I noticed that someone else was lingering in the shadow of the old hall. He was standing apart from the others, and it was only when I took a step towards him that I realized it was Stanley Clay. Slowly he came over to me, while all the time keeping his eyes on my father. 'It hasn't come back,' he said. I knew that he was talking about the nervous spasm which had been cured. 'It's definitely *gone*.'

My father saw him now and muttered, 'Meet Stanley Clay,'

to the rest of them before going back into the hall in order to retrieve the key. That was how Stanley joined the Harcombe Circle and my father acquired another disciple.

I did not lead them to Hackney Square, despite his injunction, but simply followed them. Matthew Lucas and Jasper Burden went on ahead, while I walked two or three paces behind Margaret Collins and Stanley Clay as they made their way down Old Street and past St Agnes Well. 'I want you to tell me everything,' Margaret was saying in her usual firm, brisk way. 'I've known Mr Harcombe since the year dot.' Stanley looked back at me for a moment as if he wanted me to speak for him, and with one bright glance upwards at him she noticed his hesitation. 'Come on,' she said. 'What harm can it do to tell a little person like me?' He gave a half-surprised, half-cautious look, which seemed to say: can I tell my story to her? Can I trust her to listen to me? Suddenly she reached up and put her hand upon his arm.

'I had a bit of a funny neck,' he said. And then he added, 'I've never had a person to depend on.' He looked straight ahead as he talked and had so low a voice that Margaret had to strain herself to her full height, her hand still on his arm, in order to hear him. 'This neck would move about. Like being struck by lightning, really. And people would look at me. They would look at me funny.' Then once again he seemed to change the direction of his thoughts. 'If you live alone, you know, it's hard. It's hard not to think about it.'

'That's true,' Margaret said. 'I don't care what they say.' I had noticed before, in her conversation, how she would allude to imaginary accusers in order to defy or to mock 'them'. 'I suppose,' she added, 'that Mr Harcombe helped you?'

'It didn't hardly seem possible —'

'Go on. Don't mind if they laugh at you. What do they know?'

'But he put his hands on my neck, and then it was gone. The lightning was gone.'

'It was a miracle. That's what it was.' Margaret laughed

out loud and, taking her hand from his arm, began to walk as if she were balancing a book upon her head. 'It was the same with my back,' she said. 'But just look at me now, Stanley. Look how I can manage.'

I was still following two or three paces behind them but, as they described their freedom from pain or hardship, I was filled with a peculiar depression of spirit. It seemed strange to me that they should now be so cheerful, while I sensed even then how sorrowful their lives would always remain. The dwarfish woman. The awkward and disturbed young man. Going into the night ahead of me, while I lingered behind. Yet perhaps that was the secret of their sudden access of happiness: to enter the night without fear and to find each other there. Margaret began to sing, in her high cracked voice, 'Felix keeps on walking . . .' And Stanley replied, in a low hesitant voice, 'Keeps on walking still.' Then again he started talking about his old ailment, as if somehow he were still puzzled by its absence from his life. 'The only time it went away,' he said, 'was when I tuned up the pianos.'

We had come to Hackney Square and the others were waiting patiently for us at the front gate, the gaslight falling aslant upon their pale expectant faces. Jasper Burden was whistling softly to himself, and tapping one foot upon the pavement. He was a young man who worked as a waiter at a supper-room in the City, and he could not help grinning whenever he talked; he seemed perpetually to be watching a wonderful private joke which was happening somewhere just behind one's back. 'I heard a terrible story the other day,' he might say, and then he would begin to smile. 'I can't help it,' he used to add in apology. 'It's just my way. So there was this murder, see . . .' He would be grinning now all the time, and would have to break off occasionally: he would put his hands across his chest, incline his head, and laugh and laugh. I used to laugh with him, too, and we would stand there together unable to speak. 'You've got to,' he would say, drying his eyes with an old piece of cloth he carried in his pocket, 'you've really got to. Anyway, where was I?' Whenever he heard a popular tune being sung or played in the street, he would give a little yell of pleasure and his body seemed to ebb and flow with the music – his sudden movements and turnings making him seem so much like a stream of water that there were times when I thought I could see *through* him. Such wild energy seems to me, in retrospect, to have been a strange thing; and there were to be times, in the future, when I was also afraid of his laughter. But there he stood now, slim, pale, dark-haired, under the gas-lamp in Hackney Square.

Matthew Lucas was beside him. He was middle-aged, but he had a raw, questioning, unformed quality that might generally be associated with youth. I knew dimly about his past – that he had been in an orphanage and then for some time in an asylum near Rotherhithe. My father used to mention this as if it were the most natural and unsurprising thing in the world. As a result I was never afraid of Matthew Lucas, although there were many people who were. He had a look of ferocious concentration, as if he had only just that moment entered the world and was both alarmed and puzzled by what he had found there. He was always questioning my father, seeking out the truth, as he saw it, acquiring knowledge, and on those occasions the look of concentration gave way to one of wonder and of pleasure. He was an ungainly man with a large pock-marked face, and his drab clothes emitted a not unpleasing smell somewhere between dough and putty; I discovered later that this was also the characteristic smell of the institutions into which he had been admitted. Now he pushed a tea-van through the streets, but he never discussed the way he earned his living. I believe he was ashamed of it. My father had cured him of what was then known as neuralgia: I had been present at the time and I still remember how his huge, unwieldy body had shaken and rocked under the power of the healing. I remember, too, how Matthew had sobbed as the burden was lifted from him. He had become devoted to my father and, on an evening such as this, he eagerly waited for his arrival and for the thoughts which Clement Harcombe would present to the Harcombe Circle.

There was one other person who had joined them in the lamplight – Gloria Patterson, a young woman whose beauty was then less obvious to me than the look of scornfulness which she carried with her everywhere. She worked as an assistant at Gamages, which was where, Margaret said, she had picked it up. She displayed another striking characteristic, too, for she wore clothes which would only have been suitable on a middle-aged or elderly woman. Black coats which came down to her ankles. Heavy shoes. Large, shapeless hats. She seemed to enjoy appearing oddly or preternaturally aged – and this despite the radiance of her face, so perfectly formed, so smoothly shaped, that it reminded me of the wax fruit on display in the window of the pie-and-mash shop in Tabernacle Close. She lived with her parents in a small terraced house just a few streets away, as the Harcombe Circle knew, but she behaved as if she were the grandest and most pampered daughter of luxury. She had a sharp east London voice but, when she spoke, she gave the impression of being quite divorced from her surroundings. Why she became attached to my father is another matter; perhaps she believed that she was the reincarnation of some ancient queen, and wanted him to discover more about her occluded past. In fact, as I recall now, there was one picture I could always see: it was of her in a narrow golden boat, looking down at the clear waters beneath. No doubt it was one she impressed upon me with the full force of her own imagining because, as I have said, I was in some ways a receptive child.

And so the three of them waited by the gate while I approached in the company of Margaret Collins and Stanley Clay; they seemed to be swaying slightly in the gaslight and, although this was no doubt the effect of the flickering shadows, I was reminded of the three sunflowers which grew outside our window in the late summer. Three lives brought together for a moment, lives which seemed to possess no meaning even for those who held them, lives which were like the indecipherable relics of words rubbed from a wall – and yet somehow they were part of life itself and, as I approached them with the key in my hand, I was filled with the same thin depression which issued from the very streets of London and which now seems to me to be associated with all the scenes of my childhood there. For what did my own life mean? I believe that my depression sprang from the fear that I, too, would become like them – another pale, baffled, defeated, tremulous human figure standing in the London lamplight. It had begun to rain, and the wet pavements looked as if they might turn into streets of silver.

Stanley and Margaret were now walking beside me, but he held back as we approached the others; he had seen them at that night's meeting, and no doubt on many previous occasions, but he was afraid of them. For some reason I ran ahead of him; without talking to the others I hurried down the narrow stone path, opened the front door and then ran into our lodgings. I went into my own little room, flung myself down on to the bed and put a pillow over my head. It was as if I were protecting myself against intruders, and in the darkness I could feel at peace once more; my eyes and head were sealed against the world. But that mood could never last. Even through my pillow I could hear muffled sounds, and after a moment I sat up and listened intently to their voices in my father's room – diffident, embarrassed voices, easily sliding into silence. I opened my mouth wide several times, imitating the sounds they made, and waited with increasing impatience until I heard my father's footsteps in the hall. Then I rushed out to greet him. 'Hello, dad. This is a surprise.'

'Life is full of surprises, Tim.' He walked past me and ruffled my hair; he had a light, jaunty tread, and indeed seemed to have recovered all of his good spirits. 'Timmy, put the kettle on,' he added. 'The Harcombe Circle has to be

watered before it can grow.' He was rubbing his hands together, no doubt in anticipation of an evening's conversation
with these companions.

By the time I had prepared the tea and brought it to them
in a cracked green pot, Matthew Lucas had begun. He was
leaning forward eagerly, his elbows on his knees, his moon-
shaped face gazing at my father. 'I was reading the *Daily
Mail*,' he said, with an extraordinary look of urgency upon
his face, 'I was reading about that haunted house in Chiswick.
How all the furniture was moved around. And how they saw
a hand floating in the room. Is that right, Mr Harcombe? Is
that how it happened?'

For some reason he expected him to know everything about
this event, and my father laughed. He was sitting in his usual
chair, beside the fire, and he called me over to him. 'You
remember the verse, don't you, Timothy?' he asked as he put
his arm around me and settled me on the arm of the chair.
And then he sang out:

'I hear a voice you cannot hear that says I must not stay.
I see a hand you cannot see that beckons me away.'

He held on to me tightly, and I could hear the rain beating
against the window-panes as he continued to talk in his usual
light voice. 'There are no haunted houses, Matthew. Only
haunted people.'

Jasper Burden got up from the table, against which he had
been resting. 'This is going to be a good one,' he said to
nobody in particular. 'A real good one.' Then he lay down
upon the floor.

'There are certainly haunted people. Haunted by the past,
by their own past or that of others. Haunted by everything.'
He took his arm from my shoulder and went across to the
wireless placed along the opposite wall. It was his new possession – the latest model, as far as I remember, with a curved
horn attached to it which acted as a loudspeaker. He was
fascinated by such things and, before he bought this new

valve set, he had a crystal box in the same room. He used to be hunched over it for hours at a time, wearing the head-phones, listening to those faint signals and crackles coming through the ether which he called 'the sounds of the universe'. It was a miracle, as far as he was concerned, quite as extraordi-nary as anything he achieved in the old hall; indeed I think that in some way the wireless confirmed his magical sense of life. 'Think of yourself like this,' he said. He switched it on, waited for it to warm up and then started to tune it in. 'Some people resemble this. They come across the waves in the atmosphere and then convert them into sounds. Sometimes they can control it. Sometimes they can't.' He had picked up a man's voice, who for some reason was reciting a list of names and numbers, and he turned off the set.

Matthew Lucas was listening intently. 'But where do the waves come from?' he asked in his usual urgent way. 'Does that mean there is some other place? Some place different from this? When you talk about waves, it makes me think of the sea. But that can be a very cold place. People can drown in that.' Somehow my father had evoked all his fearfulness. 'I've never seen the waves, I've never been there, but I've heard about it. And it makes me feel cold.'

'There's no need for that.' It was Margaret Collins, who had hoisted herself up into a small wooden chair and sur-rounded herself with cushions so that only the upper part of her body was visible. But she sounded as brisk and as comfort-ing as ever. 'There's no need for you to feel cold, Matthew. Not waves of water, you see, but waves of voices. Or waves of music. Waves of lovely warm music lifting you up into the other world.' This was what it meant for her: to be lifted up; to be made straight and tall; to dwell in some other world than this.

There was so much brightness and animation upon her face as she talked that Jasper Burden clapped his hands in glee. 'I can hear it,' he said. 'I'm one of those people who can hear it. Look, it's making me dance now.' He got up from the floor, where he had been lying stretched out in front of the fire, and executed a few waltz steps with an imaginary partner. Then he started dancing faster and faster, whirling around until he collapsed exhausted on the floor once more. 'But if there is a world beyond,' he said, as he lay there breathless, 'why can't we see it? I see everything so clearly *here* – I really see and hear everything. That's why I'm such a good waiter. So what stops me from hearing those sounds you talked about, Mr Harcombe? Why do some people have the gift and not others?' My father merely smiled, and waited for someone else to answer; that was often his method, to allow the Circle to argue together until eventually he arrived at some kind of resolution.

'I'll tell you why. We're too mired down.' Matthew Lucas spoke with the same intentness as before. 'We're too bogged down. We can't really see anything. Nothing at all. I'm not saying that it's our fault. I'm not saying that it's anybody's fault. It's just the way things are. We spend our time working, making ends meet. It's not for us to see beyond that. Isn't that what we're talking about, Mr Harcombe?'

'Oh, but there are times –' Margaret began to say.

'Yes. At death.' It was an unfamiliar voice, that of Stanley Clay, and everybody turned to look at him – except my father, who was staring thoughtfully at the ceiling. Gloria Patterson directed her usual scornful glance at this new face and, suddenly embarrassed by the attention, he lowered his head. 'Or when you see somebody die. Perhaps then something comes through. But I have seen a terrible death.' He had his fists clenched together, and I knew that he was talking about the death of his father. 'I've seen somebody shout and scream to the end. There was nothing there. No music. Not that time.'

'But that's the beauty of it, don't you see?' Margaret Collins dislodged one pillow from her chair in her eagerness. 'If you think you're in prison, you can try to escape. That's why we come to Mr Harcombe's meetings, because we can escape *them*. We can see that this isn't the only world. There are other worlds. Other voices. And it's such a wonderful sensation to be part of it – even if just for a moment, to be lifted up and allowed to see it.'

'Yes. I've felt that, too.' Stanley Clay kept his head down, but he was talking more eagerly now. 'And not feeling like a failure no more. Because none of this' – he put his hands out, gesturing first at himself and then at the others – 'none of this matters. Not a bit of it. Some of you were in the hall two nights ago, when I was cured.' Jasper and Margaret both nodded, while Matthew kept on looking at him intently. 'I was cured of my funny neck, you see. And I felt so much lighter – I can't put it no other way. I felt *lighter*. And it wasn't just because I'd been cured. It was because I had seen something different. Something larger. You know. Heard something else.'

'Music.' It was Jasper Burden who gave a little shout of triumph. 'All that beautiful music. I want to hear it, too.' And as I listened to them discussing these things, the 'waves' and the 'music', I realized how much more at peace they were in an alternative world than in the real one. They were happy in this room with my father but, as soon as they left this place, they would once more become awkward and alone.

'Music. Voices. Call it what you will.' My father resumed as if nothing had been said to interrupt his train of thought. 'Our new friend, Stanley Clay, put it very well. Have you met Stanley properly? Yes? He said it very nicely; there *is* something larger, something of which we're all a part. You saw it this evening, just as you have seen it many evenings before. And surely you know all about it in your own lives? At those times when you are suddenly filled with elation, don't you feel then that you are part of a larger world which is moving you forward –'

'But when you're unhappy . . .' Stanley broke in, and in his eagerness it was clear that he had rarely, if ever, spoken of such things before. It was for him a new form of freedom; in the very words he was now choosing, he was attaching some kind of meaning to his life. 'When you're unhappy, you become small and narrow. You never connect with no one else. You think the sky is going to fall in upon you.'

'That's it, Stanley Clay. Thank you for interrupting me.' My father said this without a trace of irony. 'That is why the larger world, the other world, is a world of love. It doesn't fall upon you. You fall upon it. It's all around us now. I can feel it. I can touch it.' He had his arm around me once more, as I sat on the chair beside him, and he patted my shoulder. 'It is the world where we no longer know suffering and sickness and misery, and all the things that cut us off from others. It is a world of love. And aren't you all happier,' he went on, 'now that you know?' This seemed to me, at the time, a perfectly appropriate conclusion.

'I'm always happy,' Jasper Burden replied.

For some reason this struck the others as very funny; there had been such an air of tension and insistent questioning within the room that perhaps only laughter could break it. I laughed, too, although I did not know why. But I was also very tired. I rose from my father's chair in order to go back to my room, but I only got as far as the door. The laughter had faded as quickly as it had come, and now suddenly I felt such a wave of sorrow and of misery that I could not bear it: I put my hand up to my face, leant against the wall, and then fell to the floor.

I must have lost consciousness, for at the next moment I saw my father's face looking down at me. 'Timothy has had a fall,' he said quietly to me. 'Just a little fall.' But I could see his anxiety, and I realized that it was my duty to alleviate it.

'Yes, dad,' I said. 'I'm fine.' The others had got up and were standing around him. 'Yes,' I said again, 'I'm fine.' And then they melted away.

I woke up the next morning and put my arm out from the side of the bed; I felt someone's hair. I pulled back my hand in horror, at the touch of some strange thing which had come to my room during the night, but at the next moment I realized that it was the hair of my father's head – and that I had been placed on the sofa overnight while he slept on the floor beside me. Through the red curtains I could see the first faint stirrings of the rising sun and I lay very still, feeling the light upon my face. I did not want to wake him, not yet, but I could hear him twitching and snorting in his sleep: he seemed to be suffering from bad dreams. For some reason this disturbed me, so I rose as quietly as I could from the sofa and started to tiptoe back to my own room.

'Don't go.' It was my father's voice. He had been awake all the time. 'Timothy, won't you come back here a minute?' I returned to the sofa and sat upon the sheet he must have placed around me last night; he was leaning with his elbow upon a cushion he had used as a pillow. 'I wanted to talk to you,' he said weakly.

'What about, dad?'

'You know.'

It was as if he had fainted last night, not me, and I realized at once what he wanted me to say. 'I'm fine now. Honestly. I think I was just very hungry last night.'

'That's it!' He sat up and scratched his chest. 'I knew it was that! So eat, Timmy. Eat!' Then he started singing, 'Yes we do have bananas. We have some bananas today.'

I was preparing some bread and butter for myself in the kitchen, just as he had instructed, when he came up behind me and patted me on the head. 'I was telling them last night,' he said, 'that Tim will go a very long way indeed. You will go far.' Despite the enthusiasm in his voice, he sounded almost apologetic. 'Great expectations for you, Timmy. In the years ahead.' He was staring out of the kitchen window into the bedraggled back garden, the haunt of weeds and broken bottles. 'Timothy,' he said in a changed voice. 'Timothy, will you look after me when you're rich?'

'I'll buy you a palace, dad.'

'With golden doors?'

'And golden windows.'

'You *will* look after me, Tim, won't you?'

'Yes, dad.' I was embarrassed by him, and I turned my back in order to finish the bread and butter I had made for myself.

He stood looking out of the window for a few minutes, and then, as usual, his mood abruptly changed. 'You need some fresh air, Timothy Harcombe,' he said. 'You need to be taken out of yourself. You worry too much. In fact, you need to be taken out altogether. On an expedition.'

There were going to be no lessons in any case since it was a Saturday, and it was not long before we left the house. My father seemed more than usually preoccupied, however, and he trailed along behind me as I began to walk in no particular direction. 'Stanley Clay is very odd,' he said. 'Do you think the sky ever could fall in, Timothy?'

'No, dad.' I was kicking stones into the gutter, watching them as they rolled away. 'But Jasper Burden was upset. I think he believed it.'

He did not reply and, when I turned around, I saw him grinning at me. 'Tim, he was the happy one!' He said nothing more, but after a few moments he caught up with me. 'They're all upset in their different ways,' he said. 'Everyone's life is like that, Tim. Frail. Always very frail.' Perhaps this explained his earlier conversation, when he asked me to 'look after' him when I had become a rich and famous man. 'It takes only one accident, one crisis,' he continued, 'and everything is torn away. The whole edifice collapses, and there is nothing beneath our feet any more. That's when we start falling.' He had never spoken like this to me before; he stopped for a moment and passed his hand across his face. 'I try to cheer them up, you know. But it's very hard sometimes, Timothy. Hard to know what to do for the best. Everyone is so frail.'

'Come on, dad.' He had started trailing behind me again, and I took his hand in order to drag him forward.

'I got a letter from your grandfather the other day,' he
said, still holding back. 'Your mother's father.' He had not
mentioned this person before, and it seemed to me to be so
remote a connection that I was scarcely interested at all. It
had never occurred to me that I stood in relationship to
anyone else, and I was only puzzled by my father's reference
to him. 'He's very interested in you, Timmy. You are his only
grandson, after all.'

'So what, dad?'

'So . . . so I want you to be friendly with him when he
visits. He's coming a long way to see you.' We continued our
desultory walk and in the course of it, by degrees, my father
managed casually to mention the fact that my grandfather
and grandmother lived in Wiltshire; that they were now in
their mid-sixties; that their name was Sinclair. This last fact I
already knew and indeed, in those childish days, it often
seemed to me that the original name of my mother – Cecilia
Sinclair – was somehow a living presence within the house.
Not my mother herself for, as I have said, I knew nothing of
her; but the name remained, like the photograph of her, a
familiar companion.

My father stood still for a moment, then leapt up and took
a leaf from the hanging bough of a plane tree. 'Timmy,' he
said. 'How many leaves would you estimate were on this
tree?'

'Five thousand, two hundred and sixty-five.'

'That's a good round number, Tim, but tell me this. Now
that I have taken away this one leaf, is it still the same tree?'

'Of course, dad. It's always the same tree.'

He seemed genuinely pleased by my answer. 'That is good
to know, Timothy, isn't it? That things can change and still
remain the same?'

We had been walking along Kingsland Road, by accident
as I thought, when suddenly my father turned abruptly off
into Salt Street and stopped at the burial ground beside it.
'You know,' he said. 'This is a coincidence. This is where

your mother is buried. Shall we go and visit her?' I was too surprised to do anything but follow him, as he made his way past the crumbling stone pillars which marked the entry into the burial ground itself. I had no way of understanding then the reason for this unexpected visit but, as it seems to me now, he had come to placate her. It was an old cemetery filled with broken gravestones, untended graves and mausolea displaying indecipherable phrases. A recent gale had blown down an oak tree, which now lay across several graves; the headstones had been smashed into large fragments which littered the ground. I liked this place. As I followed my father down the mossy paths, I experienced no sensation of dread or even apprehension; I felt, somehow, more truly myself. Is it possible that a small child can have some intimation of its own death? Is that what I recognized?

My father, who was always in communication with the dead, seemed unaccountably dismayed or fearful as he searched for my mother's grave. He could not remember where it was, and so instead we searched for stones of more recent manufacture. It was really only by accident, in fact, that we came across it – a pearly-white headstone with the words CECILIA HARCOMBE, 1891–1913 inscribed upon it. Underneath there was a phrase in gilt lettering, HAIL, BRIGHT CECILIA!, which now my father gingerly leaned forward to touch. Then he began to cry. After a moment he looked around and tried to smile at me. 'Don't worry, Tim, I won't do anything to embarrass you.' But he was still crying when he straightened up and looked down at the gravel which covered the grave itself. 'Twelve years,' he said. 'Twelve years without her.' He turned his back and started walking away. There were some Michaelmas daisies growing within the cracks of the ground: I picked as many as I could and laid them on the grave before hurrying to find him. 'Has she ever spoken to you?' he asked me. 'Has she ever contacted you?'

At first I was astonished by his question, and then I felt afraid. 'Dad! What are you talking about!' He looked at me for several seconds, a quiet steady look, and I ran away from him. I wanted to flee from him, yes, but in some sense I also wanted to flee from my mother and my mother's grave. I wanted to abandon them, one living and one dead.

He caught up with me just as I came to the entrance, and put his hand upon my shoulder. 'I only meant to ask,' he said, 'if you ever think about her?'

'No.'

'Not ever?'

'No.'

'Not a tiny bit?'

'No!' I was not being entirely truthful, however; while I stood by my mother's grave for those few moments, I had been reacquainted with a sensation which I had known since infancy and which I knew to be somehow connected with her – some fugitive impression of security, some intangible serenity, some echo of restfulness.

'What did you think of the words on the stone?' my father asked me. 'I made them up myself.'

'You should have brought flowers,' was all I could think of saying. 'You shouldn't just have left her.'

There was an ex-serviceman begging outside the gate, and my father went across to put a coin in the tin he was carrying around his neck. 'I always feel sorry for them,' he said. 'Not that I could have gone myself. I had you, Tim, didn't I?' I did not understand why he mentioned this now, although I suppose that for him the war was somehow connected with my mother's death. 'But I attested. I never got a white feather. Not me.' We walked back along Salt Street and, when we turned the corner into Kingsland Road, my father broke the silence. 'Let's make a day of it, Tim. Let's go to the pictures.'

There was a picture-house a few hundred yards away from us, the Electric Theatre, and we hurried there in order to catch the Saturday matinée; there was a notice outside in dark brown capitals: WHERE YOU SEE THE LATEST LIFE-SIZE MOVING PICTURES. My father loved this place almost as much as he loved the music-hall in the Commercial Road; its elaborate stucco had been painted lime-green and, within the foyer, the carpets and curtains were of a deep purple. It was an improbable place, in one of the poorest parts of London, but I believe that it was the very extravagance and unreality that my father enjoyed; he enjoyed the darkness of the auditorium, too, with its faint smell of dust and sherbet and tobacco, with its atmosphere of subdued expectancy as the pianist played before the beginning of the performance. It occurs to me now, in fact, that it might have been this atmosphere he was trying to recreate at the meetings in the old hall, where we saw different pictures.

The production was *Great Expectations*, and the pit was almost full when we bought our tickets for the balcony. It was about to begin as we arrived, but my feeling of relief at having settled on to our wooden seats only just in time was tempered by a certain unease. For after the titles had appeared on the screen and the piano accompaniment had begun, the opening scene was in a graveyard very like the one from which we had come. Could it be that my own mother was buried there among the other graves? For a moment I expected to see her sitting upon the gravel and the daisies, with the same expression which she had in the photograph in my father's room. I leaned forward, staring into the screen, as Pip began clambering over the resting places of the dead before coming to a halt before a row of small gravestones. There was a vista of flat grey marshes, of mist, of an obscure sky; and then quite suddenly the hands of the convict, Magwitch, grabbed the young boy and turned him upside down. I was conscious of nothing now except those figures upon the screen. And then it happened.

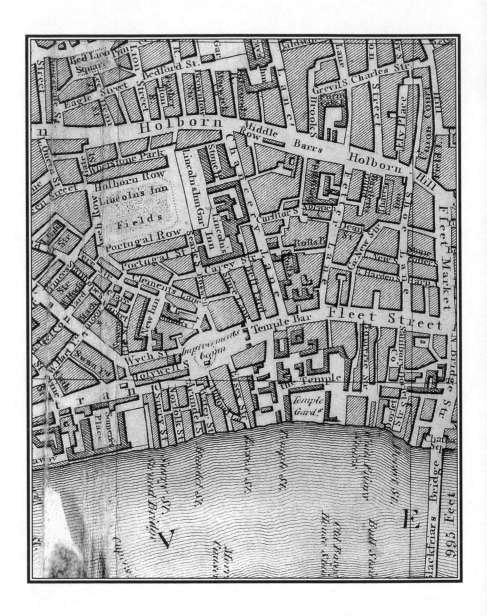

FOUR

H E WAS TURNED UPSIDE DOWN. His world upside down.
The mild sun had swung around and, as he turned, he
was startled by a feeling he had never known before – a
feeling close to that of parting or loss, but interfused with a no
less poignant sensation of wonder. Whatever held him now let
him fall, gently, on to the ground; he lay there for a few
moments, as dazed as if he had been through lightning. Then
he sat up, rubbed his eyes three times, and looked around. He
was in a garden, long since fallen into ruin; there was a paved
space in its centre, where once some statues might have been
placed, but the stones were now all cracked and moss grew
over them in clusters of grey and green. He could have been
in his mother's graveyard again but, when he looked around,
he found himself in the shadow of a large house; the lower
windows were walled up, the higher ones barred, the old
brick and stone of the structure almost completely obliterated
by ivy which clung even to the stacks of the chimneys.

'Begin again.' Someone was talking inside the house. 'Begin
again. Begin the world. Although I am an old man, night is
generally my time for walking among other public buildings,
in a certain town. It was the best of times, it was the worst of
times, in these times of ours, though concerning the exact
year there is no need to be precise. The first ray of light which
illumines the gloom, in the year 1775, sat in the corner of a
darkened room. London. An ancient English cathedral town?
How can the ancient English cathedral town be here! No.
Begin again.' Timothy crept towards the house but he could
see nothing within. He could still hear the voice because a
door had been left open and, when he came closer to it, he
saw that it led into a dark hallway. 'My father's name being
Pirrip now, what I want is, Facts. Whether I shall turn out to

73

be the hero of my own life, or whether that station will be
held by anybody else, these pages must show. Yet how does
anything begin? Should I look further back?'

Timothy entered the hall and followed the sound of this
steady, earnest voice until he came to an uncarpeted recess
just beside a staircase; there was another door ahead of him
and, when he pushed it open, he saw the figure of a man
sitting in a great armchair in the corner of a darkened room.
His eyes were bandaged, and he was playing a solitary game
of cards upon a small table in front of him. Timothy could
not understand how he saw the figures or the numbers of the
cards, but he seemed to be playing very determinedly and
very briskly even as he spoke the words which Timothy had
heard. 'Begin again,' he was saying now. 'Begin again.' He
cocked his head to one side as though he were listening to the
quietest of voices. He had a small beard and slender, very
slender, hands with carefully manicured nails; everything
about him seemed so quick and so neat that Timothy
wondered how he was content to remain here, sightless, in so
forlorn a house. Surely he would prefer to be exploring the
world?

He was immediately aware of the boy's presence, and raised
his head from the cards. 'You are expected to begin, too,' he
said. 'I see the same things always, because I see only the
past. But now is your chance to break the spell of this place.'
He raised his arm and pointed to the hall and staircase behind
Timothy. 'Go on. Climb as I once climbed.' The boy had no
choice but to obey, and so he turned away from this strange
man and approached the stairs. As he stepped upon the first
of them the wood creaked beneath his foot and, as he climbed,
the creaks and groans redoubled. They seemed to be leading
up to an infinite darkness but, as Timothy mounted higher,
his surroundings became clearer and more tangible: he
reached the first landing and saw ahead of him a corridor
lined with paintings of battles and theatrical episodes, of sea-
scapes and carefully detailed domestic interiors. 'That is how

everything used to be,' he said. 'Just before my father's time.' The house had become quiet once more. At the end of this corridor he could now see an open door and, without thought, he started walking towards it; as he did so he felt a faint breeze upon his face, but it was no ordinary passage of air, since it seemed to Timothy to be made up of whispering voices. It was a stream of words. He stopped at the threshold of the room and peered within. Heavy curtains had been drawn to exclude the light, but he could see that a fire had been made in the old-fashioned grate; it seemed about to expire, however, and the smoke from its charred logs hung in the close air. Some candles had been lit along the chimney-piece, and the boy was soon able to discern a long table with a white cloth glimmering upon it; there were certain objects lying scattered across it – plates, candles, books – but they were so entangled with cobwebs that he could scarcely make them out.

And then he noticed it. He noticed a human figure standing upright in a far corner of the room, without movement of any kind; the flickering light of the candles threw its shadow upon the ceiling and the walls, but the figure itself remained quite still. As still, Timothy thought, as if it were waiting to be born. When his eyes grew more accustomed to the gloom, he realized that it was dressed entirely in white and leant upon a crutch-stick held firmly in an immovable right fist. There was no time here, no movement and no decay. The boy became as motionless as the figure in the corner, and it seemed to him that the darkened room and its occupant had some close connection with the neat little man playing cards downstairs. Everything was waiting.

The flame of the candles flared up for a second before steadily growing higher; Timothy could once more feel the strange breeze of words upon his face and, to his horror, the figure itself began to stir. He watched as the crutch-stick started to move, the hand rising upwards, and then the stick was brought down upon the wooden floor with a thud; there was an answering rap from somewhere else within the house, and the boy understood that the figure in white and the man with the bandaged eyes were in some kind of communion. Now it was moving from side to side, sighing continually – he had been looking at an old woman, an old woman who began to walk slowly across the floor of the chamber, tapping her stick at every pace, and terrifying Timothy with a sustained low cry. Eventually she put out her hand towards him. 'I know why you are here,' she said. 'Come here, child, and take my arm.' Reluctantly he stepped forward in order to support her. 'Are your hands clean?' He nodded helplessly. 'Come here, then, and take me.' He could smell her age as he approached her – the smell of cobwebs and lavender and damp umbrellas and musk and dust all mixed together. She grasped him firmly, then began walking back and forth across the room. 'Do you know who I am, child?'

'No.'

'Do you know nothing at all?' He remained silent at this. 'And yet,' she added, looking down at him, 'you must also play a part. You must have a meaning. Go down again and ask him.' The boy hesitated, no longer certain of anything. 'Go on!' she screamed. 'Go downstairs and speak to him!' So he left the mildewed room, now very bright in the candlelight, and started to walk back down the corridor to the mysterious man on the floor below. Would he have taken the bandage from his eyes, and (this was what for some reason frightened the boy) would he then see Timothy at last? He had one foot on the staircase, when he heard a wild cry from the old woman; his first thought was to flee from this house, but then instinctively he turned back and hurried towards the room he had just left. It was suffused with a more intense light and he reeled back in horror as she rushed towards him, arms flailing, the side of her white dress enveloped in flame. He leapt past her, grabbed the old cloth from the long table in the middle of the room and, as all the plates and books fell with a crash to the ground, flung it over the burning garment. The flames were gone: the folds of the stale cloth had rapidly extinguished them, and there was left only the faint smell of burning from her seared and charred dress.

The old woman sat down upon the floor and started to laugh. 'I leant against one of the candles,' she said. 'I looked down and I was aflame. Now help me to my feet, if you please.' She was entirely wrapped in the cloth, and looked to Timothy like some priest or ancient princess. 'I am not hurt,' she went on, 'but if you had not heard me –' She stopped suddenly, put her finger to her lips and crept over to the open door. 'This will displease him. He wants to control everything. But this time I will *not* die.' She laughed again. 'No more broken words. No more incomplete sentences, as if only *he* could finish them. I will be alive now until the end!' Then she put her arm around Timothy, much to his discomfort, and walked with him around the room. 'Tell me, child,' she said, after several such revolutions, 'what is your name? Your real name?'

'Harcombe. Timothy Harcombe.'

'Well, Timothy Harcombe, I think I am going to be able to reward you. I think I am going to have that chance.' It was at this point that they both heard footsteps on the staircase and, as the wood creaked, she whispered in a sudden agony of hysteria, 'He's coming! Let's hide!' Infected by her nervous haste, Timothy allowed himself to be bundled into an old and capacious wardrobe; she followed him and quietly closed the door. They remained very still, although Timothy was almost suffocated by a number of limp white dresses which were hanging all around him and which seemed to him like the skins of dead people. The old woman had put her eye against a small hole in the wood, bored by insects which no doubt infested this room; she was tense with fright or anticipation and she hardly seemed to breathe until, quite suddenly, she poked Timothy with her elbow and burst out of their hiding place. 'It's Estella!' she shouted. 'It's only Estella!'

Timothy followed her and, much to his astonishment, found himself in the presence of a young woman who closely resembled Gloria Patterson. Had she not been in his father's room only the evening before? But the evening before what, exactly? Although he could still recall the incidents of his waking life, if that was what it truly was, they seemed to him infinitely less memorable and less real than what was happening to him now. In this strange world in which he found himself everything had some inner momentum, some secret wish to live and grow; nothing here was random or incomplete, but seemed to possess an innocent sufficiency. Perhaps there were no real tears here but, then, perhaps there was no need to cry. What happened to tears, after all? They merely evaporated and became part of the wide air. Here, everything remained – as clear and as substantial as the room in which he now stood.

'Do you admire her, Timothy? You look as if you admire her very much.' The old woman had brought Estella in front of the fireplace, and now stood beside her. 'Tell me how beautiful she is.'

'Very beautiful.'

'Do you think you can own her, Timothy, when you grow older? For even here, you know, we grow older.' He did not know how to reply to this, and merely lowered his head. He did not wish to look at Estella at all. 'Will you be married, Timothy? Is that to be?' The old woman was asking these questions so eagerly that it seemed to the boy that she was herself searching for some vision of the future. 'Well then, mark this,' she added in a lower and more defiant voice. 'She is betrothed to another. Tell Pip this when you see him. She is betrothed to another.' Timothy had no idea what she meant; he glanced at Estella, but turned his head away when he saw that she was looking scornfully at him. 'And tell him also,' the old woman was saying, 'that I never did have any money to give to him. Now go downstairs and explain to *him* what I have done.' She was leaning once more on her ebony stick, and banged three times upon the floor with it as the sound reverberated through the house.

He obeyed her but, as he walked slowly away, Estella took him to one side. 'You may think you know me,' she said. 'But you do not know me. And I tell you this, Timothy Harcombe. If you have a heart to break, I will break it. Now go.' He ran down the corridor, glad to be away from that fearful room, and descended the staircase. He had no thought of revisiting the man with the bandaged eyes, despite the old woman's entreaty, and he wanted only to leave this house; he crossed the hallway towards the open door, not daring to look back, and with great relief went out into the ruined garden.

Except that the garden was no longer there. The boy found himself in a landscape of marsh and mist. A wind came from the house behind him and, as the mist began to roll away, he could see a distant, thin line where the marsh and sky met; he looked out towards that horizon and thought that he could see a single glimmering light creeping to and fro across the flat land. This was a place of gloom and solitariness, and Timothy found himself crying out, 'Where is he? Where has he gone to?'

'Here I am.' The voice behind him scared him so much that he ran forward without looking back. But then someone called his name and, thinking that this might be his father, he faltered and turned around: it was not his father, it was the man who had been playing cards in the darkened room. His eyes were no longer covered by the bandage, and he was looking out across the marshes. 'Do you see that glimmering light, Timothy, out over yonder? Follow it, and all will be well.' He had very bright eyes, and the boy found himself staring at him. 'Go on,' he said gently. 'No harm will come to you. Not here.'

So Timothy followed the light, finding a solid path among the grass and reeds of this miserable region; he had not gone very far when he realized that the light itself was not wandering or moving over the face of the marsh but, rather, shifted and wavered as the mist rolled across it. He advanced towards it, and realized that it came from a lamp within an old barn or dwelling which had long since been abandoned. It was constructed of wood, with a roof of ragged tiles, a door hanging idly off its top hinge, and there was one window knocked into its side; it seemed so much part of this ruined and desolate place that it might have grown here as naturally as the tall grasses. He walked up to it boldly enough, but came to a sudden halt when he heard a man's voice crying out from within, 'What is this?' And then, after a moment, 'Who is this? Help, help, help!'

He did not know what to do. He could not turn back and ignore those cries, but he was too nervous and uncertain to go forward. Instead he crept over to the far side of the building, away from the window, and then very slowly approached it at an angle from which he could not be seen; he kept very low, ducking among the reeds, which grew thickly around this place, until he came up beneath the window itself. He raised himself silently and carefully until he could see inside – and there, against one wall of a bare room, he saw a young man fastened tightly to a ladder while in front of him danced another figure holding a hammer with a long, heavy handle. The window had no glass, so dilapidated had this building become, and Timothy could quite clearly hear everything that was said. 'Oh you enemy,' the man with the hammer was chanting. 'Oh you enemy of Orlick! You lied about me, you wolf! You accused me of your sister's killing. You accused me of a hunting and a harrying of Biddy. All lies, you enemy! All lies.'

The young man tied to the ladder was so pale, and in so much pain, that he was scarcely able to speak. 'I was told it was your doing. I was told so. By one who knows.'

'It was you, villain!'

'How could it be me? I was so young then . . . Remember little Pip, Orlick. How could it be me?'

'I tell you it was your doing. I tell you it was done through you. It was you who wrote it down. It was you who made up all the lies and the schemes. It was you who told the story.'

Orlick was working himself into a greater and greater rage and now, with his back to Timothy, was hopping from foot to foot while swinging the hammer closer to Pip's skull. He had not seen the boy, but Pip, with his face towards the window, noticed him at once. He had looked at him briefly, as if imploring help, and had then looked down at a bottle of gin or some other liquor which his antagonist had placed on a table near the door. It was clear to Timothy what he should do, and so he crept towards the open door as Orlick continued his tirade. 'Why is it you, enemy, who always tells the story? Why not Old Orlick? Talking of yourself and telling lies of others, making game with us, thinking you owned us all. But those days is past. No more words now. Not from you, you enemy!' Timothy had crept in through the door and approached the table; he took the bottle, now half empty, and then, as Orlick danced and gibbered before Pip, he raised it and crashed it down upon his skull. Orlick dropped to the floor, stunned; Timothy at once stepped over him and untied the ropes which held Pip to the ladder; he was free in a few moments, and with a savage yell of triumph he danced upon the prostrate body.

'I tell the story,' he shouted, 'and I finish it! I will make game with you until the end!' He stopped, embarrassed suddenly to realize that Timothy had been watching his exultation. 'We must go to Rochester, you and I,' he said to the boy, 'and take this wretch with us to the gaol. Then on to London, and to glory.'

Everyone in this world seemed so clear and so definite that Timothy was no longer surprised by the young man's eager dispatch; he was accustomed to sudden transitions of place and scene as well, so he was not in the least discomfited when he found himself in the streets of London with his new companion. They were walking down a poorly lighted thoroughfare, narrow and malodorous, while all around Timothy could hear the striking of church clocks, the barking of dogs and the rattling of carriages. 'There is no place like it,' Pip was saying. 'For coincidence, you know. I can hardly walk down a street without being greeted by a very old friend.' They had come out by the river, beside a stone bridge; there was a plateau of mud just beneath them, and Timothy could make out the remains of old iron equipment, rope and netting which now lay useless upon the bank. The river was so dark, and the leaden expanse of sky seemed so much a continuation of its darkness, that he might have entered some chamber in which each object and each sound was for ever trapped. Then it all disappeared. A sudden gust of fog obliterated everything from sight and, for a moment, he felt himself to be suspended in some cloudy medium; it was almost as if he had ceased to exist. But the fog lifted as quickly as it had fallen, and everything reappeared as it had been beside the dark river.

But now Pip turned away from the Thames, and Timothy followed him down a grander and wider thoroughfare. 'And lucky chance, and accidents!' the young man was saying enthusiastically. 'Why, there's nothing *but* them in this place.' The boy looked around as they trod the pavement together – looked out at an old house on the corner, with its shutters closed and doors barred; at a brightly lit shop on the opposite side of the way where under the flaring light of the gas various pairs of gloves were displayed; at a shallow courtyard, filled with rough stones, in which a horse reared up, its breath issuing into the mist. This was like no other street he had seen before. It seemed to go on for ever, and he had the curious sensation that there was nothing beyond it; yet the shadows were deeper, the colours more distinct, the outline of the mansions and tenements under the round moon like the crayon marks of a child. Pip and Timothy passed several people intent upon their own business, some sighing and looking down upon the ground, others gesticulating or muttering to themselves; but there were others who looked first at Pip, and then at Timothy, with a puzzled expression. 'Oh yes!' an old man shouted from the middle of the street. 'Are you here, too?' He laughed very loudly, but Pip seemed not at all disconcerted. 'Very nice old party,' he muttered confidentially to the boy. 'Knows everybody. And, if I am not very much mistaken, this is where we turn off.'

They had come to the Temple, and Pip led him through several courtyards and passages until they came to the last house by the river. 'Garden Court,' he said. 'My humble chambers.' Together they climbed the narrow staircase and, on the top landing, entered the young man's well-appointed rooms. Someone had lit a fire and Pip at once stood with his back to it, warming the calves of his legs and smiling at Timothy. 'Well now,' he said. 'Now that we have completed one stage of our adventure, we might as well go on to the next. Tell me your name.' Timothy did so, and Pip nodded thoughtfully. 'Now, if you like,' he went on, 'you can tell me everything that has happened to you.' And so the boy told him about the dark house and the old woman in white whom he had rescued from the flames. This intelligence seemed to surprise, and even alarm, the young man. 'Please stop there a moment,' he said. 'Are you sure it was *you* who saved her from burning?'

'I was the only one there. Except for –'

'Very well. Go on with your story.'

But as soon as Timothy began to tell Pip about his encounter with Estella, the young man blushed and turned towards the fire. Then the boy remembered that he had a message from the old lady: he recalled it perfectly, and it was strange how in this place he could bring back even the tiniest details at precisely the time it was necessary for him to do so. 'Oh Mr Pip,' he said, trying to regain the young man's attention now that he was rummaging among the coals with a wrought-iron poker. 'The old lady said that Estella is betrothed to another.' Pip stiffened and held the poker in the air. 'And she told me that she never did have any money to give you.'

He put down the poker very gently before the fire and turned to Timothy. 'Is that really what she said?' Timothy nodded. 'And nothing more?'

'Nothing.'

The young man went over to an armchair covered in red leather and held on to the back of it very tightly. 'But how can that be? When all my expectations had been raised upon her?' He glanced at Timothy with something very like horror. 'I supposed her to be the one who made me a gentleman. I believed her to have promised me Estella when I had finished my time here. And now you tell me – you, who rescued me, now prove to be my undoing – is it true that –?' Pip's remarks were becoming more and more disjointed; he pulled away from the armchair and began to walk around the room in smaller and smaller circles. Until eventually he came to a halt and abruptly sat down in the chair. 'But then,' he said, 'who am I? Who made me what I am?' He sat looking into the fire for what seemed to Timothy to be a very long time – except that, in this place, he found it difficult to measure time at all; it was always changing, rushing forward from event to event or coming to a sudden silent halt, but always circling around him.

'Look at me,' Pip was saying. 'My appearance, my manner, everything. Just look at me. If none of it came from Miss Havisham, then truly I am in the dark. What have I inherited? And from what – from whom – have I inherited it? I walk, I talk, as if everything were of my own volition, as if I understood precisely what it was that sent me rushing through the world. But now it is as if I were possessed by a stranger. Literally possessed. Words cannot tell what a sense I have of the dreadful mystery that is my own self. Timothy, these must seem wild words. But they are breaking out at last. I had a knowledge of this which I kept from myself for all the long years. Here, take my hand for a moment. Please do.' The boy stepped forward reluctantly and put out his hand, which Pip grasped in his own. 'Do you understand yourself, Timothy

Harcombe? Do you know why your eyes are blue and your hair is brown? Do you understand why it is that you walk quickly, and that you often rub your forehead with your hand? Do you know why you speak as you do, or how you have acquired all the words you use? Do you understand any of these things, Timothy Harcombe?' The boy slowly shook his head. 'Well, then, we are in the same boat, you and I. May I shake your hand?' In fact he was still holding the boy's hand, and now began pumping it vigorously up and down.

It was at this moment that they both heard a noise from the landing below; it sounded like a footstep, except that it seemed suddenly to stop or to hesitate. Pip took up a lamp and opened the door. 'There is someone down there, is there not?' he called out.

'Yes,' returned a voice from the darkness below. Timothy recognized something in the voice – yes, it was his father! It was his father who had come for him, and who was about to guide him out of this strange world. He was not disinherited, after all.

'What floor do you want?' Pip called out again, putting the lamp in front of him so that he might see this stranger.

'The top. Mr Pip.'

'That is my name. There is nothing the matter?'

'Nothing the matter.' The man had climbed the final flight of stairs and, as he said this, entered the room. It was not his father. It was another man altogether, dressed in an old great-coat and with a scarf wrapped around his neck. Yet there was still something about him which seemed familiar to the boy – even more so now that he took Pip's hands and smiled as he surveyed him. 'I am delighted by your attentions, naturally,' Pip said, not without a trace of irony. 'But pray, tell me, what business have you here?'

'I have come to see you and to speak with you. That is all. That's my business.'

'Forgive me,' Pip replied, with an expression of mild distaste. 'My friend and I are very tired. Can you postpone this affecting scene until tomorrow?'

The stranger smiled. 'You are a game one,' he said admiringly. 'I'm glad you grew up to be such a game one.'

Pip looked at him more intently. 'Do I know you?'

'Surely you understand?'

'Understand what?'

'May I have something to drink?' Impatiently, and with an air of half-suppressed expectancy, Pip poured him a glass of port; he sipped from it briefly, and then put it down upon the floor. 'Pip,' he went on. 'Tell me, Pip, how have you done since you were left an orphan on those terrible marshes?' The young man stepped back and almost went into the fire, but then he muttered something about coming into property. The stranger smiled again. 'Might I ask what property? Might I ask whose property?'

'I have no – at this moment I cannot tell you.'

'Could I make a guess, I wonder, at your income since you came of age? As to the first figure now. Five?' Pip looked across at Timothy wildly. 'Concerning your great expectations,' the stranger continued, not at all displeased by Pip's manner, 'could we say that you mistook Miss Havisham to be their originator? And could we say that a certain Estella always seemed to be part of, well, your portable property?'

'Who are you?' Pip was struggling for every breath that he drew. 'Who *are* you?' As soon as the man had mentioned Miss Havisham, Timothy knew precisely who he was: this was the man in the darkened room, the man with the bandage around his eyes, the man playing a solitary game of cards.

Pip swayed for a moment and then turned blindly to find a high-backed sofa against the wall; as he moved towards it the stranger rose quickly and caught him before he fell. He placed Pip on the sofa and sat there beside him. 'I will tell you who I am, Pip,' he said gently. 'I'm your second father. You are my son, although in truth more to me than my son. I nourished you and fed you from a distance. I watched over you. I planned the very life you lead now. I created you, just as you are now.'

Pip kept his head turned away; biting his lower lip and clenching his hands together, he looked towards the fire. He remained silent for a few moments after the man had finished and then, still looking towards the fire, he spoke in a faltering voice. 'There are so many pictures,' he said, 'in these burning coals. Just where that glow is now – do you see, that dull glow? – I can make out traces of my past. And of my future. I could spend my life looking into the fire, you know. At the pictures. The visions.'

'That's it, Pip,' the stranger replied. 'That is precisely what I mean. Visions. I have had visions of you since the day you first emerged into the light. I said that I was a second father to you but, really, you could be my second self –'

'No. Please. No more.' Pip's tone was so urgent that the man fell silent at once. The three of them remained quiet, as it seemed to Timothy, for a very long time; he had an alarming fancy that someone had stopped reading them, if such a thing were possible. Then to his surprise he saw that Pip was pointing towards him. 'And Timothy Harcombe,' he said. 'Did you help to fashion him too? Is he part of your pattern?'

The stranger looked directly at the boy, and Timothy noticed at once how keen and comprehensive his gaze was; it was as if, in the hot air of this secluded room, he was measuring up his entire young life. He could not have said of what he was afraid, for his fear was altogether undefined and vague, but there was a great fear upon him. 'I am not sure,' the man said. 'I don't think so. He could not have existed without me, I believe, but he does not belong to me. He has come from – from somewhere else.'

Pip now regarded Timothy with something like exultation. 'So cannot I be like him, too?' he asked. 'Why should I be trapped in the vision you have of me? There are other visions, after all.' He rose unsteadily from the sofa and looked down at the stranger. 'I want no father. I want no second self. I don't want to be chained to you!' He beckoned to Timothy and then, catching the boy's arm, he rushed out of the room;

he still had his key in his pocket, and with a flourish he locked
the door before running with Timothy down the staircase.
'Come,' he shouted behind him as the boy followed. 'We have
taken him by surprise. We have escaped from him. If he loses
all sight and knowledge of me, then perhaps I may be free.'
They came to the foot of the staircase, breathless, and Pip
turned to him. 'Shall we go on together?' Timothy did not
know how to reply, since he had no wish to lose himself
further in this strange world. 'Come. Here is my hand. Do
you stay with me, you real – or visionary – boy?' They heard
the noise of a door being forced somewhere above them and,
before Timothy could reply, Pip grabbed him and led him
through the courtyards of the Temple. They hurried away
from the river and made for safety towards the maze of alleys
around Fleet Street and Newgate Close. Timothy was now so
invaded by Pip's own hysterical panic that he began to sob as
he ran, and from time to time cast back fearful glances. For a
moment he thought that he glimpsed the strange man in
pursuit but, when he looked back, he was gone. To his terrified
imagination he seemed to be everywhere – and yet, at the
same time, nowhere to be directly seen.

So Pip and Timothy hurried on together, through close-
packed streets and along empty avenues, among the tenements
of the poor and beside the white mansions of the rich; the boy
had no notion of how long or how far they wandered, but it
seemed to him that they were moving in a circle – that all
these contrasting and bewildering scenes were part of one
another. There could not be riches without poverty, or crowds
without sudden silence and isolation. Each thing meant
nothing by itself but, when it was seen in contrast or oppo-
sition to the next thing, the pattern began to emerge. He was
about to explain this to Pip when he realized that others were
beginning to join them in their headlong career – a young
girl guiding an old man, a family of strolling players, a young
child on crutches, an old woman in a wheelchair, and many,
many others were excitedly hurrying behind Pip and

Timothy. He was surprised by the number of pale-faced children who now accompanied them, when suddenly he caught sight of Estella and Miss Havisham. How could they be here? And there, most curiously of all, was Orlick. How had he escaped imprisonment, and how had he discovered his tormentor?

He had no time to consider these things for the whole concourse had come to a halt beside the Thames: there was nowhere else to flee from the stranger, and instinctively Timothy raised his arms as if imploring help to reach the other side. In the grey afternoon light the river had become all the more sombre, and seemed to be bearing away all his hopes of light and life; it was a dark river, moving through a dark city. Yet the sombre scene did not affect any of his companions, who, to Timothy's surprise, began to board a variety of craft – steamships, yachts, barges, pleasure boats, skiffs and wherries – which seemed set to embark on a journey to the open sea. The boy almost lost sight of Pip in the confusion, until he saw the back of his green coat as he was being helped on board a sailing-ship. Timothy hurried after him and just managed to reach it before the gang-plank was lifted, and now he stood on deck as the ship left its moorings with the general flotilla. There was a steamship ahead of him, the *Aurora*, and he could make out on its deck the profiles of Estella, Miss Havisham and Orlick; they seemed to be eating and drinking with great merriment, and then he was astonished to see them dance together as their vessel moved slowly through the heart of the great city. They passed under Old London Bridge and Timothy looked out at the oyster-boats, the chain-cables, the hawsers and the buoys which mingled promiscuously along the banks; he saw the ship-builders' yards, which echoed to the sound of pumps and hammers and engines, as well as the decaying wharves with their huge timber supports jutting beyond the black mud. He looked up for a moment and glimpsed through the smoke and mist the spires of the old churches which rose above the grey streets;

when he looked down at the river again just past Rotherhithe he could see the scavengers, many of them children, trailing their arms and hands in the polluted water. Night was falling, and the flares from lit torches accentuated the darkness around the river; Timothy could no longer tell what were shadows and what were objects, so obscure the scene had become. Many of the others were now dancing on their vessels and, in the flaring light, they cast enormous phantoms of themselves across the water: Timothy watched their shadows as he gripped the wooden rail and stared down into the river.

After a while his sailing-ship came out into a clean stretch between woods and hills, manoeuvring carefully between the low shallows and mudbanks which litter the region of Gravesend when the tide is out. The light now seemed to come from the river rather than from the sky and, when the vessel stopped, Timothy realized that he was back in the marsh country where his adventures had first started; all around him he could see the flat and monotonous vista with its dim horizon. The vessel had stopped by a part of the shoreline which jutted out from the marshes, and Pip disengaged himself from his laughing companions. He came up to Timothy and patted him on the back.

'Well,' he said, 'my friend and brother – my visionary friend – you and I must part.'

Timothy felt his mouth become dry, so great was his fear of being abandoned. 'Where are you going?' was all he could manage to say.

'We are going to the open sea. That is where we belong. The sea. The sea of life!' He pointed through the darkness. 'For you know,' he added in a quieter voice, 'we can never die.'

'But who are you?'

'Oh yes. We know very well who we are. But who are you? That is the real question. You must leave us now, before we continue our journey. You do not belong here.' And, before Timothy knew what was happening, he found himself being raised by many hands off the ship and then lowered gently on to the point of land by the marshes. The vessels set sail again at once, and Timothy watched his old companions as they sang and danced on their way to the open sea.

He was alone, and all his old longing for his father returned. 'Where is he?' he called out into the air, as he had called out once before. 'Where *is* he?' There was a narrow path of small white stones which led inland and the boy, frightened of becoming lost upon the marshes and with no other course to pursue, began to follow it. He walked on and on; he slept for a while in the hollow of a large grey rock, and then he walked on again; he walked on until, to his relief and astonishment, the path led him back into the ruined garden of the house where he had seen Estella and Miss Havisham. Yet it was not as it had been. There was no house now, but only the crumbling wall of the old garden. The space, where once the building had stood, had been cleared; there was a rough fence around the area and, looking over it, the boy saw how some of the old ivy had struck root anew and was growing across low mounds of rubble. A mist had gathered here but, as Timothy pushed through the fence and wandered around this barren place, he could trace the outline of the old house – where the door had been, and where the hallway. He looked back along the desolate garden walk and suddenly glimpsed a solitary figure coming towards him. He stood very still, but then stepped forward when he realized that it was the man who had once played a game of cards in the darkened room of the old house, the man who had come to Pip's lodgings. 'I am greatly changed,' the man said with a smile. 'I wonder you know me.' The freshness of his strength had indeed departed from his face but he had the same keen, bright eyes.

'I know you now. You are Charles Dickens,' Timothy replied quietly. 'Do you often come back?'

'I have very often hoped and intended to come back, but I have been prevented by many changes in the narrative. Poor, poor old place!'

'I was wondering,' the boy said, 'how it came to be left in this condition.'

'It has served its purpose and must give way to other places. Other houses.'

'Is it to be built on, then?'

'In a sense, yes. I came here to take my leave of it before its change.' He smiled, and all his old quickness and brightness returned for an instant. 'Houses are always built on, Timothy. One gives place to another. Foundations laid upon foundations. The end of one is the beginning of another. And this one, now, is coming to its end. Can you not feel it? It is getting darker here, and colder. The inhabitants of this place have all gone their own ways, their adventures finished, and whatever stories have been told beneath the roof of this old house have come to their conclusion. All the feelings experienced here, all the words spoken, have been released. Nothing left except ruins, and ghosts, and darkness.' He smiled again. 'It is always the same,' he said more cheerfully. 'It is always renewed. And now you, too, must be on your way. This is no place for you. You are beginning your own journey. Go back the way you came.' He pointed towards the patch of ground where Timothy had first found himself; the boy walked towards it and, when he looked back for the last time, he saw the stranger taking a pack of cards from his pocket. Then suddenly he felt the light upon his face.

FIVE

As my father and i left the darkened interior of the picture-house, the world seemed for a moment to have been reborn; the natural light was so bright and so vivid that it might just have been created, and I had the curious feeling that I had walked into some other dream. Perhaps it was the strangeness of this sensation which led me to confide in my father since, as we walked down the Kingsland Road, I remember taking his arm and telling him of the scenes concerning Pip and Estella which I had just witnessed. I told him everything or, rather, I whispered to him; I do not know why I whispered, since there was no one near us, unless it was in recognition of some shared secret. For I still believed that in some way he was responsible for my dreams, and that he watched over me even as I slept. I assumed, too, that there was some connection with my presence at the meetings: when I was with him in the old hall I saw the phantoms, after all, and were they really any different from these visions which invaded me?

I was telling him about the previous dream, in which I had walked with Alice and Christian; he was smiling, and all the time he bent his head near my own so that he could hear me whispering. I tried to explain to him how different Alice and Christian were from Pip, or Orlick, or Estella. I could still see the three of them, with their other companions, drifting down towards the open sea; they were all involved with each other, and with that world which I had entered for a short time. But Alice and Christian had nothing to do with the landscape in which I had found them; they were isolated figures, withdrawn from the world, as much strangers to themselves as to each other. So it had been a different kind of dream. I could think of nothing else to say, and we walked together in silence for a while. Eventually he put his arm around my shoulder, and drew me closer to him. 'That's a strange story,' he said. 'A very strange story.'

'But it's not a story, dad. It's real. It all happened to me. And you're part of it, too, dad, aren't you?'

'Yes, Timmy. I know all about your dreams. Of course I do. But let's not tell anyone about them for the moment. Let's keep them to ourselves.'

'Not even the Circle?'

'No. Not even the Circle.' We walked towards home in silence again; he had withdrawn his arm from me and he was whistling, with his hands in his pockets. 'Tell me this, Timothy,' he said after a few minutes. 'Are the wild flowers in London different from the ones in the country?' I shook my head, unable even to feign interest. 'There are daisies,' he said. 'You get those in parks . . .'

'And in cemeteries.'

'Yes. They grow up between the stones.'

'What about sunflowers?'

'But they're not wild, Timmy.'

'They are in our garden.'

'No, Tim, they are trained. They're trained to follow the sun. Everything follows the sun in our house.' He started whistling again, then abruptly broke off. 'Would you like to go to the country,' he asked me very casually, 'and get away from here for a while?' Suddenly I experienced some great fear. 'Just for a little while?'

'No, dad. I like it here.'

He said no more, and we walked the rest of the way in silence. For much of that evening my father seemed irritable and depressed but, when he saw my own unhappy expression, he smiled and rose from the armchair where he had been sitting. 'Would you like to hear an adventure, Tim?'

'What kind of adventure?'

'You know. The special kind.'

'Sherlock Holmes?'

'Go and get it from the shelf, Timmy. Before I change my mind.' Knowing that he was quite capable of doing that, I hurried into my own room and took down the volume of Holmes stories from the bookcase. He used to read them to me from time to time, and I can still remember those hours under the lamplight, the small fire burning in the grate, the curtains drawn, the low sound of my father's voice. He did all the characters, the clipped and abrupt tones of Holmes as well as the warm and unctuous responses of Watson, and in my memory those contrasting voices are inextricably mingled with the shadow of the lamp quivering upon the wall, the vague murmur of the fire, and the warmth of the small room where my father sat beside me reading the tale: 'If we could view the strange coincidences of our destinies, the burden and inheritance of the years, the wonderful chain of events, working through generations, and leading to the most extraordinary results, it would make all fiction with its conventionalities and foreseen conclusions most stale and unprofitable. Now, Watson, I am going to tell you a most mysterious story . . .'

There were even occasions, as on that particular evening, when, lulled by the sense of comfort and enclosure, I fell asleep; I knew that I was sleeping because I found myself dreaming of a strange room, in which a man gazed out of a window at the yellow fog. I was about to enter the room when it was gone and I heard my father's voice. 'You see, Timothy,' he was saying, 'I would like you to have a holiday.' The book was closed, and so the Holmes adventure had come to an end; my father must have been talking to me without realizing that I was no longer awake. 'And you'll like your grandfather. When he comes to see us.'

I was alert in a moment because I was invaded by the same fear I had experienced before. 'Who is he?'

'Your grandfather. Your mother's father.'

'I've never heard of him.'

'Of course you have. I've often mentioned him to you.'

'You have not.'

My father looked away. 'Well, I mentioned him to you today.'

'Why is he coming here, dad? What does he want from us?'

'He doesn't *want* anything, Tim. He just hasn't seen you for a while.'

'He's never seen me.' Again my father looked away, and I spoke out in a louder voice. 'And why does he want to see *me*?' I could not imagine for myself an existence or an identity beyond that of my father.

'He just wants to pay a visit, Tim.'

I was too tired to say any more. I did not even want to ask him about the 'holiday' he had mentioned, perhaps because I was too frightened of the answer I might receive. Everything now seemed so uncertain, and I could sense my young life drifting away in a direction I could not foresee. I went to my room and slept.

He arrived the following morning; my father, who must have known of his impending visit for some days, had chosen to tell me about it at the last possible opportunity. 'William Sinclair,' my grandfather said, holding out his hand to me. 'Grandfather Bill.' I can see him as vividly now as I did then. He was a short and stocky man, quite bald, with a peculiar snub nose which gave a slightly infantile cast to his features. He also had the clearest blue eyes I had ever seen. I looked up at him as he shook my hand, and for an instant I glimpsed an image of my mother – not as she was in the photograph but rather as she might have been, some spectral resemblance hovering over my grandfather's face and general bearing.

'I don't suppose you're interested in me at all,' he said. 'I don't suppose you care tuppence.' This was my first intimation of how direct my grandfather was, how little allowance he would make for the fact that I was a child. 'But I am interested in *you*, Timothy. Very interested.'

I could sense my father's uneasiness as he stood beside us. 'Would you like a cup of tea?' was all I could think of saying.

'Just like your mother.' He laughed. 'Always polite. Always

good-humoured.' It was the first time anyone had compared me to her, and I was strangely delighted; it was almost as if I had acquired another self and for a moment I felt somehow lighter, less bound down to that time and that place.

'Why don't you do that, Tim? Why don't you make us all some tea?' My father sounded more solemn than usual. As soon as I left the room I could hear them talking in low voices, and instinctively I knew that they were talking about me. They stopped when I returned to ask if my grandfather took sugar; and, when I came back to ask if he wanted milk, they stopped again. It was like a game in which I, the victim, could exert a little power over his aggressors. Eventually I brought in the tea, and my grandfather patted the seat next to him on the sofa for me to go there. But instead I stood in a corner by the wireless, clutching my mug in both hands.

He did not seem to take offence at that but merely smiled at me. 'Not much room here,' he said very cheerfully. 'Not enough room to swing a cat.'

He was addressing me but I did not know how to respond. I had never considered our lodgings in that light before; they were so imbued with my father's presence that they had seemed illimitable. But, yes, they were small.

'We don't find it so.' My father was replying for me. 'You know the phrase, much riches in a small room.'

'Not many riches here, either,' my grandfather added. It was the same direct response, quite without any trace of hostility, and it occurred to me that my mother might have displayed the same characteristics. Once more I felt a certain lightness of spirit, and I glanced over at her photograph. But it was gone; my father must have taken it down just before my grandfather arrived.

'Don't forget my work, William.' My father sounded angry, but now he hesitated. 'My real work. Not –' He glanced across at me and stopped.

'Of course,' my grandfather said. 'Your work.'

'Something is accomplished. I don't pretend to understand

how, and I claim no credit for myself . . .' Again my father hesitated as both men looked across at me. 'I can't explain to you things you haven't seen. But there is something –'

'Does Timothy know all about this?' was my grandfather's question.

'Of course not.' I had no idea why my father told this deliberate lie, but I said nothing. 'The boy has no connection with it.' It was as if he were trying to defend me, although, at that time, I did not understand why it should be necessary.

My grandfather got up from the sofa and stood near the window; he had put his hand on the shelf where my mother's photograph was usually placed. 'What did you used to call her?' He had his back to us both, and he was looking out at Hackney Square. 'Bright Cecilia?'

My father glanced at me and, once again, I had the impression that he was defending me. 'That's what she was,' he replied.

'What she is.' I said this quite without thought, and then ran into my room: I knew instinctively that my father had put the photograph beneath the small bookcase there, and now I brought it back in triumph to my grandfather. 'Would you like to see a picture of her?' I held it out to him. 'Here,' I said, even as I sensed my father's embarrassment. 'We always keep it in a special place.'

William Sinclair took up the photograph and sighed. 'There's a lot of your mother in you, Timothy. I can see it in your face.' He looked at it for several seconds, tracing her outline with his finger, and then returned it to me with a certain gravity. 'I'll tell you what,' he said. 'Would you like to see the house where she was born?'

I held on to the picture very tightly. 'Will dad be coming? I mean, will father be coming?'

'I'll be coming down after a little while, Tim.'

'He has to stay here,' my grandfather said. 'He has to mind the shop.'

I looked at my father, who put out his hands in a curious gesture of submission.

My grandfather stayed with us for the rest of that day. My father had, rather ostentatiously, set me to work on my studies; but I could not concentrate upon them while my future remained so uncertain. It was as if my mother – the shadow or ghost of my mother – had somehow entered my life and I had become a stranger to myself. I could hear them talking in the next room as I lay upon my bed, a book unopened beside me; for some reason my heart was beating so fast that I put one hand against my chest to feel it. At one point I could hear my grandfather clearly saying, 'And what about the poor boy then?' I assumed that I was the 'poor boy' he meant, but the phrase had no real meaning for me; I was more alarmed by the way he was talking to my father. It was the first time that our lodgings had been entered by someone who did not necessarily believe in his powers and who did not in some way depend upon him; this disturbed me and I sensed, too, that my father was also at a loss. Indeed, as far as I can now recall, it was this which truly frightened me.

They left the house at twilight and, as soon as I heard the door close behind them, I rushed into my father's room and watched them from the window: they were walking around Hackney Square, talking all the time. On occasions my grandfather would make an emphatic gesture in the air, and my father would nod or look down at the ground. They must have walked around the square three or four times and, when finally I saw them returning to the house, I ran back into my room and opened the book which still lay upon my bed. My grandfather knocked on my door and I looked up into his bright eyes. 'What's that you're reading?'

'The history of England.'

'I'll be seeing you tomorrow, then,' he said, putting out his hand. 'Tomorrow morning. Bright and early.' He said this so confidentially it was as if I were a willing partner in the scheme. 'You can tell Mrs Sinclair about the history of England.' He turned to leave the room, but not before asking very innocently, 'Do you see visions, too?'

'No.' For some reason I believed that I was protecting my father by saying this. 'But my father does.'

'Yes. I know. He told me.' He was smiling at me. 'Tomorrow morning, then, Timothy.' He shook my hand again and left me.

Then, before I knew it, my father was in the room beside me. He put his arm around me but, in my despair, I shook him off. 'I don't want to go,' I said. 'I don't want to leave here.'

'Not even to see the house where your mother lived?'

'I don't want to go.'

'It will be good for you to have a holiday, Tim. Think of it as a holiday. Get to know your grandparents. See all the countryside.'

I got up from the bed and walked past him; for some reason I was fighting for breath. I went into his room and stood by the window. 'So why don't you come?' I shouted.

He had followed me: I could see his pale reflection in the window now that the daylight was fading fast, and I watched as he put out his hand towards me. 'Your grandfather has a motor-car,' he said. 'You'll be travelling in it.' I was intrigued by this, but I was determined to say nothing. 'An Austin 7. A real beauty.' Then he sighed and put his arm down by his side. 'I will come. I'll try to come. I promise.'

But these words made the impending separation seem all the more real and therefore all the more painful; they were already filled with an awareness of his absence. And in truth it seemed, as I looked out of the window, that I might as well not exist – that I did not exist. 'How long shall I be gone?' I asked him.

'Not long. Just a little while. You see,' he added, more enthusiastically, 'it will be good for you to have your own life, Timmy.'

'But I don't want to have any life. I just want to be with you.' I was about to cry, but I could not; I felt too desolate, too insignificant, for that.

'Of course you have a life. You have many lives, don't you know that?'

'Is that why I have to go away?'

He seemed confused by my question, and, indeed, I had no idea why I asked it. 'Of course not. I want you back here with me very soon. Think of it as an adventure, Timothy. Just an adventure.' There were two or three dead flies on the window-sill; they had died trying to reach the light, and I bent down and blew their frail bodies on to the floor.

I packed my few belongings that evening in my father's battered brown suitcase, which was, he said, one of the relics of his 'travelling days'. 'Like father, like son,' he said, with more enthusiasm than I could muster. 'Moving on. Always moving on.' I said nothing but I made sure that I packed some of our books; I knew now that the memory of my life with my father was something which would have to be retained by my own efforts, and I wanted some reminder of the past. I lay upon my bed that night and stared up at the ceiling, waiting for him to come and read to me, but he did not do so.

My grandfather arrived early on the following morning. 'The early bird catches the worm,' he said. He must have seen the look of horror upon my face, because he stood squarely in front of me and grasped my shoulders. Once more I noticed only the brightness of his eyes. 'I can see you're afraid,' he said in his usual direct way. 'Don't be afraid. I love you. Now I expect you want to be alone with your father for a moment.'

I shook my head and ran out past him through the hallway into the street; it was raining and, when the first drop of water fell upon my wrist, I realized that my life was about to change for ever. My grandfather came out carrying the brown suitcase; there was a knock at the window and, when I turned, I saw my father waving to me. Instinctively I tried to wave back but my arm seemed too heavy to lift; I just stared at him helplessly, until my grandfather took me by the hand and led me across the street.

There was a motor-car parked there – an Austin 7, just as
my father had said – but I had never been inside a car before,
and the strangeness of it seemed to be leading me further
away from any previous life I had known. My grandfather
opened the door for me but I was not sure what to do. 'Get
in,' he said, kindly enough. 'Don't worry. It can't start without a driver.' So I clambered into the brown leather seat next
to his own and held on to it very tightly. I watched, fascinated,
as he started the engine and then put his foot down on the
pedal; slowly we drew away from Hackney Square, but I did
not look back. Instead I clutched the leather seat and watched
the familiar houses and the familiar shops passing by; and yet
they were no longer recognizable. I had lost all connection
with them as I sat in this strange vehicle, and at once they
had become opaque objects in an alien landscape; if I ceased
to exist in the same way, then so did they. We drove away
from east London through narrow streets of small houses in
brown and yellow brick, past offices and tenement buildings,
past small parks with cast-iron railings like spears pointing to
the sky; we travelled west through Holborn and Oxford Street,
Notting Hill Gate and Shepherd's Bush, until we came out on
to the new road leading us from London. I had never left the
city before and those narrow streets were so truly my home
that, when I first saw fields and hills, I was invaded by a
great fear. They signified absence to me – the absence of my
father and the loss of my old life. Every stream was bearing
me away from myself, every hill was burying me, every field
was laying me waste.

'Where are we going?' I eventually asked him, although I
knew well enough.

'Didn't your father tell you?' I shook my head. 'Wiltshire.
We're going to Wiltshire.'

'How long will it be?'

'We should be there in a few hours, in this car. There's
some lemonade and sandwiches in the back.' And so we
travelled on, blowing up great clouds of dust as we drove

through the small towns and villages along our route. My grandfather sometimes glanced at me as he drove steadily along the road, but for most of the journey he left me to my own thoughts. 'I'll tell you what,' he said suddenly. 'We'll play a game. Wiltshire coming up, by the way. Do you know "Yes and No"?' As far as I understood it, this was a game in which one person had to guess what was in the other's mind by a process of elimination; I must have seemed distracted, because my grandfather explained the rules to me several times. 'Now,' he said at last. 'Tell me what I'm thinking about.'

'Wincarnis Tonic.' I was staring out of the window at some sheep huddled in a corner of a field.

He looked across at me in astonishment. 'How on earth did you guess that, Timothy?'

'It was the first thing that came into my head.' I sounded nonchalant, but even in my unhappiness I was pleased to have impressed him.

'Let's try again. What am I thinking about now?'

I closed my eyes, screwing up my eyelids as if I were involved in some grand process of divination. 'A pogo stick.'

When I opened my eyes and looked across at him, he was staring at me in bewilderment. 'Astonishing,' he said. 'Try once more.'

I looked out of the window again, at a single horse with its head bowed towards the ground. 'A flower girl,' I said.

'You are a very unusual person.' The vehemence of his words alarmed me, and I turned towards him; we looked at each other silently for a moment before I resumed my contemplation of the passing landscape. A strong wind had started up and I watched the patterns which it created in the long grass; I thought I could see faces among them, the faces of the land staring up at the sky, but then the wind passed over and erased them.

My grandfather said nothing for the rest of the drive until we reached the outskirts of a small town. 'Upper Harford,' he announced to me. 'Close to journey's end.' And once more I felt afraid. We travelled for two or three miles through a landscape of undulating hills and pastures, then crossed a small bridge and made our way along a narrow road with hedges on either side of it. My grandfather stopped the car at the end of a white lane, just under a tree. 'I always park it here,' he said. 'In case of rain.' He lifted my little brown suitcase from the back and then, sensing my anxiety, he waited quietly until I climbed out of the car and followed him down the lane. I have never forgotten, and shall never forget, that short walk. It was a bright day in late November. The weak sun seemed to lay a hand on the back of my neck, and I looked down at the small white stones beneath my feet; faint spirals of dust issued from the ground as I walked along and I knew that, in such a place, nothing would ever change. The lane, the white stones and the dust would always be here. And, in my memory, would it always be a place of sorrow and desolation?

'Here we are,' my grandfather said. 'Home.' I know now that it was only a modest farmhouse but, at the time, I saw in front of me a grand mansion. There was a wide wooden gate leading on to a gravel path and then, at the end of it, the whitewashed and thatched front of the house itself. A small figure emerged from the porch, and seemed to be waving. 'That's your grandmother,' he said as we walked up the path towards her. After I had taken a few paces I could see that she was shaking rather than waving – not an indistinct nervous tremble, but a continuous and visible physical movement. Her whole body shook and, as she stepped slowly off the porch to greet me, she put her hand against a small wooden seat. 'Timothy,' she said in a tremulous, quavering voice. 'You look just like her.'

My grandfather came up beside her, and she leaned against him. 'Just like her, Mrs Sinclair? That's exactly what I said.'

At that moment I just wanted to escape from them. 'Can I use your toilet, please?'

'Up the stairs,' my grandfather said. 'On the right.'

I rushed past them and ran up a staircase; there was a door open on the landing and I went inside. It was a small bed-room, looking out over a lawn and a pond at the back of the house, and with a sudden sensation of intense weariness I flung myself down upon the bed. And there, for the first time since I left my father in Hackney Square, I wept. Perhaps it was the sight of the lawn, or the silence, but something even-tually calmed me; I must have slept but I remember no dream – except, that is, for the briefest sensation of someone entering the room and watching over me.

My grandfather was standing just beyond the threshold when I awoke fully clothed upon the bed. 'This used to be your mother's room,' he said. 'You found it straight away. You are an astonishing person.' I hardly knew that I was a person at all, and for a moment I simply stared at him. Then I noticed a small dog lying at the bottom of the bed. 'That's Friday,' my grandfather said. 'Because he was born on a Friday. He's a very old dog now, but he likes you. He used to belong to your mother when he was a puppy.' I soon dis-covered that Friday was a cairn terrier, thirteen years old and now quite grey, and in the days to come he became my constant companion. 'You must be hungry.' For some reason my grandfather was smiling broadly and seemed about to burst into laughter. 'Astonishing people are always hungry. Come into the kitchen.'

I followed him downstairs, and was greeted by my grand-mother who was leaning forward upon the battered kitchen table in order to steady her quivering limbs. Everything shook and rattled as she fried some eggs for me – the plates, the cups, the knives, the frying-pan, all seemed to vibrate in sympathy with her condition as she made her way from the gas-stove to the table. My grandfather paid no attention to the noise, however, and continued to address me as if he had known me all his life. 'You'll like it here, Timothy. It's a different life from London. Quite different. You see, we have forests and streams and hills.'

'We have hills in London, too. Campden Hill. Primrose Hill.'

'And we have fields and cottages, Timothy.'

'Swiss Cottage,' I said.

He laughed loudly, but my grandmother shook her head. 'Don't contradict the boy,' she said, as if it were her husband's fault. 'Don't get him excited. He needs a good rest.' The cups and saucers were rattling in her hands as she brought them over to the table. 'Don't get him all bothered about cottages.'

'Perhaps,' my grandfather went on, 'Timothy would like to go down to the pine forest after his tea.'

'Don't go upsetting him.' Again she intervened as if her husband had been viciously denouncing me. 'Don't go putting ideas into his head.'

'It's only a forest.'

'He may have seen enough forests at home.' With great effort and deliberation she put the eggs in front of me, clinging to the edge of the table as she did so.

'I've seen Epping Forest,' I said.

'This *is* his home, Mrs Sinclair.'

I recalled the peace, even comfort, I had felt in my mother's room and I experienced a brief sensation of horror. How could this be my home, when I was so far away from my father? How could I dwell in two places without, in some sense, tearing myself apart? My identity had been established around my father's presence and I could not envisage any life without him, yet I was curiously at ease in this house. Where did I truly exist? Suddenly I became very hungry and I ate everything my grandmother put in front of me – thick slices of bread and butter, wedges of cake, cheese. She gave me a glass of milk, spilling a few drops on to the floor, and I drank it quickly despite its slightly unfamiliar taste. 'All the milk is pasteurized now,' I announced, 'because of the government.'

'Not here. Not in the country.' She saw my face and added quickly, 'But we can get you some if you prefer it.' Everything had become so strange that, as I finished the meal, I felt I was consuming my own past.

'Have you ever been to school?' my grandfather asked me as I put down my spoon. My grandmother did not interrupt on this occasion, but sat next to me. I shook my head, because my mouth was full. 'I thought not,' he added without a trace of disapproval; it was as if he had known about me all along.

'But my father teaches me every day,' I managed to say, after swallowing the last piece of cake. 'He teaches me everything I want to know. You said I knew a lot, didn't you? You said I was astonishing.' It is hard now to distinguish between those facts which I guessed at the time and those which I learned later, but this I did understand very quickly: one of the reasons why my grandfather had taken me away from London was to send me to school, in the belief that my welfare and my future were being neglected by my father. He thought he was protecting me – saving me from a wayward existence with a suspicious parent, a charlatan who professed to see visions and pretended to heal people. This was his true opinion of Clement Harcombe; he never admitted as much, but I sensed it clearly. So I, the only child of his only daughter, was to be given a proper future just as she would have wished; Cecilia Sinclair would not be forgotten, and her son would come into his inheritance. He had acted out of concern and love for me, as I knew, but one thing puzzled and disturbed me even then: why had my father allowed William Sinclair to take me away? Why had he not refused him access to our lodgings in Hackney Square? Why had he not struggled to keep me? In time, however, all these things would be revealed.

'I don't particularly want to go to school,' I said now, as the three of us sat in the kitchen together. 'I'm quite happy as I am.' In fact I was afraid, not of school itself but of the children whom I would have to meet there; I knew no one of my own age, and the idea of doing so filled me with horror. What kind of child shuns the company of other children? Yet, secretly, I did.

'There you go again.' My grandmother was addressing my

grandfather as if I had not spoken at all. 'Talking out of turn and frightening the boy half to death.'

'I'm not frightened.' I turned to her but I did not know whether to address her as 'grandmother' or 'Mrs Sinclair'. So I called her nothing and I knew that, as a result, I sounded curt and difficult. 'I'm not frightened of anything.'

'Of course not.' She had taken no offence and with her trembling hand patted me on the shoulder. 'Your grandfather is a very argumentative old man. He's well known for it, aren't you, Bill?' He nodded and smiled at her. 'Now,' she added, 'is there anything else you want?'

'I'd like to listen to some music, please.' I don't know why I made this unusual request, but my grandfather looked at me in delight.

'Just like your mother,' he said. 'He wants to listen to the gramophone, Mrs Sinclair.'

'Now don't go putting words into his poor little mouth . . .' Her head was shaking from side to side, as if she were somehow denying my request.

'He wants to hear his mother's records,' he went on softly. My mother listening to music: this was another picture to put beside the mental image I had of her. 'Now where did we put them, Mrs Sinclair?'

My grandfather found the gramophone in the attic where my mother's few possessions had been carefully preserved; it lay there beside a wooden box of records, a wicker-basket filled with half-empty bottles of scent, several dresses and skirts neatly folded among layers of tissue paper and, most extraordinary of all, a small musical instrument. 'Here's a violin!' I exclaimed, quite as if it were some discovery of mine.

'A mandolin,' my grandfather explained. 'She liked to play the mandolin.' I put it down gently and covered it with a piece of tissue from the pile of clothes next to it.

The gramophone itself, with its large brass horn and clockwork motor, was very dusty. The wood was chipped and scratched but it was not damaged, and together we carried it downstairs. I had been given my mother's old room as my own, and I placed it beside my bed. Carefully I wound the handle and put on one of the old-fashioned twelve-inch records which she had collected so many years before; then I lay down and listened to a piano piece which was being played. Friday was at my feet, in the same position he had found for himself that afternoon. Seven o'clock. I could hear the chimes of a clock downstairs and I got beneath the covers of my bed, feeling the sheets upon me like a cold hand. I was listening to my mother's own record in her old room and, as I lay there, the very sounds became imbued with her presence. But I sat up in bed, alarmed, when I heard a sudden distortion of the music – not so much a break or jump, but a lengthening of the notes. And then I believed that I could hear a woman sighing. But this may have been just the perception of a bewildered child: perhaps I had heard only the usual hiss and crackle which accompanied the music as it issued from the brass horn. I lay down again with my right arm covering my eyes, my left arm curled above my head; and I knew, even then, that this was how my mother had slept.

So ended my first day away from home. Other days passed, although I cannot now remember how many; that time was marked for me only by strangeness. My grandparents were always very kind to me but I did not want to come too close to them, since it seemed to me that I would somehow be betraying my father. There was a long sloping lawn behind the farmhouse which led down to a pond and then, on the other side of a rough track, a pine forest. In those early days that forest became my refuge and, in a sense, my hiding place; but whether I hid myself out of guilt or fear, I cannot now recall. Certainly I did not want to disturb or burden my grandparents with my presence, despite their kindness to me, but, more importantly, I wanted to seem busily occupied in the hope that they might forget about the school which my grandfather had mentioned on the first evening. I suppose I had the faint expectation that I, too, might be forgotten.

So I remained apart and each morning would make my way towards the pine forest with Friday; the old dog had taken to me so much that he would follow me everywhere and lie patiently beside me when I rested. I would trace the paths between the slender pines, the piles of fallen needles like clouds beneath my feet, and breathe the scented, secluded air. It was for me an enchanted place, quite beyond the reach of the world, its softness and secrecy promising a kind of immortality; for, yes, I thought of such things even then. There was one tree in particular against which I liked to sit, its gnarled grey roots forming for me a perfect resting place, and when I leaned back against its trunk I could see the sky glimmering through its feathery and striated branches. I did not care to look up at the open sky, while the darker and more overgrown parts of the forest frightened me: but this protective canopy of wood and pine needles, through which the bright day glittered, was the very image of peacefulness and repose. It summoned up some quiet part of myself, which somehow gave me strength; I think of it even now, in this latter time, when I cannot sleep or when I daydream, and all the years of my life count for nothing.

Eventually I would rouse myself from my trance; with Friday padding alongside me, I would leave the forest and go back across the lawn towards the farmhouse. The darkness of winter gradually gave way to the warmer days of early spring and my life seemed to be suspended in their general brightness; my father had not visited me here and, after a while, I ceased to expect it. I remember feeling very tired sometimes, and there were occasions when I would lie down upon the lawn with my face buried in the grass. But I was never lonely, not even when I looked up at the house and my mother's room, because in some way the ground itself seemed to be my companion. I whispered words into the earth and imagined them travelling through the infinite recesses of the globe, and there were times when I listened for voices which might comfort me in my distress. For I knew then, as I know now, that this was not a dead landscape.

One afternoon my grandmother, seeing me lying upon the lawn, called me to tea in her tremulous voice. Reluctantly I got up and walked towards the house, just in time to see her retreating into the kitchen – the very curve and shape of her back outlining the terrible physical discomfort from which she suffered. Everything was laid out as usual upon the table, except for the brown tea-pot, which slowly and unsteadily she was now putting down beside the sink. And, as I watched her, I recognized my mother in her face; or, rather, I saw her as my mother. I saw my mother as an old and infirm woman. I went up to her and, for the first time, put my arms around her. I could feel her shaking violently as I embraced her and, in that moment, I understood precisely the very depths and limits of her condition; I understood, also, her sensation of being cut off from the steady rhythm of the world. This was how it felt to be her: to be somehow apart, tenuous, easily discarded. It was then that I began to shake violently and uncontrollably. She sensed that something was wrong and with a cry let me go. I stood there quivering and trembling in front of her, my head swaying from side to side, but when I could look up I saw that she was now perfectly calm and still. My body continued to shake, and in my horror I fled from her into the garden; I ran down on to the lawn and flung myself upon the ground as my limbs continued to be agitated by all the terrible nervous seizures I had previously witnessed in her. I do not know how long I remained here, but slowly the tremors abated. It seemed to me at the time as if they were being transmitted into the ground, that they were being drawn downwards through the earth; and, as the entire landscape took this disquiet from me, my own body became calm again.

It was twilight when I arose, now quite still, but I did not want to go back into the house. I felt that I had committed some wrong against my grandmother; I knew that I had cured her, just as surely as my father cured the sick at our meetings, but I still felt that I had robbed her of something. I walked across the track into the pine forest, but in the gathering dusk it gradually became unrecognizable. So I retraced my steps and, as I approached the house once more, I could see my grandparents in the kitchen talking together; my grandmother was still very calm, all traces of her nervous disorder gone. I stood outside the window, watching them, uncertain what to do. Then my grandfather saw my pale face in the darkness and, with a smile, beckoned to me; I came into the house but hesitated by the kitchen door. 'I'm sorry,' was all I could think of saying. I did not look at my grandmother but rushed past them and ran to my own room. I knew that they would not disturb me there, and in the silence I could hear their low voices. Then suddenly I was out of the room and climbing the stairs to the attic; there, in the twilight, I saw my mother's clothes lying neatly folded as before. I went over to them and stroked the dress on top of the pile; it was violet, I remember, and made of some shiny material like silk. Whenever I see that colour now, I think of my mother. I took the dress, buried my face in it, and then surprised myself by bursting into tears. For some reason I put it on, hastily, clumsily, struggling to get it over my ordinary shirt and trousers until I stood there, dishevelled, in my mother's old dress; then I picked up the mandolin and began to play. I do not know how long I might have remained, but after a few moments Friday came up the stairs to find me and, seeing me in so strange a condition, began to bark. With a sudden sensation of panic I removed the dress, folded it back with the others, and hurried down again to my room. I was panting as furiously as if I had run a long distance and, with the dog still barking at me, I lay fully clothed upon the bed.

I could have slept only for an hour or so when I was suddenly roused by a loud rattling noise; it was a curious sound and cautiously I went over to the window, from where it seemed to have come, only to jump back when two pieces of gravel were thrown up against the pane. That was the noise I had heard. I looked out and there beneath my bedroom window was Stanley Clay. As soon as he saw me he started waving, and I opened the window as quietly as I could. 'There you are,' was all he said.

'What are you doing here?' I was trying to whisper, not wanting to disturb my grandparents, who were probably even now reading the newspaper in the parlour.

'Come on!'

'Where?'

'Home!'

It was clear to me that Stanley had been sent by my father; he was here to take me back at last. I leant down towards him eagerly, just as if I were about to shake his hand. 'One minute,' I whispered. Quickly I packed my few books and clothes in the brown suitcase, which I kept beneath my mother's bed, and very quietly I left the room. Friday had been lying on the landing outside and, yawning, he rose to greet me. I kneeled down to embrace him for the last time and murmured some soothing words. I could hear voices coming from the parlour, so I crept downstairs and very cautiously opened the front door. Stanley was standing by the gate at the bottom of the drive and, checking my impulse to run, I stepped softly over the gravel until I reached him.

'That was quick,' he said. He was looking down at the ground and spoke in his usual low voice; he seemed embarrassed at having acted in so daring a fashion and now did not quite know what to do.

'We should get away, Stanley, shouldn't we?' I looked fearfully back at the house.

'Oh yes.' The idea might just have occurred to him. 'Margaret's waiting for us. Down the lane.'

And indeed I could see her some yards away. The moon was almost full and on this cloudless night the lane became a track of silver light; everything was quiet at that hour and the moonlight itself seemed to be part of the silence. 'Here I am!' Margaret shouted quite unnecessarily as we came towards

her, but she was flustered and excited by her part in the
adventure. 'I'm here to save you! Let's go, Timothy, before
they can catch us.' We might have been the children in the
story-books who are pursued by giants – and perhaps, for her,
that was really how it seemed. 'Come on!' She was now
almost screaming. 'They might be coming!' I was caught up
in the wave of her own sudden panic and the three of us ran
down the lane, Margaret looking anxiously back in case the
ogres were already in pursuit.

It was a few minutes before we stopped, and I was able to
catch my breath. 'Where are we going?'

'To Mawbro,' Stanley replied.

'Where?'

'Marlborough.' Margaret answered for him. 'That's where
we catch the motor-bus back to London. It's the way we
came.'

'And how do we get there?'

'We walk,' she said very firmly. 'Shanks's old pony.' And
so we began our trek through the night.

'How did you find me?' I asked her after a while, but she
kept her anxious watch over the deserted countryside and did
not seem to hear me.

'Mr Harcombe told us.' It was Stanley who replied; he was
much more at ease now that he could concentrate his gaze
upon the road ahead. 'He told us where you had gone.' So
my father had sent them, just as I suspected. 'He told us all
about it at the last meeting.'

'That must have been yesterday then,' I replied, having all
this time kept careful note of the days when we would have
gone to the old hall together.

'No. That was five months ago, Tim. Just after you left.'
Stanley hesitated. 'Mr Harcombe hasn't held no meetings
since.' This puzzled me very much, since they were at the
centre of my father's life. Why had he so suddenly stopped?
'It's not the same without you,' Stanley was saying.

'Why?'

'It's just not the same.'

'What does my father say about it?'

Stanley was even more hesitant than before. 'We haven't seen Mr Harcombe for a few weeks.'

'But I thought he sent you here.'

'Not exactly, Tim. Not in so many words.'

All the time Margaret was marching beside us, pretending not to be concerned with our conversation but occasionally listening to what was being said. 'We know he wants to get you back from them,' she added now. 'He doesn't want them involved with you.'

I remembered the image of my mother which I had seen upon my grandparents' faces, and I remembered the peacefulness of her room. 'They were nice to me,' I replied. 'And they had a good old dog.'

'Oh yes. They're always nice until your back is turned.' She had looked at me for a moment, but now she resumed her fearful watch for 'them'. 'What did you do there?' she asked a few minutes later.

I did not want to tell her about my life with them, because I realized that she would somehow interpret it to their disadvantage. 'I listened to the gramophone,' I said.

We rested for a while beside a derelict barn and then carried on walking. It was an hour or two after midnight when we approached Marlborough, and the three of us were so tired that we decided to sleep in a field on the outskirts of the town. But Margaret managed to rouse us at dawn, and we found our way to the motor-bus depot.

On the journey back to London I talked fitfully to them and, slowly, I began to understand the course of events in my absence. After the last meeting the Harcombe Circle had come up to my father outside the old hall and asked him why I was not on the stage beside him; he had appeared unhappy, even a little anxious, but told them everything that had happened during my grandfather's visit. The meeting itself had not, it seemed, been a success; somehow, according to

Margaret, 'the spirit had gone out of Mr Harcombe' and in fact he had cancelled all subsequent meetings. Naturally the Circle were dismayed, but, when Margaret and Stanley had called at our lodgings a few weeks ago, my father had refused to open the door to them; he shouted out that he was very busy and would contact them later. This was so unlike him that I became seriously alarmed as we travelled back to London through the morning. I could not imagine what had disturbed him so profoundly; nor could I understand why Margaret should believe that it had some connection with my own departure. Yet this was the reason why the Harcombe Circle had met and decided, as she put it, to 'mount a rescue': they assumed that my father was alarmed, or dejected, by my unaccustomed absence from his life and that my sudden re-appearance would resolve the problem. My father had told them about the Sinclairs and the area of the country where they lived, so it had been a relatively simple matter to find me.

We entered London in the late afternoon, and I was as awake and as alert as I had ever been. Margaret was still keeping watch through the rear window as we drove into the depot at Ludgate Hill, in case 'they' had followed us so far, and even I felt uncomfortably nervous as we reached the end of our long journey. We boarded a tram which took us by Whitechapel High Street, and then we walked back to Hackney. As soon as we came to the square I ran towards our lodgings. I hurried down the path with my key in my hand and, as quickly as I could, flung open the door while calling out 'Dad! Dad!' I went into his room, expecting him to be at his usual place near the fire, but there was a space where his armchair had been. I knew at once that he was no longer here. I turned around just as Stanley and Margaret entered behind me: the room was quite bare, the furniture gone, the maps and engravings taken down from the walls. Margaret put her hand up to her mouth, and I looked at her in horror. Then I rushed into my own room, but it was also empty. My little bed and bookcase had been taken away. 'Dad!' I cried out in despair. 'Where are you? Where are you?' There was no answer.

A N
E S S A Y

CONCERNING

Humane Understanding.

In Four BOOKS.

Quam bellum est velle confiteri potius nescire quod nescias, quam ista effutientem nauseare, atque ipsum sibi displicere ! Cic. de Natur. Deor. *l.* 1.

LONDON:

Printed by *Eliz. Holt,* for **Thomas Basset,** at the *George* in *Fleetstreet,* near St. *Dunstan's* Church. MDCXC.

SIX

'WHERE IS HE?' A SMALL boy, dressed in a page's blue uniform, regarded him curiously and then burst out laughing. 'You're a dreadful sight, you are. Where is he? He's upstairs, as usual.' The boy lit the stair gas and Timothy leaned against the oak banister for a moment: his heart was beating so fast that he must have been running before he entered this unfamiliar but well-appointed residence. It was the first unaccountable event in an unaccountable day, which can be compared only to the strange case of the missing Portuguese lampstand or the extraordinary affair of the one-eyed Russian consul, which may or may not be revealed to the world at some later date. 'Go on then,' the boy muttered. 'Do go up.'

So Timothy climbed the broad staircase; there was a barometer on the wall ahead of him and, when he came to the landing, he saw a light shining through an open door. He knocked briefly and then, mustering his courage, collecting his thoughts, and fired in any case by his desperate determination, he walked in. In the dim light he saw the great detective sitting in a cane chair, his back towards him; some smoke was curling towards the ceiling from a pipe or cigarette. 'Pray be seated,' he said without turning around. 'You are a child of about twelve years old, wearing a most peculiar variety of trouser, and you have been running for several miles. At the moment I am not at liberty to inform you of the processes of my deduction. Suffice it to say that I have never been mistaken.'

'I'm sorry, sir,' Timothy cried. 'But you must find my father. My father has disappeared!'

The famous detective did now glance around at his importunate visitor. 'You are not a street child,' he said. 'Yet you are not dressed as if you came from the great band of the educated classes. Sit down, do, and add something further to the very significant information you have just given me.' He rose from his chair and for a moment leaned over a highly polished silver coffee-pot which had been placed on a narrow table just beside him; it seemed to Timothy that he was looking at his own reflection upon its curved surface. He walked over to the window, pulled back the wooden shutters from one side, and surveyed the yellow fog which was even now rolling down the deserted thoroughfare in the general direction of Tyburnia. He was dressed precisely as Timothy might have imagined, or expected, with his steel-grey trousers and blue waistcoat surmounted by a black frock-coat of the most fashionable cut. 'Do begin,' he said, still looking down into the foggy street. 'Relate to me all the facts as you understand them.' And so Timothy narrated to him everything that had occurred, as well as the incidents which had been described to him by Stanley Clay and Margaret Collins. He concluded with the description of the lodgings in Hackney Square, stripped bare of their contents, and his father gone. 'This is a case of some interest,' the detective said. 'This is what I might call an *affair*.' He spun upon his heels and was suddenly looking across the room at Timothy. 'So what is your next step, Master Harcombe?'

Timothy hesitated. 'That is why I have come to you, sir. I do not –'

'Quite so. Then you and I will most certainly proceed to the scene of the mystery. Tell me,' he added more softly, 'what precisely is it that you suspect?'

'I cannot be sure, sir. But there is so delicate a harmony between my father and myself that I should know – I should *feel* – if any harm had come to him.' Timothy stopped for a moment, bewildered by the strangeness of his speech even though he knew it to express the true state of his feelings. 'And I do not feel it. He is not in any mortal danger.'

'I anticipated every word you have just spoken, my young

friend, and I have already taken steps which I hope will justify your confidence. But there is still a mystery in this case to be resolved, and I have not yet found the thread to lead me out of the labyrinth.'

Timothy listened intently as he spoke, but at the same time the boy could not help but notice the furnishings of the room in which he was sitting – the elbow-chair by the fire, the table covered with cuttings from the public prints as well as almanacs and railway timetables, the small sandalwood box of gold-tipped cigarettes, the piano. The piano? What was a piano doing there? 'We need a name for this,' the detective was saying now. 'We need a name before we can proceed. Would you consider "The Adventure of Hackney Square"? No. It sounds badly. Would you be very upset by "The Case of the Disappearing Father"? An excellent title, I think.' Timothy was now so eager to start their inquiry that he merely nodded. 'That is agreed between us, then, and we can begin our adventure. Come. There is not a moment to be lost.' He startled Timothy by suddenly rushing across the room and grabbing his scarf and ulster from a coat-stand beside the door. Then he hurried out of the room with the boy following behind, and as soon as they had emerged into the street he hailed a cab with a ferocious whistle. 'To Hackney,' he shouted up at the driver. 'And go like the devil himself!'

Timothy did not care for the interior of the vehicle, which smelt of animal fur mixed with damp umbrellas, and he was perched uneasily upon the coarse leather of its seat as they sped past tenements and terraces, archways and lonely brick-fields. 'Mr Holmes,' he said at last.

'What did you say?'

'Mr Sherlock Holmes?'

'And who may he be?'

The boy was astonished. 'But *you* are Mr Sherlock Holmes. I came to you in Baker Street.'

'You most certainly did not. My lodgings are in Berners Street and my name, as everyone knows, is Austin

Smallwood.' Timothy was too bewildered to reply, and sat in silence until his companion spoke again. 'Who is this Sherlock Holmes?'

'He was a detective, sir. He is a detective.' It had now become so delicate and difficult a problem that Timothy did not know how to reply. 'He was invented by a writer.' He noticed the sudden look of horror upon Austin Smallwood's face, and once more he lapsed into silence until they arrived at their destination.

But this was not the Hackney he remembered. He recognized the square, but the small brick houses which formed it looked too fresh and too well defined; they looked too bright to be real. A smell of plaster, clay and mortar pervaded the area: then Timothy noticed that there was a building-site at the south end and that several houses were still in the process of being constructed. The scene of his childhood was enduring its own beginning; just as age brings character and temperament, would the square itself reveal its own true nature only after the passage of time? Or was it that these houses would slowly become imbued with the spirit of the place – with the spirit of London and its past? Austin Smallwood was already writing in a small leather-bound notebook, but now he closed it with a definite snap. 'Where is the empty house?' he asked the boy.

'All these houses look empty, sir. They are all so new.'

'No house is ever without its inhabitants, my young friend. Remember that, and now, if you please, point me towards it.'

It was just behind them, although Timothy hardly knew it. Its small garden was covered with fresh earth, its door and window-frames painted a light green, its brick a pristine yellow. They opened the gate and, to Timothy's surprise, the detective dropped at once to his knees and – with his face no more than two inches from the ground – began inspecting the loose earth and gravel by the steps which led to the front door. 'There were three of you last night,' he said, with his face still directed towards the soil. 'A child, a heavily built man in his twenties and a female dwarf.'

'I believe I already mentioned them to you, sir,'

'Pray leave such matters to me, Timothy Harcombe.' He sounded a trifle annoyed, but he continued his close and painstaking investigation of the ground. 'Yes,' he was muttering now. 'Yes. Yes. Now we have it.' Excitedly he beckoned Timothy over to the patch of loose earth he was now scrutinizing. 'Two other persons have come this way in the last twenty-four hours. One a man of middle height.' He paused. 'His companion was a very beautiful young woman.'

'A woman!'

'There is no need to register surprise. Men are often accompanied by women, even in this area of London. Follow me, and you will learn something else to your advantage.' He opened the front door and slowly entered the hallway, keeping his eyes upon the floor and upon the lower part of the walls. 'Here?' he whispered to Timothy, pointing to the lodgings which the boy and his father had occupied. Timothy was so chastened by the unfamiliar emptiness and silence of the house that he merely nodded. 'Quite so. Enter ahead of me, if you please, and tell me immediately if you notice anything out of the ordinary.' The rooms were as bare as on Timothy's last visit, but they were not without interest to Austin Smallwood. There were no curtains hanging from the window and it was a bright day outside; nevertheless he took a small lantern from the capacious pocket of his ulster. 'A bull's-eye,' he murmured. 'Invaluable in the East End.' He brought out a pencil, a pair of tweezers, a silver cigarette-case, a white envelope and then a magnifying glass with which he proceeded to examine the window-sills as well as the wooden boards of the floor. 'A cutting from a woman's finger-nail,' he announced suddenly. And then, a few minutes later, 'A man's hair.' Slowly he got to his feet and, standing in the centre of the room, took out a gold-tipped cigarette and put it to his lips without lighting it. 'You informed me, Timothy, that your companions found your father much disturbed when they last visited him. He was not disturbed because of your disappearance, however wounding this may be to your feelings.' The boy shook his head, as if disclaiming any such response. 'He was alarmed because he was hiding, or sheltering, a young woman who wished to remain unknown. Who did not wish to be exposed to the vulgar gaze, *if*, for the purposes of the argument, I may call your friends vulgar on this occasion. May I?' Timothy nodded. 'I promise not to do so again. Your father then left with this same young woman only a few hours before your sudden arrival with the female dwarf. But they have not travelled far.' He inhaled upon the unlit cigarette. 'I have solved this part of the case to my entire satisfaction, but one question remains: why did your father cancel the meetings in the hall after your departure to your grandparents' house? Once we have resolved that, we have found the key to the entire mystery. Follow me, if you please.' He left the house quickly and with a deliberate, almost theatrical, gesture he summoned the driver who had been waiting with his hansom at the corner of the square. 'To the meeting hall in the City Road,' he shouted up at him, before pushing Timothy inside the musty interior of the cab. 'And drive like the wind!'

Once they were seated, Austin Smallwood lit his cigarette. 'For the purposes of fumigation. May I?' He settled back against the decaying leather and, as he looked out at the yellow brick houses, blew the smoke against the grimy window. 'There is such a pleasure in deduction from first principles,' he announced to Timothy. 'Such a joy in clear, distinct and complete ideas. I am very much part of the English tradition, you see. From the particular to the general. From analysis to synthesis. That is what we call the English movement.' At this point the cab was jolted by a ridge in the newly paved road between Pitfield Street and Old Street, and the detective laughed out loud. 'Such a tradition,' he said, 'is no less true because there is nothing in the world which fully represents it. At least that is what Locke said. Have you read Locke, by any chance?' Timothy shook his head, unwilling to admit that he had never even heard of him. 'You must do so immediately. English philosophy is quite as beautiful as English music, and indeed may be said to illustrate it. Rational. Contemplative. Locke believed that there are certain principles which lie beyond history and historical change. There is an organic unity between past and present, and an inner sense which responds to it just as the physical senses respond to the material world. That is why, my young friend, you must move from sense impressions to the imagination and from there to the historical understanding. Music. But you do not read English philosophy. You read detective stories.' He opened the window for a moment, tossed out his cigarette and then immediately lit another. 'Although, don't you think, they are much the same thing? And now, if I am not mistaken, we have arrived at our destination.'

The cab-driver had stopped only to ask the way, however, and then proceeded a few yards further along the City Road before again coming to a halt. 'Here we are and here we go,' he called down to his passengers through the trap.

'What a charming expression. But am I correct in thinking that you were directed to this place?' Austin Smallwood was questioning the man as intently as if he were also involved in the case. 'Think carefully before you answer.'

'That's the size of it.'

'Then I am convinced that you have found the right locality. Let me note it down at once.'

But the hall was not there. Or, rather, Timothy Harcombe was looking at the ruins of a much older building in the area where the hall should have stood: it might have been a church or a mansion, but only the remnants of the outer walls were left. The surviving stones were blackened with soot or grime, and there was an iron brazier in the middle of the abandoned site; a fire must have recently been started within the brazier, however, because the flames were now leaping up towards the sky. There was such an air of dereliction about this place that the boy could hardly speak, and he stood by the side of the road for a moment. 'This is wrong,' he said at last. 'Something is wrong.'

Austin Smallwood had already leapt across the remains of the ancient wall and was closely examining some specimens of fallen masonry. He called over to Timothy, who reluctantly stepped over the wall and joined him. 'The building has only recently been demolished,' he said. 'You will perceive how only two sides of the stone are discoloured. And what do you make of this? An inference, please, from these extraordinary items of evidence.' He walked over to a large pile of coarse sand and put his foot upon it as if he were its conqueror. 'And what of this?' He moved towards the fire in the brazier and began to walk around it, staring into the flame. 'Pray do not argue with me,' he said, not taking his eyes away from the fire. 'The old building is being destroyed, and a new one is being constructed in its place. It has always been a meeting place, and will remain one still.' Quite suddenly he dived towards the brazier and retrieved a paper from the ground beside it. 'Now give me your opinion on this fascinating document,' he said, holding it out to Timothy. 'Keep nothing back. Tell all.'

The paper was thick, with its edges curled and charred. It had also been torn in half, and only the right-hand sides of the words printed upon it were visible. Timothy could see *combe* and, beneath it, *er* and *ian*. 'Harcombe,' he said, with a surprised glance at the detective. 'Could it be the name of my father?'

'And what of the other letters?' The boy shook his head. 'Try preacher or healer. Then try magician. If this is truly your father, then he has come much further than you think. And now we will return to Berners Street, where we will analyse the events of this very interesting morning. After you, if you please.'

Timothy walked back to the cab and sat wearily in the seat with his head bowed. Austin Smallwood glanced at him for a moment and, in a gentler tone than any he had used before, started to talk of other things. 'Tell me more,' he said, 'about Mr Sherlock Holmes. You were gracious enough to confuse me with that gentleman, and I readily admit to being interested in him.' So as they travelled back to the detective's lodgings, Timothy told his companion as much as he could remember about Holmes's methods, adventures and habits. Austin Smallwood seemed particularly intrigued by the fictional character's mode of reasoning. 'You see,' he remarked, putting up his hand to stop Timothy's account of 'A Case of Identity', 'we have returned once again to Locke. The mind, in all its thoughts and reasonings, has no other object but its own ideas. And yet a little before that he explains that there is so close a connection between ideas and words that they cannot be untangled. Everything is made up of words, therefore –'

'I recall something else, sir. The name of the author was Arthur Conan Doyle.'

'That is precisely what I meant.' Austin Smallwood seemed only a little discomposed by the boy's interruption. 'Do go on with your extraordinary narrative.'

At this moment, however, their cab turned into Berners Street and the driver lifted up his whip and waved it once in the air. As soon as they came to a halt the detective jumped out and, with a flourish, held open the narrow door for Timothy. 'Now,' he said, as he led the boy into the house which they had left earlier that morning, 'now we must return to first principles. We must hit the right chord. Did I explain to you that philosophy and detection resemble music?' They ascended the stairs to the detective's study, and, as soon as they entered the room, he went over to the piano. 'A necessary preliminary,' he said as he lifted the polished ebony lid of the instrument and began to play. Timothy did not recognize the melody but he seemed instinctively to understand it – lyrical, mellifluous, the cadences soaring and then calmly descending, the harmonies so firm and clear that they seemed to hover in the air for a moment before dissolving. He thought of the landscape through which he had passed with his grandfather on the day of his departure, with the gentle line of distant hills and the softer gradient of the pastures; he thought of the pine forest and the slender trees against which he rested; and then he thought of the yellow fog gliding through the streets of this city itself.

'William Byrd,' Austin Smallwood announced, as the music ceased. '*Passing Measures*, naturally in my own adaptation. I believe it was Byrd who said that God is in essence a musician, because he creates harmony within the universe. We are all looking for that harmony, Timothy. We are all detectives, looking for the pattern.' He was distracted for a moment, and looked at the boy strangely. Then he turned back to the piano and played some stray notes. 'I have, as you un-doubtedly know, been engaged upon the definitive study of medieval and Renaissance music.' Timothy gave no reply. 'And I have made a curious discovery. It is perfectly clear to me now that English music rarely changes. The instruments may alter and the form may vary, but the spirit seems always to remain the same. The spirit survives. I suppose that is what we mean by harmony. And besides,' he added a moment later, 'music helps me to think.'

'About my father?' The boy was eager to continue with the quest again, after all they had discovered in Hackney Square.

'About your father. And other matters.' He hesitated again. 'I have also been thinking about your friend, Arthur Conan Doyle. I trust that was his name? Of course. I have a perfect memory for such things. From what you tell me of his most entertaining stories, I am led to believe that he has read the works of Mr Dickens. "The Adventure of the Blue Carbuncle" is no more than a fantastic reworking of *A Christmas Carol*. I would also say that he has attended the plays of Mr Oscar Wilde, although he pretends to dislike them, and that he is strangely fascinated by that gentleman's fate. He was brought up as a Romanist and has seen service in India. He has also practised as a doctor. I would deduce that he has travelled extensively in Germany, and has a fascination for the Middle Ages. I believe that he carries a magnifying glass as well as a pocket pistol, and is most interested in psychic phenomena.'

'How can you tell so much, sir?'

'A mere trifle. Elementary.' Austin Smallwood turned back to the piano, began to play a melody, and then stopped abruptly. Timothy noticed that momentary look of horror, or agony, which he had seen upon his face before. 'I wonder,' the detective was saying, 'I wonder if Mr Sherlock Holmes realized that he was a mere invention of someone? He was clearly a man of some perspicacity, and he may have tried to unravel the clues to his creator. Was that his last case?' Timothy noticed once again the sudden expression of horror. 'But, if that is so, should I begin a similar adventure? Who invented me?' He got up from the piano and walked slowly over to the window. 'You see, my young friend, a person like myself can only really exist in stories. Or perhaps in dreams. Don't you agree?' The boy was so struck by the truth of this, and by the detective's own clarity of expression, that he could think of nothing to add. 'I am tall. I am slender. I dress perfectly. I am a scholar and a musician. I solve all my cases. What else is there to say?' He sighed and looked out of the window into Berners Street. 'Look at the yellow fog. Was there ever one so thick as this? Or so comforting? Were there ever streets like these? So strangely dark? Listen to the forlorn cry of the urchin just below us. Did you ever hear such a thing except in fiction? And then there are all the coincidences and improbabilities which beset us . . .' He had his back turned, but Timothy could see the detective put a hand up to his face. 'Perhaps,' he said after a moment, 'perhaps you believe that I am nothing more than whimsical. Or that my wits have gone astray. Well, then, pray explain this.' He quickly walked over to the table beside the fire and snatched up some papers. 'Here, you see. Written down exactly as it has happened!'

Timothy took the papers from him and was astonished to

see a neatly handwritten document with 'The Case of the Disappearing Father' as its title. He read on a little and was no less surprised to find an account of all the events of that day. 'All my adventures are narrated,' Austin Smallwood exclaimed before Timothy had a chance to reach the end. 'All the time I am being invented, or created, or what you will. And do you know the worst aspect of this affair? I cannot see the conclusion. How is this particular plot going to end, for example? How are we going to solve the mystery of your father's disappearance?' He took the papers from the boy and clutched them to his chest. 'But there is also a larger question. How will I come to the end of my adventures? I go on from day to day as if I were immortal, and yet there is someone else. Someone who is writing everything down.' He glanced at the pages with disgust. 'And yet,' he said, smiling now as he continued to stare at the handwriting, 'and yet there may be clues even here.' He held the pages to the light. 'The watermark is quite unusual. I have expert knowledge of these matters and there is only one stationer in London who supplies paper of this kind. Now if I could give them some description of the person who might have purchased it –' He broke off and, to Timothy's surprise, lay down on the Turkey carpet with the papers close to his nose. 'A man is responsible,' he said. 'I deduce that from the sturdiness of the "p" and the "d". The boldness of the "q" and the "t" also informs me that he is thirty-five or thirty-six years old. I know that he is self-educated because the handwriting conforms to no academic model. And do you notice the way his letters dip below the line?' Timothy could hardly notice anything since the detective remained prostrate upon the carpet. 'Surely the mark of some dark interior life? Out of what depths have I come?' For a moment he seemed pleased with himself. 'From caverns measureless to man I have emerged in Berners Street.'

Timothy clapped his hands. 'That's it! I remember now! I remember how I know the name. My father was born in Berners Street. He told me about it once.'

Austin Smallwood rolled over and looked severely at the ceiling. 'Yet another of those coincidences which could occur only in fiction. No doubt the happy event took place in this house. In this very room. Everything returns in a circle. Everything has been done before. Everything has been said before. It is the same pattern. The same music surrounds us.'

'But don't you think that the coincidence can help us?' Timothy said, excited by the realization that his father also knew this place. 'My father understands such things. He sees things which other people cannot see. He could help you discover . . .' He paused, unable to think of the phrase.

'The author of my being?'

'Yes. Of course. Oh do let us find my father and ask for his help.' Timothy bent down and picked up the last page of the manuscript, which the detective had dropped upon the carpet. He started reading it so earnestly that it was as if he, too, were searching for some clue to his eventual destiny. 'The story doesn't end in Berners Street,' he said. 'It begins here, but it doesn't stop here.'

'And so?'

Timothy paid no attention to the question, but in a clear, calm voice began to read from the last paragraph: 'The great detective, accompanied by the boy, returned on that same day to Hackney Square, having been given a curious message, delivered *sotto voce* by an old woman dressed in the colourful costume of an oyster-seller, that they would learn something to their advantage. My dear friend, Mr Austin Smallwood, of whom every reader is aware, pausing only in a momentary fit of abstraction induced by the absence of gold-tipped cigarettes from his person, left his chambers as quickly as decorum would allow and with an elegant wave of his hand claimed the attention of a hansom. With a gracious yet firm gesture he manoeuvred the boy, Timothy, to an adjacent seat before addressing the driver in his customarily measured tones, "To Hackney! Swiftness is all!"'

Smallwood had listened to all of this with attention. 'I

think nothing of the style,' he said. 'But it is suggestive.' He felt the interior pockets of his dark frock-coat. 'And it is also accurate. I do *not* have any cigarettes!' He went over to the mahogany table and picked up his cigarette-box. But he did not open it; he began passing it from hand to hand as he stared at nothing in particular. 'So we are to learn something to our advantage if we return to Hackney Square. I believe I know the identity of the old woman who conveyed this very interesting information.' He was still holding the cigarette-box in the air as he spoke. 'Is that what we must do then? Go back to the beginning of our quest?'

'It can do no harm, sir. And perhaps, in finding my father, you are meant to find someone else as well.'

'And yet,' the detective went on, not hearing Timothy, 'he has shown too much of his hand in every sense. The writer – the author – has outlined the next stage of the adventure and has therefore given us the advantage of surprise. What if I were now to change the plot myself? Would that not be the most remarkable thing?' He put down the box, and laid his hands upon it. 'Could I then become a free agent, after all? Let me speculate. Let me consider.' He began walking up and down the room before coming to a sudden stop. 'Timothy,' he said, putting his hands upon the boy's shoulders. 'I am about to give you a sovereign. Take a cab to Hackney Square, as we have been directed, and wait for me there. I will meet you outside the house at dusk. Remember that. Dusk. As a mere boy – if you do not mind me mentioning that fact? Good. As a mere boy you will pass unnoticed in the vicinity, and you will take the opportunity of making some inquiries of your own. Strangers in the neighbourhood. Sudden migrations at night. And so forth. I will not ac-company you, and will thus frustrate our author's schemes. I have plans of my own. Now go immediately.' He took a coin from his pocket and tossed it at the boy, who, in his excitement at being once more in search of his father, hurried from the room without saying a word.

He emerged from the house and, now that the fog had lifted, lingered by the corner of Oxford Street until a cab should pass. A young man in a garish check jacket seemed to be watching him from the other side of that thoroughfare and after a few moments walked up to him. 'Hello, Mr Harcombe,' he said. 'Nice to see you again.' Then he winked and, before Timothy could respond, he hurried away towards Tottenham Court Road.

'I know that voice,' the boy said out loud. 'I know that voice very well.' But who could have recognized him in this time, and in this place? Who could have known his name? He had no opportunity to consider such matters, however, because at that moment he saw a hansom coming towards him.

As soon as Austin Smallwood observed the boy being driven away, he entered his small bedroom and went over to a panelled section of the wall just beside his dressing-table; there was a concealed lock there and, after a moment, he slid back the panels from a dark alcove. It was in this place that he preserved his famous disguises, although there were occasions when he believed that they preserved him. Here was his costume as a common labourer, the grime neatly rubbed into the soiled fustian; and here were the ragged trousers and peaked cap of an ancient match-man. There were many of them, each one representing a clear and distinct idea of the character he wished to impersonate. He did not hesitate, but reached out for the one he needed to undertake the last stages of the present adventure.

That afternoon an elderly woman, dressed in the brown shawl and stained yellow bonnet of an oyster-seller, made her way through the narrow streets and alleys of the East End. The wind had cleared the yellow fog and in the sudden brightness everything looked newly made – the house-fronts, the stalls, the carts, even the people themselves, seemed to have been freshly printed and rolled out upon the earth like some vivid presentiment of life. The oyster-seller herself was a bustling, energetic, gossipy old party who looked as if she knew everyone's business. And everyone knew her: or, rather, she conformed so much to type that she was instantly recognizable. There had always been women like her in this area of London and no doubt there always would be, but who could say whether they created the city or the city created them? It was as if the same spirit or the same character were constantly being reborn, just as the atmosphere of the East End itself had been sustained through the long years. Indeed Austin Smallwood had his own theory about such matters, based upon his familiar methods of observation and deduction; he believed that people of the same mental and physical type recurred in each generation, that they inhabited the same areas and even performed the same tasks. He had become interested in recent experiments with electricity and electrical magnetism, and had come to the conclusion that there were also patterns of energy which formed the very shape and texture of human lives within each specific place. He even began to wonder whether there were not other invisible agencies at work—spirits which inhabited people and locations.

So it was that the garrulous old party made her way along streets, down alleys, past closely packed tenements, which were as sordid and familiar as she was. She walked among coster girls, and baked-potato men, and sellers of boot-laces, and cockney serenaders, and street children, all of whom streamed through the narrow thoroughfares as if they were lost in some dream of London from which they would never awake. She was seen outside some model lodgings for the poor just beyond Shoreditch Church; she was seen loitering beside a wagon full of old books in Postern Street; and, most particularly, she was seen entering Whitmore's, the stationers, in Crucifix Lane. Indeed she had only just left that establishment and was approaching the public bath-house on the corner when a young man fell heavily against her and almost knocked her to the ground. 'Come on, you,' she said. 'Put 'em up, you. Show me yer knuckles. I'm an old 'un, but

I'm game.' She lifted her tattered skirt with one hand and shook the other in his face as she started to dance around him. But he did not answer; he was breathing only with difficulty and, when she started to wrestle him to the ground, she realized that there was a knife sticking in the back of his neck. 'God love us,' she screamed. 'Who has done this dreadful thing?'

A crowd was beginning to gather around the two of them when suddenly another young man ran across the street; he pushed his way through, at the same time holding up the palms of his hands. They were covered in fresh blood and, as the crowd shrank back, he started to laugh. But no sound came from his open mouth. Then he performed a somersault and left the marks of his bloody hands upon the ground: for some reason the oyster-seller thought of the wheel in the old English song, the wheel that keeps on turning, the wheel making its own music, the wheel at which the story-teller sits. The one who had been stabbed, and perhaps killed, was now sprawled half upon the cobbled pavement and half upon the muddy road; the other was putting his hands up to his face, and smiling as he smeared the blood against his cheeks. But there was something wrong here, something missing; the old woman knew the sudden atmosphere of a place where blood has been shed, and she sensed nothing of the kind here. Then all at once she realized that these were street acrobats, conjurors who conducted their mime for the small coins that would be thrown to them at the end of each performance. But it was not at all clear that the gathering crowd, which became more menacing now that the initial shock had subsided, realized that they were watching a pantomime of the old type. She backed away and, looking around fearfully, noticed that the fog was once more coming down upon these ancient streets. 'Everything is coming apart,' she whispered to herself. 'The fantasy is beginning to dissolve.'

Taking advantage of the confusion, she ducked within the porch of the public bath-house and began to take off her clothes – her stained yellow bonnet, brown shawl and tattered dress were soon in a pile on the steps of the building when, of course, Austin Smallwood finally emerged from the depths of his disguise. The great detective was perfectly dressed in frock-coat, waistcoat and iron-grey trousers; but he was without his ulster, and he began to tremble as the cold fog swirled around him. 'It will soon be dark,' he muttered, for some reason still using the voice of the old woman he had recently become. 'I must meet Timothy Harcombe and acquaint him with the truth. For the truth, they say, is stranger than any fiction.' So in the gathering dusk he hurried towards Hackney Square, where the boy had agreed to wait for him.

Timothy had been loitering beside the iron railings of the square for some time; despite Austin Smallwood's instructions, he had discovered nothing about his father's sudden disappearance. The windows of the lodgings were still without curtains, but no light came from within; he imagined that the rooms were as bare as they had been during his last visit with the detective, and he felt so bereft that he had great difficulty in holding back his tears. To be in this place without his father – well, it was almost too hard to bear.

'I am always in the right place at the right time, am I not?' Austin Smallwood was standing beside him, calmly lighting a cigarette. 'Now tell me, quite precisely and in the proper sequence, exactly what you have observed this afternoon.'

'Nothing, sir. I have seen nothing.'

'And nothing can come of nothing. Think again.'

'No one has come. And no one has left. There is no one here at all.'

'In that respect, at least, you are quite wrong.' He took the boy's arm, and together they began to walk around the square just as if they had embarked upon a casual stroll. 'Will you allow me to speak confidentially? You will? Good. Do you remember how I was able to identify the watermark of the manuscript we inspected this morning? I have just come from the stationer who sells it, and he assured me that he delivered a ream of just such paper. And do you know to what place it was delivered?'

The detective paused for so long that Timothy felt obliged to answer. 'No, sir.'

'It was brought to the very house you have been watching all afternoon.'

'How could that be? This is a deserted house. A new house.'

'Nothing is ever deserted. Nothing is ever new. You, of all people, should understand that now.' Austin Smallwood seemed to regret his last remark, and started to walk more quickly than before. 'And here is something else,' he said. 'While pursuing my investigations, in the costume of a specialized character about which I am not at liberty to speak, I was informed that seances are being held in precisely the same dwelling.'

'Seances! No, sir, not seances. My father –'

They had returned to that part of the square where the boy had been waiting, and Austin Smallwood had already darted towards the house itself; in the gathering dusk he began to scrutinize the clay in front of it, and he beckoned to Timothy. 'Several people have passed this way in the last hour. And you tell me you saw nothing?'

'Perhaps,' he replied, not knowing quite what he meant. 'Perhaps I was seeing it as it used to be. I mean, as it will be.'

'Only work in one tense at a time, my young friend. You will find it simpler.' He put a finger to his lips. 'Say nothing, if you please. Now we must be inconspicuous.' He crept towards the door, Timothy following him, but it was firmly closed. The detective took from the pocket of his frock-coat a small piece of wire which he inserted into the mechanism of the lock and, within a few moments, he had sprung it; quietly and cautiously he entered the dark hallway. The boy was only a few steps behind and, as soon as he came close to the front door of his old familiar lodgings, he could hear a voice coming from his father's room. He thought that he recognized it, but how changed it was: 'I brought to his mind,' the voice was saying, 'an accident which had occurred to him some years previously, and which I was impressed to tell him was the cause of his suffering. I am so sensitive to anyone who comes near to me in a diseased state that I not only myself feel but accurately describe their symptoms. For I hope you remember that I have a mission entrusted to me. It is a great and holy one. I cannot speak to you about a thing which you have not yet seen, and therefore cannot understand. I can only say that it is a great truth. Now let us prepare for our contact with the spirit world.' There was a shuffling of feet from behind the closed door of his father's room and a sudden low murmur of voices; Timothy and Austin Smallwood took that opportunity quietly to open the door. 'At first a heaviness of my feet comes on,' the voice continued, 'and then I feel as if I am fainting away on the brink of a precipice. But do not be alarmed on my account. There is a moment of suffering, but then all is agreeable. In this state I speak, and sometimes write.'

Austin Smallwood tapped the boy on the shoulder and whispered in his ear. 'The manuscript. He writes the manuscript.'

There was silence, but then, after a few moments, a low moaning began; it grew louder and, as it gained in intensity, the boy softly crept within. His eyes quickly grew accustomed to the darkness, and he could see that there were several people sitting around a circular table. There was a figure just beyond the table who seemed to be in an unnatural posture – his head was thrown back, his arms outstretched in front of him. Then he brought his head forward, while his eyes remained closed and the muscles of his jaw rigid. It was at this moment, as the sound of rapid and shallow breathing filled the room, that Timothy realized that he was indeed in the presence of his father. But he was much altered: he seemed younger in one sense, and yet imprinted upon his features was the shadow of another face. There was an older man somehow around him – Timothy could not explain it to himself any other way – a man with a small moustache, thin mouth, greying hair and startled eyes.

Austin Smallwood took the boy's arm and gently led him out of the room. 'You knew him, I suspect?'

'It was my father.' Timothy felt quite sick with amazement and apprehension. 'And yet he was different. He was stranger. He was somehow changed.'

'He sees us changed, too. At this precise moment he is seeing us as if we were in a vision.' The detective was very grim. 'He has been imagining my adventures. It is he who has been writing them down. Don't you understand now? He is the author of my being. And of yours also.' Timothy was too alarmed to speak, and slowly bent his head forward. 'We have found your father at last. And, my young friend, he is bringing us to life even now. He is dreaming of us both.'

SEVEN

WHEN I OPENED MY EYES I saw Stanley Clay and Margaret Collins standing on either side of me. I must have lost consciousness, because they were looking down at me with obvious concern. 'Aren't you going to say, "Where am I"?' Stanley asked me.

'Where am I?' I replied politely.

'Home,' he ventured to say. But, in the circumstances, it was a forlorn word. My own small bedroom, where I found myself now, was stripped of its furniture and of any associations with my past; no doubt it was as bare as it had been when the house was first built.

'You was . . .' he could not think of the word.

'Resting. Having a little rest.' Margaret spoke for him.

'You was resting for a few minutes. It was a long journey, Tim, wasn't it?'

'Where is he?' I was almost pleading with them. 'Where has he gone?'

They looked at one another. 'He must have a good reason,' Margaret said eventually. 'He always has his reasons.'

We might have been talking through yellow fog, so flat our voices seemed in this confined space. Stanley helped me to my feet and, even though I knew what I would find there, I went back into my father's room. All the life he and I shared had been taken away; it was as if someone had gathered it up, packed it into a box, sealed it, and then thrown it into an abyss. But could the atmosphere of a life, the meaning of a past, be removed as easily as the furniture and rugs? Even then I sensed that this was not so, that a harder and somehow more impersonal residue was left behind. The mornings of study, the evenings by the fire, the conversations, the silent companionship – all of these things had gone, but the room itself had been changed by them for ever.

'You'll be coming to stay at my house,' Margaret was
saying, as if the matter had been decided weeks before, 'you'll
be nice and safe with me.' She still made it sound as if we
were being threatened or attacked by 'them', like children in
a dark wood, but for once her fear did not communicate itself
to me. I had more serious matters to consider. 'Where *is* he?'
I asked again. But of course they had no answer.

The sun was setting behind the houses when Margaret
Collins led me away from Hackney Square; as we walked
past the iron railings, she reached up to take my arm. 'I'm
looking forward to your sunflowers,' she said, anxious to find
anything to divert my anxiety. 'They'll be growing very tall,
Timothy. They'll be able to see further than I can.' She lived
only a few streets away, in Blackall Cut, and her roof was
bathed in the tangerine light of a spring evening when we
arrived outside a gate which had a sign, THE ISLAND, affixed
to it. I had never visited her before, and it was with a certain
reluctance that I followed her: for some reason I held in
horror the houses of other people, as if I were in danger of
being buried alive within them, and there were times when
different rooms or furnishings, even the air itself, acted upon
me like a drug in which I lost all consciousness of myself. Was
I about to be swallowed up again? Upon her front door was
the same motto, THE ISLAND, and she laughed out loud when
she saw me glance towards it. 'That's what I call it,' she said.
'Like Robinson Crusoe, I keep my own company.'

She led me into a sitting-room which was a miracle of
intricacy and neatness: all the chairs were of the usual size
but fitted between so many wooden chests and cushions that
it was easy for Margaret to move from one to another and to
arrange herself comfortably. The kitchen was of a normal
size, too, but she had adapted an ingenious series of boxes
and planks which allowed her to walk about with as much
agility as if she were of average height. It entranced me and,
tired and dispirited though I was by the events of that day, I
could not help but smile. She noticed this and clapped her

hands in shared enjoyment. 'Do you see,' she said, 'how I've fooled them? They think I'm too small to manage, but I'm as safe and as snug here as anybody could be!' It was indeed her own little world, and I was to learn later that her great delight lay in reading *Robinson Crusoe* over and over again. She even read it to me in days to come, but she always stopped at that point where the castaway sees the savages upon the shore and realizes for the first time that he is not alone.

'You can have a cup of tea,' she was saying, as I stood and looked around at The Island. 'Then you can have a sleep. We can't make any plans while you're so light-headed.' And indeed I must have seemed so – the flight from my grand-parents' house, the long walk through the night, the coach ride and the disappearance of my father had left me quite dazed. But it was only now that suddenly, and unexpectedly even to myself, I burst into tears; I heard a dog barking as I cried and cried, cried about nothing, cried about everything. Margaret looked at me, her head cocked to one side, but she made no attempt to touch me or to console me; even as I wept, I knew that she had cried many times like this in the same room. I stopped eventually. The dog was still barking in the distance, and now the sound was a comfort to me. 'There now,' she said. 'Let's go on as if nothing like that had happened, shall we?' I nodded, embarrassed. 'I'll pretend that I was out of the room, making your tea; and then I'll come back with it.' She performed her part admirably. She brought me tea, complete with some ham sandwiches cut up into the smallest possible portions, but I was so tired that I could eat nothing. So she led me upstairs to a bedroom that looked out over the other terraced houses of Blackall Cut; although I was still fully dressed, I lay upon the bed and fell at once into a profound sleep.

I did not wake up until late the following morning. I opened my eyes to such unfamiliar surroundings that I experi-enced a sudden panic: it was as if I had been sleeping in some hybrid world, made up partly of my mother's room and partly of my own small bedroom in Hackney Square. I even thought I could feel the old dog, Friday, lying at my feet again; but there was nothing. I was alone. Suddenly I heard voices coming from a room below my own, and at that moment I remembered all that had occurred. Stanley Clay was talking to Margaret, and I thought I could also distinguish the low voice of Matthew Lucas. I heard my own name mentioned, at which point I could no longer bear to remain in this strange bed. I went downstairs and, as I approached the kitchen where they were sitting, I also heard them discussing my father. They stopped talking as soon as I appeared in the doorway. 'I'm sorry I slept so late,' I said. Stanley was looking down at the floor, and even Margaret seemed confused by my unexpected entry. 'What were you saying about my dad?'

'I was saying,' Matthew Lucas replied, looking straight into my face, 'I was saying that we haven't heard from him.'

'We don't know where he is, Tim,' Stanley added.

'But I expect he went on a holiday.' Margaret led me over to a wicker-chair and patted the cushions around me. 'He didn't know you were coming back, did he?' This was true enough, but it hardly accounted for the fact that he had removed all the furniture from our lodgings. When I mentioned this point, Margaret was not at all discomfited. 'But don't you see? It was probably all going to be a surprise. He must be moving to a new house. That was why he wanted you to stay with your grandparents.' It was an explanation at least, and one that, in my desire for reassurance, I was willing to accept for the moment although I knew well enough that it was a false one; even in childhood, it is possible to entertain two opposite states of consciousness at the same time.

'We're very pleased to have you back,' Stanley said. 'We missed you.'

So the four of us sat together through the morning, and gradually my companions described to me in more detail how my father had behaved after my departure – how ill at ease he had become, and how he had abruptly broken off the last meeting he held in the old hall. He had escorted Gloria Patterson to her parents' house afterwards, and had then been seen by Stanley wandering down Brick Lane in the general direction of the river. I knew him in those vagrant moods; many times I had accompanied him on just such expeditions, when he became as much a child as I was.

The door-bell rang and I jumped out of my chair – surely my father had heard of my return and was coming to find me? Margaret, perhaps also expecting to see him at last, allowed me to run to the door; when I opened it, Jasper Burden was standing there. He had his back to me and was whistling a popular song of the day, 'Passing the Time Away' I think it was called; when he turned around and saw my stricken, disappointed face he stopped in astonishment. 'Now there's a funny thing,' he said. 'I was just thinking about you.' He crossed the threshold. 'Don't worry,' he added. 'It may never happen.'

'What may never happen?'

He did not reply but, instead, executed an impromptu tap-dance in the passage. 'I just can't help it,' he said, laughing. 'I'm built that way.' I ducked as he tried to ruffle my hair, and then he joined the others in the kitchen. 'Where's Gloria?' he asked. 'Where's my girl?'

'She's not your girl,' Stanley muttered.

'Just a figure of speech, my friend. And, oh, what a lovely figure it is.'

In fact nobody seemed to know what had happened to her, but the absence of the last member of the Harcombe Circle did not greatly affect them and soon they were talking eagerly again. 'Why wasn't it the same, Timothy?' Matthew Lucas asked me after a few minutes. 'Why did everything change after you had gone?' It was the eager and insistent questioning I had known before, but now it was directed towards me rather than my father. I had no answer for him.

'It all started coming back,' Stanley added. 'You know. Feeling anxious, Tim. Just as if the whole world was closing in on you. It doesn't strike you all at once. It strikes when you don't expect it. It comes into the room and takes over . . .'

'That's what happens when an old thought pops into your mind,' Margaret muttered, almost to herself. 'Anxiousness comes back with it. All of your previous feelings just waiting.'

'But with you and Mr Harcombe,' Stanley was saying, 'all of that seemed to vanish. I used to think about it all the time. Where has all the fear gone? Then you was away and, just like Matthew said, it all changed.'

I still did not know how to reply. They were treating me as if I were an adult, as if my absence had given them some new sense of my identity. And I realized, also, that they could quickly become as dependent upon me as they had been upon my father. 'Dad told me that those feelings never go away,' I said. 'That they come from your parents and grand-parents. You know, before you are born.' I could not recall any occasion when he had discussed such matters with me but, nevertheless, these were his words I was using.

'That's right,' Matthew Lucas replied. 'You never really stop worrying. Creating pictures in your mind of all the things that can go wrong. Looking ahead. At least,' he added, rub-bing his hands and staring directly into my face, 'that's how it is with me, Timothy, isn't it?'

'Isn't it funny,' Jasper Burden broke in as if Matthew had not spoken at all, 'one minute you can be terrified to death, and then at the next you can be singing?'

'Are you always like that?' Margaret asked him, not with-out smiling.

'Like what?'

'Blowing hot and cold?'

'When I *am* hot and cold. And isn't everybody? Sometimes I take hold of myself and ask myself, Now listen, Jasper, what exactly is going on here? Why are you so frightened of life now, when you were excited about it last night? Why are you so nervous of a certain thing happening now, when a few moments ago you couldn't care less about it? What exactly *is* going on?' He paused for a moment before bursting out in laughter. 'And do you know the funny thing? There never is an answer. Most probably there never will be. Until my dying day.'

'Not even then,' Matthew added.

We carried on talking through the morning, and slowly I began to lose that feeling of isolation which had afflicted me since my father's disappearance; there were even moments when I thought he was in the room with us, just as before, and when the others left I was no longer afraid.

I stayed with Margaret for the next few weeks, and slowly grew accustomed to her habits: it was a great truth with her that the world did not welcome her, and did not want her, so she went to some trouble to keep it at a safe distance. I believe there are many people who, no doubt for good reason, feel the same way. She had no wireless and read no newspaper, so her awareness of life was essentially limited to this particular part of east London. And yet even here she remained somehow outside the ordinary course of events: she was a familiar figure in the streets, but she made her own way and never stopped to talk or gossip. 'They' were in charge of the world and, since 'they' had no time for her, she had no time for them; she walked, head erect, looking straight forward, secretly longing to return to her own little kingdom – a kingdom of which I had become a temporary citizen. Sometimes she returned home, closed the door behind her and for a few moments leaned against it, her face flushed with anger or unhappiness (it was difficult to say which). 'Mr Timothy,' she often said at this point, 'I think we ought to take a stroll around the grounds' – by which she meant her garden, no more than six feet square, and around which we would solemnly tread in single file until she was quite calm again.

On most days she allowed me to accompany her on her

daily expedition to the shops of the neighbourhood, and on these occasions she would dress very carefully – 'so as not to show you up,' she used to say. We would walk together down the street and in a clear, strong voice she would maintain a stream of light-hearted conversation while paying no attention to anyone who stared or even glanced at her. I noticed that she took care to avoid Hackney Square, also, as if the sight of my old home might still prove too much for me. There was no question of my leaving the house without her, since I had now become part of her secret conspiracy against the world. About a week after my arrival, however, I told her that I wanted to see if anyone had taken over our lodgings. 'They'll be nothing to do with you,' she said. 'You should leave well enough alone.'

'Just curiosity, Margaret. Dad said I should always keep my curiosity.'

That was reason enough for her, I suppose, and so that morning we turned our steps towards the square. As we made our way, I began to entertain the hope that my father had unexpectedly returned and that I would find him waiting for me by the gate. So great was my anticipation, in fact, that I kept up a fast pace – only to stop suddenly short when we came into the square and saw a policeman in front of the house. He was walking down the path, shaking his head at another policeman who was standing in the road outside. Margaret was terrified and dragged me at once into the shadow of a hedge. 'Don't let them see us!' she whispered fiercely. 'Let's run!'

I was not so eager to leave; the policemen might, after all, have news of my father. But she had so tight a grip on my arm, and possessed such strength, that she was able to drag me away. As soon as we arrived back at The Island she locked the front door, and hurried into the sitting-room with the key still in her hand. 'What are we going to do?' she asked no one in particular. 'What *are* we going to do?' She was standing upright in a corner of the room, but now she dashed over to the door. 'Stay here,' she commanded. 'They won't come here.'

I believed that I knew why the police had come: they had come to take me away. I had committed some crime in leaving my grandparents so abruptly, and now I was about to be arrested. Margaret kept no mirrors in the house but I suddenly felt the need to see my reflection, so I went over to the window and looked at the shadowy image of myself on the glass. 'I didn't realize I was doing anything wrong,' I said. 'I thought my grandparents would understand why I went away. I should have left them a note, but there wasn't any time. I didn't know I was doing anything wrong.' I repeated these phrases over and over again, never managing to get beyond them but always going back to the beginning.

Margaret came hurrying back into the house after a few minutes and, even before she had entered the room, she was calling out to me. 'They were looking for you! But they've gone now!' This was some relief, at least, but to my surprise she went over to the window and started stealthily to pull the curtains. 'I was talking to your neighbours upstairs,' she said, and I knew at once what an effort this must have been for her. 'Your grandparents called in the police. That was why they came to the house this morning. And now they've gone to look for your father. They think you're staying with him.' All of this alarmed me even more, but Margaret reached up and took my hand. 'Don't worry,' she said. 'I'll find him before they do, and explain everything. At the moment you're what is called a missing person.' A missing person. So that was what I had become. That night I turned off the light and opened the window; I leaned out into the dark air and, the more I allowed the night to envelop me, the less I seemed to exist. A missing person.

My father arrived the following morning. He was standing in the hallway when, aroused by his voice, I left my room. He was wearing his familiar dark three-piece suit, with neatly polished shoes. 'Welcome back,' he said as soon as he saw me on the stairs. He was being determinedly cheerful, and I did not know how to reply. Then I ran down the remaining steps and embraced him. 'I didn't expect you so soon,' he said. 'Life is full of surprises, isn't it? Didn't I tell you that once?'

'I suppose so.'

'I had no idea you had left your grandparents, Tim. Not until Margaret told me. And then the police came.' He said this quite without reproach. 'Why did you run away, Timothy?'

'Do you have to ask, dad?'

He slowly disengaged himself from my embrace, but he did not entirely let me go; instead he put his hand on the top of my head, just as he used to do during the meetings. 'Didn't you get on with them?'

'I wanted to be with you, dad.'

'You are with me.' He was speaking with the same cheerfulness as before. 'You are always with me.'

'No. I mean our home.'

'Everywhere is our home, Timothy. You know that.'

'No. Our own home. In Hackney Square.'

He looked at me in so absent-minded a fashion it was almost as if he had forgotten that we ever lived in such a place. 'There may be a slight difficulty there, I'm afraid. I had to leave, you see. I had no money . . .' He seemed to hesitate slightly. 'So Gloria has kindly agreed to let me stay with her.' He looked over my shoulder and instinctively I turned, to see Gloria Patterson standing in the front room with Margaret beside her. She seemed different, and after a moment I realized that she was no longer wearing the middle-aged clothes she had adopted before. She was wearing a short skirt with a cream-coloured blouse, and looked utterly unlike the young woman who had attended the meetings.

'She left her parents.' Margaret spoke of her so flatly and impersonally that she might not have been in the room at all. 'That's how I found your father. They told me.'

'That's right,' Gloria said in a low voice. 'I moved out,

didn't I? I got my own room.' I noticed at once that there was something like an expression of triumph upon her face: she had never given me so direct a look before, and we both stared at each other until I could bear it no longer. I turned back to my father. 'But why didn't you tell the others? We were looking for you.'

'The others?' He seemed genuinely not to understand what I meant.

'Margaret. Stanley.'

'I would have done.' He glanced at Margaret as he said this, and she folded her arms. 'Of course I would have done. I just wanted to get settled first, Tim. In any case Margaret found me, didn't she? She never gives up.' I believe I noticed a trace of bitterness in his voice, but it vanished immediately.

'And what about me, dad?'

'I want you to live with us, Tim – with me. Naturally I do.' I turned away from him and climbed the stairs; he followed me, as I had expected, but when he reached my room he stood on the threshold. 'Gloria wants to live with us, too, you see . . .'

'Where?' I had already conceived a horror for our lodgings in Hackney Square, now that they were abandoned, and I had no wish to move in to Gloria's 'room'.

'Listen, Timothy. Please listen to me. I want you to stay with Margaret for a few more weeks. Just a few more. Until I find something.'

'But what about our meetings? What about the old hall?'

'It's time we started a new life,' he said, ignoring my questions. 'Isn't it exciting, Tim, to begin all over again?' I did not know what he meant, and so I said nothing. He must have taken my silence for assent, because he began talking animatedly about moving to a new area, living in a new house, and so forth. I found all of it hard to comprehend – my father and Gloria, the sudden end of our meetings, his cheerful talk about the future. Where was I in all of this? I still seemed to be the missing person. 'We had better go back to the others now,' he added. 'It's rude.' I sensed that he was only concerned with Gloria's feelings, however, and, as we came downstairs together, he looked at her nervously for a moment. She was still standing with Margaret in the front room, and then my father smiled at them as if he had successfully completed some arduous assignment. 'Do you see, Tim,' he said, 'how everyone cares about you and looks after you? Margaret, Gloria, all of them?'

Margaret came up to me; she was pressing the palms of her hands very tightly together, a gesture which indicated that she was suffering from more than usual stress or annoyance. 'He has a lot of friends,' she said. 'He's safe here.'

'You're a very fortunate person, Timothy.' He glanced past me at Gloria. 'I have to go now,' he said. 'But I'll be back this evening.'

It had already been agreed, it seemed, that I should remain with Margaret until my father had 'found' something. In fact, I enjoyed staying with her over the months – not weeks – that followed. She was such a brisk and cheerful person that I grew much more cheerful, too; and I had the strangest sensation of becoming smaller in her company. My father visited me most evenings, without Gloria, and the three of us talked for an hour or more; sometimes the others joined us, and at first it was as if nothing had changed. It was remarkable to me how easily my father could resume his old manner, despite everything, and I assumed that he was merely being kind to Stanley Clay and Matthew Lucas; they needed him, after all, and I had no doubt that he understood this. It did not occur to me, at the time, that his buoyancy and confidence had anything to do with my presence.

It was our first evening together, I think, when Matthew asked him why he had discontinued the meetings in the old hall. He got up from his chair and stood by Margaret's fireplace. 'Have you ever heard of the ghost-eater?' He did not wait for their answer. 'The ghost-eater is a member of the tribe who communicates with those who have just died and takes away their anger by eating their sins. Bread and meat are put upon the body, and he has to eat everything. Sometimes he is successful and calms the spirit, and sometimes he fails. Sometimes he even dies and then, the people say, he has eaten too many ghosts. Well, I am tired. I have eaten too many ghosts.' He smiled at me, and then resumed his seat. They never raised the question again.

He did not seem tired, however. His enthusiasm had returned undiminished, although I noticed that he now often talked about me and my future rather than his own; he rarely, if ever, mentioned the old life of Hackney Square, but instead concentrated upon the grand and indefinite plans he had for me. In the past the Harcombe Circle had always shared my father's enthusiasms but, down these avenues of my future happiness and success, they found it difficult to follow him. It was almost as if he were deliberately trying to set a distance between me and my companions. Yet there were still occasions when we all recaptured the intimacy of the past and, for me, those were the happiest times. Or, rather, now they are my happiest memories – of Matthew with his large head bowed in thought, of Stanley gazing at me or at my father with his strange, sad earnestness, of Jasper with his restless movements and intermittent laughter, and of Margaret sitting upon her high cushions with the same bright, alert expression. Of course those evenings could not last, and I am sure that many aspects of them have faded even from my memory. Everything is changed. Everything fades away. My happiness at those times now seems so distant, and such a strange thing, that I can hardly endure the looking back.

Then it happened. The fact that my grandparents had called the police, and that I had for a while been listed as a missing person, had consequences which none of us had foreseen. Through that spring and summer, while I remained with Margaret, other people were discussing my future. I had become a case, an object of interest to the Board of Guardians for Hackney and, more particularly, to the LCC education department. It was discovered during the preliminary police inquiries, for example, that I had never been enrolled in any elementary school; my father had at some point tried to explain that he was educating me at home, but this may not have helped him with the council. For at this time they discovered exactly what his work was – somehow or other these same people found out that I had acted as his assistant during the meetings in the old hall, a fact which no doubt also met with their disapproval. So there was some discussion of my being placed in a 'home', away from the influence of an 'unfit father'. Of course I knew nothing about this at the time, and my father certainly gave no indication that he was being investigated; but I feel sure that there must have been moments when he became worried, on my behalf as well as his own. Yet it was his way to remain generally cheerful and optimistic even when he had every reason to be anxious, and all I remember of this period are his good spirits. And, as is usually the case with self-assured people, his confidence was not misplaced; within a few weeks he had found a solution to the problem. At his instigation my grandparents intervened: he told them that, if they became my legal guardians and ensured that I was placed in a school close to them, the council would be reluctantly willing to let the matter rest. In the circumstances my grandparents could only comply. So it was that my father arranged for me to be handed over, as it were, to the parents of his dead wife. I do not know even now if Gloria Patterson played some part in his decision: I think not, if only for the reason that he always kept his most private feelings and judgements to himself. But the decision was taken.

I learned of it, as usual, in an oblique and unexpected fashion. My father had come around to see me one early afternoon and offered to take me on an 'expedition', just like the ones we had enjoyed in the past. I was always happy to be in his company, and so we made our way down the dusty streets in search of some area unknown to us. We had got as far as Gosset Street, leading to Old Bethnal Green, when he said, quite casually, 'Your grandfather is coming to see you.'

I could have fallen on the spot. 'Why?' was all I could think of saying.

'They miss you, Tim.'

'Do they?'

'Of course they do. You know how much they like you. And they want to see you again. Let's stop here for a moment and buy some sweets. Gloria loves her sweets.' He went inside a corner shop and a few moments later came out with a white paper bag of striped barley sugar. He offered me a piece, which I declined, and then popped one into his own mouth. 'Isn't it funny,' he said, sucking on it, 'that I never noticed this shop before? I wonder how many other things we pass and don't notice at all.'

'I don't want to go, dad.' He had no need to tell me that I was about to be taken back to my grandparents' house. I knew it as surely as if he had uttered the words.

He said nothing for a moment. 'There is no going back, Tim.'

'You mean I don't have to go back with him?'

'No. There is no going back to the way things were. Are you sure you won't have a piece? It's delicious.'

'No, dad.'

'You see, Timothy, you need a proper life. Not stuck here in this' – he waved his arm in the general direction of the small shops and houses – 'this wasteland. One day you'll grow up to be a rich and famous man. I know that. But only if you get away from here. Only if you begin again.'

'But what about Margaret? What about the others?' I was really trying to ask, What about us?, but I could not talk directly about such things.

'The world is filled with grief, Tim.' He quickened his step, embarrassed by his own tone, and then he took me by the shoulder as if he were trying to march me at his own pace. 'But there's no need for you to feel any grief. We'll never be parted, you and I.'

'Will you come and live with us?'

'I will be visiting. Yes. I will.' And then he added, quickly, 'Your grandfather is coming on Sunday, by the way.' That was in two days' time: two days left of my life in the old, familiar places. I could never understand in later years why he did not explain to me the reason I was being returned to my grandparents. Perhaps he did not want me to know that he had been branded as an 'unfit father', incapable of taking care of his only son. Perhaps he had some guilty sense that there were other reasons for his decision to send me away. There was indeed one paramount cause, which I would discover only a few days before his death. 'Everything has to come to an end, Timothy,' he was saying as we walked back from Old Bethnal Green. 'But that's only because other things have to begin. You walk from one room into another, you see.' He offered me a piece of barley sugar again, and I took it.

The last day came before I had really prepared myself for it. The Harcombe Circle arrived at Margaret's house early that morning in late August and stood around in the kitchen while she busied herself with my packing; there was really not much to do, and I believe she arranged and rearranged my little suitcase several times simply in order to take her mind from the ordeal of parting. That it was an ordeal, for all of us, there was no doubt; there was some sense of an ending and, when my father came down the path with my grandfather, the Circle grew silent and uneasy. Even Jasper stopped singing, and Margaret dashed off to the bathroom, where she could be heard blowing her nose very loudly several times.

My grandfather was as direct and as brisk as ever. 'You may not think it, Timothy,' he told me as soon as he came into the house, 'but I'm very glad to see you. Very glad.' I said nothing, caught between my despair at leaving and my affection for him, but he did not seem to mind. 'Not so much the prodigal son as the prodigal grandson. But it will all end happily, you'll see.' Then he shook hands with everyone in turn; Margaret had by now emerged from the bathroom and, when he came up to her, he bent down and kissed her on the cheek. 'So you're the young lady who looked after my grandson,' he said.

'I'm not young.' She was blushing. 'I never have been young.'

'Well, you seem young to me.'

'I seem small to you. That's all there is to it.'

'Yes. You are small,' declared my grandfather, his bright eyes beaming down on her. 'But I like small people. They know a lot more about the world than most.'

'That may be true,' she replied. 'There's a lot to know and a lot to find out.'

'I hope you'll come to know us. I hope you'll come and visit. All of you,' he added, looking around at the others. 'You will always be welcome.'

'That's right,' my father said, as if he were inviting them into his own home, 'in a way we're all part of the same family.'

But I knew as I looked at their faces that they would never be able to make the journey to this stranger's house. I believed then that I was seeing them for the last time, and I could not bear it. 'I have to find something,' I said, 'I'll be back in a minute.' Before anyone could reply I rushed out of the house and into the street. I did not know where I was going but at that moment I felt so isolated, so bereft of my past, that it was truly as if I were alone upon an island. Instinctively I ran towards Hackney Square; I could see the sunflowers in full bloom as I turned the corner, and I slowed my pace so that I could approach them more softly. I wanted to see them when I was at peace. They were waving slightly in the breeze, expansive, reassuring, their deep yellow taking the pain from me. They were flourishing here, among the dirt and the dust, and I stood amazed in front of them. I looked at them until I could see nothing else and, as I did so, I felt myself being drawn towards their vibrant centres. If only I could lie within them, the bright petals folded around me . . . So I gazed and gazed.

EIGHT

A ND SO HE STARED. AND so he sighed. And so he spent
his sorrow. The sound of his breathing, and of his beating
heart, surrounded him as he considered how he might preserve
himself in so desolate a landscape. The sky was perfectly
clear, and without the canopy of any trees the sun beat so hot
upon his face that, listless and desponding though he was, he
knew that he must find the shelter of some rock or other
opaque body. Yet, even though he might find refuge from the
burning earth, how was he to bring himself alive out of such a
place? He did not wish to open the catalogue of his sorrows,
or to number the perils and misadventures that had led him
to be cast away upon this island, yet he could not help but
reflect how miserable his end might be. Reader, about to
enter into a melancholy relation such perhaps as was never
heard of in the world before, you must take it from its beginning and continue it in order. Pray do not leap forward or
omit the moral passages, for this is an island story in which
exordium and narration are judiciously mingled; it is a map,
so to speak, upon which may be found the signs of hidden
treasure.

The boy, Timothy, should first of necessity have taken his
bearings; but he was too full of foreboding to collect his
thoughts. Instead with a rambling mind, and errant incli-
nation, he began merely to wander over the island and lose
himself in a countryside all barren and rocky. The first daze
of surprise and wonder had now passed, but still he roamed
back and forth, making no progress, no, nor hope of any.
Such is our life when we go on from day to day, without
taking any heed. But then he bethought himself a little; he
espied a hill not so far distant and he bent his steps that way,
hoping by such means to survey a larger portion of the island.

By slow degrees he climbed to the summit of this hill, and was thereupon greeted by as strange a prospect as he had ever seen. To take it in order: firstly, he saw some dun-coloured woods or forests with an abundance of good-sized trees and broken up by patches of sand; there were many good fowls, also, circulating in the air above the verdure. Secondly, rising up from the higher land some little distance from the woods, Timothy could see wild pillars of naked rock so strangely shaped that they might have been cathedral spires carved out of the very stone; some live oaks grew here singly or in clumps and, mixed with these, some tattered pines near fifty or seventy feet in height. Thirdly, upon his right hand, he observed a landslip of broken rocks very much like a ravine, in addition to patches of grass, marsh and sand which led by gradual descent to the shore.

And yet what shore was this? Like nothing he had read in his adventures, for, as he peered about, he observed that this island was in the shape of a man's hand with each finger stretching out upon the sea. The waters themselves were of the darkest blue, resembling good writing ink, as if the hand itself were only in need of a quill to compose its own history. The tide was far out, but he could hear the noise of distant breakers mounting from all around, and even from so great a distance the sound was much like music. Yet there was not a man or a sail upon that sea, and he came out with these words: 'Truly I am now alone, entirely destitute of comfort and company!' A breeze started up and shook the trees with its motion so that, from his summit, it seemed to the boy that they were nodding and murmuring to each other very like people in an assembly. He thought he saw a vast multitude of human creatures running across a plain, leaping and turning in the air as they made their way, but it was merely the pattern of the wind in the tall grasses. And, with that picture, he was set to fall into more sorrowful, isolated and forlorn a condition than before. Everything in this place had its own rare life and movement, of which he could not puzzle out the secret; this little world, this world in miniature, existed apart from him and took no heed of him. He saw in this the model of his future existence – and yet not only of his own life but that of everyone. 'The world is a sea,' he observed, 'the world is a sea in which we all must surely drown!'

He came down from the hill in sadness and disarray, therefore, and without any thought took a path which led him away from the blank and open shore towards the interior of the island. It was a curious and wayward track but one that, within the space of a few minutes, brought him to an isolated rock rising from among low bushes; it was pretty high, and white in colour, and as the boy approached nearer to it he saw a cave of narrow entrance hollowed out from its side. It was visible enough above the brush and Timothy walked towards it with some trepidation, not knowing what wild beast (or worse) might inhabit such a place. But then, much to his delight and astonishment, he found that it was a little shelter, or dwelling, with his own few possessions neatly placed within it. So do we discover, in the world, that our worst fears are unfulfilled; yet we must fear, in order that we may feel delight. With spirits more lively and cheerful the boy entered the cave and saw there how closely everything had been fitted so that it was a very haven for those suffering the shipwreck of all their hopes. The sides and floor were plastered with clay, and the entire expanse of the ground was covered with rushes; unsquared trunks of pine had been ingeniously placed to hold up the roof of this place, and so neat was the contrivance that nails had been knocked into these posts or pillars so that anything might be hung upon them. Within there were some square chests and boxes, some pieces of board set up like a dresser, and even shelves upon which Timothy could see the array of his own books. In one corner there was a slab of stone laid down in the manner of a hearth, and upon it an old rusty iron basket to contain any fire. It was a warehouse and a kitchen, a lodging and a dining-room, all in one. Yet to see his own books and his own clothing was still a matter for

astonishment with him. Had he lived here all his days without
any company? No, that could not be. He had seen sunflowers,
but had they flourished on the island or in some other place?
Where was he, and from whence had he come? He took up
his books from the wooden shelves and began to place them
neatly in order on the ground; he found his pen and ink,
together with some few sheets of paper, and these he put
against the far wall of his cavern. Then he gathered up his
few clothes and laid them carefully within a chest. For in this
place (he thought) I must take all my provisions and barricade myself within. I must take stock of myself, and order
every thing safely around me. So should we all take hold
upon our certainties in the midst of great distress, though we
do but rarely find a cave or shelter within our own selves.

He took up one of his books and thereupon began to read.
He had come upon these words, 'Just as during the plague
the richer sort did shut themselves up and let no one come
near, taking all their provisions within . . .', when he was
surprised by a sudden thought. For he remembered, in another story he had read, how a castaway like to himself began
to keep a journal of his labours and his sufferings. Surely he
might embark upon a similar voyage (so to speak) and thus
keep track of his own life upon the island? The boy began to
consider his condition, therefore, and the circumstances he
was reduced to, and prepared himself to draw up the state of
these affairs in writing. Just as he had put his own goods and
possessions in neat array within this habitation, he determined to set his own solitary life in order. He took all his
understanding from the books piled beside him, and in like
manner he might draw some comfort from his own words: as
the castaway makes his clothing from fur or his umbrella
from rabbit-skin, in another sense did Timothy begin to stitch
together a covering for himself. So may we use our books to
form a barricade against the world, interweaving their words
with our own to ward off the heat of the day.

In this fashion, then, he began to cast up in remembrance

the scenes of his past. There had been a loss, for how else could he have arrived in so forlorn a state? Yet he could in no wise recover it or bring it into his mind. When he spoke the word, 'father', his hands clinched together, his fingers pressing against his palms, and an innumerable crowd of thoughts whirled through that great thoroughfare of the brain, the memory. He commenced his writing with this cry: *Whence are we? Sure we are all made by some secret power, and what is that?* Then he went on: *Poor boy. Where are you? Where have you been? How come you here, without a father or a mother?* All the woes of his childhood, and of his present solitary condition, now found vent; and by degrees he did deliver himself from his afflicting thoughts. But the first fit of composition having passed, he grew extremely tired, and with that and the heat of the weather Timothy found himself much inclined to sleep. He lay down upon the rushes which covered the floor of his private lodging, which were very soft, and slept sounder than ever he remembered to have done in his life and, as he reckoned, about twelve hours; for when he awaked, it was just daylight.

He attempted to rise but he was not able to stir; at first he was filled with alarm, for it was as if some tiny human creatures had fastened him down with slender ligatures. But pretty soon he came to his senses, and observed that the books he had been reading had lain upon him during the night. He placed them to one side and, stumbling and yawning, washed himself by means of the water from a little spring which rose up beside the entrance to this cave; there was an abundance of excellent good raisins stored within, and with these he also refreshed himself. The sun having just risen, the boy then bethought himself to take a walk beyond the confines of his own little kingdom. There was a tall tree some way distant, and that became his mark, yet it was no easy progress towards it. The ground soon became mired and heavy, and frequently he tripped upon the coarse vegetation which sprang up around him; but by little and little he found himself to be walking on rising ground so that it became more stony under foot, with the bushes appearing in more open order. Thickets of green nutmeg trees grew among the broad shadow of the pines and, as Timothy walked among them, clouds of blue and yellow birds rose from them before wheeling and crying over the island. He walked on a little, though the tall tree was now behind him, until he came upon more undulating and sandy country where a great number of contorted trees, not unlike the oak in growth but pale in foliage, grew low upon the ground. Now he could hear the continuous thundering of the surf close by him, and could feel the cool draught of the breeze from the sea; he came out beside the open borders of a grove and found himself once more upon the strand.

Thereupon he walked beside the surf and looked out at the dark blue sea, gazing upon it so deep and so long that it might be he were looking for something stirring within it. But there was only the continual motion of the water and, tiring of his own thoughts, he determined to retrace his steps and return to his habitation. By now the tide was farther out than before, and great tracts of sand had been uncovered; the boy had gone a little way, musing with his head bowed towards the ground, when he stopped short and stood like one struck by lightning or one who has seen a spirit. For there printed upon the sand in front of him was the mark of a man's naked foot. He turned his face up to the sky and then looked wildly around. He listened intently to every passing sound, but he could hear nothing nor see any thing. He decided to reach the higher ground beyond the shore, so that he could look farther across the island, but when he reached the first clumps of vegetation he thought he saw a shape moving between the slender trees. He was in such fear that he stood quite still, but jumped back when a little spout of gravel fell rattling and bounding at his feet. Then he heard a voice, murmuring 'Hekinah Degul', and he fell into a dead faint.

There was a stillness about him when he awoke from his swoon, and a quietness about his head like cool water. Indeed he sensed, much to his surprise, that certain broad leaves had been placed over his forehead and around his temples: he put up his hand to brush them away, when he felt another hand restraining him. 'Let them be,' he heard someone saying above him. 'Let them be.'

He opened his eyes to discover himself lying upon the rushes in his own cave and saw a man of middling height, and not so very old neither, standing beside him. He was dressed in patchwork, and in so various a guise that he seemed to belong to no time, no, nor to any place beyond this island. 'I thought you were my father,' the boy said, 'when I first heard your voice upon the shore.' He was stronger now and sat up to view him the better.

The man smiled. 'On this little isle, I am like to be your father. Have you seen any other?' He started to walk back and forth within the cave, casting bright glances at the boy; and it seemed to Timothy that this man of the island, in his solitariness, was now burning with words. He must have read the boy's very thoughts, for he turned around and delivered himself of the following: 'Do not think I am a solitary. No. Not so. For in my retired imagination I remember that I am not alone but surrounded by others who came before me.'

'To this place, sir?'

'Yes. To this very place. To this island, which is an emblem of our existence. Do you not see the books around you?' He pointed at the many volumes lying where Timothy had discovered them that morning.

'My old books,' he said apologetically.

'No books are ever old. It is said that the soul of one man can pass into another and so do words, after certain ages, find men and minds like that which first begat them. The world is now as it was in times past, just as this island itself can never change.' Timothy was so surprised and perplexed that he stared down at his own books rather than look in amazement at the stranger. But the man now took up one of them, and cast the thread of his words around it. 'No, no, books are not

old. But they must needs be revived by ornate scholarship
and invention. Just as you have now come to this island and
awakened its life, so you must apply your thoughts to old
things and to the consideration of times before you. Music is
to be fetched from the passed world.' Timothy observed how
tightly he gripped in his hand the book from which he had
been lately reading, *A Journal of the Plague Year* by Daniel Defoe. 'You may look around this island where now you find
yourself and, by discovering the features of its antiquity,
understand the bounds of your own new life. By the same
token, from the English books of all ages we will understand
our own. When the bones of King Arthur were digged up,
the race beheld some original of themselves; so can we erect
and proclaim our worth upon the pillars of our forefathers.'
He must have been long in contemplation of these thoughts,
for he spoke with such passion and eloquence that Timothy
was struck silent. Indeed he had been in such a hot torrent of
words that he walked a little more around the cave to calm
himself. Then he turned to the boy, smiling still. 'No doubt,'
he asked him, 'you thought you were dead, and gone you
knew not where, when you came upon this island?'

'I had given myself up for lost, sir, certainly.'

'Well, well, even to dream that you are dead is no fatal
phantasm. Besides we live by the dead, and everything is or
must be so before it becomes our nourishment. I must kill
those bright birds yonder, which are the very emblem of the
soul, in order to maintain my self. So am I a soul-eater.' He
paused a moment. 'Have you considered where you are?'

'It is an island.'

'Certainly it is an island. But is it one you know of?'

'I seem to recognize it, sir, yet somehow I knew of it before
this time. Or perhaps I have read of it.'

'Well, as I have said, there is nothing new under the sun.
This field has been so traced that it is hard to spring anything
original from it, and in the same fashion we must transcribe
our knowledge or lend our own names to other men's en-

deavours. No one comes into the world fully clothed, for we are what we learn. You have inherited all that you possess. Do you know what is truly yours? And why did you think I was your father?' The man spoke so freely and so rapidly that Timothy scarce found an interval to make his answer; and still he continued with his discourse, walking up and down all the while. 'You honour your father by imitating him, just as we honour an author by the same means. For what we virtuously imitate we approve and admire; since we delight not to resemble our inferiors, we aggrandize and magnify those whom we copy. Yet there is also a general commemoration which is manifest through time. That is why I tell you that, while you are here, you will dream of your own country. You will hear its music in this place. For what is time but the very passage of music from generation to generation? Yet it is not enough to hear it.' He took a few steps to the entrance of the cave, and stooped down to drink from the spring which issued there. 'You must not only hear. You must also understand. To palliate the shortness of our lives, and to compensate our brief term in this world, it is fit to have such an understanding of times past that we may be considered to have dwelled in the same. In such a manner, answering the present with the past, we may live from the beginning and in a certain sense be as old as our country itself. Now, you see, I am as old as the island.' He was still holding the book which he had taken up from the floor of the cave; he opened it, seemingly at random, and began to read what he found upon the page there. '"London might well be said to be all in tears. I would that I could make him who reads this hear, as I imagine I now hear it, for the sound seems still to ring in my ears."'

'That was no music, sir,' Timothy said. 'Not in the plague time.'

'Yet music issued from it, and that in no ordinary sense. The terrible visitation spawned any number of tracts and journals such as this, but sweeter and louder notes rose from the general lamentation.'

'How could that be?' The words of this man of the island interested Timothy exceedingly and he was, as it were, lifted up from his own mournful situation so that he might see the world at a great height. The stranger (yet not so strange now) sat down beside him and, closing the book, commenced this narrative of great suffering.

'Of Daniel Defoe and Henry Purcell, true children of the plague. In the parish of St Giles, Cripplegate, John Foe comforts his young son with a *Dan, Dan, come and sit by me*; but the boy could not be removed from the window where, looking down into the narrow alley running beside, he could see so many dismal objects flitting past. And some not moving, neither, but, in their extremity, merely leaning against the walls of the very house or lying in agony upon the ground. *Dan, Dan, come away from the casement.* The boy seemed to be hemmed in by the dead and the dying, himself unable to move, fearful that the very fabric of the world was filled with rottenness and corruption. Close by, in the parish of Westminster, sat the little child, Henry Purcell, not yet seven years old; his father being already dead, his mother was near death in her imagination with all the horror around her. She had taken up her child, himself in the last stages of fear, and put him in a locked room where lozenges were burning to purify the air. He could see nothing from this chamber, but all the sad sounds of Tothill Street South encircled him: viz. the cries of the dying, the ravings of those in delirium, and the lamentations of those whose wits had not yet fled. Such doleful music.

'When the funeral pyres were out,' the man of the island continued, 'and the last valedictions over, and when men took a lasting adieu of their rotting and infected friends, then did the true lives of Defoe and of Purcell begin. For their imagination had been forged amidst all this suffering, like to a coin which can be given its stamp only by the means of fire. How came it that Defoe created an island with no man upon it, except one? It was to continue in a deeper sense the dream of his childhood, when he was surrounded by the bodies of the dead and of the dying; so in his solitary travels around the kingdom, also, and in those solitary personages of his we call heroes or heroines but who are so many atoms in the void. He took the meaning of his childhood, and played upon it with such symmetry and nice proportion that it may justly be called the music of the spheres. For music is to be found as much in books as in instruments; though they give no sound to the ear, yet to the understanding they strike a note most full of harmony. Thus he made order out of misery, and in the fears of his infancy Defoe hit upon a shadowed and hieroglyphical lesson of the whole world.'

There was a sudden roll of thunder above the island, but the stranger paid no heed to it. 'It will pass,' he said. 'It was not meant for this place. There are other sounds to which we must attend, and what more pleasant or more doleful than those of Purcell? It is said that the first Englishmen made music to quiet or excite the affections of the gods, according to different harmonies. Yet what of the boy in the locked chamber, the smoke of the lozenges around him, who could hear the cries of the dying in Tothill Street? He found in music the peace he sought for, and at that time so sadly missed, for music reflects the harmony of the soul and soars above the corruption of the flesh. It was his music which obliterated the horror, effaced the memory of his childhood, dilated him out of himself, and by degrees (or so it seemed) resolved him into the harmonies of heaven. Thus we can speak of his music as truly inspired. There are some men who, upon the hour of their departure from this world, do speak and reason above themselves: so, in the melody of Purcell's sweet laments, we hear a discourse in a strain above mortality. He has not conquered time, as some wits say, but has become a true part of it.' These were strange words indeed, and Timothy grew so perplexed that the man of the island laughed out loud. 'There is a simple moral to my lesson,' he said, and with the second finger of his right hand pointed to the volumes which the boy had placed in order beside him: 'Never forget

these books, and out of them you may build your own barricade against sorrow. I know of your misery and your aban-
donment, for how else might you have reached this island?
But think not where you are or where you may go, since, with
these books, you are in England, every where and under any
meridian. Darkness may bury your eyes, but not your imagination. You have suffered a shipwreck, yet you have escaped,
and one day will make a happier voyage. Do you understand
how you came by this island?'

'I came by way of England.'

'And that is the way by which you must return. But do not
hope to make such a journey in some poor bark without a
mast or a sail. Feel something of your ancestors within your
own self, and trust not simply to your own compass. Fill your
sails with English music. Rest here now, and we will speak
again tomorrow.' The stranger left abruptly, and Timothy
looked after him amazed. Conceive his astonishment, then,
when the man of the island suddenly reappeared with a
wicker-basket of branches or twigs. 'I quite forgot,' he said,
'that you will need some fire as much for light as for warmth.
This place grows dark.' So he busied himself with these preparations until a good blaze seemed to protect the entrance to
the cave, and then once more took his leave.

Timothy lay back upon the rushes scattered over the ground,
his head aching with words. The interior of his little kingdom
was now filled with the fantastic shadows thrown by the fire and,
though his eyes were closed and he seemed to sleep, a multitude
of images passed over him. He thought he saw his father's face,
and then the face of his mother glimmered for a moment
through the shadows; these in turn were followed by the visages
of his grandparents, and then by others, which seemed to be
passing in procession before him. Some of them were so like his
own that he smiled in recognition, but he could in no wise count
up the number of them or calculate the centuries from which
they all had come. Thus he rested, and his own face was in
repose at last: Timothy Harcombe, the bearer of so many lives.

When he awoke, the stranger was leaning against the entry and tapping his face with a slender stick. 'You are lying in ashes,' he said, laughing. The boy sprang quickly to his feet and brushed from himself some flakes of burnt wood. 'The fire has quite gone now,' the man of the island added, 'though the spirit of it still lives. Come. Let us walk a little.' They set off together, the man keeping up a fast pace, and pretty soon they had passed the wooded areas close to the cave and come to a low sandy country sparsely dotted with dwarf pines. Soon they were beyond that again and turned towards some rocky hills which lay in profusion around this part of the island. The stranger led him towards a large hole or cave which seemed to soar up within one of these hills, even to its summit, and here they lingered in order to amuse themselves with the echoes of their own voices. 'There is an ancient melody,' he said, 'in the sound of the echoing voice. It is a vocal spirit which haunts concave and hollow places like to this one. Yet here is another fancy for you. What of a world in which there were only echoes and no voices? What then?'

They walked once more into the sun, and the man seemed to breathe more freely out of the cave; he stretched his arms towards the distant shore, and then turned upon his heels to admire the ravines and trees all around him. 'This is a famous island,' he declared, 'for it is much written about. Like those who suck in the last breath of their expiring friends in the opinion that the soul passes out that way, so the spirit of one writer or another may pass into a place such as this. It is an enchanted island and, since it is no injustice to take that which none complains to lose, so it thrives upon the descriptions of many Englishmen. The treasures of time lie all around us here, and we need no map to discover them. Do you see this?' He reached up and held out a broad leaf of deep green, although he did not pluck it from its parent tree. 'It is always the same, and yet it must always be renewed; it is the same, and not the same. So this island is continually being recreated in other men's words while its identity can never change.

Shall we go on a little?' They walked in the direction of the shore, as the stranger continued with his discourse. 'And why should we not possess a similar fate? Why should we be lost in the uncomfortable night of nothing, when we may partake of the same renewal? For my part I will be content to recede into some larger spirit, some divine original, which is the ground of all our being. No man is an island.' He laughed out loud at this, as he proceeded to cross a small stream by means of three flat white stones. 'Do you see this current?' he asked the boy. 'It is lost in one place, but then rises up again in another. Do you not recognize the very pattern of mortality there? Like language itself, which perishes not with its authors, but emerges elsewhere in a refined or polluted sort.'

They passed on into a more barren part, with no water or vegetation, where Timothy seemed troubled. 'This is very like my own life,' he murmured. 'This place where we are standing now.'

'There is no need to fear,' the man of the island replied as he maintained his measured pace. 'There are others with you. Did you dream of faces last night?'

'How did you know of that?'

The man said nothing further but, instead, with a piece of driftwood drew a face upon the ground. He inscribed the eyes first and followed them with the mouth, the nose and the ears. 'A hieroglyph,' he said. 'See how it encircles us.' For indeed he had drawn it so large that it quite encompassed them both. 'It is said that in the hours before death a man may lose his own face and resemble some of his near relations.' He placed his hand against Timothy's cheek for one moment. 'This is your proper countenance and yet the lines of your father's face may lie deep and invisible here. As from our infancy we run through a variety of looks before we come to consistent and settled faces, so, before our end, by sick and languishing alterations, we put on new visages. In our retreat to earth we fall upon such looks which were before latent in us, and return to that community of originals. There is no need to fear, Timothy. All will be well. You are part of a greater destiny than you now understand.' They left that place without another word, the face on the ground for ever marking the spot where they had spoken of such things.

They had advanced close by the shore, and the man of the island took a flute from the pocket of his patchwork coat. 'What was it I told you once? To remember your English music, so that you might be transported out of this island state?' At this point he blew some sweet notes from his instrument and, between airs, recited this poem to the boy as if it were a part of the melody:

> 'Teach your endeavours so my words to read
> That, learning them, by me you may proceed.
> Death may abrupt me, but succeeding glory
> Bids you go on to a more lasting story.

'Thus,' he said, bringing the flute to his lips again and preparing to play, 'thus do I make myself immortal.' And, as he played, Timothy began to dance; it was a dance of intricate steps and slow pace, but one that the boy had by heart and not by rote. He danced on until he grew tired and lay down upon the strand to sleep. The man continued playing for a short while, and then he took the boy in his arms and carried him safely homeward. He carried him towards the sea, that is, so that now once more there was only one set of footprints upon the island.

NINE

M Y FATHER HAD FOLLOWED ME to Hackney Square and now carried me towards the motor-car; I had been staring at the sunflowers in a kind of trance, it seems, and since he could not lead me away he took me gently in his arms. He put me in the back, while he sat in the front seat next to my grandfather; I do not remember saying one word during the entire course of the journey, but my father hardly stopped talking as we left London and drove west. 'One thing you will find in the country,' he said, 'are sunflowers. Hundreds of them.'

'*We* don't have any,' my grandfather replied.

'But you have plenty of other flowers, don't you? Down where the rambling roses grow.' Nothing seemed to disturb my father's good mood, and it was as if we were embarked upon some wonderful holiday. It was the same whenever he travelled: the shortest journey by tram or underground would release his high spirits. Perhaps he was always looking for an escape. 'Think of the hills and streams, Timothy,' he was saying, 'and all the expeditions you can have.' I wondered how he could forget the expeditions we had made together through the streets of east London, and I stared from the back of the car at the retreating view as he began to sing in a low voice, ' "I'm happy when I'm hiking. Pack upon my back." ' I thought at the time that he was trying to encourage or console me, but now I believe he was also trying to comfort himself. ' "I'm happy when I'm hiking. Off the beaten track." There's nothing like the English countryside, is there?' I looked out at the passing trees and, when the wind stirred them, they seemed to be shaking with laughter at me. 'Yes,' he added, 'I wish I was in your shoes.' He was sitting with his arms folded, hugging himself almost, with no particular expression upon his face. 'And that's another thing,' he said, as if he had been delivering a speech to both of us. 'You can go to a good school now, Tim. That's the important thing. A good education.'

'The important thing,' my grandfather replied, 'is the boy.'

'Yes. Of course. That's what I said.' He became silent now and, after a while, I could hear the sound of his steady breathing as he slept.

Eventually we drove into Wiltshire, and reached what had become for me a familiar destination. We left the car in its usual place and I stood between them, with my battered brown suitcase in my hand, as we contemplated the white lane I knew so well. That afternoon will always live in my memory, as I smelled the dust baking in the glare of the sun and realized that he was about to leave me. 'Time to make a move,' my grandfather said, but my father seemed to be hanging back; he really did not want to enter the farmhouse, but I took his hand and we walked towards the wooden gate. He kicked a stone to the side of the lane. 'Don't do that, dad,' I said. 'You'll get your shoes dusty.'

My grandmother was waiting for us by the front door, and for some reason my father became uncomfortable in her presence. I noticed that her incessant shaking had not returned but, at least for the moment, she did not care to mention that fact. There was in any case a diversion when Friday, the old dog, bounded up to me; I bent down and buried my face in his fur so that I would not have to talk to them. 'Timothy loves dogs,' my father said proudly, assuming it to be some great merit on my part. He followed my grandparents into the house, leaving me on the porch with Friday, but he did not stay for very long. 'I have to catch a train,' I heard him whispering to them. 'I have to see someone.'

'Always on the move, Clement.' My grandmother was also talking in a low tone. 'Just like the old days.'

I did not understand what she meant by that and, when I joined them in the parlour, it was as if they had been caught divulging some shared secret. But that sensation passed in a moment. So we sat there, talking of nothing in particular but thinking of everything, until the taxi-cab arrived to drive him to the station. 'Well, old boy,' he said, as he rose slowly from his chair. 'This is it. I'll be back soon.' I believed that he could have tried a little harder to console me, but he did seem genuinely unhappy now that the time of parting had come. If I had known then what I know now, I would have embraced him; but I held back. I did not know what to say. 'Don't forget,' he said, 'I love you.'

When the three of us were alone together, my grandfather stood in front of me and put out his hand. 'Here's my hand,' he said. 'In a minute I shall want you to shake it. We're going to make a bargain, Timothy. You promise never to run away again, and we promise to look after you faithfully. You never let us down, and we will never let you down. Now what do you say to that?' All this was expressed in his usual forth-right manner, not as if I were a child at all. 'Now, Timothy, will you shake it please?'

'It's a bargain,' I said and took his hand. Indeed I had no intention of running away again, because there was no place to which I could possibly flee. This was indeed my home. I had no other.

They accompanied me upstairs to my old room (or, should I say, my mother's room), which had been redecorated in honour of my return; my grandfather had painted the ceiling a dark blue with small white stars across it, so that it seemed as if I were looking up from my bed at the night sky. He had also brought in a small bookcase, a table and chair; the gramophone was still there by the bed, where I had last seen it on the night I ran away. They left me to unpack, and with a sudden sensation of helplessness I began to place my few possessions in order; the more anxiety I felt at the unknown future, the neater I became. Ever since that time I have always thought it to be one of the most poignant of human activities – to bring one's few possessions to a strange place.

No doubt patients with a fatal illness, when they enter the room in which they are going to die, neatly fold away their clothes and tidily arrange their belongings. When I came down into the kitchen, it was time for tea; in those days I found it a mournful ceremony, because I associated it with age and twilight, but we talked easily enough. I knew that my grandfather had something more to tell me, however, and he waited until my grandmother had cleared away the cups and plates before he got up, put his hands in his pockets and started walking around the table. 'Do you think,' he suddenly asked me, 'that you could put up with a little teaching? Nothing too boring. English literature. History. That sort of thing?'

'Dad taught me all of that.' I was already referring to him in the past tense and I began to breathe more heavily. 'He used to call it English music.'

'And that's exactly what it is.'

'He taught me everything.'

'That's the point, Timothy.' My grandmother sat down next to me and with a glance reduced my grandfather to silence. 'He doesn't have anything else to teach you, and now he wants you to learn from other people. There is so much within you . . .' She hesitated slightly, no doubt recalling the evening when I cured her disorder. 'So much to bring out. We want you to develop, Timothy. We want you to do very well.' Now that the quavering of her voice had gone, it was surprisingly bright and clear, and for a moment once again I saw the image of my mother somehow existing around the old woman who sat beside me.

'I don't mind,' I said. 'As long as I can live here with you.'

'This is your home, Timothy. Your mother's home.' She looked up at her husband, who was standing quietly behind us. 'So don't you go bothering the boy with any more talk about schools. Show him the pictures we found upstairs. Go on.'

My grandfather rushed out of the room and a few moments later returned with a small photograph album. 'It was in the attic,' he said. 'Under her clothes.' He opened it out upon my knees and pointed excitedly over my shoulder as I turned the pages. 'Here she is in her Sunday best,' he said. I recognized her at once, even though she could have been no more than fourteen or fifteen years old; she was standing on the back lawn, with the small pine forest visible beyond her. With something of a shock I realized that I had lain down upon the grass just there, where my mother had once stood looking at the camera. There were several other photographs of her; she always wore the same serious expression and, so it seemed, she was always looking at me.

'Do you see,' my grandmother said, 'how much you resemble her? You have the same mouth. The same eyes.'

'Yes,' my grandfather added, 'they are very much the same.' This made me feel curiously happy, and we sat together harmoniously in the gathering dusk.

Summer was coming to its end and, in my remembrance, those gradually shortening days were the most peaceful of my life. They were not the happiest – I still felt my father's absence too deeply for that – but, after the sudden and unexpected changes of the previous few months, there was comfort to be found in my grandparents' steady routine. I took Friday with me everywhere, just as my mother had once done; sometimes he would run ahead of me and follow some familiar path through the forest or the fields, and then I knew that I was walking in her footsteps. I found my old tree again, among the other pines, and when I rested beneath it the feeling of strength and calmness flowed back towards me – as if, by sitting there, I was somehow beyond the hazards of time. Sometimes I imagined to myself that I was stranded with my dog upon a desert island, and then the strangest sensation would invade me; I seemed to be taking part in a story which had nothing to do with me, but from which I could not escape. Yet I kept on repeating it, in my imagination, each time I made my way into the pine forest.

Then, towards the close of that summer, the time came for

me to attend my first school. It was called St William's, and was an ancient grammar school for boys situated in the nearby market town of Upper Harford: I knew all this within a few days of my return to my grandparents' house, so eager were they to enrol me there, but it had no reality for me except as a vague sense of menace which imperilled my secluded hours in the pine forest. Perhaps that is why I still dreamed I was on a desert island. My grandfather knew two of its governors, and so there was no difficulty in my being placed there; it was agreed that my history should be known only to the headmaster, and indeed I think I posed something of a 'challenge' for him – for what was I but an apparently uneducated child from the East End of London?

My grandfather accompanied me on the motor-bus that first morning, and I might as well have been escorted to a place of execution. A week before we had purchased the green cap and grey suit, as well as the old-fashioned stiff collars, which comprised the standard uniform of the school: in these uncomfortable and unfamiliar clothes I felt an impostor, and I blushed continually at the very conspicuousness of my false position. We walked up the high street towards the ancient gates of the school and my grandfather left me there, solemnly shaking hands with me as if we were never to meet again; I guessed that he would turn to look at me and, sensing his bright eyes upon my back, I did not dare linger there or run away (much as I longed to do), but instead felt compelled to go through the gates and enter the large yard in front of the school buildings. There were groups of boys already standing around, all of them with a faint air of expectancy, but I was too bewildered to be afraid. I had spent no time in the company of other children, and now, in the presence of so many of them, I felt quite dazed and faint. I moved stiffly through them – some of them (or so I thought) looking at me curiously as I did so. I did not know where I was going but I needed to find shelter from the sudden infliction of so many lives, and I quickly made my way towards the school buildings ahead of me. One of the doors was open and I found myself in a hallway which had what was for me the exotic smell of chalk, rubber bands and stale food.

'Outside.' Someone was standing in a doorway beside the hall. 'Go outside. Wait for the bell.' I turned around and walked back into the yard, hardly able to breathe; I pretended to tie up the laces of my shoes, keeping my face away from the other boys, and then I stood by myself against a low wall. A few moments later I did a curious thing: I put my hands in the pockets of my new trousers and sat down upon the wall, whistling and banging my heels against the stone as I did so. A bell rang somewhere and, as the others walked into the school, I simply watched them; it was as if I needed to play no part in these proceedings at all. But suddenly the yard was empty and in panic I ran towards the door from which I had so recently come; the hall there was empty, but I could hear the sound of distant voices. I had been left behind. I hurried down an adjacent corridor, in the frantic belief that this would lead me in the right direction. 'Walk. Don't run.' It was the same figure who had stopped me before. 'The assembly is that way.' He pointed to the other end of the corridor, and I made my way down it as slowly and as casually as I could. To my relief the other boys were still standing around and talking, some of them pretending to fight with one another, while others rocked on their heels or moved from side to side with the bright, undirected energy of the young. And then the man appeared again. He could only have been a few steps behind me, and I realized at once that he was the headmaster; in the profound silence which greeted his arrival I kept my head bowed in case he should remember me, and I cannot say that I heard any of the remarks or exhortations which he delivered on this first day of term. I understood only one thing: that the 'new boys' were supposed to find the number of their classroom on the notice-board. This I managed to do, and was directed down another corridor which smelled of dust and fresh paint. It was how I had always imagined the interior of a prison or hospital.

'Oh do wait.' Someone was calling to me and, when I turned around, I saw a boy of my own age lurching down the corridor; his right shoulder and right arm were bent backward, as if held by a invisible string, and he limped badly on his left leg. I thought at first that he was imitating my own self-conscious movements in this unfamiliar place, but, when he came closer, I realized that he could walk in no other way. 'I am a cripple, you see,' he said quite calmly as he came up to me. 'And sometimes I need a little bit of help.' We had stopped outside the same classroom, and I held the door open for him. Many of the other boys obviously knew him, and whispered to each other as he struggled into the classroom with his awkward, disjointed movements. He had put one hand on my shoulder in order to steady himself but, in my embarrassment, I moved away from him. He did not seem to notice this. 'Here's a desk for us both,' he said. There were two seats together in the central row, and now he tugged at my sleeve to catch my attention. 'My name is Edward Campion.' So it was that Edward and I encountered each other, the beginning of a friendship which was to have lasting consequences for us both.

The first lessons, and indeed the first day, passed so quickly that I remember nothing of them now – nothing, that is, except for the pleasure I took in opening my new exercise books and finding the fresh, neatly ruled pages billowing in front of me. With my fountain pen I wrote my name and form on the green covers, and it was as if I were performing a benediction. Edward watched me with undisguised pleasure, although his own hand was more unsteady and his name emerged somewhere between a blot and a scrawl. 'There,' he said, looking warily at his own signature. 'That'll do.' We spent most of these first days with each other, and he stayed by my side during the intervals in the yard (or, as I came to call it, the playground). Many of the other boys took part in what seemed like elaborate games: I did not care to join in, and Edward could not do so, and in a sense we were forced into each other's company. I felt a certain humiliation in being associated with him, I remember that clearly enough, especially since he was treated with open ridicule by many boys. He did not seem to notice their contempt, and it was not until many years later that he confessed to me how he wept each night at the insults he pretended to ignore during the day. Many of the others directed the same contempt at me for being, as it were, attached to him; they also called me 'Cockney' because of my London origins, although within a matter of days I had acquired the softer cadences and 'burr' of their native accent. I did not consciously adapt my voice; it simply changed.

'I've always been the same, you see.' Edward and I were sitting on the low wall which I had found on my first day at the school. 'My father says' – this was how he often opened his remarks – 'my father says that in the old days I would have been dead by now. A hundred years ago,' he added, more emphatically, 'I would have been lying in the street.' He seemed to take pleasure in the thought of his own extinction. 'My father was at the Somme,' he went on. 'What did your father do?'

'He sank the Germans at Jutland,' I replied at once, making up this extraordinary past quite spontaneously. For some reason I did not want Edward to know my father's true occupation; although I was still proud of his work and believed in it as strongly as ever, in the context of my new life and my new school it also seemed somehow ridiculous and even improper. Edward said nothing, although I do not think he believed my story. Indeed that is one of the most curious facts I discovered about other children: belief was somehow suspended and the distinction between truth and lies, between fact and fiction, was by common consent discarded. And yet, on reflection, I realize that Edward was the exception to this; he never strayed from the plain truth, no doubt because in his own life he had, by some process of courageous reasoning, prepared himself to face the worst.

'If you weren't you,' he was saying, 'who would you rather be?'

'I'd like to be my dad. I'd like to be a war hero.' I believed I was blushing slightly, so I went on quickly, 'Who would you like to be?'

'I would like to be you.'

'Why?' I laughed at this.

'Because you're the only one here who cares about me.'

No one before had ever expressed such a sentiment, and I pretended to ignore it. 'I've got some friends in London you would like.' It was the first time I had mentioned my old life to Edward, or to anyone in the school.

'I've never been to London,' he replied. I was astonished by this; somehow I assumed that everyone knew the city as well as I did. 'One day,' he said slowly, 'we can go there together. We can see the dome of St Paul's. My father says it has the largest golden cross in the world.'

'And we can see my friends.'

He did not reply, and I sensed that he did not want to hear about these other people. The bell sounded for the next lesson, and I helped him down from the wall. 'We'll go to London together then,' he said. 'That's definitely settled.' He was happy when any part of his future could be 'settled', I knew that, and he kept his hand on my shoulder as we walked back towards the school. He always liked me to be beside him when he entered the classroom, but on this particular afternoon I noticed a curious thing. I was limping slightly.

And so those first days passed. In the late afternoon I would take the motor-bus from Upper Harford, which dropped me at the end of the lane I knew so well. I always walked slowly down it, kicking my shoes in the dust, the mild sun of early autumn still warming my back as I entered the house. I generally completed my homework in my own room, had supper with my grandparents and then took Friday for a walk in the pine forest. Of course the quiet routine of my new life did not mean that I had abandoned or could ever forget my past; there were still times when the belief that I would never again see Margaret Collins, or Stanley Clay, or any of them, left me feeling so sorrowful and bereft that I lost all purchase upon my present reality. Then indeed my new life seemed very much like a dream, and I would walk through the forest with the strangest feeling of emptiness; it was as if I scarcely existed any more. It was not necessarily an unpleasant sensation, however – I knew that, if I lay upon the ground or rested against a tree, I would be filled simply with the motion of the turning world. And there was some comfort in that. I would not be wholly lost.

After a few weeks I was no longer the stranger in the school and, in any case, I was never very unpopular with the other boys. My friendship with Edward was now accepted, and had won me a certain churlish respect even among those who whispered behind their hands about 'Campion the Cripple'. I was known as 'Flash', and this because I always seemed to be in movement, always hurrying from place to place. In the classroom I would turn my head from side to side, provoked by any noise or sudden movement, quickly noticing everything around me. I hardly realized this at the time, of course, because it was so much part of my life in the world that it seemed perfectly ordinary behaviour. Certainly I could not have understood the reasons for my nervous alertness but, looking back upon it now, it seems to me that I was afraid. I resembled one of those small birds which, even when it appears to sleep, darts glances from side to side for fear of predators or rivals. I, too, was never still; I would knock my knees together under the desk, much to Edward's displeasure, or bang my heels against the floor. I do not remember if I had been so nervous in lodgings with my father, but I do not think so. It was only in his absence that the world became more urgent, more unsettled, and more threatening.

If the other boys did not call me 'Flash', they still called me 'Cockney' even though I had long ago lost whatever London accent I had once possessed. I discovered another useful talent of that kind, too, when I found that I could delight my classmates with impersonations of our teachers. I had only to think of them and I could, as it were, conjure them up. I also told stories. I lied about myself and about my past in order to acquire more popularity still. My father was a famous war hero and my mother was still alive: she was a famous opera-singer. I also had an older brother who had emigrated to America and made his fortune in the oil-fields of Texas. My father had a big car – a Daimler. My parents were so busy in London that I had volunteered to come and live with my grandparents in the country. These lies came quite naturally to me because, as far as I understand it now, they sprang from my own sense of insufficiency; I could no more tell my school-fellows about my real father than I could explain my mother's death. Yet this is the most curious thing of all – I believed every word of these stories as I invented them, and even found myself disappointed at returning to my grandparents' house when I had such a notable family elsewhere. Of course I took care not to invite anyone to the farmhouse, not even Edward, and I was terrified that my grandfather might one day meet one of my classmates and discover all the lies I had been telling. It was partly fear of this eventuality, I suspect, that made me so nervously rapid and abrupt in all my move-ments. Edward never censured me or questioned me about such things, however, and instead simply accepted them as part of myself. He did not even seem to think any the less of me because of my lies, and it is even possible that he under-stood some of the reasons for them – that he understood me better than I understood my own self.

He had lived in Upper Harford all his life, and so he knew it very well; it was an ancient market town, and he explained to me each successive stage of its history from the time of early Saxon settlement. Sometimes, after school, he would take me to a spot where there were traces of an old medieval wall or the remnants of some ancient stone house. He was a familiar figure in the town itself and often on these expeditions the people would make way for us as he struggled forward, his whole body lurching and shuddering with the effort to maintain a straight course. I still recall one winter afternoon when the sun was so low in the sky that it had become a globe of blood trembling upon the horizon. We had walked a little way out of town, crossing the River Har by a footbridge in order to visit a small settlement which, according to Edward, dated from the twelfth or thirteenth century. With delight he pointed out to me the outlines of some rect-angular buildings and, as he sat upon an outcrop of stone and blew into his hands to warm them, I paced around the line of one of these ancient houses. 'My father says that the same people have always lived around here,' he shouted across to me. 'The same families, I mean. We all look alike, don't we?' Just as there were times when he seemed to find a strange fascination in the idea of death or extinction, so there were occasions when he took real pleasure in losing his identity within some larger group – whether it was his family, the school, or this area itself. And in a sense he was right: I had noticed before how the faces of my classmates bore a faint resemblance to one another. With my dark hair, and very pale skin, I was a stranger in more ways than one. 'So you see,' Edward was saying, 'I'm probably related to the people who once lived here.' His body was swaying all the time, back and forth, his face sometimes momentarily twisted out of shape by a spasm as he leaned against the stone. 'In those days there wasn't any school, so I would probably have stayed at home.'

I was still pacing along the contour of the small house when I was suddenly filled with a sensation of the most intense horror. I was no longer able to listen to Edward, but instead felt the infliction of other voices and other lives. I could feel the sickness rising within my body, and there seemed to be some weight or burden inside me which I had to expel; there was a stench like smoke all around me, and the crying of small children somehow mixed within it. I bent over, pierced by intense hopelessness, and then all at once the experience was gone. I looked up to find Edward staring at me strangely. 'Are you feeling sick?' he said, putting one hand up to his face.

'I was. But I'm better now.'

'You were limping,' he said. 'Just like me.'

'There was a stone under my foot,' I replied, and then with exaggerated care I knelt down upon the freezing ground to remove an imaginary object from my shoe.

'I was telling you what my father says. He says that everything is inherited. You know, like a legacy. But then I want to know where I come from.' I knew that he meant his poor, twisted shape. 'I must have come from someone, but nobody seems to know. Do you think there was someone like me in this house?'

'Yes,' I said. 'There was.'

It was about four months after this that I finally invited Edward to meet my grandparents. I really believed that he accepted my lies about my family, as I have said, and I feared no revelations; in any case I had mentioned him so often that they continually pressed me to bring him to tea. So it was that on a spring afternoon of the following year Edward and I boarded the motor-bus which took me home after school; all through the journey he maintained a commentary on the various features of the landscape which we passed. 'Look,' he said, 'there's Dan's Hill! And there's the old coaching track, there, past the black barn!' I had already been told the stories surrounding those places, but I pretended now that I was hearing them for the first time.

My grandfather was raking the gravel path when we came up to the gate; I had already warned him that Edward might be self-conscious about his physical condition, and he took care not to look at us until we had come close to him. 'So this is the young man who knows all our history,' he said, shaking Edward's hand solemnly. 'I was very impressed when Timothy told me about you.' Friday came bounding out of the house to greet me, and Edward at once bent down to embrace him; he almost fell sideways but I caught him, and the dog itself was not alarmed. He licked Edward's face, and then ran in circles around the garden.

'Come in, come in!' My grandmother was calling us from the door. Edward walked unsteadily towards her and, as soon as he reached the porch, she took both his hands. 'I've been waiting to meet you,' she said. No doubt she remembered her own old nervous seizures, because she smiled at him and kissed him softly on the cheek. 'Now that we're all acquainted,' she said, 'we can have some tea.'

'Tell me,' my grandfather asked him when we eventually sat down together, 'what do you think of the state of the country today?'

'I think it's very good,' Edward replied. 'My father says that TB has practically gone now. Of course he still pays into the sick club.' He had an awkward way of eating; he was forced to lower his head to one side, so that his mouth was level with the fork or spoon, before he could make contact with the food. 'My father says that it's a whole new world now. A different world.'

'Your father is a very wise man.'

'Yes. He is.' He nodded several times. 'He works for the government. In the post office.'

'Is that what you want to do?' my grandmother asked him.

'Oh no. I would like to be a doctor. I want to look after people.'

The sheer incongruity, even impossibility, of this ambition did not seem to occur to my grandparents. 'You'd make a very fine doctor,' she replied. 'You have very good hands. Just like Timothy here. They must run in your family too.'

'I don't know.' Edward was suddenly more defensive. 'My father says that everything is inherited. But I don't know.'

We were all silent for a moment. It is hard to know how long the silence would have continued, but there was a sudden knock upon the door. My grandfather went to answer it –

and who, to my astonishment, should return with him but my father and Gloria Patterson.

'Hello, darling,' Gloria said to me as soon as she entered the kitchen. 'We took a chance and came down.' She seemed much changed; she was more self-confident, even assertive, and she was wearing a grey tailored suit which came down just below her knees.

My father was standing a little way behind her, but now he came forward and patted me on the back. 'Hello, Tim,' he said. 'I've been looking forward to seeing you.'

'Hello, dad.' I looked up at him from the table, and resisted the impulse to rise and embrace him. 'We weren't expecting you.' I could think of nothing else to say, especially in the presence of Edward, who was visibly disturbed by the sudden entrance of two strangers; as soon as he saw the beautiful Gloria, he began shaking violently. 'Edward has to go home,' I said quickly. 'He has to catch his coach.'

My father looked at Edward for a moment and then glanced at me warily, as if he believed that I was keeping something from him. 'I'll go with you,' he said, 'and we can have a chat on the way.'

'No.' I was near panic at the thought of my real family's life being disclosed to my friend. 'We have to go a special way. I'll be back in a little while.' Before anyone could object to this arrangement, I helped Edward to his feet; he barely had time to stammer out his thanks to my grandparents, when I opened the front door and led him out towards the gate.

'I'm sorry,' he said. 'I couldn't help myself. Were you embarrassed by me?'

'No! Of course not!' I was horrified that he should even consider the idea.

He said nothing, and I do not think he believed me. 'She's very beautiful,' he added as we turned into the white lane. He seemed much calmer now, even weary.

'Who is?' Of course I knew whom he meant.

'Your mother. She's just as beautiful as you said.'

I did not know how to reply. I did not want him to believe that Gloria Patterson was my real mother; and yet, since she was indeed beautiful, Edward would tell our schoolfellows and I might gain some advantage. My own mother *had* been beautiful, too, so was there any need to correct his mistake? 'Yes,' I said. 'Everyone thinks she looks young for her age.'

I accompanied him to Upper Harford, and then returned immediately. They were all still sitting in the kitchen when I came back into the house, and at once I experienced their tense and uncomfortable state. 'Here he is!' Gloria exclaimed as I slowly entered the room. 'Here's our dream boat!' Edward was right: she was indeed very beautiful, and what I know now to have been her insincerity and vulgarity seemed to me then only aspects of that beauty. She was holding my father's hand under the table but, on my arrival, I saw him withdraw it; as if in compensation for the gesture, he held it up to me in greeting.

'The wanderer returns,' he said. 'From over the mountains and streams.'

'Edward just lives in town, dad.'

'I liked your friend.' He had resumed something of his old expansive manner, and now he tapped his forehead with his finger. 'Didn't he remind you of some of the people we used to know?' I realized whom he meant – Stanley Clay, Matthew Lucas and the others – although I wondered why he should consign those familiar companions to the remote past. 'I'm glad you've made friends, Tim,' he added, quickly. 'And your grandparents have been telling me how well you're doing at school. All our predictions came true, didn't they?'

'I like it here,' was all I said.

'It makes a change, doesn't it?' Gloria clearly did not want to be left out of this conversation between my father and myself. 'We like to come down to the country now and then, don't we, Clement? It's interesting.' She glanced around her with a barely suppressed look of boredom. 'And this house must be worth a bob or two.'

'I don't know about that,' my grandfather replied. 'We've always lived here. You may have heard of Timothy's mother, Cecilia. Well, this is where she was born.' He was looking at me as he spoke, with his usual frank gaze. 'He has his mother's old room now. Perhaps he would like to show it to you.'

'I remember,' my father said, 'when Tim had his own room in Hackney Square. I couldn't have managed that place without him.'

'Shall we go outside?' Gloria broke in. 'I'd love to see a bit of the area. Before we have to leave.'

But my father had not finished reminiscing. 'I miss those days,' he said. 'Listening in to the wireless. Going for long walks. Do you remember our walks, Tim? We could have gone on for ever, couldn't we?' Again I wondered how he could bear to bring up the past.

'The best walk,' my grandmother said, 'is down memory lane.'

'There is a theory,' he went on, 'that the first fifteen years of your life are the most important. I hope that's true, Tim. And I'm sure you're happy here.'

I could bear it no longer, and I jumped up from the table. 'I have some homework to do,' I said and rushed upstairs to my room. I lay down upon my bed and, for the first time since my arrival, I wept. A few minutes later I heard a familiar step, and then my father knocked upon the door. 'Timothy,' he said gently. 'Can I come in?'

'What do you want?'

'I want to come in. Isn't that what I said?' He opened the door and stood at the foot of the bed. 'You have to realize, Tim, that I mean everything for your own good.'

'Everything was going so well. Why did you have to come back and ruin it?'

When I saw the stricken look upon his face I instantly regretted what I had said, and yet I had meant it. His arrival, and his reminders of our shared past, had taken away the contentment I was beginning to feel in this house. 'I'm sorry . . .' he began to say. 'I didn't mean . . .' He stopped again, largely, I think, because he was beginning to appreciate my feelings. 'Perhaps I shouldn't talk about the past so much,' he said. 'But they were good days together, weren't they? What's the point of forgetting them?' Something of his familiar enthusiasm returned as he spoke to me, and he paced up and down the room in the way I knew so well. 'And they're not over yet. The good days will come again. One day, Timmy, I'll be able to explain everything that has happened to you. Everything was done for your benefit. For your future happiness. Believe me. Do you think I could have let you go otherwise?' I did not understand then what he meant; but I do now. Suddenly he sat down next to me upon the bed. 'Are you still having those dreams, Timmy, the dreams you told me about?'

'I don't like to be called Timmy any more, dad. My name is Tim.'

With a sigh he got up from the bed, and began walking up and down once more. 'So this used to be Cecilia's room. I never saw it before this moment. Isn't that strange, Timmy? Tim. Never till this moment.' He sighed. 'Do you ever dream about her?'

'No, dad.'

'Do you promise?'

'Yes. I promise. What difference does it make?'

'No difference. No difference at all.' He seemed about to add something, but then said only, 'Will you come downstairs with me now?'

I never could disobey him, and so I followed him back into the kitchen, where Gloria, tapping her foot upon the tiled floor, was clearly impatient to leave. All thought of the country walk had vanished. 'It's been ever so nice,' she said, 'but now we must love you and leave you.' My grandparents did not seem eager to prolong the visit, either, but my father tried to hold back. I believe that he did not want to leave me in this abrupt way, but Gloria was already busily looking for her hat and coat. 'It's fox,' she said. 'Ever so expensive.'

'Look after your grandparents,' my father called out to me as he reluctantly left the house with her. 'I'll be back.' I did not see him for another three years.

Three years with my grandparents. Three years at St William's. It was, I suppose, a typical education in an English grammar school – the learning by heart, the set essays, the examinations, all contributed to the idea that knowledge was simply information to be acquired and then discarded as quickly as possible. It was a technique or exercise, which the cleverest boys could master easily; that was all. I had no difficulty in understanding whatever studies were placed in front of me but, perhaps for the same reason, I did not find it quite so easy to take them seriously or to discover in them any further purpose. There were occasions in the classroom when we would chant the various tenses of French verbs – I have done, I do, I shall be doing – but to me each tense seemed problematic; I had no real belief in my future precisely because I had no real connection to my past. Or, rather, I had no trust in the future because I had no faith in the past. So I existed in a kind of limbo, a period of enforced calm which often passed for contentment or even happiness.

There was one saving grace in my life, however. I became interested in music and, as I grew older and progressed through the school, my principal enthusiasm was for the music lessons which were conducted twice a week by an extravagant and boisterous man who, as far as I was concerned, could not have been imagined outside a classroom. Mr Armitage's true domain was the music-room; here he would loudly improvise a few chords upon the piano, or sing at the top of his voice, or conduct an imaginary orchestra as he played one of his collection of classical records. Many of my classmates laughed at his impetuous behaviour, but he never seemed to mind. 'Music is a divine madness, boys,' he used to say. 'Don't you wish you had caught it? Sing! Play! Do something to lift your mediocre little lives!' All this was said in the highest good spirits, which were themselves infectious; and there were times when he had the whole class roaring out a chorus or declaiming a ballad. But my most powerful memories are of more subdued occasions, when he would put a symphony or concerto on the gramophone; then he would gaze quietly out of the window, occasionally rocking back and forth in his chair while the music surrounded us. At those times I would be lifted out of myself, and become so much part of the music that I lost all sense of my present reality. Even Edward became still.

Mr Armitage had a particular passion for early English music, and many of our lessons were spent discussing the work of Tallis, Byrd, Dowland, Purcell and others. In those days there were very few gramophone recordings of such music, but he would play examples for us on the piano. He was also a Roman Catholic, as he used to point out in his usual emphatic way by calling us 'heretics' or even 'atheists', and he reserved his greatest enthusiasm for what he called the Catholic composers of England. That is no doubt why he had a strong affection for John Dowland and, sometimes almost in tears, he would describe the course of his tormented life. 'What could he do, boys, but wander around Europe? But despised and rejected though he was, he never forgot his English music! A melancholy creature, of course. A great, melancholy creature.' Here Mr Armitage would break off and, breathing heavily as a result of his exertions during this lecture, would stand gazing out of the window in silence. Then he would perform for us some of Dowland's songs. He was a large and very solid man, in appearance something like a rugby player or a boxer, but he had a voice of singular purity and sweetness which astonished the most fractious class into silence. I recall very little of those songs now, but lines from one of them have for some reason always remained in my memory:

His golden locks time hath to silver turned,
O time too swift, O swiftness never ceasing.

What a strange spectacle it was, this large and ungainly middle-aged man expressing sentiments such as these in a pure melodious voice which filled the music-room and echoed around the corridors of the school.

Mr Armitage also dwelt at length upon the music of Henry Purcell. 'What a short, strange life that was, boys! Tell me what you heathens make of it.' Purcell had been a Catholic, too, and he recited to us all the miseries of the composer's life – his childhood during the Great Plague, the premature deaths of his own children, and the terrible burden of work which destroyed him at the age of thirty-six. 'Do you wonder,' he would add, 'that he composed such doleful music?' Then he sang a line from one of Purcell's works – 'Remember me, but ah! forget my fate' – in such a high, piercing voice that the memory of it disturbs me still.

But Mr Armitage's greatest reverence was for William Byrd, whom he described as 'the father of English music'. 'Another Romanist, boys,' he declared. 'Not some lily-livered Protestant courtier.' In our lessons we discovered that Byrd was so great a master of music that he excelled in songs, madrigals, anthems, voluntaries, preludes and fantasies; that he had no rival either in keyboard music or in music for stringed instruments; that he had changed the entire shape both of sacred and secular music. His masses – 'that's a Catholic expression, so bow your dirty heads' – were the finest achievements of English polyphony, and his sacred songs surpassed any previous work in motet or fugue.

'So tell me, little boys, why were there so many great Catholic composers in England?' None of us had an answer. 'It's all in the cadence. The line of beauty. The Catholics get it from birth, in the rhythms of our Latin mass and benediction. It's the same as the English genius for the rising and falling melody, for the undulating cadence. Do you understand now?' Sometimes I felt that he was teaching himself at the same time as he was teaching the class, but that only added to the excitement which he managed to impart to us.

'Come on pagans,' he would say. 'Try and hear the music, too.' Then, to the accompaniment of stifled laughter, he began to chant to us some of the phrases from Byrd's masses before breaking off to deliver another short lecture.

'Do you know what we can do? We can date the beginning of a real and continuing English music to the sixteenth century. The gentle cadences. The clear harmonies. The sweet melodies. The purity, boys, the purity of the music. That's what we still hear today. The music lives on. Have you heard Elgar or Vaughan Williams?' There was silence in the class. 'Bax? Holst? Arthur Bliss? Well, my ignorant friends, the music never dies. The old music is still part of us. It's always part of us. It's always the same melody repeated through the centuries, reaching every generation.' Then he got up from his chair, in which he had been rocking violently in time with his words, and started striding around the music-room with a finger to his lips. I had never heard of any of these composers before, but something of what he said excited me because it corresponded with an inchoate sense of my own self.

It did not take long for my schoolfellows to discover that my 'mother' was very beautiful: Edward Campion had blurted it out soon after he had met Gloria. I was not at all unhappy about the mistake; as I suspected, it merely increased my popularity among my contemporaries. I was less pleased, however, by the continuance of my lie that she was an opera-singer. Even Mr Armitage had heard this and one afternoon, after the others had filed out of the music-room, he asked me her 'professional name'.

'Cecilia,' I replied. 'Cecilia Sinclair.' And then I added, hurriedly, 'She's living in Paris.'

He did not bother to inquire further, perhaps out of respect for my feelings concerning an absent mother, but he seemed delighted by her name. 'That *is* exceptional,' he said. 'A singer with the name of Cecilia. Do you know what it means, Harcombe?'

'No, sir.'

'Cecilia is the patron saint of music. A Catholic saint, of course. Her day falls on the twenty-second of November. Curiously enough, Purcell died just the day before.' Then, much to my embarrassment, he began to sing in his clear and piercing voice:

'Hail! Bright Cecilia, hail! Fill every heart
With love of thee and thy celestial art.

'Everyone wrote poems to her,' he said. 'And music was always being composed in her honour.' I thought of my own dead mother, and I was filled once more with the same curious nostalgia which had invaded me when my grand-parents had shown me the photographs of her. 'It is never quite the same poem, or the same music,' Mr Armitage was saying. 'It changes as it's handed down from composer to composer, from generation to generation. But, you know, the melodies and cadences have a strong affinity with each other. There is always something inherited, and there is always something new.'

'Yes,' I said. 'I know.'

Mr Armitage recognized soon enough how interested I had become in the music he taught; and, after I had become a 'senior' in the school, he would allow me to sit with him in the music-room and listen to his favourite recordings. One afternoon he brought with him what he called his 'great prize'; it was the oldest book I had ever seen, bound in dark leather and so large that I had to lay it upon my lap in order to open it. It was entitled *A Plaine and Easie Introduction to Practicall Musicke*, and with great delight he pointed out to me its dedication to William Byrd; with my finger I could feel the indentation of the old type, and for a moment I had the strangest sensation that I might somehow fall into the spaces which had been hollowed there. 'I want you to listen to something,' Mr Armitage said as he went over to his piano. 'It's by Byrd. I found the music in London last weekend.' London. My London. But now somehow associated with the discovery of ancient music.

His voice filled the music-room and the Latin chant soared around me; then he got up and put his arms out in the air. 'Listen,' he said in a low tone and in a voice quite unlike his usual one, 'this is what I was singing.' He began to translate the words for me: '"All the days in which I am now your servant, I wait until my change comes. Leave me, therefore, that I may lament my sorrow a little. Before I go and return no more, to a land that is dark and covered with the mist of death." Sacred music, Harcombe.'

I cannot say that I understood what he had just recited to me, but the very plangency of his voice expressed to me a meaning as deep as any of the words themselves. He sat down again at the piano and began to play; the notes rose or fell in prolonged and solemn cadence, but to me it seemed that they were all connected in quite another sense. It was a line of light, a line that moved among the phrases and melodies of music just as it did within the images and colours of painting. It was the light that brought all things into harmony – and, yes, it was present too in the curving and bounding line of the landscape which surrounded me as I sat in the music-room through this late afternoon. All these images occurred to me as I listened to Byrd's music, the open book still on my lap, but gradually there stole over my awakened senses a larger spirit; it seemed to me that the notes were following a line of light which led forward to a sweeter and greater harmony, a harmony which encompassed me and the music master, and the room, and then everything beyond it, so that all things moved in unison. It was the roll of creation itself, the continuous disclosure of a pattern that never changed but was always enlarged, human being with human being, past with present, the earth with its inhabitants; the line of light encompassed us all, and in this music resounded the harmony of the universe. I no longer held the book in my hands, for it was now also part of my being, and I closed my eyes. I remember only that the music master was reciting some lines as the mild sun touched my face:

'Like Orpheus sitting on a high Thracian hill
That beasts and mountains to his ditties drew . . .

TEN

' . . . So doth he draw with his sweet musicke's skill
Men to attention of his science true.'

THE VOICE WAS STILL BEHIND his back, but changed
somewhat and in more solemn guise. 'Oh I cry you
mercy,' the grave old man continued. 'You are like a pot
with a wide mouth, gaping at the simplicity of my words. Yet
I mean to teach musicke not eloquence and, falling to such
discourse, I will be sure not to stumble like the ass with too
great a burden. I will show you matter, not filed speech or
rhetorical sentence. I will not put simplicity in plumes of
feathers any more than I would deck a carter in a cloth of
gold: for this is English musique, and nothing Italian.' He
came to a halt for the moment and stepped forward before
the three scholars, one of them being the boy Timothy. 'You
know my mind,' said he. 'Musicke is the science of making
musick, either for church or chamber, and not some trifling
air to drive you out of your dump.'

Timothy looked aslant at his two companions in this place,
for could that be his gentle friend, Edward Campion, sitting
close to him? No, this scholar had no weakness upon him: and
yet the face was very like, as it were some distant original.
And, as he revolved that thought in his mind, the lesson
proceeded.

'In these latter days and doting age of the world, there is
nothing more subject to calumny and backbiting than that
which is most true and right. But let the wolves fall into their
own toils, for you will escape them if you be true scholars of
musick. Your young minds are to be trained upon music, not
so that you will be incited to wantonness by mere bauble and
outward show (such things as make our art to be so vilely

reputed among the vile), but that your very souls might be administered by law and reason. I can find nothing that is more great, more healthful, more honest, than musicke. It drives away cares, persuades men to gentleness, represses anger, nourishes arts and increases concord.' And so Mr Byrd continued with his discourse.

He was a very ancient man, wearing a dark cloth gown like an artist's gown, with hanging sleeves and a slit. His beard was cut short, now much more white than red; he possessed a slim belly, but he stooped somewhat as if he had been for too long bent over his studies. Yet he turned to the door with great alacrity when there was a sudden gust of healthful air. 'Shut it, I pray you,' he exclaimed, 'or all our sheets will be overturned and thrown into confusion. And now, you see, I have lost my theme. What was it?' He rubbed the rings upon his fingers, as if seeking there some motto for his discourse.

'It was the story of all our scholarship, sir.' So spoke Master Boyce, scratching his head therewithall.

'Yes. I have it. I have the thread once more. I cannot cease to pray you diligently to practise, for that only is sufficient to make a perfect musitian. In my opinion he who can but rightly imitate this one precept is on the right road: yet it is not so easy a journey, either, to excel in the three parts of our art. As some will excel in descant and will be but bad composers, so others will be good composers and yet bad descanters extempore upon a plain song. Again one will be so excellent in parts of voluntary upon an instrument as you would think it impossible for him not to be a good composer and yet, being enjoined to make a song, he will do it so simply as you would think a scholar of a year's practice – such as you soon will be – might easily compose a better.' He cracked his knuckles exceedingly, seeming secretly pleased by his sad lesson. 'There is another matter also. When you have set down a point, though it be right yet you ought not to rest there, but should rather look earnestly how you may bring it more artificially about. A musitian ought rather blot out

twenty good points than to suffer one point pass in his composition unartificially brought in. But I am going too far forward
in my eagerness to give you true precepts. Let us go back a
little and, as they say, begin at the beginning. For there is no
way to enter this wood but one. And yet not so much a wood
as a garden, a well-garnished garden of most sweet flowers,
which the more it is searched the more variety it does yield.
This is English music.' Timothy looked about him at the
chamber in which the three scholars pursued their close
studies. It was a room of the old sort, with sundry carvings
and thick-leaded windows; in front of him there stood an
oaken desk for their good master and behind it, in the corner
beside the fireplace, lay an ancient lute upon a threadbare
livery cloak. Beneath the window there stood a treble-viol
and, as the wholesome breeze blew through the open casement, the boy thought he heard its strings vibrating through
the sweet air. It was a goodly prospect of parks and fields,
with the Thames running beside and with many arbours to
avoid the vehemence of the sun. Yet the true sweetness was
all compact within this chamber itself, where musick and the
laws of music reigned.

It was the next day following when Mr Byrd came in,
clasping his hands together as one pleased. 'What a morning is
this,' said he, tapping Timothy upon his head with an ebony
rule, 'and how bright is the sunshine, cleaning the air and
banishing the vapours which threatened rain. Now I must
take heed of this example and, with my own light, banish the
vapours rising in your pretty brains. So tell me this, what is
musicke?' He gazed at them, until the scholar next to Timothy
raised his hand. 'Well now, Master Goodfellow?'

'The most ancient definition of music is by Plato, sir, as set
out in his *Theages*.' The squab had his lesson by rote. 'Musick,
says he, is a knowledge whereby we may rule a company of
singers or singers in companies.'

'A fine definition, certainly, but one narrow in conception.
What say you, Master Boyce?'

'Music, sir, may be divided into two parts.' He put his hands upward to illustrate his argument. 'The first part is called elementary or rudimentary, teaching to know the quality and quantity of notes, and everything else belonging to songs.' He put one of his palms flat down upon his desk, and laughed. 'The second may be called syntactical, poetical, or effective, treating of sounds, concords and discords, and generally of everything . . .' His other hand hovered still in the air.

'Everything?'

'Of everything serving for the formal and apt setting together of parts, for producing of harmony either upon a ground or upon a voluntary.'

'And you, Master Harcombe, what say you to this?'

Then Timothy began to speak, the words coming from he knew not where and going he knew not whither. 'Musicke, my master, is a knowledge of tuning, which consists in sound and song. Otherwise known as the world's music, because of the motion which the celestial orbs do make, or human musick which our selves practise.'

This said, Mr Byrd stood by the casement and elaborated upon the great theme. 'As for the first,' said he, 'it is commonly known that the motion of the world is not without sound. How can this wheeling frame of the world whirl about with a dumb and silent motion? And from this turning of the heavens there cannot be removed a certain order or grace: thus the world's music is truly an harmony, caused by the motion of the stars and the violence of the spheres. As for the second, human musique is the concordance of diverse elements in one compound by which the spiritual nature is joined with the body. What other power can solder and glue that spiritual strength, which is endued with an intellect, to a mortal and earthly frame? Only that musicke which every man that descends into himself finds in himself.' He took up his lute and seemed about to play upon it, but then bethought himself of his lesson. 'And of human musick we may distinguish these kinds: organic music, harmonic music, inspective music, mensural music and plain music. Do you understand now what I have said to you before? He is truly to be called a musitian who has the faculty of reason, not he who has only the fashion of singing. All the ancient musicians ground their practice upon speculation, for these were the great musicke masters, and since their death the knowledge of the art is decayed with a more slight or superficial understanding come instead. In these days, as has been our manner in many other affairs, we rush to do things blindly like the mouse in the fable: such are the men who think they know enough already, when they can scarce sing their parts with the words. All their arrows come from one quiver, yet still they miss the mark. But this is the world, my masters. I take as little account of the ignorant as the moon does of the barking of a dog.' So did William Byrd begin his lesson, an old man, the father of English music, on this fifteenth day of April in the year of the reign of our sovereign lord James, by the grace of God king and defender of the faith, re 1608. Sixteen hundred and eight. The spheres revolve, making their own musique, as Mr Byrd looks upon the bright faces of his scholars and continues with his discourse.

'I must instruct you in the art of musick, therefore, and in all those moods, ligatures, pricks of division and alteration, augmentations, diminutions, and proportions which it is fit you should know. So you will learn to divide your skill: into sober and slow-timed notes for church tunes or into full and solemn musick for descant. For if in allegory musick has been accounted divine, therefore it cannot be more naturally employed than when it is conversant about heaven. And then again you must turn your skill upon more airy and soft pleasing sounds, as in your madrigals or fa'la's of five or six parts; from there it is but a short way to go into light and effeminate musicke, such as pleasant amorous songs or sarabands.' Hereupon Mr Byrde did tread a light measure, and whirled about in a perfect circle once. 'If you have a grave matter you must apply a grave kind of music to it, if a merry subject you must render your musicke also merry. So that when you would express any word signifying hardness, cruelty, bitterness, and other such like, make the harmony like unto it – that is, somewhat harsh and hard but yet so it offend not. When any of your words shall express complaint, dolour, repentance, sighs, tears, and such like, let your own harmony be sad and doleful. Now if your subject be light, you must cause your musicke to go in motions which carry with them a celerity or quickness of time, as minims, crotchets and quavers; if it be lamentable, the note must go in low and heavy motions as semibreves, breves, and such like. Also when you would express sighs you may use the crotchet or minim rest at most, but longer than a minim rest you may not employ, because it will rather seem a breath taken than a sigh –' Here he broke off and gazed out of the casement window. 'It is no marvel,' said he, 'to watch a snail after a rain to creep out of his shell and wander all about, seeking the moisture. Do you under-stand me, Master Harcombe?'

Timothy could not puzzle out this conceit, and shook his head. 'Is it a comparison?' he asked his master.

'Yes, my addle-pate.'

'Then it is a dark one,' he murmured. 'Not a plain one, sir.'

William Byrd laughed at this. 'Then in plain terms, I see that you three scholars are wearied with your studies within. Why should we not take opportunity of this fair morning and snatch a mouthful of the wholesome air?'

They gladly assented to this, and Mr Byrd led them out of the chamber into the gardens beneath; he could descend the winding stone stairway only with slow and hesitant steps, so great his age now was, while the three youths followed him with proper reverence: he being *Britannicae Musicae parens.* When they came out into the light he looked up at the sky (or, as it were, the heavens) as if aspiring to go there at last, but then with a laugh took the arms of the two scholars who walked slowly on either side of him. 'Observe,' he said, 'the fields and grasses yonder, arrayed in such beauty, and fashioning a gentle curve to the horizon. You see how the land does rise and fall, as a pilgrim will bow down in adoration? It is the line of England. And you must remember this in all your studies: we were not made for our selves, but to do good to our country.' They walked on among the green, the breeze gently breathing upon the beds of wholesome pot-herbs and the knots of sweet-smelling flowers, and all the while making a whispering noise among the tender leaves. 'The scent delights with refreshing,' Mr Byrd continued as they came into an arbour where were arrayed little chairs carved out of the trees. 'Like music it is ever fresh and ever renewed. And now that I have begun upon this note, why do we not continue our lesson in this shady and secluded place? Do you hear those birds above us, who in more natural or piece-meal sort do imitate our singing? They possess wildness without artificiality, yet in our own musick for voices we must follow more closely the observances of reason and authority. Thus if you make a ditty in the grave style it must be comprehended under the name of a motet: this kind of all others requires most art, for it moves and causes most strange effects in the hearer. This music being the chiefest for art is notwithstanding little esteemed (a lamentable case) and, in this present age of the world, is in small request with the greatest number of those who most seem to favour musique. So much for motets, under which I comprehend all grave and sober sound.'

Mr Byrd gazed at the faces of his young scholars and fetched a sigh from his breast. English faces, was his thought, and how long must it be before I leave them for ever? The pain of death does not perplex me, only that it be an everlasting farewell to humane beings such as these I see before me. Well, well, there is music in me yet: the almond tree bears most fruit when it is old. 'Of light musicke,' he continued, 'the best kind of it is termed madrigal, a word for etymology of which I can give no reason; yet usage shows that it is a kind of musicke made upon songs and sonnets such as many poets of our time have excelled in. It is next unto the motet the most artificial and, to men of understanding, therefore the most delightful. If you will compose in this kind, my young masters, you must display an amorous humour, for in no composition shall you prove admirable except you put on and possess yourself wholly with that vein wherein you compose: the thrush never sings with the nightingale. In your madrigal, therefore, you must be wavering like the wind, sometimes wanton, sometimes drooping, sometimes grave and steady, or erewhile effeminate, for the more variety you show the better shall you please. In this kind of musicke our age excels. The second degree of gravity in this light music is given to canzonets, that is little short songs wherein art can be shown being made in strains with every one repeated except the middle. The last degree of gravity, if it have any at all, is given to the villanella or country song which is made only for the ditty's sake. They and all other kinds of light musick, saving the madrigal, are by a general name called airs. Not like the airs we breathe now on this bright morning, but of a more rational sort.'

He halted in his lesson again, driving strange thoughts along the thoroughfare of his mind such as these that follow. At the moment of my death will I comprehend the musique of the spheres at last, which all my life I have strained to hear? Will I be taken up into the empyrean, of which I have sought the traces within the muddy vesture of this earth? If so I sit upon thorns until I be gone, gone into that region of harmony whence all our musique derives. I may lose these humane faces and these humane voices, but I shall look upon another Face and hear another Voice; and all my airs will be at last completed. Yet perhaps I earnestly aspire to such things since I am come to my end: these young scholars are at their beginning and eagerly seek their own music. How much of that will be my own in imitation (as I did imitate the great masters), how much sweetly set forth as the natural air of their own country, and how much the spark of some divine original? They know not now, but in time they will learn that all true music springs from origins much greater than themselves. That is the meaning of my death, as I suppose, to return to that source from which all my music flows.

'The principal kind of musick which is made without a ditty,' he continued in a moment, 'is the fantasie: that is, when a musitian takes a point and wrests or turns it as he likes, making either much or little of it according as shall seem best in his own conceit. In this more art may be shown than in any other musicke, because the composer is tied to nothing but that he may add, diminish and alter at his pleasure. This kind will also bear any allowances whatsoever tolerable in other musick, except changing the air and leaving the key, which in fantasy may never be suffered. The next in gravity to this is called a pavan, a kind of staid musique ordained for dancing, and most commonly made of three strains whereof every strain is played or sung twice – a strain, by the bye, you may make to contain twelve or sixteen semibreves, as you please, yet fewer than eight I have not seen in any pavan. After every pavan we usually set a galliard, causing it to go by a measure which the learned called *trochaieam rationem*, consisting of a long and a short stroke successively.' He stopped short and, taking his eyes away from their inward vision, looked around him. 'I see, Master Harcombe, that you are in a perplexed state with my strokes and semibreves and such like. You look as if you will never leave breaking your brains until you puzzle out my meaning. No matter. We will return to our theme another morning, when once more we are secluded within. There it will become our *chamber music*.' He smiled at this conceit as he rose from his wooden seat, and in slow procession they made their way out of the shady arbour.

'This garden,' said he as they walked back between the fair and choice flowers, 'makes me think of our English masters, whose music, like these sweet violets and fragrant primroses, is laid out for our content. The curving lines of those lawns and meadows yonder is like their own lineage – that is, Farefax, Taverner, Shepherd, Mudy, White, Persons, and, pre-eminent in all, my old master Mr Tallis. All of them admired musicians, famous for their work. The fault of White,' said he, bending low to pick up a fallen twig, 'was only in pricking, for breaking a note in division without looking to the rest of the parts, but this is by the way. All of them conceived their best path lay through the old music, that is the musicke of the country before this time. And remember this, that it was in England we brought to completion the art of the virginal. So you also ought to imitate those who have been observers of true precepts, join your selves to them and embrace them as good masters. Even as a picture painted with diverse colours does more delight the eye to behold than if it were done but with one colour alone, so in our English music we have such a variety of diligent and artificial compositions as you may profit by.' He passed a hand over his withered face. 'I am an old man now, but once, as young and fresh as you, I had a fine spirit and would rather choose to make a whole new song than to correct one which was already made. I believe that now to have been my errant wit. Yet I knew how to sing a part of a song perfectly: supper being ended, and the music books according to custom being brought to the table, my mother was wont to present me with a part and request me to sing to the company. To this I gladly assented, though in my enthusiasm I was as likely to invent new melodies as to keep to my book.' The scholars laughed at this. 'But you must not be too ready to condemn me, my young masters, seeing it was the general fault of the time: in those days I have heard him highly commended who could upon a plain song sing hard proportions, harsh allowances and even country dances. Indeed he who could bring in the greatest profusion of them was counted the jolliest fellow.'

He halted both in his step and in his discourse, as if the weight of past time had for that moment fallen down upon him. 'Yet I was taken from this easy course by proper studies, for it was then that I came upon my esteemed master, Mr Tallis. He, seeing me so toward and willing to learn, ever had me in his company. Because he continually carried a plainsong book in his pocket, he caused me to do the like; and so, if we were walking in the fields or studying together in his chamber, he would sing the plainsong and cause me to sing the descant. It is the same chamber as we use now, for it is the same Chapel Royal as then.' He broke off again and looked up at the casement, seeing not the open window so much as his vision of things before. 'When I sang not to his contentment,' he continued, recovering himself, 'Mr Tallis would show me wherein I had erred. "What," he would say, "can a composer be without descant? Do you admire those ignorant asses who take it upon them to lead others, none being more blind than themselves?" Mr Tallis had a tongue as sharp as his wits. "Those malicious caterpillars," he added, "who live upon the pains of other men?" So I thought it best to imitate him (though I was no caterpillar), and every lesson which I made was a counterfeit of his; at all times and on every occasion I would foist in some of his points, which I had as perfectly in my head as my paternoster. And, because my master did not dislike that course, I continued still therein. Thus did I begin the world. Mr Tallis also caused me so diligently to apply my prick-song book that, in a manner, I did no other but sing practices: to skip from one key to another, from flat to sharp, from sharp to flat, from any one place in the scale to another. There was no song so hard but I would venture upon it, no mood nor proportion so strange that I would not go through and sing perfectly before I left it.' He plucked a leaf from an ancient oak and observed it in the palm of his hand. 'My voice is quite gone now,' he said. 'I am like to an old crow still wheeling around the sky. But the spirit of music is still strong within me. The spirit is not broken, no, nor yet even touched by time. Remember the herb basil, which the more it is crushed the sooner it springs forth, or the poppy which flourishes when it is trodden with the feet. But I will break off here and release you to the bright morning. Good day, young masters, good day.'

When Mr Byrd had left them, they fell to talking among themselves. 'Not an old crow but an old swan,' observed Master Goodfellow as he watched him walk slowly to his apartment next the Chapel Royal. 'Even to see him is to think of times long gone. He was well settled in the cathedral church of Lincoln some fifty years before this, and was even then a renowned musitian. For, as he told us, he had been raised under Tallis.'

Master Boyce continued in the same vein of praise. 'I have his works by heart, all his psalms, his sacred chants and songs. He was as skilled in the sonnets and pastorals as he was in the songs of sadness and pietie. But wherefore do I say "was"? "Is", not "was". The exercise and love of his art have exceedingly increased in these latter years, and his labours in musique are more esteemed and delighted than ever they were before. He still writes songs of sundry natures' – he broke off to watch Mr Byrd, with his head bowed, entering through the gate of his little house – 'and yet it is in sacred musicke that he excells.'

'I have heard,' Master Harcombe said, 'that he is still of the old faith.'

'Yes. He has been a Popish recusant and no doubt still professes that belief in the quietness of his own soul. Yet he was called into the service of Elizabeth, and is still a gentleman of the King Majesty's chapel. For of course he is still the father of English musicke: no faith can deny that.'

Master Goodfellow had been turning about a tree, whistling merrily as he did so, and now he broke in with, 'Have you heard his song of pietie, "Why Do I Use My Paper, Ink and Pen?"? It is filled with a mighty musical fury, which has caused him to show much diversity in small bounds.'

'True,' Master Boyce replied, 'but he was moved to do so by the words of his text. Does he not continually tell us that words have their own secret power, to reflect upon which will bring our notes to their highest virtue?'

But the admiration of Master Goodfellow was not to be breached. 'I thought good just yesterday to set down a fugue by Mr Byrd, which, for difficulty of composition, is not inferior to any which I have seen. It is both made by rising and falling, and likewise the point is reverted note for note: how hard this is to perform upon a plain song, none can perfectly know but he who has tried to do the like.'

'There was a time,' Master Boyce returned, 'when he and Tallis made a contention upon the plain song of Miserere, which caused them to strive and to surmount one another, each making the other censure of that which he had done.'

'Which contention of theirs,' Master Goodfellow recalled, 'without malice, envy or backbiting, but by great labour, study and pains, caused them both to be excellent in that kind and to win such a name, and gain such credit, as will never perish so long as musicke endures.'

So long as music endures: Timothy Harcombe then saw time as musicke. And so, he thought, Mr Byrd will never die. But now his two companions took him by the arm, and together they walked through the fields singing in unison.

> 'A bird I have that sings so well
>   None like to him their tunes can raise,
> All other birds he doth excell,
>   And of all birds most worthy praise.
>
> 'This is my Byrd of endless fame
>   Whose music sweet, whose pleasant sound,
> Whose worthy praise, whose renowned name,
>   Do from the earth to heaven rebound.'

'And today,' Mr Byrd announced to them as he entered that next morning, 'today we will speak of the artifice of composition, without which nothing can properly be done: the great music masters have given us much to imitate in this guise, for how can a workman work who has had no pattern to instruct him? You may rob, or you may unwillingly fall into the same chords: it is no matter.' He seemed in disturbed sort, and hushed them as they muttered among themselves at this beginning of the day. 'I pray you,' he said, 'be silent now. I must have deliberation, and quietness also, else I shall never instruct you in any thing.'

'You shall rather think us stones,' replied Master Good-fellow, 'than men.'

He laughed at this. 'I see that you live in a good opinion of yourself. Yet you must not be stones but scholars still. And look upon this.' He took out from his carven desk a scroll, so old and parched that it made a cracking sound as he unrolled it. 'Here,' said he, 'is the evidence of old time which I lately discoursed upon. Of a time even before I was a boy.' They looked at one another, but dared not laugh. 'There were then four manners of pricking in the art of composition: one all black which they termed "black full", another which we use now which they called "black void", the third all red which they called "red full", and the fourth red as ours is black which they called "red void". You may see it clearly upon this antique paper.' He held out the parchment towards them. 'That order of pricking is quite out of use now, and indeed the red itself is gone almost out of memory so that few know what it means. As for the forms of notes, there were within these last two hundred years but four known or used by the musytions: those were the long, brief, semi-brief and minim. The minim they esteemed the least or shortest note singable, and therefore indivisible; its invention they ascribed to a certain priest (who he was I know not) in Navarre. But who invented the crotchet, quaver and semi-quaver is uncertain. Are you taking note of this, Master Boyce, or has it all gone through your head like the wind in a cave?'

'No, sir. I am reflecting upon it.'

'Good, good. Then I may quiz you still. Follow me right closely with your answers now. I shall be the pavane, and you the galliard. What is a key?'

'A key is a thing, sir, compacted of a letter and a voice. And, like as a key opens a door, so does the key open the song.'

'How many keys are there?'

'Keys are twenty-two in number, and are comprehended in a three-fold order.'

'And how many intervals may there be?'

'The usual intervals are nine – a semitone, a semiditone, a ditone, a diatebaron, a diapente, a semitone diapente, a tonus diapente and a diapason.'

'Good. That is good, Master Boyce. I see that you have thoroughly learnt all that I have attempted to instill into you.' The boy smiled in satisfaction with himself, while his two companions gave a look at one another. 'And remember also that every key has a peculiar air proper to itself: if you go into some other than that wherein you began, you change the air of the song. Which is to say that you wrest a thing out of its nature, as making the ass leap upon his master or the spaniel bear the load. The perfect knowledge of these proper airs was once in such estimation among the learned as therein they placed the perfection of musicke. Yet though the air of every key be different one from the other, some prefer by a wonder of nature to be joined to others like the lamb and the dove. Or like lovers who intertwine themselves –' Master Goodfellow snorted at this and Mr Byrd broke off for a moment. 'I see, sir, that you are in sprightly mood today. So now you may be the galliard to my pavanne, and come up behind me. Pray, sir, what is the tone?'

'A tone is a rule judging the song in the end. Or . . .'

He stumbled for a moment, while Mr Byrd gazed at him. 'Or?'

'Or it is a knowledge of the beginning, middle and end of every song, showing the rising and falling of it.'

'Rising and falling, like to the curve of the English landskips which are even now coming into the fashion. But this is by the way.' He smiled at the boy. 'Well learned by rote, my good scholar. Pretty soon we will see how you fashion this in your practice. Tell me now, Master Harcombe, what is a figure?'

'A figure, sir, is a certain sign which represents a voice and silence. A voice because of the kinds of notes which are used, and silence because of the rests, which are of equal value with the notes and are measured with artificial silence. Such for instance is the semi-brief, which is a figure round in the form of an egg. Or a large, whose length is three times as much as its breadth and has on the part towards your right hand a small tail.' He did not understand how he knew the truth of this, for the words had shot out of him like pebbles from a sling.

'All this, young masters, is excellently well said, leaving us only with the true meaning of notes which we will all chant and not speak. You remember the verse, for you indited it within the month, so each of you take turns severally to sing it.'

And so Master Harcombe began:

> 'To attain the skill of music's art
> Learn gamut up and down by heart,
> Thereby to learn your rules and spaces,
> Notes' names are known, knowing their places.'

Then Master Boyce took it up with:

> 'No man can sing true at first sight
> Unless he names his notes aright;
> Which soon is learnt. If that your *Mi*
> You know, where e'er it be.'

To which Master Goodfellow answered:

> 'The first three notes above your *Mi*
> Are *fa, sol, la*, here you may see,
> The next three under *Mi* that fall,
> Them *la, sol, fa*, you ought to call.'

Mr Byrd clapped his hands at this. 'I pray you now, my good boys, sing no more but take your papers and write me your music.' He gave to each one of them a slip or note. 'Try now to make two parts upon the plainsong which you see before you. The closer the parts the better the harmony, as you know, so do not put them too far asunder or else your harmony will vanish. Take heed of scattering your parts, also, for it makes your music seem wild.'

He moved to the corner of the chamber and picked up the lute which was lying there upon the old cloak. 'Do not be too hasty. Even as someone with a quick hand playing upon an instrument, showing in voluntary the agility of his fingers, will by the haste of his conveyance cloak many faults which if they were stood upon would mightily offend the ear – so do those musitians, because the faults are quickly overpassed, being in short notes, think them no faults.' He lay his fingers across the strings for a moment, and then put down the lute. 'Do not you do likewise. Instead remember all that I have taught you and in these ways you may make infinite variety, altering some note or driving it through others. Now fall to work.'

And so the three scholars bent over their desks, scarce taking their eyes from their papers except to raise them to the ceiling, while their master did pass away his time with sundry tossings and nods as he worked upon his own composition. Some times he wandered amongst them and looked upon their scratchings with 'I pray God it be good when it comes, for you have made it long enough' or 'You have the eye of the lynx, in spying the figure there.' They worked on until the heat of the sun filled their chamber and even the sounds of the singing birds were stilled. From the open casement they could hear only the calls of the wherry men upon the river and the faint noises of children in the open meadow. Then Mr Byrd tapped his hand upon his desk. 'Come now,' he said, 'the hours have passed. Pray let me see what you have accomplished.' So he began to study their compositions, roughly written though they were. 'Yes,' he said to Master Boyce, who was ever the first to come forward with his copy. 'You see here, for seeking to repeat the plain song, the musick is as altered in the air as if it were another song.' The boy blushed for shame and, when his master saw this, he relented a little. 'Yet these are good devisings here, and here, and easie to be understood. The first part is tolerable and good, as I say, but the ending is not so good; the end of your ninth note is a discord, but then upon another discord you have begun the tenth.' The scholar was about to speak, but Mr Byrd put a finger to his lips. 'I know that you are about to excuse the tenth note, in that it is in binding wise, but though it be bound it is in fetters of rusty iron and not in chains of gold. No ear hearing it but will at that first hearing loathe it. Come forward with your copy, Master Goodfellow.'

The second scholar approached his master and gave him his papers, which Mr Byrd did examine at one glance. 'You have set it in such a key,' said he, 'as no man would have done, except it had been to have played it in the organs with a quire of singing men.' He went on then, more gently. 'First of all in the second note is taken a discord for the first part of the note, and not in the best manner nor in binding. The like fault is in the fifth note and, as for the two notes before the close, the end of the first is a discord to the ground and the beginning of the next likewise a discord. You are like to a tailor with a pair of left-handed shears.' Then he called forward Master Harcombe, to whom he addressed these words: 'In the seventh bar your counter and tenor come into a unison, whereas it is an easy matter to put in three several parts between your counter and your treble. Would you put a patch of fustian in a damask coat? Then again, here in the eighth bar your tenor and base go into a unison without any necessity. Lastly your close in the treble part is so stale that it is almost worm eaten.' He smiled at the boy, who seemed in doleful sort. 'But it is not quite out of joint, and you will improve with time. Time healeth all things, Master Harcombe, even the understanding. Be attentive to me now, and I will try to make four parts out of my own invention.'

So the three scholars observed him as he worked closely and swiftly upon his own composition; and, as he worked, he threw out a commentary. 'Some musicians,' he said, 'make no account of keeping their key, but follow only that vein of wresting in much matter within small bounds; seeking to show skilfulness in following of points, they miss the mark whereat every good musician should shoot, which is to show cunning with delightfulness and pleasure.' He worked on quickly, pricking in his notes, his face bent so close to the paper that there was scarce room for him to breathe. 'It is the same musicians,' he continued, looking up suddenly at his scholars, 'who are content to be wranglers and take occasion to backbite.' He finished one page and then hitched up his sleeve the better to begin again upon a fresh sheet. 'They do in huggermugger, or even openly, calumniate that which either they do not understand or maliciously wrest to their own sense. But, as Augustine said by one who had spoken evil of him, they shall find that I have a tongue also. He snarls at one who will bite again. Now let me see.' He stopped for the moment and gazed at the page he had worked upon, letting the tip of his tongue show. 'Must every part maintain that point wherewith it did begin, not touching that of other parts? I think not. Come forward, my masters, and be my critics also.' They willingly left their desks and clustered around him, like so many young fruit upon an old vine. 'It is the fugue of the plain song, as you may see, and the point will excuse the sudden harshness, will it not?' They all nodded. 'And now to the close.' He held down the sheet with one hand and, with the other, filled the rules with his slender strokes; and, to Timothy, the curving of the notes as he indited them was like a line of moving light. The line of beauty, serpentine. 'Sudden closes,' said he as he worked on, casting up a bright glance at his three scholars, 'belong properly to light music such as madrigals, canzonets, pavans and galliards, wherein a semi-breve will be enough to cadence upon. But as for the motets, and for other grave musicke, you must come with more deliberation in bindings and in longer notes towards the close. Just as I am doing now. And, there, it is finished.'

So saying he ended with a flourish and laid his hands flat down upon the sheets. 'I am too ancient to descant,' said he, 'and indeed it is no more to the taste of our time than it is to my own age and infirmity. But my spirit is not so weak that I cannot give voice to music of my own devising. You must not think,' he added, after gathering up his sheets and beginning to hum a little to himself, 'that he who can artificially put three or four or more parts together may at his ease sing one part upon a ground without great study, for singing ex- tempore upon a plain song is indeed a piece of cunning. Yet here, you see, we have our memory all before us.' He waved the sheets in front of them. 'Indeed, is this not a chamber of memory wherein we sit and study?' Then, gazing around this room and taking stock of all that it contained, he began to sing in his aged voice; yet it was still pretty firm, and had as much sweetness as if he were once more the tender youth who walked among the fields. He pointed out those parts to the others, where they were to join in with their own voices, following the notes as they did so, and they sang on together until the end.

Mr Byrd could not help himself, but laughed at the conclu- sion to their labours. 'I heard you striving to bring in the point soonest,' he explained, 'and to make the hardest propor- tions. You sing as if you had but lately come from a barber's shop, or had been walking among fiddlers all the days of your lives. Well, it is no great matter. The best song that ever was made is seldom or never well performed at the first singing or playing. Besides a song that is well and artificially made cannot be well perceived or understood at the first hearing, no more than a book at its first reading, but the oftener you shall hear it the better cause of liking it you will discover.

Indeed commonly that song is best esteemed with which our ears are most acquainted, be it ever so harshly welcomed upon its first arrival into this world. Does an author signify his meaning for the idle or incurious? No, but it is stored up in time for those who approach it with care and patience.'

He seemed elevated by his recent labours, for at this moment he took up the treble-viol, tuned its six strings, and then moved to the casement window. Looking out upon the meadows and the few humane beings who wandered there, he began to play a slow, sweet air which so entered Timothy's breast that he was as like to weep as to do any thing. But Mr Byrd was ever the musitian, endeavouring to compose the rules of his art even as he practised it. 'If there be an odd note at the beginning of a tune,' he explained, 'then you strike it by drawing the bow backwards; if there be no odd note, then your first note is struck with the bow put forward. Like so.' He broke off again, but continued gazing out of the window at the world. 'When you come to practise upon the instrument, let the third, fifth and sixth be your usual chords: they are the sweetest, and in your musick you must seek to please the ear as much as to show cunning. Such is the line of beauty, as it rises and falls in our English music.' These last words seemed to halt him in his discourse as if in the very phrase, *English music*, he heard the strains of his own destiny.

'But now,' said he in more cheerful sort, 'what is most excellent for recreation after our solemnities? What makes the body active and strong, as well as graceful in deportment?'

The three scholars knew of what he spoke, for their master came from a dancing generation, as it is still termed. '*Orchestrice!*' called out Master Boyce.

'We will have none of your Greeks here,' replied Mr Byrd. 'It is known by us as our good English dance.'

'"All in a Garden Green",' cried Master Harcombe.

'"Blue Cap",' responded Master Goodfellow.

'"Hit and Miss",' echoed Master Boyce. And in airy mood, now that their serious studies were done, they set out in competition with one another, endeavouring to recall to their mind all the dances of their own day and of their master's time.

'"I Loved Thee Once, I Love Thee No More".'

'"Lady, Lie Near Me".'

'"Under and Over".'

'"If All the World Were Paper".'

'"New New Nothing".'

'"Touch and Take".'

'"Have at Thy Coat, Old Woman".'

'"Saturday Night and Sunday Morn".'

'"Punk's Delight".'

And so they carried on, rounding on one another with these English names betokening sport and merriment: 'Jog On'; 'Maid Peeped Out of the Window'; 'Heart's Ease'; 'Parson's Farewell'; 'Grimstock'; 'Chirping of the Lark'; 'An Old Man is a Bed Full of Bones'; 'Lull Me Beyond Thee'; 'Dissembling Love'; 'Drive the Cold Winter Away'.

Mr Byrd was like to weep as he heard all the dances of his youthfulness, when England was so green and so merry. 'Do you know "Jack Pudding",' he called out to them, 'which proceeds long ways for as many as will?' He seemed moved by his enthusiasm as he recalled those ancient steps. 'Wherein we go about each other, not turning our faces, and then again? Come. I will show it you.' So he performed the steps, until with much practice his three scholars had got them by heart. Now, as the evening came upon them and chased the shadows into their chamber, they all danced together gravely, turning about and turning about again. So leave them dancing, these scholars of musick, and sing in cheerful voice:

'Fare well I say fare well: fare well and here I end:
Fare well melodious Byrde: fare well sweet musicke's friend.'

ELEVEN

THE MUSIC WAS STILL RESOUNDING in the room when I awoke, but I did not want to open my eyes; I was reluctant to leave that world which I had inhabited for a moment. Only a moment had passed, because I could still hear Mr Armitage reciting some words as he played the piano, and I could still feel the late afternoon sun upon my face. It was the sun of the present world, however, and not that glorious image which William Byrd had once seen. I had returned. This was my first dream since I left London; I was not afraid, but the sudden visitation after so many years left me restless and uneasy. It was as if part of my old life were once again stirring within me. I had not told my grandparents about my dreams since I associated them with my father, and with the city itself; now my connection to that time was being revived. But to what purpose?

My period at school was in any case coming to an end. And I was in my seventeenth year when, on the last day of the last term, I walked out through the gates with Edward Campion. We had said nothing about this imminent parting for the simple reason that it seemed no parting at all; we both assumed that we would carry on meeting and talking in the customary way. I believe now that there can be no real sense of loss or separation without the recognition of death; we were too young to consider any such eventuality, and simply moved on with our lives into some indefinite but illimitable future. Even if I had felt any sadness about leaving the school I had attended for the last few years, I would have taken care not to reveal it to him. So we walked that day, as usual, to a tea-shop on the high street; we would sit here for hours, discussing all those ideas and feelings which we were experiencing for the first time. Edward liked the place – principally, I suspect, because the waitress knew his family and was quite accustomed to the nervous spasmodic movements about which, in these later adolescent years, he had become far more self-conscious. He was now both more vulnerable and more defiant; he felt keenly the effects of his isolation and his difference, while at the same time he pretended almost to revel in them. His pride was as fierce as his anxiety and he had become increasingly suspicious, even resentful, of other people – except me. I believe that he recognized some strangeness, some difference, within me as well; certainly it was only in my company that he preserved the eagerness he had displayed as a boy. It did not bode well for his adult life, but that was some years away in the open future.

'I've been reading a very good book,' he said as we sat in the tea-shop on this last day. '*The Secrets of the Fallen World.* Do you know it?' I shook my head. Edward had become interested in philosophy, just as I had discovered music, and now his conversations often concerned various abstruse or metaphysical questions – abstract matters, perhaps, yet somehow I knew that they were directly related to his own precarious and embattled life. 'You see, Tim, we live in time. But in the fallen world time simply recurs. The same events or situations happen again and again. The same people are born from generation to generation. The years and the centuries are part of a cycle. No wonder when you understand the pattern, you begin to feel a sense of futility or despair. You don't even have to understand it to feel its effects. Doesn't that make sense, Tim?' He looked across the table at me with his large, bright eyes; he sounded so intense, so enthusiastic, that he might have been proclaiming the secret of his own life.

'Yes,' I replied. 'Yes. It makes sense.'

'But there's a way out. Let me read it to you.' With difficulty he leaned down, took a book from his satchel, and then eagerly scanned the pages for the section he wanted to find. 'Here it is. "The divine vision is a vision of the eternal present, or the release from the cyclical nature of time in the fallen world. It can be reached only through an act of the imagination, although it resembles the unconscious experience of the child or of lovers . . ."' Edward lowered his voice for a moment here, and seemed to have omitted a passage. '"Only through that act of imagination can we see the images of eternity in the recurrent forms of this world. It is to see identity persisting through changes, to see the archetypal form dwelling in substance. That is why we are moved by the features of an ancient landscape, because it provides the best possible approximation to that unchanging identity which is the eternal present. Past acts or past traditions are not necessarily lost in time, therefore, because they can be recreated in the imagination; not relived as part of the endless cycle of the generations but restored in their absolute and unchanging essence. Thus do they become part of that eternal present through which the imagination lives. Similarly the evidence of past civilizations, of past lives, can be renewed and enter that state of permanent reality which the imagination bestows upon it."' Edward stopped reading and, staring silently at the page for a moment, put down the book. 'Do you agree with that, Tim?'

'I think so.' I had scarcely been listening to the words, and I realize now that they were very much like other philosophical analyses in the Twenties. I had been staring out of the window at the main street of Upper Harford, recognizing certain people as they passed, thinking of nothing in particular but invaded by a vague sensation of disquiet.

He noticed my inattention and perhaps felt rebuffed. 'I suppose,' he said, after a few moments' silence, 'that you'll be going back to London now. Now that you've finished school.' In truth the idea had not really occurred to me; my immediate future was so vague that I had been afraid to impose any definite pattern upon it. Then there would have been a possibility of failure. 'You don't really need this place, do you?' Edward said this as calmly as he could, but he looked away as he spoke.

I knew what he really meant, and I could not bring myself to inflict any further pain upon him. 'I don't know,' I replied. 'I was thinking of getting a job here.'

'That's a good idea,' he said. 'Why not?' Some of his animation seemed to have returned. 'We could work together during the holidays.' He was not leaving school as I was; he had elected to stay and apply for a university course in philosophy. 'We could get a summer job in the post office,' he was saying now. 'My dad could arrange it.' But even as he spoke I knew that his first intuition had been the right one: I would have to return to London. As I stared out of the window, I realized that my time in this place had come to an end; now that my schooldays were over, I no longer belonged here. I had always been a stranger and, if I stayed, I would become a stranger to myself as well.

I returned home in a state of miserable indecision. I could not remain in Upper Harford but I was dismayed that, despite my promise, I would be leaving behind my friend – Edward would then truly be alone, and I doubted if all the words in all the books he read would help him. As I walked up the white lane towards the farmhouse, I kicked the dust beneath my feet and it rose around me in billows; I seemed to myself like some wicked being, appearing out of the smoke to wreak havoc on the innocent. My grandfather was working in the garden, which was his custom in the evenings of early summer, while my grandmother was preparing supper in the kitchen. Everything was exactly as it had been when I first arrived here and, in those intervening years, I had come to expect and even to need that order. My grandparents now seemed more cheerful and energetic, however, than at any time before; it was as if my presence in the house had rejuvenated them. They had not even been downcast by the death of our dog, Friday: we had buried him in the garden, with full ceremony, and a week later my grandfather had brought back a puppy of the same breed. We christened it Monday.

I opened the gate, and my grandfather put down the shovel

with which he had been clearing away some earth. 'Last day,' he said in a tone which was a curious mixture of sympathy and hopefulness.

'Yes. The last day.'

'Some people say that they're the best years of your life. But they're not. Nothing like. The best years are when you know what you're doing.'

'That's just it. I don't know.'

'But you do have time to find out.'

'Now don't you go worrying the boy.' My grandmother was hastening down the gravel path towards us. 'He must be upset enough as it is. It's not every day that he leaves school.'

'It was every day,' I replied. And then I smiled. 'Every day for the last three years.' I had a sudden feeling of elation for, if this was the end of something, it was also a beginning. No one yet knew how much I might achieve and, strange though it seems to recall it now, I had a vision of myself surrounded by music. I ran up to my room and then, taking Monday in my arms, I started dancing wildly around until I collapsed exhausted upon my bed. My schooldays were over.

We sat at the kitchen table that evening, as we always did, but my grandparents seemed unsettled; they wanted to discuss my future but were unable or unwilling to put the matter directly to me. 'I'm not sure what to do,' I admitted, breaking the silence at last, and then I added something I had been determined not to say. 'Edward wants me to work in the post office with him. Just for the summer.'

'Don't decide anything too quickly, Timothy.' My grandmother hesitated, and I knew well enough that she was torn between her desire that I should continue to live with them and her hopes for my future. 'You have to do something that is good for you. Something that helps you.' I realized then how difficult it would be for me to leave them.

'That's not the job for you,' my grandfather said, ignoring his wife's look of concern. 'You have great gifts. Don't waste them.'

I believed that at this point he was going to mention my father; I could not have endured that, but, fortunately, my grandmother forestalled him. 'I wonder,' she said, 'what your mother would have wanted for you. Is there something you can do with your music, for instance?'

'I want to ask dad's advice,' I replied.

They were silent for a moment, as my grandmother looked down at her hands, then at the ceiling, and then at her husband. 'That's a good idea,' she said. 'I never thought of that.'

My grandfather had started to clear away the plates, but now he turned to look at me. 'You know,' he said at last, 'he hasn't contacted us for three years. Not since his last visit.'

'That's not true! He's written letters to me, hasn't he?' In fact he sent me a card each Christmas, with a scrawled message to the effect that I should work hard and look after my grandparents. Of his own life and activities, he said nothing. 'He always remembers . . .' My voice trailed off.

'I suppose so.' He continued to look at me. 'But are you sure that he wants to see you?'

He said this so mildly, so without malice, that I felt obliged to answer in the same quiet tone. 'I expect so.'

'Why don't you write to him first? Before you pay a visit?'

And so I did: I explained to him that I had left school, and that I wanted his advice about the next stage of my life. He had written his address on the last Christmas card he had sent me; it was in west London, so I knew that he had moved some way from our old neighbourhood. What other changes might I expect to find? I waited for his reply with increasing impatience, but then, about a fortnight later, his letter came. It was a short one, but he made it clear that he would be happy to see me and that he would help me 'to the best of my ability'. I remember the phrase even now, so formal it seemed, but I was too excited by the prospect of my visit to be affected by any misgivings. I wrote to him again, giving the details of my arrival, and then spent the next few days anxiously anticipating my return to London.

Everything had changed now – the farmhouse, the fields, even the pine forest itself, seemed charged with my imminent departure. They had become at once more tenuous and yet more real than before; I knew that they would remain here after I had gone, and so for the first time they acquired an objective existence. But I might never see them again: even as I watched them, they were becoming evanescent memories. My impatience was mingled with something very like grief, therefore, when I thought of my grandparents. I had told them that I would return within the month, and that I had no intention of leaving them; I tried to believe this but, even as I expressed these comforting sentiments, I had the strangest sensation that I was going away from them for ever.

It was a dull and cloudy day when we arrived at the railway station outside Upper Harford and, in the diffuse grey light, they seemed older and more frail. I took my grandmother's arm as we waited for the train that would bear me away to London. I may have imagined it, but I believe that I felt her body shaking slightly; it was only a faint tremor but nevertheless it communicated itself to me, and made me more afraid for her than I had been since my arrival all those years before. Yet there was very little that could be said – very little to say – on this grey morning of my departure.

'Come back soon,' she called out as eventually I boarded the train. 'We'll miss you.'

'I won't be long,' I said. It was as if I were leaving for a morning or for an hour; but in truth the interval would be much greater than that.

I believe my grandfather suspected as much, because he came up to me as I leaned out of the window and put his hand against my cheek. 'Remember,' he said. 'Be true to yourself. And then you will be true to others.'

I watched them standing quietly together as the train pulled out of the station; the steam gathered all around them in clouds but, when it cleared for a moment, they were still gazing after me intently. I waved, and then they were gone.

I had not been in London since I had left with my father and grandfather; it had become unfamiliar, almost threatening, and as the train made its way through the suburbs to Paddington Station I could feel the tension rising within me. It was as if I were pushing my way, physically, through a crowd which might overwhelm me. I do not recall experiencing anything of this kind before—this sensation of millions of lives surrounding my own – but, when I last lived in the city, perhaps I possessed no real awareness of my own self. Now everything had changed, and it was with a newly awakened self-consciousness that I walked from the platform into the main concourse of the station.

Although my father had not bothered to give me any definite instructions, I knew in which direction I had to travel. The street in which he lived, Albion Lane, was close to the Portobello Road; so I purchased a twopenny ticket and took the underground train to Notting Hill Gate, where, with my street map in hand, I walked a little further north. This area, where Notting Hill becomes North Kensington, was quite new to me. I had really only known the melancholy and ancient streets of east London, but here the houses displayed white stucco rather than dark brick; they were larger, too, and the streets were much wider. I might have been walking among palaces, so grand they seemed, and I certainly never noticed the actual shabbiness and seediness to which much of this grandeur had been reduced – not until, that is, I found the decaying house in which my father lived. Albion Lane was a short thoroughfare running off the Portobello Road: now, in recollection, I see a row of mouldering white houses, with peeling pillars, patched balustrades and rusty iron railings. In my recollection, too, it is always the same grey and misty day, the dampness clinging to the very stones of the steps which led to the basement area where I would find my father. I glanced up at the house as I descended, and felt so strong a sense of melancholy and dilapidation that it was as if the building itself were somehow approaching its own death. I knocked loudly on the door of the flatlet, but it was only after some delay that my father came out.

'Hello,' he said very cheerfully, as if we had parted just the day before. 'Welcome back.'

He looked very different to me. He had not grown smaller or thinner, but it was as if the outline of his body did not quite match the outline which I had held in my memory. There were creases upon his forehead, too, where none had been before. We shook hands. It seemed the only thing to do. Then, as I crossed the threshold, I asked him where Gloria was. I had not been thinking of her at all, as far as I knew, and the question surprised me as much as my father.

'She doesn't live here. I mean that she doesn't live with me any more. She went away.'

'Where did she go?'

'I have no idea. She just went.' He grinned at me, and for a moment he seemed to be just as I remembered him; then a more preoccupied, anxious look settled upon his face once again. 'Well,' he said, looking away from me, 'this is it. This is home.' It was a small room cluttered with newspapers, dirty glasses, cups, discarded clothes – all of them scattered over the dusty carpet and furniture. I recognized the sofa on which my father used to sleep, in the old familiar days of Hackney Square, and the armchairs we used to place before the fire while listening to the wireless. But these were no longer familiar circumstances; my father's previous life had an order and purpose which were reflected in the neat arrangements of our lodgings, but here everything seemed to exist in a state of confusion. He sensed my reaction even as I glanced around the room. 'Not like Hackney Square, is it, Tim?'

'No.'

'But I've got electricity. I was one of the first to be connected up.'

'That's good.' There was little else to say. In any case all the misgivings and reproaches I had felt over the last three years were now reawakened as we stood uneasily with one another. 'Dad, why didn't you come and see me?'

'I can't. I couldn't, Timmy. I had so much to do.' He hesitated. 'No, that's not true. Just look around. I feel like I'm buried here. I can hardly move.'

He had never spoken so openly to me before and, as he stood beside me, I realized the state to which he had been reduced. 'But you look all right,' I said, trying to dispel this sudden mood of hopelessness, 'you look fine.'

'Oh, there's nothing *wrong* with me.' He was trying to recover his self-possession. 'But I am getting older, Tim. And some people lose hope, you know. Circumstances change, and some people just burrow away and hide. Some people can't deal with life.' His mood had lightened as he spoke, and now he laughed out loud. 'Look how much you've grown,' he said. He tried to place his hand on my head, just as he used to do during the meetings in the old hall, but he pretended not to be able to reach it. 'Look how tall you are. We could wear the same clothes.'

For some reason the idea horrified me, but I was determined not to show it. 'As you say, dad, circumstances change.'

'Come on.' His good spirits seemed to be reviving all the time. 'Why are you so gloomy? Brighten up. You've even got your own bedroom.' In fact it was no more than a small space off the main room, with a bed in it. I suspected that it was where my father usually slept but, when I asked him about this, he shook his head. 'I'm going to be on that,' he said, pointing towards the sofa. 'Just like the old days.'

And that evening it was indeed as if we had been reunited in the old spirit; I was quite happy once again to listen to his stories and to lose myself in his exuberance. He did not mention Gloria, nor did he refer to the conditions of his present life, but instead revived all the subjects we used to discuss with one another. He seemed to revel in memories of the past, too, but he also took a curious pleasure in detailing the changes in the area we had once known so well. 'The picture-palace in Kingsland Road has been extended,' he was saying. 'Do you remember the old place?' I remembered it very well; I had once seen *Great Expectations* with him there. 'It's gone over to sound.'

'What about the others?'

'The other picture-houses?'

'No. The others. Our friends. Stanley Clay. And Matthew. And Margaret. How's Margaret?'

'The truth is, Tim, I haven't seen any of them for years.' He gave me a hesitant and almost timid glance. 'I just lost contact. You know how it is.' I knew very well, because he had also 'lost contact' with me, but I said nothing. 'I think,' he added, suddenly embarrassed by what he had said, 'that I'll get myself a little drink. Anything for you?' I shook my head. I did not remember him drinking before, but it was only another change to put beside all the others. He came back with a half-empty bottle of whisky and began pouring some into a tumbler. 'You know,' he went on, as if nothing had been said, 'I don't think our old friends will ever forget us.'

'But you've forgotten them, dad.'

'Do you have to? Do you have to go over and over the past?' I was under the impression that this was precisely what he had been doing, but I was too surprised by his sudden flash of anger to reply. 'Take some advice, Tim. Never look back. Look ahead. That's what I've been doing.' He started pouring more whisky into his glass, although it already seemed full enough to me. 'I'm carrying on with my work, as you know.' In fact I had no idea what he was doing, since this was the first reference he had made to his present life. 'I don't have the meetings any more. Not without you . . .' He hesitated. 'Without you they wouldn't be the same, would they? But I can do the planets for people. And the tarot. I'm very good with the cards. Then of course there's the Ouija board. That's all the craze now, Tim.'

In the days of Hackney Square he had never mentioned such things: indeed I believe he would have dismissed astrology or the tarot as of no account beside his own activities. And now, in that confession of weakness or of failure, I could suddenly see him from the outside. I saw him as others must surely have seen him: growing older in this Notting Hill flatlet, reduced to telling fortunes. 'Of course,' he was saying, 'I tidy up the place for my clients. They always come in the evening, you see, which leaves my days free. Liberty Hall, really.' I knew as I looked at him that those days were empty ones.

'I would like to see Margaret again, dad.' I wanted to go back to the old days and rid myself of the image which I had suddenly conceived of him. 'I never thanked her for looking after me. You remember the time.'

'Didn't I just say that I remembered everything?' Again there was a sudden flash of anger, but he managed to control it. 'Tell me about the future, Tim. Tell me your plans.' In truth I had none and in that respect, at least, I suppose I resembled him. Instead I described to him my life with my grandparents and my time at school; I even mentioned Edward Campion, although apparently he had forgotten the occasion he had arrived unexpectedly at the farmhouse with Gloria and seen him there. He kept on filling his tumbler with whisky through the evening but, since I had never known him to drink before, I was unable to recognize what must have been his drunkenness. He hardly seemed to be listening to what I was saying but, instead, simply looked at me in a slightly puzzled or dejected way.

'It's not the same without you, Tim,' he said, breaking into my increasingly hesitant attempts at conversation. 'It never has been the same, you know. Not since you left.'

For the first time in my life I felt sorry for him and, in that rush of pity, I spoke out. 'I can stay with you, dad. I don't have to go back.'

'But what about you?' He picked up the bottle with slightly trembling hands. 'By the way, always remember to call me father. Not dad. *They* call me a magician.' He carried on talking as if he were making perfect sense. I did not understand who 'they' were, but he was paying no attention to me now; he was staring at the wall, and seeing nothing. 'That's probably what I am. When people believe in you, you see, you can do anything. Almost anything. But do you know what I would really like to do? Do you? I would like to take a glass of water and turn it into a bottle of wine. I would like to take this chair and make it gold. I would like to float up to the ceiling, while they watched me, and then rise through the rooftop into the air. I would like to be able to vanish. I would like to be invisible.' He stopped, and slowly looked towards me. 'So you will stay, will you?' Then he sunk down into his chair and fell asleep.

He was still asleep there the next morning as I left the house. It was just after dawn, but I wanted to see Hackney Square as I always remembered it: at its quietest time, the gardens and the houses proclaiming their own still presence in the early morning, all of their human life somehow withdrawn and silent in the slowly brightening air. I got on the bus and climbed the outside stairs, so that I could sit on the top deck in the open. When I am asked what I miss most from those far-off days, I always mention the same thing – the open-roofed buses! So I climbed up and, from a seat at the front, I looked down at London as I crossed the city from west to east – the wide streets and public gardens of Kensington giving way to the commercial streets of the West End and to the narrow thoroughfares of the City, before they in turn were displaced by the brooding terraces of Hoxton, Hackney and Spitalfields. The city itself slowly grew darker and heavier during that journey, as if the atmosphere of the past had rolled like thick smoke into the east. And yet I loved that atmosphere: I could sense it even before I jumped down from the bus and started walking along the City Road in the direction of Hackney Square. I loved the smell of the streets and alleys, like something still burning, and the memory of

my own past intermingled with the lives of all the others who
had once dwelled here.

I decided to make a small diversion so that I could pass
through Blackall Cut, where Margaret Collins had taken me
after my return to London on that fateful day; I am not sure
if I would have had the courage to knock upon her door, but
in any case the decision was not to be mine. As I turned the
corner I saw that the whole small terrace of houses was being
torn down and, as I stood there in my first surprise, the large
stone ball of the demolishers' crane swung down through the
front wall and window of The Island, her old home. Two or
three neighbours had already gathered to watch this spectacle
and I turned to an old woman whom I vaguely recognized.
'The council are building an estate,' she said. 'Terrible, isn't
it?'

'What happened to Margaret?' I asked her. 'The woman
who lived there?'

'The dwarf? Oh, she was killed years back. She was run
over by a newspaper van. The horse trampled on her. Terrible.'

The dust and grit from the demolition gusted towards me,
and my eyes began to water. A dog was barking somewhere
in the distance, and I recalled how Margaret had once comforted me in the room which was now being destroyed. I
could see the rose-coloured wallpaper still clinging to one of
the interior walls and it was at that moment I became aware
of her death. Or, rather, I was conscious of my own sense of
loss: it was as if someone had left my body and was walking
away, leaving me diminished, weaker, bewildered. So I turned
out of Blackall Cut, and continued my journey once more
towards Hackney Square at a slower pace. The square itself
had not changed, although, like my father, it did not quite fit
the outline of my remembrance; but the old house was there
and, as I ran across the road, I could see that the sunflowers
were about to bloom. There were curtains drawn across the
window (no doubt the new occupants were still asleep), so I

opened the gate and knelt down on the damp earth beside them. They were my old companions, too, and I put out my right hand; as I touched their stems, I thought of Margaret who had once been smaller than them.

A few minutes later I left them and walked back along the iron railings of the square. I turned into Grant Street and, as I passed the grocer's shop on the corner, I stopped to look into the window as I had always done as a child; but I stepped back suddenly when I saw Gloria Patterson serving behind the small counter. She was laughing at something a customer was saying while putting some apples on the scales; there was so much grace in these trivial movements that I understood at once why my father had been captivated by her. The idea that Edward Campion still believed her to be my mother somehow comforted me even now, and I could not help smiling as I continued on my journey. Until, that is, I thought of Margaret again.

By the time I returned to Albion Lane my father had woken and was attempting to clear away the debris of the previous evening; he was in a kind of daze, barely returning my greeting when I arrived, and was picking up various objects only to put them down again in the same place. 'I'm sorry,' he said. 'I must have been blotto last night.' I volunteered to help and with a wave of his hand, as if introducing me to the disorder for the first time, he went back to the armchair where he had spent the night. I was eager to retrieve something from the chaos around me, and the shocks of that morning lent me a ferocious, almost obsessive, energy. Within a few hours I had transformed my father's flatlet into a model of cleanliness and neatness; I swept the floor and dusted the furniture, I washed up the glasses and plates which he had left lying everywhere, I even managed to clean the windows which looked on to the basement area. Then I went outside and washed down the stone paving. 'Margaret Collins is dead,' I said as I came back through the door. I could not bring myself to mention Gloria to him.

'Is she?' He was still sitting in the armchair. 'It was always difficult for her. Dwarves never live for long.' His attitude to someone whom he had once known so well dismayed me, but then, to my horror, he put his face in his hands and began rocking backwards and forwards in the chair. 'What has happened?' he asked me, suddenly looking up. 'Why have I grown so cold?' He took his hands from his face and said, more calmly, 'Thank God you're staying, Tim. I need you.' After a few moments he added, more cheerfully still, 'I hope you like meeting new people. They're not the same around here, Tim. They believe in other things. Communism. The future.' He laughed. 'And for some reason they believe in me.'

Over the next three or four days, I did meet some of my father's clients. He no longer referred to them as his 'circle', as he had in Hackney Square, but there was no doubt that they were in a certain sense his followers; he had not lost his gift of inspiring others, although he tended to speak on themes different from the ones he had announced in the old hall. Those who came to him now were less interested in the world of spirits, because there was no longer so great an awareness of death; in these first months of the new decade, in 1930, the atmosphere was less oppressive, less formal, than it had been in the period immediately after the Great War. People were not so frightened, and more ready to confront – even to mould – the future. So my father now spoke of the stars, or of the tarot, as if there were some alternative way of ordering the world; it was no longer a question of understanding death, but of facing life itself. In general his new clients were more excited, more alert, more willing to talk about change: so he discussed with them secret lines of power or esoteric sources of energy. The phantoms had been exorcized, and in their place had arrived the fearless messengers of some new order.

The people around him were also younger than the members of the Harcombe Circle, and seemed strangely indifferent to the concerns which had once animated Stanley Clay,

Matthew Lucas and the others. None of them had jobs, as far as I could tell; they spent all their time lounging in my father's room or sitting in the saloon bars of the neighbourhood. But where the fear or reality of unemployment had once terrified and haunted the members of the Harcombe Circle, the young people who came to Albion Lane seemed to consider it a public matter to be fought and solved in a public way. If Matthew and the others had carried with them everywhere an air of perplexity and defeat, it was largely because they were also burdened with the fear of having no real place in the world. No such problem existed for my father's new friends, who believed only that the world had to be changed to fit their aspirations. The Harcombe Circle had been terrified of the meaninglessness of life, whereas these more recent disciples seemed much more concerned with its possibilities. They did not walk nervously through the streets in grey, subdued, shapeless clothes; they lingered on the corners of Notting Hill, greeting each other across the way, shouting cheerfully from the open windows of their lodgings, conveying such an atmosphere of freedom that it was impossible not to be affected by it. I had never before encountered people with so optimistic and determined a manner, and it intoxicated me. I, who had no real sense of my own future, was relieved to find that it might be decided for me by forces larger than myself. In the past I had always feared that the fate of Matthew Lucas or of Stanley Clay would also be visited upon me – that I would go through life with only the consciousness of my failure. With my father's friends, such anxieties seemed absurd and even irrelevant. For some weeks, therefore, I allowed the days to drift idly by. I had written to my grandparents and asked them if I could stay with my father for the rest of the summer; they could hardly refuse, I knew, especially since I had persuaded him to write to them with the news that he was actively helping me to find work during this temporary period. That was untrue, of course, but I hardly cared.

Yet, strangely enough, I was still troubled by my father's confused and irregular life; his work seemed so different from that upon which he had once been engaged, and so much less important, that I began to fear for him rather than for myself. I was young enough to accept the succession of empty days but, whenever I considered his life, I felt that he was being somehow left behind. He did not really share his clients' political beliefs, although sometimes he pretended otherwise, and he found it difficult to take their more earnest conversations seriously. He had been drinking less now that I was staying with him; nevertheless, he seemed empty, as if he were being hollowed out by the passage of time.

One morning he was more than usually tired, and I agreed to tidy some letters and bills which had accumulated over the past weeks. 'Why can't I help you properly, dad?' I asked him quietly, as I continued arranging the papers on the table.

He did not reply for a moment, and then started studying with great interest a scrap of paper on which he had jotted down some planetary conjunction. 'I told your grandparents that I would find you a job. A proper job.'

'But this would be a proper job.' I stood in front of him, clutching some papers in my hand. 'I could put all these in order. I could keep a record of the clients. I could take charge of the accounts.'

He looked up at me then; he was himself incapable of keeping accounts of any kind, which probably explained the fact of his constant indebtedness. And yet still he held back. 'But not like the old days,' he said with a curious expression upon his face. 'It mustn't be like the old days. I promised your grandfather.'

'Promised him what?'

He hesitated for a moment. 'You should have a career of your own, Tim. Make your own life. Not become like me.'

'There's no chance of that, dad.' And he laughed.

So it was that I began to work once more with my father. It took no time at all to prepare his papers and accounts, and

I soon began to help him in other ways. I interviewed his clients in advance, questioning them about their date of birth and about other specific matters which would help him to cast their horoscopes or read the cards in their presence; even though I talked only briefly to them, I was able to pass on hints and suggestions which helped my father during his more formal consultations. The old relationship of Hackney Square was now fully restored. I noticed also that his optimism and energy had started to return, but there was an even more curious development in these first weeks of working together: my father seemed to recover his powers of healing, and it was not long before he turned his readings of the stars or of the tarot to more familiar use. He told his clients that astrological conjunctions determined the health of the body, just as certain sequences of the cards led him to detect the presence of illness, but I suspected even then that these were simply his new explanations for a gift that had quite suddenly been revived.

We never discussed this change or, rather, I believe my father avoided talking about it; it became our secret, but one which we kept from one another. 'Did you notice anything?' he would ask me quite casually after I had talked to one of the new clients.

I would then explain to him, equally casually, whatever I had sensed at the time; I might say, for example, that I thought there was something wrong with a client's back. On occasions my own understanding of the person before me took on a private aspect. 'I started getting a headache,' I remember saying once. 'The middle finger of my right hand went numb for a minute,' I said on another occasion in response to a client who was suffering from a pinched nerve which my father was able to heal.

As his confidence grew, so did his reputation; the callers at Albion Lane became so numerous, in fact, that there were times when we felt obliged to make visits rather than to receive them. I always accompanied him on these 'expeditions' (as he liked to describe them), just as I always remained in his room during the treatments at Albion Lane, and indeed my presence seemed as welcome to the clients as it was to him. I did not then understand the reasons for this, although I suspected that the presence of a child – for I was, in many respects, still only a child – helped to break down the formal barriers between two adults and thus assisted my father in his interventions. Sometimes I played a more active role: there were occasions when I would stand behind, or even hold, the person about to be healed in case of a paroxysm or fall. My father would stare at me in the act of healing and I watched fascinated as his pupils started to move upwards and I could see only the blank whites of his eyes. Then, if I held the client, I felt the sudden shock of warmth which always accompanied my sense of another life.

There were times, of course, when he did not succeed in curing pain or in alleviating more nebulous ills. One such occasion I remember still, for it marked the beginning of an even more difficult journey. We had gone out to Chiswick in response to a letter which had spoken of a 'terrible visitation'. Something about the phrase appealed to my father and it was with the barely concealed excitement of anticipation that we arrived at the appropriate house at the stated time; it was an old house, its façade of plain brown brick contrasting with the white fronts of the houses beside it. 'Eighteenth century,' my father said just as a middle-aged woman came to the door and asked us to enter. She tried to smile but it was a forced and nervous grimace, and then at once she began talking rapidly – thanking us for coming so promptly, apologizing for the condition of the house, and so forth. Certainly the interior was in a state of disrepair: the large room at the back, into which she took us, had cracked plaster and peeling wallpaper. It was also pervaded by a smell of dampness, and a large mirror above the empty fireplace was blotched with moisture just like patches of cold sweat upon a human face. Then I noticed something more curious still: the ear-piece of the telephone was lying off its hook and the wireless was covered with a black cloth.

The woman was shaking visibly, and now took out a packet of Old Gold cigarettes. For some reason she offered me one, and not my father, but I refused. I had my own routine to undertake. 'Can I ask you a few things,' I said, 'before we begin?' We sat down at opposite ends of a stained and faded couch, while I went through the usual questions. She answered them listlessly, while all the time she eagerly watched my father as he wandered around the room, touching objects with his fingers and glancing out of the window at an abandoned garden.

'Have you seen it yet?' she suddenly asked him.

'Seen it?'

'My tormentor. Of all people, I thought you might have seen it.'

'Not yet.' And then to cover his confusion he added, 'What exactly am I looking for?'

'It used to come under cover of night and darkness,' she replied, turning to address me. 'But now I see it at any time.' Her eyes were very wide. 'And hear it, too. It talks very softly, but it makes sure that I hear everything. Sometimes it comes through the wireless. And the telephone.'

My father came over and stood in front of her, with his hands in his trouser pockets. 'And what precisely does it say?'

'Can I talk in front of the boy?' He nodded. 'Horrors.' She leaned forward on the sofa. 'Horrors I might have done. Horrors I might do. All the terrors of the future. Sometimes it sits over there . . .' She pointed, without looking, at the brass fender around the fireplace. 'It sits there and repeats them over and over again. Terrible things. Drumming them into my head until there's no room for anything else.'

My father took a deep breath. 'And how will we recognize this thing?'

'Tiny. Like a man, and yet not a man. Too small to be a man. And yet more like a man than any animal I have ever seen. It lives here with me in the house.'

I was frightened of her, and I could tell that my father

shared the fear. But he leaned down towards her now and put his hand upon her shoulder. She did not move, but at that moment such a look of agony and fear passed across his face that I stood up, shaking; he raised his hand and fell back from her. And at that moment I thought I saw a shape, or the shadow of a shape, passing quickly across the far end of the room. It was only in the corner of my eye, so to speak, and I may have been quite mistaken. But of one thing I was certain: there had for a moment been another presence in that room. And then it was gone. The woman raised her head and slowly opened her eyes, but she was not looking at us. She was gazing upon some interior vision, and she, too, was afraid.

We all remained silent, until my father cleared his throat. 'I think,' he said, 'that we should come back at another time. I have to consider this. I have to think.' Still she said nothing. 'Don't worry,' he continued, taking me by the sleeve and pulling me out of the room. 'We'll show ourselves out.' As soon as we had closed the door and walked into the street, he gave a loud sigh of relief. 'I thought,' he whispered to me, 'that we would never get out of there alive.'

'I saw something, dad.'

'I know. That's why I wanted to leave. I was afraid that something might happen.'

'What? To me?'

'You never know, Timothy.' His relief at leaving the place was so great that, to my embarrassment, he did an impromptu dance upon the pavement. 'Now tell me,' he added quite casually. 'Are you still having those dreams?'

I assumed that he had forgotten about them. He had not mentioned them since the day he arrived so suddenly at my grandparents' house, and I was surprised by his question. 'I'm not sure. It all depends on what you mean by dreams.'

'You know what I mean.' He said nothing for a few moments. 'That's why I wanted to get you out of that place. You're too susceptible.'

245

'What *do* you mean, dad?'

'You always were such a nervous child, Tim. Frightened of everything.'

'I was?'

I had no idea I possessed any definite characteristics at all, and I wanted to ask him more about my younger self when he changed the subject. 'That poor woman is haunted by . . . by something.'

'By a shadow.'

'Whatever it is, I wanted to get you away from it. What if you were to start dreaming about that? What then? Now here,' he added, suddenly altering his tone, 'is a house I've always wanted to see. What a coincidence.'

'You always say there's no such thing as coincidence.' I was annoyed with him, perhaps because he had deliberately avoided talking about my childhood. But he was no longer paying any attention to me; we had been walking beside an old wall, and now he went ahead and stood in front of a wooden door upon which was fixed a painted sign: THE HOUSE OF WILLIAM HOGARTH. ARTIST. WEEKDAYS: 10 – 5. 'It's just a museum,' I said, still angry with him. 'I hate museums.'

'Don't be absurd, Timothy. It's part of your education. And you can tell your grandfather I took you.'

Reluctantly I followed him as he opened the door and walked through a small garden towards the house itself; it was a tall, narrow building and seemed to me to be indefinably unsettled. Perhaps this was the effect of its surroundings, however, since it was now standing among modern streets and roads; behind its roof I could see smoke belching from two or three factory chimneys. The garden was filled with the noise of the encroaching city but, as soon as we entered the house, everything became as still and as silent as if we had closed the door upon the world itself.

There was an attendant sitting beside a table, and he remained very still as we entered; he looked at us both and smiled, but I sensed that we had interrupted his own silent communion with this place. My father nodded to him without saying a word, as if he too were affected by the general quietness, and started climbing a narrow staircase: he always felt quite at ease on such occasions and immediately started taking me around William Hogarth's house as if he owned it himself. 'This,' he said as he led me through two rooms on the first floor, 'is where he would have done his work.' The rooms were bare enough, and along the rough whitewashed walls had been hung a series of engravings. I could not yet accustom my eyes to the shapes and figures in these pictures so, instead, I peered at the titles beneath them. 'A Harlot's Progress', 'The Laughing Audience', 'The Distrest Poet', 'Morning', 'The Enraged Musician', 'Gin Lane', 'Cruelty in Perfection' and 'Analysis of Beauty' – the proximity of the last two causing me even then to wonder what kind of artist this might be.

I entered another room while my father still lingered in the one I had just left, and I was about to turn back for him when I glanced up at a large engraving on the wall beside me. It seemed to show the interior of an asylum, with two cells set off from a wide corridor; in one of them a gibbering maniac knelt on a pallet of straw beside a crucifix, while in the other a naked man sat with a crown upon his head while he urinated upon the ground. On the wall of the corridor a deranged old man was drawing symbols of ships and globes, and behind him I could see a madman staring at the ceiling through a wad of rolled paper. The artist had written some verses beneath the engraving and I put my face very close to it in order to read, 'Madness, thou Chaos of the Brain'.

Then I saw something move: one of the figures in the picture shifted in agony. All at once I remembered the sudden movement of the shadow in the house from which we had recently come, and the horror of that moment touched me at last. I wanted to sit down I felt so faint, but instead I stumbled backwards and fell to the floor.

TWELVE

'COME,' HE SAID. 'THIS IS no place for you. Unless you wish your own wits to fry.' Timothy looked up in astonishment and perceived that, without any doubt, he was in a passageway of Bedlam. He could hear the rattling of the chains and the roaring of the mad, yet it was the smell that induced in him trepidation and horror: for it was the smell of death in life. The stains of piss against the wall were like the patterns upon a costly coverlet, while loose piles of shit had been left upon the wooden stairway which led to the upper chambers. The bodies of the insane gave off the odour of rotting meat, for so promiscuous were they in their intercourse, one with another (except for those that were solitary raving), that they had ceased to have a separate stink.

The boy rose from the ground, scarce able to endure the noisome sights and stench, while his companion smiled and clapped him upon the back. 'Take care,' he said. 'We must thread our way through this labyrinth of suffering.' He spoke truly, for there were obstacles upon every side. In front of them crouched an ancient man, who had made his cap out of sheet music and was playing upon a violin. 'English music, no doubt,' his companion murmured, 'but played without any inheritance or authority.' Indeed sounds of no comfortable sort came from this poor instrument, but sundry shrieks and cries which mingled with the voices of the mad. Next to this sad musician, on the stairway, sat a man among the heaps of ordure; his hands were clasped together, with his whole frame in a heave of sighing, while his eyes were fixed upon some phantasm of his melancholy. He was not bound in fetters, but was yet more securely chained to one burdensome thought from which he could not shake himself. He was a very model of sorrow, and Timothy could not forbear from sighing with

249

him. He did not stray from his companion, however, but, as he followed, his ankle was gripped by some creature lying all naked upon the ground; with one hand he held on to Timothy, while with the other he made great gouges in his own skin and flesh. An attendant, or gaoler, came hurrying towards him. 'Leave off,' he shouted, lashing the unfortunate object with a wooden rod, 'Fuckster, leave the gentleman.'

'But I am a gentleman,' the maniac cried out. 'A gentleman born beneath the man. Which is to say, beneath the moon.' Then he began to pull the eyelashes out of his head.

Timothy could endure no more and, as soon as the gaoler had released him from the grasp of this wretched creature, he took the arm of his companion so that he might be the more speedily removed from this place. Yet at this moment another gaoler, dressed in drab fustian, hailed them from the upper landing. 'Mr Hogarth,' he called. 'Mr Hogarth. Come to see our new demoniack, clapped up in a private chamber. He has a very good skull, just shaven, and is fit to be drawn.'

'No, no.' William Hogarth waved his hand above the boy's head. 'We have seen enough. We have circumnavigated this globe of misery.'

And so they went out together through the massive barricadoe, and entered the Moor Fields bordering upon the asylum. Timothy took in great lungfuls of air, so that he might purge the contagion which sometimes lingers in the fetid breath of the mad. 'Come, we will walk,' Hogarth said to him briskly. 'Walking is the best medicine, as they say. And I tell you this: he that shall walk with vigour three hours a day will pass in seven years a space equal to the circumference of the world.'

It was already broad day when they turned left into Wormwood Street and, as they passed an old portion of stone wall just before Leman's Pond, the artist put out his hand. 'Do you see that waving line which the shadows of our heads make against the wall here? In common walking, upon which you and I are now so pleasantly engaged, the body creates an undulating motion like a wave or moving landscape. It comes from no mechanic art of posture, but is the natural line of the body in the world. A line among other lines, working together towards an harmonious unity.' He looked up at the sun at this juncture and took a white linen handkerchief from the pocket of his coat, so that he might wipe the moisture off his brow. 'This sweat is not from Bedlam,' he said with a laugh, 'but from the bright day. I prefer the milder rays of dawn, with its modulation of the light. It causes more pleasing vibrations on the optic nerve.'

'And upon the skin,' Timothy ventured.

'Yes. The heat of the sun may leave us all bewildered. I have often thought,' he added, 'that the engraving of a landscape does a little resemble the first coming of day. The black copper-plate is like night itself until the artist introduces lights upon it; he must make frequent impressions as he proceeds, so that each proof appears like the different times of a foggy morning until one is clear and distinct enough to furnish a daylight piece. So in our work do we imitate the motions of the world.' They walked by a seller of oil, going upon his daily round, whose ladder was put against a lamp; but he was insecurely placed and spilt a little of the oil as he poured it into the box. It fell upon the ground and was likely to have splattered the coat of the artist, but with a sudden quick step he moved away from it. 'No oil,' he said, smiling at his escape. 'No dirt upon me.'

He continued with his theme as they turned right into Broad Street. 'Of course,' he said, 'dawn is not the best light for shadows. For that we need broad day. And the best light for seeing the shadows of objects truly, is that which comes in at a common-sized window when the sun is not directly upon it. As you may observe in there.' He pointed to a good-sized window in the house opposite to them, and Timothy could see the shapes of several ancient women bowed down in mourning; in a moment they had passed, but not before Hogarth had crossed over and glanced in at the scene. He returned to his companion, a little breathless. 'My skill,' he said, 'is not so much in painting the light of dawn, or any such exercise, but in delineating the characters and faces of the English people. The methods of the French and Italian painters are cried up at present but, as they say, we must all work with our own tools. I do not want my country, in this age, to be utterly blotted out of remembrance. Did you see those faces within?' He glanced back at the window, but carried on walking as if he wished always to be moving onward. 'Yet I must add this. No face, be it ever so singular, can be perfectly conceived in character until we find it connected with some remarkable circumstance or cause. The old crones there seemed to be at the end of a vigil, or some such.'

And so, thought Timothy, what were the circumstances that formed you? What is the cause of your appearance in the world? For Hogarth was a short, neat man of quick step and bright eye; his nose was snub, and he had a small white scar upon his forehead, which he would gently stroke on occasions. He was dressed in a sky-blue coat and had a scarlet neckcloth; and as they walked through the crowded alleys into Bishopsgate Street, he seemed to be truly the lord of this place.

He had seen the boy glancing up at his face, and now returned his look. 'You understand,' he told him, 'how all my delight is in motion. Movement is the key to all exercise of energy and the imagination. It is what the painters call the spirit of a picture, lending it the greatest life that it can possibly possess, yet we may see it everywhere around us. Look there upon that brazier. No form is so fit to express the grace of motion as the flame of a fire. Look upon these crowds of people, passing before us and around us with such large, flowing, gliding outlines. It is the same spirit of motion. It is known that bodies in movement always describe some line or other in the air, as the whirling round of a firebrand apparently makes a circle. So what is the line or outline which these citizens form? It is the line of our age. It is the line of our country. Shall we continue our own motion and make a curving line into Grace Church Street?'

Timothy assented to this, and together they embarked upon the next stage of their journey. 'I can remember the time,' Hogarth said, 'when I have gone moping in these very streets with scarce a penny in my pockets. Indeed I can place myself among these scenes even further back: I was born a cockney, or cock-a-neg, or cock's egg (and thus a fool), and as a child I used to wander merrily here. Yet I think I observed everything even then, and could impersonate the very movements and attitudes of the people I encountered. We have from our infancy a delight in imitation, and the eye is as often entertained by mimicry as it is delighted by the exactness of counterparts. Observe that child there, all dressed up in a bag-wig and velvet breeches. Is he not the perfect likeness of an adult in miniature, and therefore the fount of laughter?' Timothy looked at this child, this prodigy of fashion, who at that moment unfastened his breeches and pissed into the gutter. There was a poor girl close by him; she was no more than four years of age, and seemed to be searching for something among the cobbles.

The illustrious artist was now ahead of him and, as he hastened to draw level, he could hear him continuing with the narrative of his life: '. . . which was why I was indentured to a silversmith in Cranbourn Street. It was laborious work though not entirely profitless to me, but I grew tired of serving another master; so, after my time was gone, I set up on my own account as a copper-plate engraver near Leicester Fields. It was in this way that I began upon the art of painting – or, rather, I should say that I stumbled upon it in the manner of making sketches from my own observations of London.' He put out his hand and seemed to draw a few pencil strokes in the air. 'I endeavoured the habit of retaining in my mind's eye whatever I saw without drawing upon the spot, so that on my return to my lodgings I could put down all parts and objects with my pencil. It was my childish gift of impersonation, without a doubt, but now transferred to quite another sphere. Thus I strolled about, always advancing in my art, while the most striking things presented themselves and made the strongest impression upon my mind. Whether they were comical or tragical, however, I concentrated only on such subjects wherein these men and women were the actors.' He broke off and gazed at such people as were hurrying past. 'These were the very scenes which had not often been executed before, and I found out likewise that they were such as had seldom been done in the manner of which I imagined them capable. I could never describe what I had not seen, and I could not hope to move those whose interests and opinions I did not understand. So my own desire of excellence impelled me to fix my attention upon English life: English nature was to be my subject, and English people to be my audience. In previous years our art was corrupted by the ignorance and caprice which taught us to learn tricks from the Italian masters or the French *cognoscenti*. But I hoped to retrieve a truly native strain. It is said that atoms retain their substance while they alter their appearance, that they can be varied and compounded while yet not being destroyed, and it is the same with our English genius. It may flourish for a while and then decay (as it has in these latter years), but its true spirit remains intact and ready to be gathered up by each succeeding generation even to the end of time – or of England. I saw everything with a new meaning as I walked these streets, therefore, since my purpose was to create English art.'

They came to a halt when a slattern threw a bowl of foul stuff into the kennel only a little way ahead of them and two children hurried over to see if it contained anything to eat. A sturdy beggar, carrying a cudgel and with his teeth bared like those of a dog, rushed from the shadow of an ancient tenement and knocked them backwards in his own hot haste for food. Hogarth took the boy's arm and quickly stepped away from this scene. 'It is not enough to hit upon a subject, howsoever terrible or delightful it may be, since nothing in art can ever be attained except by due attention to harmonious proportions and to the principles of nature. This is not simply beauty or grace, though they must be present in some degree, but rather what I call the whole order of form. Look,' he added quite suddenly. 'He is fit to be tied.' A young man, all bedaubed with mud and grime, was standing by a new-built church and calling upon God to save him from demons. Hogarth stood and watched him a little, before going on his way with Timothy. 'So what may be a beautiful form? When a vessel sails well the sailors call her a beauty – the two ideas have such a connection. And again that church we just saw, diminishing from its basis to the tip of its spire, that has its own simplicity and variety.'

'Fuck your mother, you shit-skulled son of a whore!' A coachman was leaning across his horses to threaten a chairman who stood in his path.

'Piss up my arse, you buggaronie!'

'And so from these two examples,' continued the artist, 'from the ship and the church, we find but one idea: when the parts answer one another, and with so exact a uniformity, then we discover beauty. It is the harmony of things that do stand, or swim, or fly without losing balance, and within them is to be discerned the harmony of the world. Yet simplicity alone may not stand the test: the eye is also rejoiced to see the object turned and shifted so as to vary these uniform appearances. The shape and colour of plants, flowers, leaves, the painting in butterflies' wings, or shells, seem of little intended use other than that of entertaining the eye with the pleasure of variety. Indeed it can be said that the art of composing well lies in the art of varying well. For is not the world itself filled with distinction and mutability? Odd numbers are more satisfying than even numbers, just as we prefer the oval to the circle and the pyramid to the cube. The painter must diversify his scene, therefore, and gratify his audience with the unexpected touch of life. Why do you think I still haunt these streets? The great world of order contains within itself irregularity, and he who knows most will have the greatest power of expressing it. Truth is always found where it is honestly sought.'

They had come up now to Great Eastcheap when Hogarth held the boy back. 'What do you see in front of you?' he asked him. A bear was being led towards the pit by Star Court, its muzzle so tight upon it that Timothy observed great welts upon the animal's face. He could also see the filthy garments of the poor who brayed and yelled at the bear, and there were marks of disease upon several of their faces. 'What do you see?' Hogarth asked him again, placing his hand upon his head. The boy told him what he saw. 'Good. That is good. Now look again. Think for yourself and use your own eyes. Look more closely, and tell me what you see.'

And Timothy saw a patch upon a woman's face, hiding the canker of syphilis; a starving dog in a corner, too weak to hold up its head; a drayman so drunken that he was sleeping with his pipe still in his hand; the bloody phlegm coughed up by a child in the shadows; a blind man pushed aside and all but trampled upon by the feet of the hurrying chair-men. Hogarth listened to the boy's account before he continued. 'Yet tell me this. How are we to bring order and beauty out of this irregular world? Do you yet have the key? Come, let us climb our famous monument and see if we may find it there.'

Thereupon they crossed over by way of Pudding Lane and took a few steps southward to the great tower erected after the Fire. They entered through the iron gate and began the steep ascent of the stairway, turning and turning about as they made their way to the summit; the very stones seemed to smell of those who had gone this way before and, as it were, reeked of mortality. Yet Hogarth snuffed it up as if it were the very breath of life. 'Make haste,' he said, laughing, as Timothy sighed at the labour of the ascent. 'Mark how far we have advanced, and you will find that our toil will some time have an end. It is the same with all things: great works are performed not by strength alone but by perseverance.' So he continued with his light step, Timothy following not far behind, until they reached the pinnacle of the edifice and could look out clearly over the city. 'Do you see,' the artist said as he pointed to the river, 'do you see that little ship moving beside the shore? Breadth, and simplicity, and intricacy, all in one.' He turned back to the great city beneath him and gazed upon it for a few moments. 'Now do you understand?' He kept on looking out at the rooftops, the smoking chimneys and the spires. 'It is nature itself which provides what we may call the aerial perspective. Do you sense that interposition of air which throws a general soft refining tint over the whole prospect? It is the light of London. For mark this well – each country, and indeed each city, has its own especial brightness.' He moved around a little and, taking Timothy's arm, showed him the prospect with such pride that he might have been the master or proprietor of it. 'Of course,' he observed, 'it is difficult to understand with exactness an object so vast in its extent and various in its parts. But do you see the way in which our buildings, our churchyards and our streets form such graceful lines and masses one with another? There are no knots or obstructions here, and our rational sight is enlarged as we become masters of the meaning of the city. Perspective views of buildings are always pleasing to the eye, but here we have the additional grace of variety as we walk around and compose ourselves to each view. It is for this reason that a painter will take a building on the angle rather than in front: he will throw a tree before it, or the shadow of an imaginary cloud, or some other object which may add to the same purpose of gaining variety. But here it is all before us without any need for such devices: here is intricacy and unity close combined, the seeming crookedness and irregularity of our thoroughfares making an harmonious pattern which is to be seen only in this city. It has all the grace of a living object for, just as London has its own proper light, so does it possess its own fitting shape. Indeed it is very much like an instinct, acting in the mind and determining the will of the people congregated here. Now do you begin to see, Timothy, how order may be found in the very chaos which you have recently observed? Here ends my lesson. We may take ourselves again to the level of the streets, from which we have come and to which we must return.' He laughed at his own allusion, and led the way down the stone stairway.

They retraced their steps when they came out from the monument, and went towards St Giles by way of Grace Church Street and Lombard Street. They had just come into Cheapside when they were near to being pushed over by an elderly female wearing a dress cut too low and with blue ribbons upon her head. Hogarth touched the white scar upon his forehead and looked upon her retreating back. 'See how she goes, Timothy. To what heights of folly does fashion run?' He tapped the boy upon the shoulder, as if he might indeed give him an answer. 'What is it called? The modish world?'

'I do not know, sir.'

'Well, I care not a fig for it. And yet I observe it. I observe the cut of every coat and the flow of every dress. I have observed, too, how the average eye grows reconciled even to a disagreeable dress, as it becomes more and more the fashion, only to return to a dislike of it when a new fashion takes possession of the mind. It is the same with words, and with certain songs, which become a part of the very air of this city before being utterly forgotten. These tides of taste perplex me, for I cannot see where they have come from or whither they depart. And is it true of all created things, to be known for a moment before subsiding into darkness?' He had grown melancholy at this thought, but then he laughed again. 'Did you observe her sour old face? As bitter as green fruit and not more wholesome. I have seen many like. And that is the secret. Yes, that is the secret.' He grew more lively and vigorous again, as he hurried westward through Newgate Street and Holborn. 'The tides of fashion may alter, may ebb and flow, but some things never change. Characters remain the same, and all the affections or jealousies which comprise our mortal state: these I have taken care to observe and to copy. My task is to look upon the various aspects of the present world, where these people can be seen to exhibit themselves in dumb show, but my business is with the true shape of man. It is like our language, which may vary in its present expression but comes from some remote and undying source. So it is with these faces all around us. English faces, each one with its own particular stamp or token. Yet, in total, a general inheritance from some original we know not what.'

Timothy looked about him: at the smooth-skinned and the coarse-skinned, the small-featured and the large-featured, with a variety of mouths and eyes which now in his imagination seemed to form a line between past and future. For what faces would spring from these faces? 'Even here,' Hogarth was saying, 'even here there is an order among confusion. Do you know that, though every feature grows larger and larger until the whole person has finished growing, the pupils of the eyes still keep their original size? Now look upon that coun-tenance.' Timothy followed his glance and observed an old man, his skin so heavily lined that it seemed as if it might fall from him. His mouth was turned down like a horseshoe, and yet his eyes were as hard and as bright as jewels. 'You see there the eyes of the child, persisting through time. Thus I can trace human nature, through all its variations. Not every-thing is lost, and in this small example we may understand the laws and lessons of eternity.'

The old man was a street musician, which astounded Timothy. For at his great age who could believe that he would play a flute and caper in the mud? He had so woe-begone an expression, also, and yet he was dressed in the very height of flaunting colour with a red coat, blue cravat and threadbare yellow breeches. The artist laughed out loud. 'I have no need to enlarge or exaggerate,' he said, 'for there is nothing in declamation or in burlesque to match up to the reality itself.' The old man had begun to play the old air 'London Pride', and Hogarth listened as if he were spellbound by the song. 'I remember this from infancy,' he said, 'and it has not changed neither. Still the same song. The song of the city. Eternity. I could tread an ancient measure to it even now.' He gave a little skip, in imitation of the old man still dancing with his sour face in the filth of the streets, then suddenly came to a halt. 'We must be careful how we tread now,' he said, walking slowly around a corner. 'We are entering a world without music.'

For they had come to Gin Lane, where there was such a tumult of misery as had never before greeted the dismayed eyes of the boy; even as he stood there, he saw a baby falling from the arms of its mother, who was so drunken that she could hardly move her head. And what was there from the man beside her (no, not a man, but a living skeleton!) but coarse, harsh laughter? It was as if this world of pain and woe were less than a jest to him, and one which must surely pass. A female child, about six or seven years old, lay as one stupefied upon the threshold of a tenement: there were two men, not so far gone in drink, who were eyeing her greedily. All manner of vices seemed to find their home here; in these noisome rooms or dens, which were no more than privies or jakes, sorrow was always the bedfellow of depravity. Timothy could scarce breathe as he followed Hogarth through this battleground of the sick and the maimed, for those who had no bodily ills were fast sinking beneath the weight of mental wounds. They cried and begged in corners, and seemed, as it were, to slink away from the light.

'You see here,' said the artist as he pulled aside a threadbare blanket to find an ancient couple sleeping beneath, 'how every dreadful circumstance of drinking is brought into view. Nothing but poverty, misery and ruin. Here is distress even to madness or death, and not one house or building in tolerable condition but decayed and fallen like all the inhabitants of this place.' To the boy the ancient pair seemed at peace, in a world away from all this sorrow, yet he said nothing. His companion's eyes were very bright as he stood in the middle of the lane, and Timothy recollected the eyes of the ancient

ballad-singer who danced amidst his woe. Hogarth was pointing upward at the church of St George, which was, as they
say, no more than a breath away. 'Once when I came here,'
he said, 'I observed the tower-part of that steeple to be so
exactly the colour of a light cloud behind it that, at the
distance I stood, there was not the least distinction to be
made. It seemed as if the spire were suspended in the air.'

'So you can find beauty even among this misery?'

'Not so much beauty, though undoubtedly it must be
present, but form. Order. Proportion. Everything in human
life must be known and these scenes, which cry aloud to be
viewed with horror and with pity, should be made as in-
telligible as possible. Have we not already seen the order of
the city from our aerial perspective? It is my task to imitate
or represent that order within my own art, so that the characters and expressions are well preserved within the precious
amber of formal proportions. My figures are to be considered
in the same light as those which a mathematician makes with
his pen and which convey the truth of his demonstration.
Only when you view my works do you understand the reality
that is mirrored within them.'

It seemed to the boy that the artist was strangely elevated
by the horror around him, yet he seemed in disturbed sort
also: as if in this extremity he needed now to cry up the
practice of his own art. Close by him a very young man was
propped up against a doorway, as pale as a cloth and looking
to Timothy much like a corpse until he gave out low signs of
mourning. 'Oh God,' he whispered. 'Oh God.'

'For these scenes,' Hogarth continued, 'are copious without
order, and energetic without rules. Wherever we turn our
view we see perplexity to be disentangled, confusion to be
regulated into the symmetry of opposing forces, choice to be
made out of boundless variety, barbarities and absurdities to
be refined into true pictures of suffering. The shape of the
world cannot be altered by accident or caprice, but there are
some trifling artists in whose pictures the truth can no more

be ascertained than a grove, in the agitation of a storm, can be accurately delineated from its reflection in the water. I am not one of those. Out of this chaos and maze of variation, I seek the perfect line. Let us be on our way.' Yet, as they hurried from Gin Lane and skirted Montagu Fields, he could not forbear to add this: 'Do you find a coldness or indifference in me? No. It is not so. It is the task of art to establish principles, and to exalt opinion into knowledge. That is not coldness, but warmth; for it is the warmth of the understanding. Tell me, have you ever seen such a pert face as that?'

Timothy had already glimpsed the young woman ahead of them, though he dared not miss any part of his companion's discourse; yet it was apparent now that she knew the language of the town, for she turned and smiled at them. The boy seemed to recollect her face, but he knew not from where. 'We shall follow her,' Hogarth said, 'to see where she goes, whether to an assignation or what you will. We may call it the harlot's progress.' He laughed at this, though Timothy blushed to hear the word. She had kept up a steady pace in the meantime, and was already gone some little way into the Oxford Road when they turned into that thoroughfare. 'Pursuing is the business of our lives,' the artist said, once more wiping the sweat from his brow with his handkerchief, 'and even abstracted from any other aim gives pleasure. With what delight do we follow the well-connected thread of a novel, which ever increases as the plot itself progresses, until we end most pleased when that thread is most distinctly unravelled? Watch your footing in the shit there. It is all over the street. So if you have been vigilant, my young friend, you will already have found that thread in my own various discourse, which unites all its parts together.' He gave Timothy a humorous glance.

'English art?'

'Yes. English art. English writing. English music. What you will. You have pursued my theme through its winding walks and the mind, like the eye, takes its own pleasure in waving or curving lines. Look, she has turned into Berners Street. Quickly forward.' They hastened to catch a glimpse, and saw her enter a house upon the other side. 'Let us inspect this place,' he whispered. 'If I am not much mistaken, it is a house of assignation.' They crossed to that side of Berners Street and approached the dwelling, which was of a modern sort and very prettily adorned with a Venetian door. There was a sign upon it. 'A dancing-master,' the artist said, on going up to it. 'A French dancing-master. But it signifies nothing.' They then heard the strains of a viol da gamba coming from a room within, and he stepped from the porch in order to view the scene through the window. 'Look,' said he. 'Here are some females dancing in company together. Truly it is like some vision.'

Timothy stood beside him and all at once observed six young women, sometimes in profile and sometimes not, treading the steps of a stately dance. He saw the turns of the head and the twists of the body as they passed one another; he saw gentle bowing and presenting hands, each young woman keeping equal pace with musical time. Hogarth was smiling all the while and he clapped his hands softly to the pace of their steps. 'These females,' he said to the boy, 'come nearest to Shakespeare's idea of the beauty of dancing. Do you recall

> "When you do dance, I wish you
> A wave o' the sea, that you might ever do
> Nothing but that; move still, still so?"

'Of course,' he added, 'it will be so only in art, for if it were possible in a real dance to fix every person at one instant of time, not one in twenty would appear to be graceful, though each were ever so much in their movements. Nor could the figure of the dance itself be at all understood. In my own drawing of this scene I would create gentle winding contrasts, most of them governed by the precise serpentine line.' He broke off suddenly. 'What is this? This is no true dancing academy, for look who comes.' Into the room at this moment stepped a little capering old gentleman in a spencer-wig, together with a fat man in riding habit; close behind them followed an awkward fellow in a bag-wig. 'This is, as I thought, a house for whores. They dance in order to entice their prey.' Once again he took out his handkerchief, for the heat of the day was upon him. 'Yet it is a pretty enough dance, and the minuet is allowed by the dancing-masters themselves to be the perfection of all dancing. I once heard an eminent master say that it had been the study of his whole life, that he had been indefatigable in the pursuit of its beauty, yet at the last he could only say with Socrates, *he knew nothing.* See how these caterpillars begin.'

Now the three lechers attempted to caper about the room, but they must have been drunken already, for their dancing was composed only of wild skippings and jumpings and distorted gestures. 'Do you see,' Hogarth said, 'how their limbs are raised and let fall almost together in one time, and in parallel directions? You would think that they had fewer joints than ordinary and were no better than the hinges of a door. It is sad stuff, but it is comical.' So he continued watching, until the viol da gamba stopped and the dancers came to a dead halt. 'They are so tired,' he observed to Timothy, who was still crouched beside him, 'that they cannot rest without falling. But will they be able to rise again?' He knocked the boy with his elbow. 'That whore yonder begins to disrobe a little and, oh, do you see the line of grace?' The woman seemed about to take off her gown, and the artist came still closer to the window. 'The human frame,' he whispered, 'has more of its parts composed of serpentine lines than any other object in nature. You see how easily the eye glides along the various wavings of the flesh . . .' At this moment the woman caught sight of him and gave out a little scream. Hogarth jumped back from the window as one stung and the dancing-master (or bawd-master), a little, prim, pocky-faced fellow, lifted his fist and seemed to threaten him. 'We will go on our way,' Hogarth said, discomposed somewhat. 'These French whore-mongers will be the ruin of this country.'

They walked quickly out of Berners Street, the artist giving several glances behind, but as soon as they came once more into the Oxford Road they found themselves among a mob which was even then making its way along the thoroughfare. Hogarth at once saw a wooden cart being dragged amidst them and shouted out to Timothy, 'They are on their way to Tyburn. It is a hanging job.' He pressed eagerly forward through the multitude. 'Do you see the victim tied to the cart?' The boy stood upon his tiptoes to see the man about to be hanged: his coffin was beside him and he had one leg resting upon it as if it were a proper stool. 'He looks like a cunning rogue,' the artist said. 'It is Jack Butler, condemned for beating in the skulls of his four children. If he had a very handsome face he might have concealed his wicked mind, but I believe that no villain can be truly handsome. By the natural and unaffected movements of the muscles, caused by the passions of the mind, every man's character will in some measure be written upon his face by the time he arrives at forty years of age. Observe the aspect of this Butler here, and see how in an ill-natured man the frequent frownings have brought into his visage the appearance of villainy. He will be well hanged. The people welcome it even now.' Indeed the mob had grown so large that Hogarth and his companion were buffeted and jostled on every side. 'Be sure of your purse,' he shouted to the boy, 'there are many here who would gladly lift it from you.' A nutmeg-seller, with a child in her arms, was crying out her wares to all who would listen, yet in the general uproar Timothy could see only her mouth opening and closing like that of a great fish stranded upon the shore. But there was one sight that impressed upon him more deeply; it was that of the man condemned, his face now so pale and his features so indistinct that it seemed no more than a white cloth against the street or white cloud against marshes.

'It is reckoned a charge of depravity in mankind,' Hogarth said, looking upon the faces around him, 'that it should delight to injure another without benefit to itself. But the scenes at Tyburn are ancient indeed – some say the Druids once sacrificed there – and it is as if it were an oblation to the city itself. For my own part, I would have thought that scarce any man had leisure from his own distress to estimate the comparative misery of others. And yet so it is. So it is. You know,' he added, 'I would like to see the hanged man dissected after this event. Shall we go to the Royal College in advance of the corpse?' He noticed the boy's perplexed and doleful countenance at the news of this, and so stopped short. 'It is in the character of the artist,' he explained, 'to trace the changes in the human form before it crumbles into dust. It is not in his power to change sublunary nature, or relieve the world at once from misery and cruelty. Look around you. Do you not see too many diversities of temper and rude collisions of contrary desires? I may order them into their appropriate forms, as I have explained to you, but I cannot ever obliterate them. Enough of this.' He clapped Timothy upon the back. 'Take heart, my young master. We will avoid the College and coach it to the Gardens. Enough of misery. It is time to release you from these scenes that so distemper you.' So they walked back in the direction they had come, quite away from the stench of the mob (though it came back in gusts as the wind blew towards them), and at the corner of Broad St Giles they hailed a coach to Vauxhall Gardens.

It was a pleasant sight indeed, after the horrors of the condemned man, and they strolled among the walks, the fountains and the waterfalls. Upon the walls of various arbours had been painted many instructive and merry scenes, to which Hogarth paid not the smallest attention; yet there was one upon which he advanced, going close up as it were to smell the very paint, and which he judged most harshly. 'This image of a fortune-teller is too dry and stiff,' he told the boy. 'The flesh is painted on too thick and has what we call a sticky manner. Well, it *is* manner and no matter. This is a place of ease and not of art. Would you care for the sight of a painting that moves?' The boy readily assented to this, and so they walked towards a little covered section among the trees where, much to his astonishment, he saw in a picture the very movement of life itself: some water running down a hill, or so it seemed, and turning a mill-wheel before becoming the simplest froth and foam. Hogarth said nothing but gave a nod to himself and walked briskly away into a grove beside this place. 'We may sit here for a while,' he said when Timothy came up to him, 'and listen to the strains of the music playing over us.' Indeed he was perspiring again and now put his head back against a tree to rest himself while the musicians of the gardens performed some light airs. He closed his eyes and seemed to be slumbering, whereupon the boy amused himself by taking a stick and beginning to draw in the dust around him. Then the artist opened one eye. 'No doubt you are drawing the sounds of music which you hear,' he said. 'It comes in through your ears and then passes along the muscles of the body until it emerges from your hand. The body, like art itself, is all one. It was for this purpose that Mr Lake contrived a harpsichord to play harmonious compositions of colour. The prism colours were his notes, which the keys of the instrument were to make appear at will.' Timothy laughed at the absurdity of this and threw away his stick. 'No, no. It is all true. I have seen it myself. Even if I had not observed it with my corporeal eye I would have understood it with my mind's eye, so to speak, for divisions of every kind are generated by the laws of music. Did we not agree that English music and English art are alike, and do we not use the phrase *harmony of parts* for both of them? There is so strict an analogy between colour and sound that the gradating shade pleases the eye in the same strict ordinance as an increasing or swelling note delights the ear.'

It had begun to grow dark, as presaging rain, and the shadows of Vauxhall Gardens were softened by the general greyer tint of the air; a roll of thunder seemed at that moment to encircle them. 'It is almost upon us,' Hogarth said, 'and this English landscape is about to dissolve in rain. Let us take shelter in that alcove there while the shower lasts.' Indeed the water now began to pour and large globes fell upon the artist's sky-blue coat. They hastened towards the alcove, to discover that it was instead an eating-house but lately established. Hogarth was moved by this to pat his belly. 'The day has been full,' he said, 'but this has remained empty.'

So they sat down beside a new and curiously carved table, and at once a pot-boy hurried over to them. 'We have shrimps,' he chanted in a high, piping voice, 'and we have cockles. We have soles and livers and calves' hearts and lobsters and salt pork. What will it be, gentlemen? What will it be?'

Hogarth ordered livers, both fried and minced, together with bread, butter and a can of flip. Timothy could not eat (he did not know why), but merely looked out at the darkening scene. Hogarth followed his glance. 'Do you see the manner in which some of the people run to escape the rain from falling on them? Some of them flee to the arbours, some shelter beneath the broad trees, while a few are yet strolling about unconcerned. But do you see also how all are connected, one with another, in a compact variety of lines governed by the principles of intricacy and harmony? It is my old lesson. I call it a kind of mystic dancing, arising from the contours of this place.'

His food had been brought to him and Hogarth ate it up exceedingly quickly while he still contemplated this scene. 'In earlier days,' he said, 'this was a place of great violence and riotous commotion. Yet now it is quite calm. Quite calm. To judge rightly of this present life we must oppose it to the past, for nothing of the future can be known. There are some philosophers who say with Plato that we must reach out of our time in order to find the images or forms of eternity, but I do not understand how this can be achieved. By sudden vision? Or by some extension of my own art? No. It is a thing impossible, for I have only the materials of the past and present ages to work upon. If there is some divine vision, I can find it only in the line of beauty. It is the bounding outline which preserves everything distinctly and harmoniously. Do you hear the pleasant strains of the musicians still, playing amid the storm? This music has its own line of beauty, for it seems to lift us out of our present state into the contemplation of we know not what – except that it be some token of past and present in unity.' He leaned over the table and touched Timothy upon the shoulder. 'May I speak plainly to you without the imputation of false pride?' The boy nodded, for he scarcely knew how to reply. 'I feel my own self to be part of it also, for what are any of us when removed from the whole? Sir William Temple once said that England affords a greater variety of characters than the rest of the world, and he ascribed this to the liberties prevailing among us, which give every man the privilege of being wise or foolish in his own way. I do not know if it be true, and we have observed many scenes today which perhaps give the lie to it, but I do know this: we have a thriving and artificial civilization, the image of which shall not be lost to posterity. In my work I have attempted to preserve it and to leave a description of the manners and customs of our English nation to future times. All our singular humours and usages might otherwise vanish into the shade, like the figures of those around us now, but then how would those who come after us understand from whence it was they sprang? No, it must not be. It cannot be. Our English music must be sustained until we reach the very last note.' He grasped his can of flip and raised it in the air. 'Happy the ingenious contriver!'

THIRTEEN

'**Y**OU FELL.' MY FATHER WAS gently lifting me to my feet. 'You tripped and fell against the wall.' Behind him I could see the engraved print of the passageway in Bedlam, but all I could remember for the moment was the shape I had seen in the house from which we had recently come.

'I can help her,' I said. 'She isn't mad.'

'It's enough to make your hair stand on end, Tim, falling like that.' He started stroking the back of my head.

'Something happened to her once, but I can help her. We have to go back.' He did not reply, so I turned and went down the stairs; I fully expected him to follow me and I waited in the garden until I heard his footsteps coming down the path.

'Hello,' he called out. 'Fancy meeting you here.' He said nothing about my determination to return to the woman's house and simply walked beside me as I made my way in that direction. 'Do you know?' he went on. 'It's a funny thing. A very funny thing. But one thought can change everything. Do you know what I mean?'

'No, dad.'

'When I'm feeling low, the whole world seems dead to me. And then of course it really is dead. Do you understand? You had one of your dreams again, didn't you?' He seemed angry for a moment, not angry at me but at himself. When I glanced at him, however, he was contemplating the world as serenely as before. 'But then I revive, I feel happy, and everything grows again. If you look at the bright side, then the bright side suddenly appears.'

We arrived at the house and the woman came to the door almost at once, with the strangest smile upon her face. It was like a smile of triumph. 'So you came back,' she said. 'You believe me.'

'I believe you,' I replied. My father was standing a few steps behind me and made no effort to speak to her. 'May we come in? I think I know what happened to you.'

She said nothing but led us once more down the dark hall; when we entered the room at the back of the house, she looked anxiously about while I kept my eyes upon her. 'Do you want to sit down?' she asked me. She did not seem even to notice my father now.

'No.' She was a little shorter than I was and, just as I had seen my father do in the old hall, I put my hands upon her shoulders. 'I know that somebody died here once. And that you think you killed him. But you did nothing of the kind. There is no need to fear it. Not now.' She looked at me and then suddenly gave out a long and terrible scream. I fell back from her, trembling, and turned wildly around to my father.

He came over and for some reason put his arm around my shoulders. 'He didn't mean to frighten you,' he said.

She had put her hands in front of her face. 'How did you know about my brother?' She looked at me and, again, paid no attention to my father. 'He died when we – when he was very young.' That was the truth of it, as I already knew: a brother younger than herself, for whom she had conceived an infantile jealousy, had died many years before. And for all these intervening years she had been affected by a sense of guilt as real, and as inescapable, as the presence she sensed within this house. Then I recognized, also, that she believed this strange shape actually to be some transformed version of her brother; it was the same size as the boy had been at the time of his death, but somehow grown old, and dark, and malevolent in the shadowy world within which it now existed. But if there was one survivor which was darker and more malevolent still, it was the continuing presence of that terrified infant consciousness inside the adult now standing before me.

'You didn't kill him,' I said. 'There is no guilt. Nothing to fear. There is nothing here now except your memory.'

She sat down upon the threadbare sofa and remained very

still. She was moaning softly to herself, her face still hidden behind her hands, when I believed that I heard a similar low moan coming from a corner of the room. She must have heard it, too, for she looked up with such an expression of surprise and delight that I could scarcely look at her face. 'It's going away,' was all she said. 'It's going away.'

We remained silent for a few minutes, anxiously listening for any sound, until my father could bear it no longer. 'I think,' he said, 'that we can go now, too. It's over.' He was right; whatever had once inhabited this house had now departed, moaning, and the woman was free.

We left soon after, my father uncharacteristically silent as we returned to Albion Lane. This was the first time he had seen me alleviate another's distress (naturally, he did not know about the incident with my grandmother so many years before), and he seemed disturbed by it. Then he started humming a little tune. 'Anyone ought to be able to do it,' he said after a while.

'Do what, dad?'

'Change the world. Alter things. I've been reading some books of magic. True magic. Not hocus-pocus. And they all agree that we have divinity actually inside us . . .' He started humming again. 'There's so much to do in the world, Tim. So much you can achieve.' It always surprised me how optimistic he remained, despite all the misery and suffering which he witnessed in his work; the happiness seemed to come from nowhere, to spring out of him unimpeded by even the most difficult circumstances. Perhaps it was the difficulties which summoned it forth. 'And you can be anything you like, Tim. A poet. An astronomer. A musician. Everything exists within you, if you know where to look. The earth, the day, the light, the sky, are all yours. And only you can bring them to life. Do you think your dreams are about that?'

'I don't know, dad.' It was not a subject I wished to discuss, not even with myself.

'In any case, there's a universe inside you.'

'I thought you said God was inside everyone.'

'Don't answer back.' He was smiling at me as he spoke. 'We've achieved a lot, haven't we, Tim?'

'Yes, dad.'

'Just the two of us?'

'Naturally.' It occurs to me now that the greatest achievement had really been to lift my father from the disorder and sense of failure which surrounded him when I first arrived at Albion Lane; but, as we walked home, I simply enjoyed his sudden high spirits.

'I couldn't have done it without you, Timmy.'

'Thanks a lot, dad.' He did not seem to notice the irony in my voice and continued humming his tune.

So we carried on with our work and over the next two years my own role increased considerably; I was no longer simply his companion and occasional assistant but, instead, took a more active part. He still did most of the talking and, as it were, charmed the clients out of themselves; but now I stood beside him, as I had done in the old hall, and he relied upon me to hold or to touch them in the course of his ministrations. Our success was so great, in fact, that we were able to move up to the ground floor of the house in Albion Lane, and it was in these lighter and more spacious surroundings that we continued our practice. I had my own room now, at the back of the house; and here, in the evenings after the last session had been completed, I would turn on the wireless or listen to my gramophone. I still had the old records which my music master had given me on my departure from St William's, and I would play these as I stared out into the garden or looked at the London sky.

I was now of an age when I thought of sex continually; yet I was scared by the very idea of it. I can say it now, although I could not even whisper it to myself then – I think I was afraid of my dead mother. I was frightened by the image of her I had seen in the photographs – frightened because it was often the one that emerged as I tossed upon the bed at night, and because it was the one that seemed to whisper to me whenever I was attracted to a girl. There were occasions when I saw someone in the street, and I began to wonder if my mother had walked like that or moved her head in that same way. I envied the young men and women when I saw them together but, even as I envied them, I shrank from them.

And then one morning, as I lay in my room and waited for the fog of my sexual thoughts to clear, there was a sudden sharp knock; I sprang out of bed in alarm but, by the time I reached the front door, there was only an envelope lying on the mat. It was addressed to 'Harcombe' and inside was a single sheet of paper with a message written in block capitals: PLEASE COME THIS MORNING TO 12, LANT STREET. VERY IMPORTANT. TOP BELL. I knew that my father was away that morning – there were occasions when he disappeared for a few hours, for reasons which I was not to discover until later – and, since the letter had not been addressed specifically to him, I decided to follow its instructions myself. I remembered Lant Street well enough; it was a small road just by Borough High Street, in a part of London which I had recently begun to explore. This had become my new pastime: in the hours when I was not assisting my father, I used to embark upon long walks through the streets of London. Sometimes I returned to the area of the East End I had known as a child, perhaps with some barely conscious wish to revive the atmosphere of the 'expeditions' which my father had once arranged, but I also became acquainted with other areas of the city. I never really had a destination in my mind. I walked haphazardly, although I always seemed to find myself in the most forlorn and dilapidated streets; there were occasions when the sight of a derelict building or a narrow terrace of houses would draw me irresistibly forward and I seemed then to be searching for some aspect of my own self among the decay. But I suspect now that there was also some confused or unacknowledged sexual motive to my wanderings; I may have been searching for some form of adventure or some chance encounter, unexpected enough to forestall my fears and satisfying enough to fulfil my fantasies. So now, on receipt of this strange message, I set out again.

It was almost midday when I arrived in Lant Street and, as requested, rang the top bell. A young boy came down the hall, peered at me through some frosted glass and then opened the door a little. 'Who are you?'

'Mr Harcombe,' I said, trying to sound as adult and as dignified as I possibly could. 'I was sent a letter.'

'You're expected then.' He started walking down the narrow hall, without looking back, and I nervously closed the front door before following him up a flight of wooden stairs. 'She's in there,' he said when we came to the first landing. 'She's waiting for you.'

And, when I opened the door, there was Gloria Patterson. She was standing by the window with her back against the light and was bathed in shadow. She could see me clearly enough, but for a few moments she gazed at me in perplexity. 'It's Timothy,' I said, blushing, 'Timothy Harcombe.'

She looked astonished and not at all pleased. But then she burst out laughing. 'What are you doing here?'

I did not know how to answer and, in any case, for some reason I could scarcely breathe in her presence. She was now very slim and had short, almost boyish, hair; she was wearing a waistless dress, which came down just below her knees. 'I think there's been a mistake,' I managed to say. 'I think you wanted my father.'

'Did I?' She looked at me almost scornfully for a moment and then answered in her quick, careless way. 'I don't know about that.'

'But you left a message.'

'I didn't leave it. My brother left it.' She seemed infinitely knowing and almost sly, but her delicate, beautiful face put all such reservations at once out of my mind. I was happy simply to be in the same room with her. 'Anyway,' she was saying, 'I've changed my mind. I don't want to see him at all. Not after what he done.' She looked at me fiercely, and then lowered her eyes. 'I suppose he told you all about it, didn't he?'

'No.'

'Don't lie. Of course he did.' Her voice was so harsh that inadvertently I took a step backward. Then she laughed again. 'You're a big boy now,' she said. 'You know what I mean.'

'He doesn't talk much about the past.' This was the truth: my father and I had returned so naturally to the conditions of our former life that I never really considered the time he had spent with Gloria; certainly he never mentioned it.

'Is that how he thinks of me then? The *past*?' She imitated the way in which I had said it. 'I'm not surprised, neither. Not after the way he treated me. Do you want a smoke?' She had taken a packet of Kensitas cigarettes from the window-sill and began to draw deeply on one of them. 'I suppose,' she went on, blowing the smoke out towards me, 'that he's got some other woman now?' I shook my head, feeling more awkward and nervous with every second. 'You're just saying that. He told you to say that, didn't he?' Again I shook my head, but she was paying no attention to me now. 'My mum and dad are dead, you know. They went one after the other. Just like that. I blame him.' She flicked some ash on to the floor, and looked down at the street. 'So it's just the two of you, is it?'

For a moment I did not realize that she was talking to me. 'Yes,' I said. 'That's right. We're working together.'

'Is that a fact?' She turned around and gave me a long, appraising look before she inhaled once more on her cigarette. 'It's the same old nonsense, is it? Like the days in Hackney?'

I recalled very well how she herself had once been a member of the Harcombe Circle together with Margaret and the others, and I felt resentment for their sake rather than my own. 'It's not nonsense. There's no nonsense about it. He helps people.'

'Says you.'

So I added, without considering what I was saying, 'He helped you once.'

'Helped *me*?' Her temper flared again. 'He did no such thing. He didn't care about me. He didn't care about anyone. Except himself. Do you know what a bastard you have for a father?' She was taunting me but, even so, I could not help the anger rising up within me. Yet this was the curious thing: the more angry she made me, the more attractive she became. I think she realized this, too, because now she smiled before she spoke. 'I wouldn't trust him. Not if I were you.'

'So why did you want to see him, Gloria?'

'Oh, I don't know.' Her mood changed again. 'Perhaps I didn't want to see him at all. Perhaps I wanted to see you instead. What would you think of that?'

'I think you'd be lying.'

She came up to me and slapped me; then she kissed me on the lips. 'Go back to your dad,' she said, 'and tell him what I did.'

I left the house in a state of extraordinary, bewildered joy. I was astounded and thrilled by her kiss – and secretly, I think, equally delighted by the fact that she had hit me. I had already discounted her remarks about my father; they seemed of no importance when compared with her presence beside me in that small room. A simple light, a simple felicity, seemed to have entered my life and robbed me of my usual constraints: indeed, as I left that dilapidated house, I no longer sensed any boundaries to my own self and I felt as if I might soar over the smoking chimneys and the London roof-tops. It was a Saturday, and on that early afternoon the main thoroughfare beyond Lant Street was crowded with casual shoppers and street traders; I was knocked and jostled as I went forward, but I hardly noticed. I did not care in which direction I walked, because at that moment the whole world was before me. Borough High Street seemed endless, the shops and offices shone with an interior light, and the people around me had existed for ever. They had become extensions or emblems of my own happiness and at that moment I laughed out loud. I had become larger than myself. Yet this was my enduring sensation as I walked down the crowded thorough-fare: the more I saw my own happiness embodied in those around me, the way that light is reflected by another surface, so it ceased to be merely my own happiness. The happier I became, the less I knew or thought of myself; I realized then how it is possible to become part of the world. Or, perhaps, to discover the world already existing within one's own being. I cannot say that this recognition was precisely the one which I had already experienced in my dreams: it was rather an intensification or a purification of those other visions. But I believe that even then I felt a strange discrepancy, between the weakness or unworthiness of Gloria Patterson and the intensity of those sensations she had released in me.

When I came to a gap in the street, I found myself entering a small park and sitting on a bench beneath a large oak tree; the first sensation had passed and I attempted to capture it before it disappeared, trying actually to experience once again what had just happened to me. Suddenly I realized that I was gulping for air, my whole body trembling, and I heard myself saying out loud, 'What has happened to me? How could *she* have done this?' There was an old man sitting on another bench, bowed over towards the ground; he had a dog with him, which was lying on the grass a few yards away and gnawing on a rubber ball. Otherwise the park was quite empty and, as I sat gazing upon the dog, which from time to time looked up wistfully at its master, I was invaded by a mood of intense sorrow. I was close to tears without under-standing the reason – knowing only that my extraordinary happiness had been suddenly displaced by inexplicable misery. I did not understand myself at all.

Then I felt the presence of someone and, when I turned my head, I saw Stanley Clay. He was standing a few yards behind me and, as I looked at him, he came over to the bench and sat beside me. He was no longer the young man whom my father had cured so many years before, and whom I had seen walking with Margaret Collins in the London dusk; there were deep lines upon his face, and he had entered that period of change which takes place just before middle age. I had not seen him for six years, but I was already so distracted and disturbed that I was not particularly surprised by his sudden appearance. 'Hello, Tim,' he said. 'Long time.'

'Stanley.' I had no idea what to say to him now. 'Do you live around here?'

'Oh no. Nothing like that, Tim. I'm still in the old place. Not many changes.' And, yes, in certain respects he still seemed to me the same: the same low voice, the same hesitant manner, the same shabby impoverishment. His hands were clenched into fists, and he knocked them together. 'Did you see her?'

'What?'

'Did you see Gloria? I watched you leave the house.'

'Yes,' I said. 'I saw her.' He looked up into the branches of the tree and sighed. I thought he was about to cry and I added, quickly, 'Do you remember the time you took me back to London? And I stayed with Margaret Collins while we tried to find my father?'

'I remember, Tim.'

He was trembling still, and I knew that he was mastered by some anxiety or obsession. Even his past was of no account. I did not want to enter that obsession, not now, and I drew away from it as best I could. 'How are the others, Stanley?'

'The others?'

'I know Margaret is dead. But what about Jasper? And Matthew Lucas?'

'I don't know what happened to Jasper. But Matthew went inside again. He broke down.' I could see Matthew in front of me, leaning forward with his intense questions to my father as if he never understood the meaning of anything in the world. 'What did she say to you, Tim?' It had begun to rain. The old man rose silently from the bench and his dog followed him.

'Nothing.' I looked at his sallow, desperate face, and I experienced a moment of intense hostility. 'Nothing much.' He was still looking at me, willing me to say something more. 'She never did say very much, did she?'

'No. That's true.' I might have offered him some revelation, so grateful he seemed, and I realized at once that it was always as if he were seeing her for the first time. 'Did she ask you to call?' he said at last, although he posed the question as if he did not really wish to know the answer. Once more I was in the room with her, and I could feel the force of her hand upon my face: and perhaps that was the truth of it, after all. She had not expected my arrival and had no particular interest in me. She probably just despised me.

'She wanted to see my father,' I said.

Stanley did not reply, but he was rubbing his hands violently together. I thought for a moment that he was struggling for breath. 'But they haven't seen each other for years,' he managed to say.

'I know.'

'So why now, Tim? Why does she want to see him now?'

I had no answer. 'I think we ought to go,' I said. 'There's a storm coming.'

He rose from the bench as meekly and obediently as if he were a child, and together we walked back down Borough High Street. Now that the showers had started, many of the street traders had put oil-cloth or canvas covers over their stalls; I happened to glance over at a tray of rings, partly concealed, and at that instant I remembered with horror the fact that Edward Campion still believed Gloria to be my mother. The woman who had just kissed me. We parted at the crossroads where the Borough Road turns into Lambeth Road and, as Stanley left me, we agreed that we would meet again. For some reason it scarcely seemed necessary to name a date, or a place.

When I returned to Albion Lane, there was a small figure loitering outside the house, and for a moment it looked so much like some image of my own younger self that I stopped short. When I realized that it was Gloria's brother, I hurried towards him; he saw me at the same time and ran up with an envelope in his hand. 'She gave me this,' he said. 'You've got to read it at once. Out here.' Inside was a note in Gloria's now familiar block capitals: YOU CAN SEE ME AGAIN IF YOU LIKE. THE SAME TIME NEXT SATURDAY. BUT DON'T TELL HIM. HE'LL KILL YOU.

When my father returned that evening, he was too tired to ask me what I had done, and I chose to say nothing about the events of that day. It was the first time, I think, that I had deliberately concealed anything from him. Gloria had come between us, and for the whole of the following week I was distracted from our work by the thought of my next meeting with her. That was my own explanation, at least, for my sudden loss of concentration. My father seemed uneasy, too, and in my guilt I believed that he had managed to discover something about Gloria and myself. Perhaps Stanley Clay had contacted him? No, that could not be. And still I said nothing.

I visited Gloria the following Saturday, as she had instructed, but when I turned into Lant Street I had the strangest feeling that someone was following me; I turned around and could see nothing except the blank side of the old church which stands at the junction with the Marshalsea Road. She was waiting for me in the same room at the top of the stairs. 'Did you tell him you were coming?' were her first words to me.

'No.'

She gave me a peculiar look, of triumph mingled with disappointment. 'That's good then, isn't it?' Very slowly she took out a Kensitas and lit it. 'So what do you think of this blouse then?'

I looked at the one she was wearing. 'It's nice,' I said.

'It should be nice. It's rayon. Artificial silk to you. And what about the stockings?' She lifted up one leg. 'I got them in Woolworth's. You know what they say. Nothing over sixpence. Do they look expensive?'

'I don't know.'

Again she seemed disappointed. 'I don't know why I bother with you.' She took another draw from her cigarette. 'So why did you come anyway?'

'You asked me.'

'Did I?'

'Yes! You did!' I do not think I had ever shouted at anyone before, but in her presence I was always pushed to some extremity of feeling; I was no longer in control of my moods and, at such a time, I became a stranger to myself.

She merely smiled when I screamed at her. 'You're just like your father,' she said. 'An animal.'

'I am not like my father! I mean he's not . . .' Then all the anger left me; I was trembling, and I sat down upon a small wooden chair near the door.

'You shouldn't sit in front of a lady until you get permission.'

'I'm sorry.'

She was still smiling. 'He had a bad temper, too. He used to beat me around a bit, you know. I could show you the bruises, but they're all gone now.' I looked up at her in astonishment; my father was the gentlest of men, and the idea of his striking anyone seemed absurd.

'I don't believe you.'

She came over to me and I winced: I thought she was about to hit me again, but instead she bent down and kissed me on the lips. 'That's a good boy. Stick up for him. Millions wouldn't.' She got up and ground out her cigarette in a tin ash-tray. 'I suppose you'd like to beat me, too, wouldn't you? Just like him?'

'No!' I was almost pleading with her. 'No. I like you. I like you a lot.'

'Is that a fact? Well, you can go now, anyway. I've got things to do.' I had been with her no more than five minutes, but I accepted her dismissal as if it were the most natural thing in the world. I rose from the chair and was about to leave the room when she called me back. 'Would you like to come next Saturday?'

'Yes,' I said.

'Then you can. And remember. Don't tell him anything. Otherwise I'll never see you again.'

I left the house so shaken after this brief interview that I was not at all surprised to see Stanley Clay staring at me from the other side of the street; I think I raised my hand in greeting, but he just turned away. It did not seem to matter in any case, since my own life had suddenly become much more mysterious than anything else in the world. I realized that in some way I could not withstand Gloria: everything she said and did shook me so violently that I was unable to command myself in her presence. It was as if I had turned into a child once more, and the smallest word or gesture absorbed my attention while all around me reality shifted as uncertainly as smoke. And was this what love meant, then? To become a child again?

My father was lying on the floor when I returned to Albion Lane. It was one of his favourite positions and I thought nothing of it; I merely stepped over him and went into the kitchen. My throat was dry and sore, as if I had been shouting the same word over and over again, and I needed water. When I returned, he was propped up on his side, staring at the carpet. 'Were you waiting for me, dad?'

'No. I've been looking at the fire.'

'What?' It was the middle of summer and the hearth was quite bare.

'The fire that dwells in all things, Tim. What other kind of fire is there?'

He said this light-heartedly enough and then got up to take the empty glass from my hand. Was this the man who had attacked Gloria Patterson? Who, by her account, had beaten her? It could not be. But I felt uncertain or wary in his presence: Gloria had managed even that change in me. 'Where were you, Tim?' he asked, very casually.

'I just went for a walk.' I knew that I was blushing and I added quickly, 'You'll never believe it, but I saw Stanley Clay. Do you remember Stanley?'

'I remember Stanley very well. He was the one we cured.'

'You cured, dad.'

'If you say so. If you say so.' He was walking up and down the room, still with the empty glass in his hand. 'Wouldn't it be nice to get away for a while, Tim?' He had forgotten about Stanley and was intent upon something he had obviously prepared in advance. 'What if we were to travel somewhere and begin all over again?' He seemed uneasy, but, as always, he tried hard to conceal his mood from me. 'A new life.'

'I like it here, dad.' I was horrified by the suggestion – perhaps I was horrified at the idea of never seeing Gloria Patterson again. 'And we're doing so well.'

'If you say so, Timothy.' He went over to a small table where I kept all our documents and accounts, and put down the glass. For a moment he stood with his head bowed. 'In any case,' he said, turning around suddenly, 'perhaps we needn't go at all.' His uneasiness vanished almost as quickly as it had arrived, and he smiled at me with the force of some new resolution. It was just like him to change his mind in a matter of seconds. 'Energy alters everything. Energy and the imagination can change the world. Did you know that, Tim? I'm just popping out for a minute. I won't be long.'

I watched him walking down the street with his usual air of self-possession, but I was still disturbed by his sudden desire to 'travel somewhere'. Had he discovered something about my meetings with Gloria? Had she sent him another letter? I went over to the table and found that he had put the empty glass down upon a single sheet of folded paper. I took it up and opened it. It was not from Gloria, after all. It was a message from a bookmaker about my father's mounting debts.

I visited her again on the following Saturday, just as she had told me; but, when I rang the bell in Lant Street, no one came to answer my call. I felt at once so lost and bewildered that I ran back into the street and stared wildly around; then I sat down upon the steps, raised my knees against my chest and waited. I do not know how long I stayed there – perhaps an hour – but, in case she arrived suddenly, I was determined not to display any signs of anxiety or frustration. And then she was beside me, searching in her handbag for her key as if she had nothing to do with me at all. She had a cloche hat pulled over her ears, but I could see the powder and rouge upon her face. She was carrying a women's magazine under her arm. 'Oh it's you, is it?' she said when she eventually opened the door.

'You told me to call.' I felt the old anger welling up within me, but at this moment I could not even look at her.

'I did, did I?'

'Yes. You did.' All week I had been preparing the words I would use when I saw her again, but now they seemed as futile as the wind that gusted down Lant Street as we stood on the threshold together.

'I suppose you'd better come in then.' I hesitated. 'OK?' she added, impatiently.

I followed her up the stairs, still hardly daring to look at her. 'Where's your brother?' I asked.

'My brother?' She seemed puzzled for a moment. 'He's out,' she said. 'Not that it's any of your business.' She had reached the landing but, just as she was about to open the door to her room, she turned and kissed me on the mouth. Then she leaned forward slightly and bit my neck. 'That's for trying to kiss a lady,' she said. 'Now you can come in.' The room smelled of face-powder and perfume and, on first entering, I inhaled deeply. 'Sit down where I can see you,' she told

me. 'I don't want you coming up behind me.' She took off
her coat and hat, letting them fall on to the ground, and then
began rearranging her hair in the mirror. I tried not to look
at her, but I could not resist glancing in her direction a few
times: on each occasion I noticed that she was also watching
me. 'What's your dad been up to, then?' she asked me at last.

'He's been working.'

'Is that what he calls it? More like cheating people out of
their money.' I said nothing. I knew well enough that she was
taunting me, but I was determined not to be moved by her.
Not in anything. 'And cheating me, too. He took a lot of
money off me and, when he knew I didn't have no more, he
left me. He just walked out and left me. That's your father.'
She looked at me in the mirror, but I got up and walked over
to the window so that she would not have the satisfaction of
seeing my face. 'I used to laugh at the lot of you, sitting
around and listening to him as if he were God Almighty. And
you know he got Stanley fired, don't you? Your precious
father accused him of stealing. Did you know that?'

'No.' I put my forehead against the cold pane of the
window, but I did not want her to stop. I wanted to hear
everything.

'And all because Stanley finally saw through him. That's
when he started beating me, too.'

'I know it's not true, Gloria.'

'You? What do you know? Your father isn't what you
think he is. I'm glad I weren't your mother.' I was clenching
and unclenching my fists as I stared at the edge of the
window-frame with its rotten wood clinging to the glass, and
all the while I knew that she was watching me with enjoyment. Then I heard her moving around. 'Unzip my dress for
me, Timmy,' she said. 'There's a good boy. It's so awkward
for me.' I stood very still by the window. 'Come on, Timmy.
Haven't you seen a lady in her slip before?'

'I don't know. I don't think so.'

'You don't *think* so? Have a look, then.' I turned around to face her, just as she stepped out of her dress without any assistance from me at all. 'Now what do you think of that, Mr Harcombe?' I could say nothing and I started to walk over to her. 'Oh no you don't,' she said, picking up her dress and holding it in front of her. 'Don't you come near me. Don't you think I had enough with your bloody father?' I knew that I was being rebuffed and deliberately humiliated; but I could not blame her for it. Neither of us could have prevented what was happening and, as I stood in the middle of the room, it was as if I had ceased to exist for myself. The space I occupied was now invaded by sounds from the outer world – a couple arguing in a downstairs room, a dog barking in a nearby house, some children playing in the street. Gloria was talking to me, loudly and quickly, but I do not think I heard what she said. Then suddenly I was myself again, standing with her in this small room. 'You'd better go now,' she said. I walked past her and opened the door.

When I reached the street I started to tremble; the sweat was pouring from my face, and I did not want to be seen by anyone in such an abject condition. So I ran down an alley off Lant Street and stood in a deserted timber yard into which it led. For some reason I repeated nonsense words to myself, letting them rise up into the air, and then I started to cry. I do not know how long I remained there, shaking and weeping, but, when I left the yard, the sweat had dried from my face and my body; somehow, in the middle of that agony, I had taken command of myself.

Stanley Clay was waiting for me at the corner of the street. 'So she gave you a hard time, did she?' He said this almost eagerly, but at the same time he put his hand on my shoulder; he had not utterly forgotten the past. 'You're old enough to have a drink, aren't you, Tim? You look old enough.' I still said nothing, but he led me towards a public house in the next street: it was called the Seven Stars, and I remember glancing up at the sign swaying in the strong wind. It displayed seven white dots against a sky of deep violet, with lines of light connecting one with another in geometrical pattern. Even now, when I look up at the night sky, I sometimes recall that sign and the misery with which it will always be associated in my mind.

We sat down at a table in the corner of the saloon bar, and I waited quietly there until Stanley returned with the drinks. Then all at once he began to talk about himself; I do not know if it was my silence that led him to speak out, or whether the sight of my unhappiness had finally unlocked some recess within his own self, but in his familiar low voice he told me the story of his last few years. How he had given up his job as a piano tuner and had become a guard in an art gallery near Lambeth; how he had taken up photography as a hobby; how he still lived alone in a block of flats by Hackney. He even found a piece of paper and wrote down his address for me. But he did not mention Gloria. I did not know how to reply to him, largely because I could think of nothing but the misery which she had instilled in me. But then I recalled something which she had said to me, something which might help to clarify my confused response to her. 'Did my father get you sacked?' I asked him.

'What was that, Tim?'

'Did my father have you fired from your job?'

'From the piano tuning? Oh no. I gave that up ages ago. Just about the time you went down to Wiltshire.'

'So my father had nothing to do with it?'

'Of course not. Anyway I prefer life in the gallery. It's quiet there. I'm not bothered by no one.' He stared straight ahead, clutching his glass with both hands. 'I can think.'

'Gloria said my father had you sacked.'

He looked at me in horror. 'Why would she say a thing like that?'

'I don't know. I don't understand her at all. I don't know how to talk to her. I don't . . .' I stopped there, uncertain, now that I had revealed something of my feelings for Gloria; but there was no longer any hostility or suspicion between us, for it seemed that we had both been cast aside.

'I know things haven't been easy for you, Tim.'

'She told you about me? About my visits?' It was my turn to be horrified.

'No, not that. I haven't talked to her. Not in months.' He could not look at me now for some reason, but began drawing patterns on the dusty table with his finger. 'About the past, I mean. She told me all about the past.'

'What past, Stanley?'

'We never understood why you had to leave Hackney and stay with your grandparents. I never should have brought you back, but I didn't know, did I?'

'Didn't know *what*?'

'Your father.' He saw the expression on my face and added, more hesitantly, 'The way he was treating you, Tim. You know what I mean.'

'No I don't. I don't know what you mean at all.'

'Gloria told me that you ran away. You ran away because he was cruel to you.'

I was so astonished and angry that I believe I stopped breathing for a moment. 'That's such a lie,' was all I said. I rose from the table and went outside into the air; I stood on the worn stone steps and looked up at the sign of the seven stars until my anger subsided.

When I returned, Stanley was moving his head and neck awkwardly, as if he feared some recurrence of his old nervous ailment. 'That's what she told me, Tim,' he whispered. 'She said that's why she left him. When she found out what he did to you.'

'She's a liar, Stanley, don't you see? She just told me that my father left her when she lost her money. It's all such a lie.'

He was looking down at the circles he had made with his finger. 'It was a lie about me being fired, too, wasn't it, Tim?'

'Of course it was.'

'So everything has been a lie. Is that about it?'

'Everything.'

'I have to go home and think about this, Tim. I can't think

in company.' He rose, and left me abruptly. 'I'll be seeing you,' was all he managed to say.

I sat alone in the public house, reflecting upon Gloria. Yes, everything had been a lie; she had lied to me, and to Stanley. Yet I sensed even then something which I understand better now: a lie, once uttered, changes reality just as surely as if it were a great truth. I no longer needed to believe that my father beat Gloria, but even the fact that she had described him in those terms ensured that I would see him differently. A light had been directed upon him from so unexpected a source that his shape, and the shadow which he cast, had become (if only for a moment) unfamiliar to me. Something else had changed also, or, rather, something else had sprung out of her lies; the extremity of feeling which I suffered in her presence, the sudden and inexplicable emotions which she released in me, gave me a sense of myself quite different from anything I had experienced with my father. I was at an age when I wished to grow and to develop, and this new awareness of myself lent some additional force to that desire. Gloria had managed to come between me and my father after all; which, no doubt, had been her intention from the beginning. I made a resolution never to see her again.

My father and I continued our work together, but from that day forward I am sure something changed. I believe he noticed some loss of interest or attention on my part; but he never complained. He seemed to be growing a little weary of the work, too, although this may have been part of a more general weariness. I realized soon enough that his sudden and mysterious absences from Albion Lane were not a mystery at all: he was spending hours in the company of his gambling friends and, as a result, his debts were becoming more and more difficult to manage. He never mentioned any of this to me, of course, but I knew.

I was going through the accounts one morning, when a letter arrived for me. It bore the postmark of Upper Harford and, since I had kept up an intermittent correspondence with my grandparents over the last two years, I assumed that it came from them. They seemed to have accepted the fact that I was staying in London with my father and yet, through all their cheerful messages, I had received the strangest sensation that they were ailing. The letter was not from them, however, but from Edward Campion. It was typewritten, because, as he explained, 'my writing has deteriorated'. I suspected that he was referring to his general condition, but there was otherwise no reference to his illness. He was about to start his studies at Reading University and he would be coming to London before he travelled there. Could we meet? 'Perhaps I will see your parents again, too,' he added at the end. 'I still remember meeting your mother all those years ago.'

My father had crept up behind me and was reading this over my shoulder. 'I don't understand what he says about your mother.' He sounded very cheerful.

'He means Gloria Patterson, dad. Don't you remember he saw you both together in Wiltshire? He didn't know.'

He turned down the corners of his mouth, a familiar token of disbelief or dismay. 'I haven't thought about her for years.' He sighed. 'Not for years.'

'But she thinks about you.' I said this before I realized what its effect would be.

'How do you know that, Timothy?' He came around the table and sat in front of me.

I could not lie to him directly, not when he was staring at me in that way. 'I saw her.'

'What?'

'I saw her once. Twice. But all she talked about was you.'

'Where did you meet her?'

'In the street, dad.' This was not altogether untrue, but I kept my fingers crossed beneath the table as I said it.

'Why didn't you tell me this?'

'It was nothing.'

'Nothing? How can it be nothing?' I had never seen him so disturbed before; I think he guessed something of the truth, and was afraid of it. He said no more but left the house, slamming the front door behind him. He returned a few hours later, apparently quite cheerful once again; he did not mention Gloria at all, but I could not help noticing some residue of suspicion and even resentment in his manner towards me. Once again she had managed to come between us.

Edward Campion arrived three days later, at the time he had suggested in his letter, and I waited by the window as he slowly came towards the house. He had a stick now to help him control his movements, but his body was still wracked by nervous tremors. 'I'm no better, you see,' were his first words to me as he climbed the front steps. We stood by the door for a moment, smiling at each other, and we did not shake hands. 'But you have changed,' he said. 'You seem older to me. Much older.'

'My father's out,' I replied. 'So we have the house to ourselves.' It was almost as if we were schoolboys again, although both of us knew that those days were gone. Now we were part of the world – a transition which seemed to have exhilarated Edward as much as it unnerved and baffled me. I had never seen him so excited and, as we sat together in my room, he explained to me his prospective studies at the new university as well as his plans for his career. But, as he concentrated so enthusiastically upon the future, I wondered what there was for me to tell him in return. I had really done nothing except live in my father's shadow; as for my future plans, well, I had none. I simply listened as Edward talked on eagerly, until the imbalance in our conversation grew so obvious that he faltered and tried to speak of other things. 'You're so lucky,' he said, 'to live in London. Do you remember how we used to talk about it? In the old days, Tim?'

'Yes. I remember.' For some reason I did not want to be reminded of those times, when we sat together in the tea-shop and speculated so intensely on what we would do with our lives.

'I suppose you go out a lot. Picture-palaces and so forth.'

'No,' I replied. 'I'm generally working with my father.' And at that moment the whole sad weight of my life fell upon me: as I spoke to Edward, all I could see ahead of me was an existence which in truth was becoming increasingly frustrating for me. And I felt humiliated, too – humiliated because I did not dare explain to Edward what my father's work was. I felt sure that he would dismiss it as some kind of ridiculous joke and, at this moment, that was precisely how it seemed to me as well. I was ashamed of my life and, I suppose, I was ashamed of my father. Edward did not press me any more, no doubt because he sensed my own feeling of shame or inadequacy. He left soon after, more awkwardly than he had come; it was not that we had ceased to care for one another but, rather, that his hopes for the future – and my lack of them – created a division between us. It was then, just after he had left the house, that I decided I would have to change my life.

But what was I to do? The arrival of Edward had re-awakened all my old hopes and ambitions, but how were any of them to be achieved? Suddenly I was thinking of Gloria once more, as I always did when I was tired or unhappy, but she was also part of the life that was imprisoning me: it would need some great effort on my part to exorcize what I now knew to be her truly malevolent spirit. What *was* I to do? As I wandered through our rooms and reflected miserably on all this, my father returned. He knew at once that something was troubling me, but he said nothing for the moment. He seemed to have forgotten our quarrel about Gloria a few days before, but there was still some reticence or uncertainty hovering between us. 'How was your friend?' he asked me casually as he laid the *Daily Herald* on the table in front of him. He used to joke that it was a method of divination, but I knew that he bought it only for the racing page.

'He was fine, dad.' I still felt some great weight upon me, and with a sigh I sat down on the sofa.

'Is he still the same?'

'Yes. Still the same.'

He looked up at me from the newspaper. 'I may not be an expert, Tim, but I think something is bothering you.'

'What could be bothering me?'

'Something is on your mind. I know that, because your eyes are drooping.'

I could not help laughing with him, but, even as I did so, my true feelings emerged. 'I'm sick of my life, dad.' I was still laughing.

'What did you say, Tim?'

'I'm sick of my life. No, I'm afraid of my life. The future looks so dark, dad, and I can't see anything ahead of me.'

He folded the newspaper away and sat down beside me. 'Listen to me, Tim. There is nothing to be afraid of. There is no darkness. When you brood on the future like this, you're just taking yourself away from the real world. You're entering some tiny space where all your fears are hidden, and that's where the darkness really lies.' It was almost as if he were giving one of his lectures to the Harcombe Circle, but he was much graver and gentler now. 'You're cutting yourself off from the world, and that's wrong. Don't do it, Tim. As soon as you get back in touch with what is real, you'll understand that you can do anything. Anything at all. Now, tell me, what do you want to do?'

'I'd like to go to university. Or to an evening institute. Something.'

'You can do that. What else would you like?'

'I want to earn my own living, dad.'

'You can do that, too.'

And so together we started to discuss these possibilities very calmly, as if it were the most obvious thing in the world to start a new life, until it was decided that I should enrol in studies of some kind while at the same time look around for other employment. The unspoken agreement between us was, of course, that I should stop working for my father. The details were still very vague, but as soon as I began wondering about the specifics of a university course, for example, he seemed to grow tired. 'Will you do me a favour, Tim?' he said. 'Put on some of your music. Please.'

Reluctantly, I went into my room and picked out a record at random; I still wanted to go over all the details that lay ahead but, when I came back, he was lying on the sofa with his legs outstretched. The music was Purcell's and he began to conduct it with an imaginary baton. 'This is the kind of thing your mother loved,' he said.

'You never told me that before.'

'I never thought of it before. In any case,' he went on, as if continuing with the same subject, 'you must learn not to worry. Not to brood. Think of this sonata, and the way it changes everything. There is no past and no future, Tim, just the two of us listening to the music.'

That was how we left the matter. On looking back now, it seems strange that the direction of my life could be altered so easily and with such little preparation. But perhaps that is always how important decisions are made. They are of such significance that they do not need to be anticipated or complicated by preliminary planning; they just occur, naturally and instinctively. So I lay in bed that night and considered the future with a hopefulness which I believed I had lost for ever; all difficulties seemed to disappear in the light of my enthusiasm, and even the prospect of a new job no longer seemed daunting. It was then I remembered that Stanley Clay was an attendant in an art gallery: surely that was the work for me, too? I could take on some temporary post at night, perhaps as a guard, and use those silent hours for the studies I was already contemplating. Everything now seemed possible, just as my father had explained it would.

I had kept the address which Stanley Clay had given to me in the Seven Stars, and on the following Sunday I went there in the hope of finding him at home. He lived near Hackney Square, in a block of flats which had been built in the last century as 'model dwellings for working men': these, at least, were the words cut into the blackened stone above its entry. I found Stanley's 'dwelling' easily enough, and he was astonished when he saw me at the door. 'She told me you'd gone back to Wiltshire,' he said.

'She was lying.' It was such an absurd lie, and one so easily discovered, that it occurred to me that Gloria might actually enjoy being found out.

'Come in then, Tim. It doesn't matter now, anyway.' He led me down a narrow passage which smelt of damp and stale food; the peeling wallpaper had a pattern of pink roses in yellow straw baskets, and I recognized it at once from my childhood in this neighbourhood. It had been used in the hallway of our old lodgings. And was that what it had been, after all – a childhood of garish wallpaper, stale smells, and small rooms like the one into which Stanley led me now? There was an old red sofa here, and a small chair on each side of the fire. It was if I had entered a sealed chamber in which I could not breathe, so great was the sensation of failure and loneliness that invaded me. Yet how could I assume Stanley was responsible for that, when I also seemed to be re-entering the atmosphere of my infancy? 'I'll just get some pennies for the gas,' he said. 'I'll make some tea.'

I followed him into his kitchen and, while his back was turned to me, I explained to him that I needed a job and asked him if there were any opportunities or vacancies in the gallery where he worked. He seemed visibly to relax when he understood that this was the reason for my visit, and promised that he would ask his supervisor the following morning. 'It will be nice to help you for once, Tim,' he said, as we sat together in the other room. He put a hand up to his neck and I saw at once that the old nervous tremor had partly reappeared. He noticed my glance, but only shrugged his shoulders. 'Nothing lasts for ever, does it? Nothing lasts for ever.' He spoke for a while about the art gallery and his work as an attendant there; but he might have been talking about someone else's life, so subdued and constrained he seemed.

Then he stopped suddenly, and just as abruptly rose from his chair. 'I'll show you something, Tim, if you promise never to mention it again. Not even to me.'

'Of course.'

I followed him across the passage into what must have been his bedroom, except that I noticed only the images which covered the walls. They were all images of Gloria – drawings, two paintings and some photographs which she had obviously given to him; they were deliberately posed, and she had even signed her name at the bottom in imitation of the film stars' photographs which she had known all her life. There was a sadness in that, as deep as the sadness of Stanley himself. But there were other photographs which must have been taken by him – of the house in Lant Street, of the front door, of Gloria walking down the street itself. There must have been at least a hundred of them, and I recalled how Stanley had told me that photography was his 'hobby'. 'I did them all with my Box Brownie,' he said. 'It's the latest.' He was silent for a moment and I did not know what to say. 'I was reading something, Tim,' he went on. 'Do you know this theory that a man and a woman were originally in one body before they were split apart? Your father would have studied it, of course.' I doubted that, but I said nothing. 'That's what love is, Tim. Looking for the other half.' He gazed at the photographs for a moment. 'Sometimes I feel it. I feel that she's the other half of me. That I can never be myself, never be whole, until . . .' He stopped, put one of his fingers in his mouth and started gnawing at the nail. 'But I know it's always going to be like this. The feeling of something missing, Tim. Of something lost. But it's me that's lost. I'm the one that's missing.' He sat down upon the bed, trembling; then he looked up at me, almost shyly, and I realized that he had never before spoken about his feelings. I doubt that he had ever said anything at all to Gloria herself. 'And if you're only half a person, Tim, then you don't feel right. You feel as if you're halfway down the pit, and you can't climb out again. I hate seeing her, Tim. It's like having a knife put in my face. But I have to see her. I can't think of anything else. It's like being dead and being alive at the same time. It's like being myself and not myself.' He stopped and got up from the bed. 'I know you hate her. And I hate her too.'

'I don't hate her exactly . . .'

But he was not listening to me. 'I know she says terrible things. I know she lies. But don't you see, Tim, that makes her more . . .' He could not think of the word and shook his head angrily. 'She doesn't want to see me now, and that's the same thing. I can't put it into words. It's like she's taunting me. So what do I do all day? I hope that she's going to change her mind. That's all. That's all I think about. All I ever want to think about.'

He bowed his head, and I put out my hand to him. It was the same gesture I had used as a child, in the old hall, and as soon as I touched him I had the same sensation – that he would never be anything other than what he was now: poor, lonely, despairing. 'It will be all right, Stanley.' I took my hand away from his shoulder. 'Everything will be all right.'

'No. It won't. Why should it be? Why should anything ever be right?' And at that moment there was nothing else: no connection with the past or future, only this infinitely extended and unendurable present misery. 'Don't worry,' he said after a while. 'I won't forget about the job, Tim.'

He remembered well enough. Within a month, after being interviewed and deemed reliable, I found myself working as a night guard in the gallery. It was called the Spencer Gallery, and housed a large collection of English painting which had once belonged to a nineteenth-century industrialist; it was close to Lambeth Bridge, on the south side, and took up three floors of an old house beside the river. I travelled there five nights a week and stayed on duty from seven in the evening until eight the following morning; it was my first job, if I discount all the time I had spent assisting my father, and I approached it with as much enthusiasm as if I had embarked upon a successful and highly paid career. My father seemed to share my optimism and after a few weeks readily agreed to my finding a small room in the neighbourhood of Lambeth. He did not wish to stand in my way, even at the cost of his own work; but I believe now, also, that he wanted to spare me the knowledge of his own increasing poverty and desperation as he sank further into debt. Stanley Clay worked during the day, so I hardly saw him. I soon learned from the others, however, that he led as solitary a life here as he did in his tenement flat. He said very little to his colleagues, and every lunchtime he would take his sandwiches and sit by the river; he remained on a bench there, and stared into the water until it was time to return to work. There was nothing else for him in this life, as I knew, and I did not often try to see him: he needed his silence. In any case, I now had my career to fashion. I still intended to enrol in some kind of course, my preference being for the study of English literature at an evening institute, but it was early autumn now and all the places for that year had been taken up; so, while I waited, I planned to use my nights in the gallery for private study. It was the perfect setting. I had a partner on night duty, but he spent most of the time asleep in the office where we made cocoa and filled in our work-sheets. In fact I was pleased to be spared his company: he was a little man with a wispy beard and watery, protruding eyes, who for some reason insisted on calling me 'pal' or 'squire'; he had a habit of making quite unfunny remarks and then doubling up with silent, mirthless laughter. I was always relieved when he eventually withdrew into the office, put his feet upon the desk and closed his eyes.

For then I had the gallery to myself. In my first weeks there I tried to apply myself to my library books; I chose a comfortable chair and would settle down with a copy of *Tristram Shandy* or *Pamela* or *Wuthering Heights*. But, in truth, I rarely progressed beyond the first few pages; I would get up from the chair and wander in the three long rooms which

comprised the gallery. The paintings were arranged chrono-
logically, so I seemed to be moving through time when I
began in Gallery A and walked along to Gallery C, but most
of them were landscapes or portraits from the eighteenth and
nineteenth centuries – Wilson, Gainsborough, Constable,
Turner, Palmer, Ford Madox Brown, Whistler. I stood among
them and, in the silence of the guarded night, I felt less
anxious than I had for many years.

The paintings seemed to glow upon the walls, all the rich-
ness of colour and the gradation of tone creating alternative
worlds in which I might lose myself – and with so many
different forms or perspectives, also, that the shape of the
gallery itself seemed to bend and shift. It was like walking
through a place of infinite recesses and sudden, echoing
depths. Sometimes I sat down on one of the wooden benches
placed in the middle of each room and stared at a particular
face or a particular landscape until I had forgotten everything
else around me. Then the very materials of the painting – the
canvas, the encrusted paint, the mottled surface of the varnish
– seemed to me to have a visible presence. It was not the
presence of the sitter or the landscape, but rather of the
person who had created them. I could hear the sound of my
own breathing as I sat there, but it was joined with the
breathing of the artist who existed everywhere within this
work. In the longest room, which stretched the whole length
of the house, there were two windows overlooking the Thames;
throughout the night the river gleamed with the reflected
light of the moon and the street-lamps, and there were times
when I would stand by a window and look down at the dark
water. It glistened and changed, yet it never seemed as fully
real as the paintings upon the walls behind me. It was too
vague, too attenuated: it lacked presence. Whenever I gazed
at it, I was always looking for some diversion, some accident,
to lend interest to it; but I never wanted anything to move or
to be changed in the paintings which I guarded.

And then one night I dreamed again. I had been working

in the gallery for about six months and had developed a system for my watches; every night I moved my chair from one painting to another, so that I could study each of them in turn. I had now arrived at a work by Gainsborough – it was the only one in the collection and had been given a prominent place in the room which overlooked the river. It was of a track within a wood (whenever I think of Gainsborough now, I remember an incomplete or endless journey), and there was something about the delicacy and detail of the paint that induced in me a kind of restfulness; while I sat in front of it it was as if I wanted to dream again, with that image of beauty to guide my sleep. Somehow I found myself getting up and walking towards the painting; or, perhaps, it was coming towards me. And then, without any surprise or hesitation on my part, I entered the frame.

FOURTEEN

HE FOUND HIMSELF WITHIN A wood, standing upon the
dark brown earth of a beaten track. But the soil was
neither firm nor hard beneath his feet; he was merely resting
upon it, since it was fine and dry enough to be scattered by
the mildest breeze. Timothy looked up and felt the power of
the sky upon his face, while all around him the brilliant green
of the trees and hedgerows was concealing pieces of the light
like a secret inheritance. It was noontide here, and he noticed
how the very tops of the trees assumed the shape of the small
and separate clouds which hovered above them. It was as if
these indistinct leaves were themselves attempting to become
clouds, to become part of the sky at last, and he experienced
a sensation of weightlessness as he pursued the track through
the bright leaves and boughs. There was so much depth and
movement in his surroundings that he felt himself being effortlessly swept forward, until he followed a curve in the road
and saw in the distance the level pink and yellow of that
place where the sky touched the land. It was the horizon of
all his hopes, like some great source which gave strength and
purpose to this scene, and yet it was one that he would not
reach. For now everything began to change; the air grew
thinner, and a translucent mist rose upwards to obscure the
pure outlines of the trees. The day itself was rolling backwards
and returning once more to the dawn. The beginning.

The wood had become dark, its trees growing so thick and
so straight that the spaces between them were mere ink lines
of blackness. This was a wood in which wild things might
roam, a true wasteland of woe. Timothy knew not his way,
and wandered in vain among hazel and hawthorn. There
were many birds perched upon branches, piping piteous for
pain of the cold. What were the sounds which swooned out of

the wood, but the roar of the wolves and of the wild swine, and of all wicked beasts that walk in the waste land? 'And yet,' he said, as he stood forlorn in this forest, 'the day drives on the dark. This place may perish and be replaced by another.'

So it was that the ground felt softer now beneath him and, when he looked down, he saw that he was treading among flowers – flowers of blue and gold, of white and vermilion, like jewels seen beneath water, and in so intricate a pattern that he could not unravel it. There was a passage of silence as he walked between the colours of the flowers, a silence like that of a cloister in which he held open a book with its white pages and with its blue or golden illuminations. He closed the book and, as he stepped out from the shade of the cool stone, he entered a walled garden. Here grew the rosemary and the gilly-flower, in square beds of earth between the small trees bearing fruit; the stone walls were wreathed with briar and fragrant eglantine, while the violet sky arched like a shell above them. The sounds of lark and nightingale revolved about him, and yet their notes were coming from beyond this place. He passed through a gate and there, in the clearing before him, he saw a tall tree rising between two deep green banks of earth. Here were the birds in profusion, all mingled together upon the branches, and he marvelled at their music as sweet and orderly as the garden from which he had just departed.

He walked on a little until he came to the crest of a hill and looked down upon a meadow filled with moss and sweet flowers; the track of a river gleamed among the grass, and beside it there ran all manner of deer while above them flocked the falcons and pheasants. A mist hung in the air, but now, as it descended to the level of the ground, Timothy noticed that even this meadow was encircled by wild crags and irregular mountains; there was no colour here, no, nor form, nor grace. In these dark regions of the world, the murmuring water turned into a torrent of woe and the warm wind fled between the precipices where no man could walk. The mist rose again as he watched, concealing the emblems of darkness, and all at once he saw a fair field full of folk. Men were moving a plough with oxen ahead of them, while four boys dragged horses with harrows across the bare earth. A child scared away crows with stones from his sling, as the birds carolled their defiance in the still air. For everything here was still, and each human figure was delineated in the same clear and even light. They stood in profile, or with faces turned towards him, and yet they cast no shadows; they took up their attitude according to their occupation, and dressed according to their rank. The merchant. The monk. The clerk. The cook. Standing together in the light. Illumination. Like the whiteness of a page that must be turned.

He started to descend this hill, when all at once he noticed that the scene had again changed before him; the mountains around him were no longer the dark quarters of the middle earth and he could see perched upon their sides, as if lowered by pulleys from the empyrean, little cities and castles, woods and hanging rocks, valleys and grottoes, lakes and towers. These were not mountains but circles of life spiralling down towards him, and in the left-hand corner he glimpsed a company of brightly dressed noblemen going forth to hunt the stag. From his vantage they seemed to Timothy to be the same size as the castle from which they had just departed; all the works of man and nature were of equal proportion here, the profusion of this world laid out in front of him as if he had been looking at the shapes made by moss or broken stone upon the flat surface of a wall.

No, not a wall, but the drawing of a wall. It was part of the drawing of a house, the landscape and gardens measured from A to G, with the secluded walks and paths, ponds and orchards, parks and avenues, all fenced around with symmetry. One area, set off from the trim parkland, was depicted as 'The Wilderness'; and it was here that Timothy now found himself. There was a house rising beyond two rows of sculpted trees, a stately mansion built of squared brick, and he walked through the prospect towards it. It was very much like a dream of a house, so firm and secure amid the perils of the world, and all the landscape bowed towards it. He entered the hall, the cool flagstones measuring his progress, and turned down a narrow passageway lined with many large and curious portraits; in that confined space, against the oaken panels which concealed the material walls, face seemed to be looking across to face. Endymion Porter. George Gower. Sir John Tradescant. Margaret Bacon. Elizabeth Riley. Jeremy Fry. Michael Wright. Jonathan Ashton. English faces peering out of the darkness. Some of them stood before carefully modelled draperies, some sat in small rooms, while some were posed in front of a prospect like the one Timothy had just seen. Those with a more magnificent air had become dim and indistinct with age, but the faces of the others were still bright. Eagerly they looked down upon Timothy, fixing him with their gaze, questioning him, pleading with him as if they wished to be set free into this formal and graceful English air. And yet in a certain sense they were already at liberty, part of the generations which would come after them.

Then he heard voices, or, rather, the echo of voices, somewhere within the house. He retraced his steps along the passage and returned once more to the great hall; there was a room beyond it, and now he could clearly hear two voices raised in argument.

'So, Pamela, we have seized, it seems, your treasonable papers.'

'Treasonable, sir!'

'Ay, I suppose so; for you are a great plotter; but I have not read them yet.'

'Then, sir, it will be truly generous in you *not* to read them; but to give them to me again unread: they are written to my father and mother only.'

'What can you write to them that I may not see? I must read them before I return them.'

Timothy crept closer and, as he peered around the open door, he glimpsed a young woman sitting by a desk; she had a quill pen in her right hand, with an ink-box and various scattered papers in front of her. A man stood over her, and now he began to speak in a quieter tone. 'Yes, by all means, every line that such a servant as *my* Pamela writes, be it to whom it will.'

It was there that Timothy left them; he did not understand what he had heard, and he did not wish to linger in a place where he might be discovered. He was tempted to go back through the passage, since he had a great desire to see the faces in the portraits once more, but he knew that it was time to move forward. He went out through the door, and found himself facing a different landscape. The ornamental gardens and stately prospects had disappeared, just as if they had been rolled up and put away within one of the carved wooden chests which Timothy had seen in the house.

Instead he walked into a wide and golden light. He was standing before a vale, through which a river fulfilled its course. I could walk here, he thought, and never count the miles – there is no tiredness or melancholy in such a place as this. I could walk towards that church, rising between the trees in the middle distance, or even towards those hills touched by the light of the horizon. And there is a bridge, spanning the river just as it retreats from my view. That must be the bridge of contentment: I can see its reflection in the gently moving water, so calm and bright that it seems to be a form of sleep.

The masses of shade and light here were like the trees and their reflection in the water, each calling to each: every detail of this scene led the eye towards the horizon, while the radiant tones of the landscape rose towards the general radiance of the sky. This was the picture of a golden age in which the earth aspired towards beauty – not a moment in time, not that, but rather the fulness and summation of time itself. It reflected some unknown antiquity of the world, just as the river reflected its banks, and Timothy knew that his own buried memories of other landscapes were somehow revived here.

He lay down upon the gently curving slope and, through the grass, glimpsed the human figures in this landscape. They were sitting or lying in the foreground like the guardians of the land, porters at the threshold of the image. Their bodies seemed to curve with the land itself, just as the backs of the animals in repose copied the line of the earth, just as the trees seemed to stretch across the air before gracefully declining, just as the clouds reflected the shape of the fields. The landscape was charged with common feeling, a sense of origin as subtle as the light which moved back and forth across this picture, taking the eye upwards from the earth and back into the sky. This was the line of beauty, the graceful double curve which seemed to Timothy to be a line of music, so soft and so prolonged it had become. It was the line of the English landscape, the flow of its being in the world, the ground of origin, the breathing earth upon which he walked and to which one day he would be consigned. And then he said out loud, 'I am in a landscape by Richard Wilson.'

He thought he heard the rumble of an oncoming storm, but after a few seconds he turned to see two horses galloping wildly across a field behind him. There was a wind coming from the river, and gusting upon it were the voices of the horsemen who seemed barely able to keep to their saddles. 'Damn my eyes, Hatchway, I always took you to be a better horseman than to overset our chaise in such fair weather. Blood! Didn't I tell you we were running to the right?'

His other words were lost, until another gust brought his companion's reply. 'Yes, Commodore Trunnion, I do confess as how you did give such orders, after you had run us foul of a post, so as that the carriage lay along and could not right herself.'

The two horses had been galloping several times around the field, managing to turn in smaller and smaller circles, until their riders successfully reined them in. They dismounted and, as they walked unsteadily to the river, they passed Timothy without noticing him; he followed them down the hill, and watched as the horses refreshed themselves in the clear water. One of the riders, by far the older of the two, was in a coat of blue broad cloth trimmed with brass buttons; he had breeches of blue cloth also, and a waistcoat of red plush lapelled with green velvet. His companion, Hatchway, was dressed in grey breeches and a loose white shirt. 'I run you foul of a post!' The commodore had obviously decided to continue the altercation, now that they were at their ease. 'You're a pretty dog, an't you, to tell me so above board to my face? Did I take charge of the chaise? Did I stand at the helm?'

'No. I must confess you did not steer, Commodore Trunnion. You were in a regular pickle.' The younger man had gone behind his employer's back, and was now hopping on one leg while making the most extraordinary grimaces at him.

'Damn my limbs! I don't value what you say a rope yarn. You're a damned mutinous –' He broke off there, too tired to pursue the argument, and instead began to survey the landscape into which they had so furiously propelled themselves. 'You know, Jack,' he said at last, 'I have been over rocks, and flats, and moorlands, but I have seen nothing to equal this. It's a regular landskip.' He put out his arms, and in a strong voice began to recite what sounded to Timothy like the words of a poem:

'The watery landskips of the pendant woods,
And flowing trees that tremble in the floods;
In the clear azure gleam the flocks are seen,
And floating forests paint the waves with green.'

Commodore Trunnion put his hand up to his eyes, the better to shield them from the glare of the sun, but then started rubbing it across his forehead and on to the top of his head.

'But where is my hat?' he bellowed. 'And my periwig! Where is my periwig?'

At that Timothy awoke. He fell forward with a start and, on opening his eyes, he realized that he was still sitting in front of the landscape by Gainsborough. 'This is the first time I have woken in the middle of a dream,' he said out loud in the empty gallery, and looked around in bewilderment. But then he recalled how on a summer afternoon, many years ago, he had sat with his father in Victoria Park. There had been families all around them – the mothers in long dresses, the fathers in shirt-sleeves and braces, the children in frocks or short trousers. But he remembered something else, even now: there had been a group of children chattering beneath the shade of a large horse chestnut tree. 'Orphan children,' his father had said. 'Poor orphans.' He could see them still, sitting on the earth and laughing, protected by the leaves and branches of the ancient tree, their legs and faces in the shadow while he sat with his father in the bright sun. He remembered how he had climbed into his father's lap and fallen quietly asleep. He wanted to sleep again now, and once more he gazed at the painting by Gainsborough; he had in fact woken only for a moment, and within a moment he re-entered the landscape.

He was back where he had started, on a track within the forest. It was dawn still, and patches of white mist lingered around him like fragments of a dream; he could see two grey posts ahead of him upon the narrow path, shining with the dampness of the air, but the masses of trees bending over the path in the middle distance were barely visible. Even as he watched, the mist was being drawn upward by the sun and, as it rose, it revealed those depths of the forest that had been obscured by the silvery vapour of the night. It was an awakening, and Timothy felt himself to be changed by it. For an instant he was possessed by the most curious sensation of surprise and recognition: this was a morning he had never seen but which somehow he still remembered. The mist had cleared altogether now and, in the distance, he could see a prospect of blue hills between the trees; perhaps they were the point to which the narrow path made its way, the true goal of the traveller.

But there were no travellers here. Timothy was quite alone among the trees on this autumn morning, with the mild rays of the sun slanting across the grey elm, the golden beech, the yellow sycamore and the crimson maple. There was a radiance among the leaves, and all the warm light of the earth seemed to rise towards the cooler tops of the trees that reflected the colours of the sky. He traced the light upwards, and noticed how the trunks gradually became more slender; the boughs themselves diminished as they grew higher, throwing off smaller and smaller branches until they ended in a general haze which hovered between the trees and the sky. Everything seemed to gleam, iridescent, as if the forest itself had been filled by a white breeze that billowed out beneath each leaf or twig and displayed its true form. There was no indistinctness here, but a soft buoyancy which entered all things, making the leaves and the clouds one element, lending a radiance to the colours shimmering around him. The sun emerged above the trees, and at once the shade deepened in the recesses of the forest: only for a moment had their true lightness been revealed. This was the vision of Thomas Gainsborough.

Timothy left the path and walked across the moss and bracken until he found a clearing where he could rest. The place was quite enclosed and, as he listened to the song of the thrush and the woodlark which echoed around it, he began to appreciate the meaning of the track from which he had just come: it was a reminder of that other world to which it led, but it also confirmed the solitude and peacefulness of the forest. It was a path which need not be taken, or one from which the traveller might stray in order to linger in this ancient world. There is the story of a dying stag which sobbed when it entered its own familiar glade, and now Timothy realized that he was crying: it was as if he, too, was experiencing something for the last time before it disappeared altogether from the earth. This was a place to which the pensive solitary might have come, attracted to the secret shades, and where he might have read the book of nature in all the plants and flowers which grew undisturbed. For it was here, not in the fields or in the ornamental gardens, that Timothy felt the true presence of the past around him; in such a place as this, as the English Druids had once found, you might consult the dead and live over former ages. It was possible here to be reconciled to the very fact of death. Now he understood that visionary gleam which seemed to dwell within everything and, as he looked upwards at the shimmering contours of the leaves against the sky, he saw the bright air as a silver radiance trembling around the world as it plunges through endless night.

Suddenly the evening came, and he roused himself from thoughts of vast embowering glades, of twilight groves, and visionary vales, in order to make his way out of the forest. He returned to the path easily enough, and could not help lingering there to watch the sun descend upon an orange and turquoise horizon which could just be glimpsed beyond the purple trees. But now he saw human figures who, at the end of the day, had come to collect wood and berries: they stretched out their arms against the panoply of branches, or bent down towards the crimson earth, and in their movements Timothy saw how naturally they assumed the same lines and curves as the trees around them – for they were an aspect of the forest, too, and could not be imagined apart from it. They laboured so calmly and so quietly that he stood quite still, so as to make no sound; and then, as the deeper shades and tones of evening began to fall, they slowly departed. They seemed to fade away, leaving only the subdued browns and dark greys of the foliage.

Timothy stood uncertainly beside the narrow track, while the sky itself dissolved into dark elusive vapours. Everything around him was now confused and indistinct, except for a red glow upon the edges of those leaves and stones which had somehow caught the last vestiges of light. He put out his hand, to see if it also reflected that light, when he heard the sound of a jingling harness close by; then, within a few moments, a lean, lank, broken-winded horse came ambling along the path with a rider just as thin and spare as itself perched precariously on its back. As they approached, Timothy noticed that the rider was a parson, dressed entirely in black and with a black hat sitting as uncomfortably upon his head as he sat upon the horse. He grasped a tattered bridle with his left hand, while with his right he was holding a book which he read even as the horse came through the forest. So engrossed was he in his volume, in fact, that he did not notice Timothy until the horse almost stumbled upon him.

'Oh by heavens,' the parson cried, 'we might have destroyed you! Halt, Rosinante, halt.' His mount was going so slowly that it would scarcely have grazed Timothy, but it came to a stop very readily. 'What a tract of country have I run,' its rider continued, 'and all the time reading in my own book of journeys.' The horse began to amble forward again, and Timothy kept pace beside them; at which point the parson leaned over and started to speak to him confidentially, as if trying to conceal something from the horse. 'Do you know the common wisdom? That all journeys must end where they began, or else we would not know that we had been abroad? Listen, my author says it here.' He sat upright again and read aloud from the book which he held in his hand. ' "Are we for ever to be twisting and untwisting the same rope? For ever in the same track – for ever at the same pace?" And then my author says on the same page – it is the first page of the fifth volume, if you wish to consult it later . . .' Timothy nodded gravely at this. 'My author goes on to say, "Shall we for ever make new books, as apothecaries make new mixtures, by pouring only out of one vessel into another?" Now tell me. Where are *you* going?' Timothy brushed some golden leaves from his sleeve but, before he could answer, the parson began talking again. 'But, of course, you must ride with us. Rosinante can carry you with great ease, since I never have one single ounce of flesh upon my own bones. My horse and I are centaur-like, as you can see, all of a piece. My name is Yorick. How do you do? Here, sit behind me.' So Timothy found himself behind Parson Yorick, as Rosinante made its way through the forest; and, as they rode, the good parson still seemed to be speaking continually. 'We ride slowly, you see, but I can compose my sermon . . . compose my cough . . . compose myself to sleep . . . as I ride on this eminence of horse flesh. And there is another thing to help me on my way. Do you see the poor skull of this beast? Why, I can sit mechanically upon him and meditate delightfully on the vanity of the world and the flight of time with the advantage of this death's head before me. Where do you come from?'

In truth Timothy hardly knew. They had reached the edge of the forest, but it was now so dark that he saw only indistinct masses and shapes, stray objects enfolded in obscurity and waiting to be born once more into the light. 'Gainsborough,' he replied.

'Why, that is a long march.'

'No. I mean –'

But the parson had already gone the way of his own thoughts. 'There is a painter of that name, too. He plays the viol da gamba, and is reputed to like nothing better than the old English music. He made a sketch of it that I once saw. Well, every road must have a beginning, as they say . . .'

He continued talking, sitting bolt upright upon Rosinante, but Timothy was so drowsy after his day in the forest that he was soon lulled to sleep by the parson's low voice and by the horse's slow pace through the open country. It was dawn when he awoke, and he looked about him as the world came to life; colours returned to their proper objects, light pervaded the scene, and the whole great form of the landscape seemed to breathe again. Parson Yorick knocked his legs against the side of Rosinante, and stretched out yawning. 'It is a new world,' he said. 'Do you feel the breeze blowing from the green hills? Here are the meadows, and beyond them Salisbury. But look there, there is the cathedral. We will leave you now. Good day!'

Timothy dismounted from Rosinante but, before he could properly thank Yorick for his kindness, the parson and his mount had disappeared. He was quite alone in the meadowland, and it was with this sudden experience of solitude that he looked earnestly towards the spire of Salisbury Cathedral: it seemed not to be a work of man but of nature, rising among the trees as if it were a part of the landscape or some guardian spirit of the river which flowed in the foreground. The colours around him subdued his troubled mind, leaving him in some unchanging relation to this grand scheme of light and shade; for it was a landscape charged with feeling, its great curves and bounding lines suggesting freshness and amplitude, the fulness of the beauty of this earth, which found an echo within Timothy himself. And, as he gazed, the river and the meadows lay within him, and the sky, never before so beautiful, sank into his heart and held him like a dream. This great cathedral rose from the green earth into the firmament, and the scene haunted him as if it were a passion of his own. He watched it for so long that he felt as if the whole earth could be removed, and yet this ancient building among its trees and water would be sustained by his own spirit of wonder. It was all one life.

He turned back across the meadow, the gleaming dew clinging to him as he walked among the long grass and left a trail of darkness across the earth. It seemed to him that he was moving from feeling to feeling, as the light and shade billowed about him within the currents of the air. As he crossed the meadow, he noticed a hare ahead of him; with her feet she was raising a mist from the dew which, glittering in the sun, hovered around her wherever she leapt. He decided to walk in her track, which made a perfect curve through the grass before coming to rest in front of a thick hedge; he followed the line of the hedge until he found an opening and, on climbing through, came out on to a patch of level ground that looked out over a wide landscape. All at once he could see the gentle declivities of wooded hills, luxurious meadow flats sprinkled with flocks and herds, well-cultivated uplands, ponds and running streams, farms and cottages, all stretching out towards the horizon in a series of radiating lines and flowing curves. The morning mist had now begun to clear, and it changed this picture to one of deeper or more variegated green; he glimpsed hedgerows like little lines of wood, small farms which were green to the very door, and wreaths of smoke sent up in silence from among the trees where gypsies made their home. Thus did the landscape connect with the quiet of the sky, in this morning of John Constable's exultation.

As the mist rose so the wind grew stronger, and Timothy observed its passage across the earth in the sudden changes of colour, in the momentary gleams of light flashing from the narrow streams, in the shadows racing across the undulating grass. The whole landscape was now filled with depth and distance, so that in the moist atmosphere it seemed to tremble like a great globe containing all the colours of the world: the grey stone of an old wall turned to violet and then to green, as the wind blew yellow and scarlet flowers against it. All the world was bathed in a luminescence invented by Joseph Wright, and even in the darkest shades lay traces of brightness – as if theirs was the darkness of buried silver rather than of lead or slate. It was the radiance of the sky which interfused all things and, when Timothy looked up, he saw the wide air filled with shape and movement. A lower ocean of dark clouds remained quite still while luminous wreaths and pillars of cloud floated across it in slow array. Spires and circles of iridescence glimmered through stratus and cumulus alike, so that it seemed as if the freshness of the earth itself had soared into the empyrean.

But now it began to change. The air grew colder and, issuing from the palest blue of the horizon, came bands of darkness that gradually covered the sky; the light left the landscape and patches of gloom appeared within the clouds as if the earth were somehow casting its shadow upon them. Steps of grey vapour climbed into the turbulent atmosphere and then, suddenly, great swathes of opaque rain swept across the land. But this storm subsided as quickly as it arrived; the rain seemed to sway and curve before it moved away, and Timothy looked up to see great masses of pale cloud smoking and heaving with the passing of the tempest. Close beside him was a withered tree, bent against the remnants of an old stone wall, which through all the wind and rain had seemed enshrouded in its own bleak music. He walked towards it, and in its crumbling bark he recognized an element more solitary and mysterious than anything else he had noticed in this landscape. In the contours of the blasted tree he could see images of ancient towers, of crags and precipices bathed in an unearthly glow; on its mottled surface there was the strangest gleam, which conveyed the moods of twilight, smoking ruins, and solitariness. Lightning must have killed the tree and left such radiance in its withered shape that he could view there John Martin's vision of the world.

And then everything began to dissolve in a billowing light, not light but clouds of light, a vaporous turbulence that filled the world with mistiness and silence; it was as if the earth and sky had become one element, tossed within storms of brightness, the horizon now soaring upwards into regions of gold, vermilion and yellow ochre. But what was this billowing colour beneath the horizon? It was the sea, the real sea! It glistened in the light reflected from its transparent green surface, conveying such a promise of ease and freedom that the tears came to his eyes; there were glints and slivers of light dancing across it, and shafts of brightness which swept downwards into the liquid depths of cobalt and ultramarine. There was nothing in the world apart from this and Timothy's

vision was filled with mist and steam; the round ocean, and
the living air, and the blue sky, were filled by a motion and a
spirit that impelled all things, all objects of all thoughts, and
rolled through all things.

He could feel the mist blowing against his face, as the forms
themselves shifted and eddied about him, until all was
suddenly calm; it was as if the colours had found the idea
which they had wished to express and needed to move no
more. He found himself looking out upon a huge sea of mist
which rested at his feet, striated by blue chasms of thought
and split by gloomy streams of vapour which spiralled downwards. He was looking at music, slowed down until it had
become a landscape – the very laws of its being revealed in
colour and in line, a line which curved as the earth curves, as
a song curves, as a dream curves. Turner's dream of England.
And as he gazed into the oceans of silent form, he could see
flights of stairs, climbing upward, higher and higher until the
last staircase came to an abrupt end at the edge of an abyss;
he watched as translucent lakes, shining like great mirrors,
turned from silver expanses of quiet water into seas that
threatened to engulf him. And now upon the rocking waters
of this world appeared innumerable faces, upturned towards
the whirling heavens: faces imploring, wrathful, despairing,
surging upwards by myriads, by generations, by centuries.

Then everything faded away, like the visions of faces before
sleep. The ocean had turned into a vast area of sparkling ice,
the surface very uneven, descending low, and interspersed
with rifts which sank deep. This sea or, rather, this vast river
of ice, seemed to wind among its dependent mountains, whose
aerial summits hung over the recesses. Their icy and glittering
peaks shone in the sunlight over the clouds, and Timothy
heard an echo of a voice, seeming to descend from them:
'Wandering spirits, if indeed ye wander, and do not rest in
your narrow beds . . .' He heard no more, but at that moment
suddenly he saw the figure of a man at some distance advancing towards him with extraordinary speed. Timothy watched

him, and then spoke out loud in his alarm. 'This reminds me of a story, of which the meaning has never been understood.' But then the mist and rain descended once more, and it seemed to Timothy that the figure had turned into a train hurtling through the vaporous smoke which it created. Rain, steam and speed all at once involving the world in wreaths of moisture as if no thing or object of sight could ever be fixed.

But then the colours swirling around one another began to lose speed and, as their momentum slowed, to separate out into their component shades or tones – into violet, dark green, a pale dead gold, and the rusty traces of many colours gleaming beneath a crescent moon. There were arches of trees, of horse chestnut and oak, and beyond them was the small dome of a hill which shone in the reflected light. This was not a wild place, not an area of storm and turbulence, but some valley of vision interfused with the colours of dying timber and of decaying stars. The valley by moonlight with the evening star: the English vision of Samuel Palmer glowing among these assembled forms like an hallucination. Timothy could count the rows of white stones on the hillside ahead of him, and he started to climb the slope of glowing green which seemed to spring up around his footsteps; he came out upon a ridge of dark red earth and saw before him a solemn moor, its furze shrouded in blue shadow, and the barer ground stretching beyond in graduating half-tints. He could see a line of stunted firs which, in conjunction with a range of gaunt thorns all stretching their limbs one way, gave some indication of the ferocity of the wind which blew across this deserted place. Yet was it so deserted? A line of upright stones, daubed with lime, seemed to give some indication of a road across this waste; and then, just as if they had emerged from the evening star which gleamed above them, two figures came running across the moor. As they came closer to Timothy, he could see that they were children; they turned off the moor, on to what seemed to him to be some rough highway, and when he advanced towards this track or road he found a sand-pillar with the letters w.h. cut on its north side, g. on its east and, on the south-west, t.g. There was a hole near the bottom of this weather-worn block and, stooping down, he perceived that it was full of snail-shells and pebbles: he took out one of the shells and, in the moonlight, saw that its spiral form was the very image of the landscape in which he stood. He could hear voices close to him now, the voices of children: they must have been hiding near by, sheltering perhaps in some favoured spot among the gorse. He listened to a young girl's words: 'If I dare you now, will you venture? If you do, I'll keep you. I'll not lie there by myself: they may bury me twelve feet deep, and throw the church down over me; but I won't rest till you are with me. I never will!' She suddenly appeared and started to run across the moor; she was laughing, but then she turned and shouted, 'Run, Heathcliff, run!' before disappearing over the horizon. Run, Heathcliff, run! Run before you are trapped in this vision where you are hiding. Run!

And then the vision faded. The moon and evening star grew paler as the sun rose and charged the world with its own brightness. In its even glow Timothy could see every detail of the valley to which he had now returned; the very blades of grass, springing from patches of mauve shadow, seemed to be exactly numbered in the vibrant air. There was no aerial perspective here to subdue all the bright colours around him, or blur the precision of the dandelion puffs and blossom, of the variegated earth and gravel, of the grey pebbles clear at the bottom of the stream: all these things were as diverse in tint and shade as they are found in nature, bathed as they were in a brilliant momentary light. It was as if the sun had suddenly emerged between clouds and, in that moment of Ford Madox Brown's illumination, all the world rejoiced. As Timothy looked out at the translucent stream and the violet grass, he was in love with transience and half in love, too, with the little girl who was watching this scene: she had been standing on just the same spot at the edge of the water ever since Timothy had paused here. Ah, his arms were really benumbed. He had been pressing his elbows on the grass and dreaming that he was standing on the bridge in front of Dorlcote Mill as it looked one February afternoon many years ago. The time when he sat beneath the shade of the great chestnut tree, and when he gathered the purple plumy tips of the reeds, and when he watched the rushing spring tide of the great Floss between the green pastures. Was this what he truly remembered now, this landscape which had the vividness and precision of a sudden memory from childhood? Or was it the memory of Maggie Tulliver seated in her little parlour above the river, with one candle that left everything dim in the room except a letter which lay before her on the table. 'Oh God, where am I?' she cried out in her loneliness. 'Which is the way home?'

Oh God, where am I? Timothy was standing beside a dark river and could faintly taste the thin sulphur of a foggy London evening. Yes, he was standing upon one of the bridges which span the Thames; he was outside the gallery in which he worked, but this was some different time. Nocturne. The darkness crept among the wharves and banks, and mingled with the shadows of the houses and the buildings beside the river; but it was so soft a darkness, filled with all the sighs of the city, that it had gathered light within itself. This was an English landscape, also, its bands of subdued colour releasing the sadness of Whistler's exile. Pale lights glimmered above the river, so that its surface seemed to rise upwards until it mingled with the darkness of the middle air; there were patches of grey and silver resting upon its banks, and in their reflected light Timothy could glimpse the fog in movement. There were footsteps behind him on the bridge and, in the foggy air, the words of two people hovered around him.

'Partly. Do as you wish, Jasper.'

'I'll go and see him, if you like.'

'I am so afraid. No, writing will be better.'

'Very well. Then he shall have the letter tomorrow afternoon.'

'Don't let it come before the last post. I had so much rather not. Manage it, if you can.'

Then they were gone. Stray words, and yet how much meaning might be conjured out of them – wreathed as they were with the atmosphere of this foggy night? No doubt they had their own bleak story, those two who walked away from him into the quiet city.

A hand was laid lightly and suddenly on his shoulder and, when he turned in alarm, he saw the figure of a solitary woman dressed from head to foot in white garments; her face was bent in grave inquiry as she pointed into the dark fog. 'Is that the road to London?' she asked him.

'Why, this is London.'

'Then I shall follow the two who walked ahead of you. Perhaps we are going towards the same destination.'

She laughed and went on her way, leaving Timothy cold and unsettled. Where was he, after all? He looked once more into the fog as it moved about him, and in its shifting iridescence he believed that he could see other forms and objects. Impressions. Points of light. The vortex. Squares of colour. Abstract shapes. Shadows. This is how it all began, he thought. Then he woke up, and found himself still seated in front of the Gainsborough landscape.

FIFTEEN

I WORKED IN THE GALLERY for three years; it seems a long time when given a duration, but it passed soon enough. Perhaps that is the characteristic of a wasted life – not how long it takes to ebb away but, rather, how quickly it vanishes. After a few months I had been promoted from night supervision to daytime duties as a guard, and I spent my hours standing silently among the infrequent visitors. They barely glanced at me, and one of the strangest pleasures of working there was the sense in which I had become invisible; I had supposed that no human presence could compete against the more enduring identity of the paintings upon the walls, but, curiously enough, many people hardly looked at them at all. They simply walked around, surreptitiously examining one another.

I in turn examined them. It might be a gesture, or a sudden movement, or the shape of a coat or a jacket – something would arrest my attention, and I would hurtle into that person's existence with such velocity and intentness that it was as if I were falling from a great height on to the earth. Perhaps it was the fact that I had no proper life of my own that left me so susceptible to others; perhaps it had something to do with my dreams. I do not know why it happened, even now; it just happened. There was an old woman, I remember, who was really more interested in the view from the window than in any of the paintings. For a moment I looked at the tattered edge of her red cloth coat, and all at once it was as if I were standing beside her in her small house: I could smell the dust on the sofa, I could see the charred pieces of old newspaper in the grate, I could hear her muttering to herself as she moved from the sitting-room into the kitchen. I knew about her dead husband, and about her son who had been away for many years. I recognized all this and then, just as suddenly, I was back in the gallery with her as she lingered by the window and watched the river moving slowly towards the sea. And all at once I thought of my father.

I had one companion, in Stanley Clay. He continued to work in the gallery and, at lunchtime, we would go down to the Thames together and eat our sandwiches on a bench by the embankment. Often we said nothing to each other, and just gazed at the water until it was time to go back, but there were occasions when he talked about Gloria. 'She passed me in the street yesterday,' he might say, or 'I asked after her brother. Do you remember her brother?' I knew well enough that he still watched her and sometimes tried to speak to her; but I realized, too, that she continued to ignore or even to ridicule him. I could see her smiling as she did so. As a result, over the months and years, he grew more sallow, more wasted. There is always one expression, passing over the face of a person in silent thought, which reveals the true being and which never really changes: now, in Stanley's face, I could see the lineaments of the young man he once was and the old man he would become.

And then one day, while we were sitting by the river, Gloria came and stood in front of us. 'What's this?' she said. 'Feeding-time at the zoo? Don't you two look pretty in your uniforms?'

Stanley was hunched upon the bench, trembling; he had his eyes fixed upon the ground and would not look up. I felt such sorrow for his condition that I was not afraid to speak to her. 'What are you doing here, Gloria?'

'I came to see the pictures, didn't I?' I laughed in disbelief, and she flared out in her old, angry way. 'That's no crime, is it? I suppose you think I know nothing. But I do. Ask your dad. I know all about pretty pictures.' She glanced at Stanley for a moment. 'And photographs.' Now he did look up at her, and she gave a triumphant smile. 'Hello, Stan. You could do with a haircut.' She turned towards me again. 'Say hello to your dad for me.' She gave that same exultant smile, and then she left us.

That was all: there seemed to have been no reason for her visit, except some wish to mock or to belittle us. Perhaps she wanted to assert her hold over Stanley, and to display it in my presence. Or perhaps, with nothing better to do, she had simply come on a whim. Stanley was still sitting hunched upon the bench, but he was no longer trembling; he just sat very quietly, his eyes upon the ground, and he said nothing when eventually I tapped him on the shoulder and walked back with him to the gallery.

I had experienced a momentary sense of guilt when Gloria mentioned my father, since I had not seen him for two years. During the first few months I worked in the gallery, I had often travelled from my small room in Lambeth to Albion Lane; I sensed even then that my father was growing more careless and untidy in my absence, but I preferred not to notice such signs. He himself never complained, or even mentioned what must have been for him a much more solitary condition. There were even times when he seemed pleased to be alone, and I suspect that he was trying to shield me from the consequences of his gambling. He was ashamed of his weakness, and of his poverty. So my visits became less and less frequent; several weeks passed, sometimes, before I returned to Albion Lane. And then I went back one evening in early November to find that he had gone. The flat was now occupied by an Irish family, and my father had left no forwarding address. He had disappeared. I can admit now that I was relieved by this. His slow decline disturbed me – not so much because of my concern over his condition, but because I saw in him some image of my own future. For I was ashamed of my own life, too; ashamed of the fact that I had settled into a dull job and a dull routine, ashamed of my inability to secure any place at a college or evening institute. I had begun to lose interest in the idea of an education, in any case, and the need to earn my own living led me to acquiesce in my failure. So I never did study English literature after all. There is no humiliation worse than the consciousness of a wasted life. It stains the spirit, forestalls hope, and destroys any motive for action or change. There were times when I believed that I had inherited all of this from my father, which was why I had watched his own slow dilapidation with such anxiety. Was it possible – was this the true nature of my inheritance, the legacy of a dispirited life passed from generation to generation? So I never mentioned my father to anyone, not even to Stanley, and the years went by.

Three years altogether before I realized that my life would have to change. I had no sudden revelation, however; what occurred was simply an unexpected but powerful desire to see my grandparents once more, and to revisit the farmhouse where I had spent some of my early years. I was sitting in the gallery one morning when I had a vision of the white road down which I had often walked as a schoolboy: I could smell the dust baking in the summer heat and even reach out to touch the hedgerows growing on either side. Then it was gone, leaving me with an overwhelming feeling of peace and safety. I had no real belief I could start a new life, because even then I realized that such a thing was impossible – no life can be wholly renewed when there are so many forces already working within it. Had I not already suspected my father of bequeathing to me his own consciousness of waste and shame? No, at the time I wanted only to leave my job and return to my grandparents for a while. I never even considered writing to them in advance: I assumed somehow that they would always be waiting for me there. I told my employers of my decision and then explained to Stanley that I would come back to London within a month or so. I was not convinced of this, but I could not bear the experience of any final parting.

Yet it was with a light heart that I travelled by train through the familiar countryside, until I finally arrived at Upper Harford Station. I expected it to have changed – somehow to have reflected the changes in my own life – but there was still the same waiting-room of local yellow stone and the same well-kept borders of flowers beside the platform. I had only one suitcase (so few were my belongings even still) and I took the motor-bus which left me at the bottom of the lane I knew very well. It was late November, the same season of the year when I had first walked down this path with my grandfather and felt the brightness of the winter sun upon my back, and it was as if nothing whatever had taken place in the interval. No doubt I was still very like the boy who had once reluctantly accompanied his grandfather towards a new home. I only understood one thing about myself and that *was* my self – there was always the same essential identity preserved beneath changing circumstances and changing moods. And somehow I understood, also, that the idea of the world I grasped as a child was the one which I still possessed; it would always be for me a place of phantoms, pervaded by my father's presence.

So, as I walked up the white lane, I began to realize why my grandfather had always talked to me in the same direct way; he knew that the small boy could comprehend as much as any adult. It was the same way he treated me now as I opened the gate and found him stooped over a bed of earth. 'Hello,' he said, as if I had left just yesterday. He straightened up and sighed. 'I always meant to plant some sunflowers here, you know. For when you came back.'

'I am back.'

'I can see that.' He shook my hand and gave me the same bright, direct look I knew so well. 'And now here's Mrs Sinclair.'

My grandmother came running out of the house towards me. 'We knew it,' she said as she embraced me. 'We knew it.' And the dog, Monday, barked around the three of us before putting his paws up against me.

As we sat in the kitchen during that late afternoon, I tried to describe to them what had happened to me over the last few years. When I explained how I had worked with my father for a while, I noticed that they looked briefly at one another. They seemed much happier with the idea of my job in the art gallery, although I emphasized to them that it was one without prospects of any kind. My grandfather stopped me when I tried to apologize for my long absence. 'You followed your instincts,' he said, 'and that was what you should have done. We always knew you'd return at the right time.'

'I never guessed there was a right time.'

'There's always a right time. And there's always a right place. Isn't that why you've come back here?'

'That's true,' my grandmother added eagerly. 'Everyone belongs somewhere.'

And perhaps she had the answer after all. I may have had a sense of my own identity, of something unchanging within me, but I had no very clear idea of what it consisted – or to what it belonged. And was that the origin of Stanley Clay's misery, the sense of not belonging?

'Have you kept in touch with your father?' my grandmother was asking me.

I did not know how to reply. I did not want them to think that I had abandoned or neglected him, but I found it hard to explain the circumstances in which I had lost all contact with him. 'Not really,' was all I could think of saying. They were obviously waiting for something more. 'He always was very independent.'

My grandfather was looking steadily at me, and I blushed. 'We believe we've seen him, Timothy. No. That's not quite true. We saw something about him. We saw his name on a poster.' Oh God, what was this? Was he wanted by the police? Had he been murdered? I think I started to laugh. 'A poster for the circus.'

'What?'

'A circus *and* a fair.' My grandmother replied for him.

I still did not understand what they meant, and my grandmother, embarrassed now, waited for her husband to speak. 'His name was there, Timothy. Clement Harcombe. Magician. And hypnotist.'

In my astonishment I laughed out loud again. 'He never was a magician,' I shouted. 'It was all real.'

'Well, that was all it said. You can't argue with a poster.'

Now I saw my father's disappearance for what it was: he had left Albion Lane in order to take up some kind of wandering life and, inconceivable though it seemed to me, he had elected to use his gifts in a fairground. But how could he have left behind all the people who consulted us? Then I remembered that he had done the same thing once before, when he had walked out of the old hall for the last time. But then to go on to this – to work as a circus performer . . .

'They picked a good spot,' my grandmother was saying. 'There's been a fair on that common ever since I was a girl.'

'And long beyond that, Mrs Sinclair. Long beyond that.' It was as if my grandfather were in some way trying to console me. 'There were strolling players there centuries back.'

'Did you see him?' was all I could think of asking, even though I did not particularly want to know the answer.

'No, Timothy, we didn't. We just saw the words. We didn't inquire any further.' It was obvious, from my grandfather's expression, that he had not wanted to make any inquiries at all.

'I'm tired,' I said. 'I think I'll have a little rest.' But I could not sleep. I lay fully clothed upon the bed in my mother's old room and stared at the ceiling which had been painted dark blue with white stars in honour of my return so many years before. Now, once again, everything had changed. I could not think of my father without pain – not for my own sake, but for the image of his humiliation and frustration. It was then I experienced something else. As I lay upon the bed, I felt as if I were wearing a clown's costume and had been plastered with a clown's white make-up. In my mother's room I was sporting a bulbous red nose, a large scarlet mouth and a ginger wig. I thought for a moment that I had entered one of my dreams, so vivid was the sensation, but the experience quickly passed over me and was gone. Then, at last, I fell asleep.

The next morning I travelled into Upper Harford with a strong desire to see my old school again. At the time my interest surprised me, since I had not thought of St William's for the past three or four years; but now I realize that at moments of great change it is customary to return to the scenes of an earlier life. There may be some comfort to be drawn from the very fact of continuity, as if the persistence of certain houses or streets affords some hope for the persistence of one's own life, or it may reflect some simple nostalgia – I do not know. Whatever the reason, I found myself on this winter's day lingering outside the iron gates of the school.

'It looks much smaller, doesn't it?' I knew the voice at once. 'Everything looks smaller when you come back.' Edward Campion was standing beside me, swaying slightly, as he always did, trying to keep his balance in the world. 'But I'm still the same, I believe. I'm not any smaller, am I?'

'No. You're the same.' I turned to face him. But then, even as we smiled at each other, I remembered all his plans about university. 'I didn't know you were still here,' I said. 'I thought –'

'You thought?' He sounded defensive rather than curious.

'Nothing. I just didn't expect to see you.' For a moment there seemed very little left to say. We both looked through the bars of the gate together at the school where we had met so long before.

'That's where you found the poor crippled boy.' Edward laughed. 'Come on. Let's have a drink. They're just about to open.'

There was a public house on the high street of Upper Harford; we had passed its dark oak doors on many occasions during our schooldays, but this was the first time I had been inside. Edward seemed to know it very well, however, and immediately started a conversation with someone behind the bar. 'Do you remember Ian?' he asked me as a young man carried the drinks over to our table. 'He was in the class above us.' We nodded at each other, but I did not recognize him. In this unfamiliar place I felt more of a stranger than ever now, and I found it difficult even to talk to Edward. We managed to discuss the old times for a while, but he seemed reluctant to mention the years he had spent at university. 'I didn't tell you I had a job, did I?' he said at last.

'Is that why you came back?'

He chose not to answer me directly. 'I'm working in the post office. I'm one of the managers.' I remembered that this had been his father's job, also. 'They all know me there. It's easier.' I knew what he meant: easier to survive among people who understood his disability and who were accustomed to his erratic, shambling gait. But he had once entertained such plans for the future – he had conceived so many hopes for himself in another time and another place. All of that seemed to have come to nothing.

Edward had been drinking very quickly, and went over to the bar to refill his empty glass; he also came back with a small measure of whisky, which he swallowed first. 'Were you asking me about university?' he said, abruptly launching into the subject I had decided not to raise. 'I finished the course and I got my degree.'

'That was good –'

He raised his hand, forbidding me to say anything further. 'I never liked it there. I never felt at home. I was always the one they were nice to, and that made me uncomfortable. I lost interest in my studies after that, you see. It was like some confidence trick I was playing on myself. Do you understand now?' I understood: he had not been able to escape his disability, after all. He had gone to university with hope and enthusiasm, but he had not been able to avoid his inheritance. And this place, Upper Harford, was part of that inheritance; so he came back. I noticed for the first time what he was wearing: an ordinary dark grey suit with a cheap white shirt and nondescript tie, while above it was his pale, writhing face. He was looking at me with his sad, tremulous eyes. 'It's much easier here,' he was saying. 'They leave me alone. I'm not the best of company in some moods.' A grandfather clock in the next room chimed out the hour. 'I have to get back,' he said. 'Now that I'm a wage slave.'

We left each other outside, having arranged to meet the following evening. Perhaps it was because I was unaccustomed to drinking, but I was suddenly seized by a fit of low spirits so acute that I could hardly walk along the high street. Even the stones of the pavement depressed me, and I realized once again that I was still a stranger here. I walked a little way out of town until I came across the old settlement which Edward and I had explored many years before – that had been the day he talked about his ancestors. But if I did not belong here, where did I belong? I started walking back. Then, all at once, I realized that I belonged with my father. Even now. Even as he was working in the circus.

I returned to my grandparents' house in a happier mood. I told them I had met Edward unexpectedly, but I was more intent upon another subject. 'What was the name of the fair?' I asked them that evening.

My grandfather knew immediately what I meant. 'Blackmore's,' he said. 'It comes here every year.'

That was the solution, of course. The fair travelled around the country, continually returning to its customary sites. 'When was it here last time?' I tried to sound as casual as I could.

'That would have been the spring,' he answered, graver now than before. 'Blackmore's comes here every spring.'

'So it will be back soon?'

'Soon enough.'

Now, in the light of everything that has occurred since, it seems to me so appropriate: life, that is, coming in a full circle. What I had thought to be an ending, with my father's disappearance into circus life, was in fact a beginning. At the time I thought the world turned upside down; but the world was merely turned around. I had only to wait, and he would come back. He would come back to me. My grandparents realized this also, but they said nothing; in a sense, they simply waited with me as the weeks passed. I had no particular plan – only to make sure that my father still accompanied the travelling circus, and then somehow to approach him. How he would react to me, how he would appear in his unfamiliar guise, were questions I dared not put to myself; I knew only that I had to see him. Certain consequences were bound to follow, but I saw no point in trying to anticipate them. I was surprised by my own calmness, and yet I managed to pass each day without impatience or anxiety.

Once more I grew accustomed to the quiet rhythm of my grandparents' lives. It was such a self-contained and innocent existence that there were times when they seemed to be very like children; although I could see how they had grown older in my absence, they had the same freshness and enthusiasm even still. There were occasions when my grandfather became very solemn, but again it was like the solemnity of a child involved in some serious game; when you are truly at peace with the world, and understand your own place within it, perhaps then existence is indeed changed into a kind of game. A serious game. It often occurred to me that my grandparents must have been essentially the same when they really were children – and that they, too, had now come full circle and recaptured the spirit which first animated them. They often talked of my mother now. 'Cecilia,' my grandmother might say, 'always liked to sit beneath this tree.' Or, 'Cecilia kept this flower garden. You'll see her blossoms in the spring.' She had become a companion, someone coming closer and closer to them whom they could invoke without grief. It was as if, in death, she had become another child with whom they could play their serious game.

I saw Edward Campion frequently, but we found it difficult

to recreate our old companionship. We managed to discuss all the old topics, but I suspect this was because we did not want to approach the more recent events of our lives; I never mentioned my father, for example, and he never referred to his period away from home. He had become resigned to his present life, although not without bitterness, and I realized very soon that his mood of resignation covered everything he said or thought. His old enthusiasm had gone, and he no longer railed against his disability as sometimes he had done; he drank instead, and there were times when I guided his stumbling wandering steps homewards. He belonged here, as he said, but that sense of belonging seemed to be accompanied by an awareness of defeat and even of futility. There was a price to be paid for everything, after all: to have returned to his origins, to have come home, meant that for him there was no possibility of change.

I was walking through Upper Harford one March evening on my way to meet Edward after his work was finished, when I saw the posters for Blackmore's Circus. I can see them still, in front of me – bright orange with black lettering, and then at the bottom the words I hoped to find. CLEMENT HARCOMBE. THE GREAT MAGICIAN. There was also an announcement that the circus, with its accompanying fair, would be arriving on the common outside town at the end of the month. I had expected to feel some sense of shame at my father's name so prominently displayed, but instead I was filled with anticipation and something very much like pride. Why I should experience anything of the kind was a mystery to me; and yet, as soon as I met Edward, I told him precisely what I had seen. He was not at all surprised. 'That's the life,' he said. 'A travelling life. Free and easy. There's only one problem, though.'

'Yes?'

'I don't believe in magic.'

'Oh I do.' I was aware how quickly, how instinctively, I had defended my father.

'You believe in anything, Tim.'

'I believe in visions. Isn't that what magic is all about?'

'No such thing.'

I was silent for a moment, considering how best to respond to his flat denial. 'But no one can live without a vision, Edward. Without the chance that magic might be true. Don't you see that?'

'I don't see anything any more.'

'Well. Suit yourself. I've seen my own visions.' It was the nearest I had ever come to mentioning my dreams, but Edward simply laughed; not unkindly, or unsympathetically, yet it was enough to prevent me saying anything further.

'I think you'll find,' he replied, 'that you can survive without them.'

'If it comes to that –'

'But it does come to that. It always comes to that.'

We had continued down Venn Lane, away from the main part of the town and towards the open country; it was the kind of walk we had taken when we were schoolboys, of no certain direction but propelled by the momentum of our argument. 'But what would life be like,' I said, 'without the possibility of magic? Or of visions? Life without hope, isn't that so?' He was not laughing now. 'And there is another kind of vision, too. Do you remember old Armitage?'

'The music master?'

'Yes. Him. Do you remember how he used to play us English music over and over again?' Edward nodded. 'Don't you think that he had a vision?'

'Of what, exactly?'

'I don't know. Of time. Of continuity. Of England. I'm not sure what I mean. Perhaps, like you, he had some vision of belonging –' I stopped suddenly as we passed an old wall at the bottom of the lane; there was another orange poster there proclaiming Blackmore's Circus, and I pointed to my father's name. 'There he is,' I said. 'The Great Magician.' We turned back and, after we had spent our usual time drinking together, I made my way home.

The circus came at the end of March as announced and, on the evening of its arrival, I travelled out to the large field beyond Upper Harford and watched its progress. The caravans and trailers had been parked in a circle, as the tents, booths and rides were taken out from the lorries and gradually assembled. It had been raining all day, and drops of moisture ran down the polished wooden faces of the merry-go-round horses; some of the stuffed toy monkeys, used as prizes in the shooting gallery, were already damp, and somewhere in the background I could hear the muttering and growling of the real animals who performed in the circus itself. The green canvas of the tents flapped in the strong wind, and a thin veil of mist covered the brightly coloured booths. How could I find my father among all this confusion? I wanted to see him now, before all these preparations were completed: I wanted to see him as I remembered him, and not as the performer which he had undoubtedly become. I crossed a path and walked on to the site reluctantly, when a very fat man seemed to bounce towards me over the wet grass. 'Are you from the council?' he asked me in a cracked and distorted voice, much like that of a boy whose voice is about to break. I shook my head. 'Then we can't have nothing to do with you until tomorrow. That's when we open, see? Easy to do. Easy to understand. Am I right?' And with that he bounced away again.

I stood quietly for a few moments, uncertain whether to trespass any further into this scene of frantic activity, when a pale-faced and extremely thin young man came out of a caravan parked near by. 'Hello, vicar,' he said. 'I'm sure you're a terrible man on your home turf.'

'Pardon?'

'No no. Do pardon me. Where do you hail from in Ireland?'

I was quite bewildered by him, and hardly knew how to reply. 'I'm looking for my father,' I said. 'I think he lives here.'

'Try the Vatican. You've got the Pope's nose.' I looked wildly around, convinced I was in the company of a madman, when he laughed and wriggled his hips from side to side. I believe it was meant to be a gesture of friendship. 'What's his name then, this father?'

'Clement Harcombe.'

'Oh. Clementi. Now that's an entirely different story. You'll find him over there. In the mermaid's grotto.' He pointed, not to a grotto, but to a caravan painted in blue and scarlet stripes. I thanked him; he bowed, and then did a series of highly elaborate cartwheels in the direction from which he had come.

There seemed nothing else to do but to approach this caravan, although I was nervous about doing so; the cadaverous young man might have misunderstood me, after all, and I had no wish to tangle with a mermaid. But then, as I came nearer, I heard a familiar voice issuing from behind an open door; I might have been back in the old hall by the City Road, listening to my father from the side of the small wooden stage where we had worked together. 'Of course there is a world beyond this one. Some people call it the spirit world, but the name is not very important . . .' Yes, this was my father; I felt the blood rush into my cheeks and, for some reason, suddenly I felt very tired. 'It isn't some world beyond the sky, some world up there . . .' I could imagine him pointing upwards, his forefinger stabbing the air as he carried on speaking. 'It's here. It's all around us. It's part of us.' He stopped for a moment, and I heard a murmur of voices; but I did not want to come too close. Not yet. 'Look at it another way. You all know how the atmosphere of an old house is quite different from that of a newly built one. There is some other quality about it, isn't there, which touches you as soon as you walk through the door? And what is that, but the spirit of place? It's not some ghost hovering over the roof, but part of the bricks, part of the furniture, part of the floor, part of the walls. That is what I mean when I tell you that the spirits are among us, and are a part of us.'

I crept towards the open door of the caravan – for some reason which I could not explain to myself I wanted to remain a secret presence while he spoke about such things. In a curious way, also, I was frightened. I was about three feet away now and, although I could not see my father, I glimpsed through the door four people who were listening to him intently. There were two very tall men lying upon the floor – even though they were curled up, they stretched from one side of the caravan to the other – and, sitting in front of them, two tiny women who were identically dressed in dark green suits and yellow blouses. All of them were watching my father, whose outstretched hand I occasionally glimpsed as he continued with his talk. 'And of course there are other spirits. Other forces. Let's call the atmosphere of that old house the spirit of place. That seems fair, doesn't it?' The two tall men nodded in agreement. 'But then there are the spirits of landscape. The spirits of a nation. You know when you are in England, don't you? How different it is from the atmosphere of France, and how different France is from Germany? We might even call this the spirit of the past. The spirit of time. It is part of us, you see . . .' Once more I heard the low emphatic cadence, which he had used to such effect in the old hall. 'As much part of us as the atmosphere of an old house is part of the house. As much part of us as our flesh or our skin . . .'

I stopped listening to him at this moment because, to my dismay, I realized that the two women had seen me; they had whispered to each other for a moment and then started beckoning me over to them. I did not know what to do. I could not turn back, not now, but I was afraid to confront my father in this surreptitious manner. But there was no alternative. I stepped over to the caravan, knocked politely on the door and, even as the two dwarves smiled at me, I entered.

My father was not as surprised by my arrival as I had expected, but there was an indefinably uneasy expression upon his face when he saw me. 'Good Lord,' he said, surveying me as if I were a stranger to him. 'This is a coincidence. Is that the right word? Coincidence?' I was not sure if he was addressing me but, before I could reply, he had turned back to his audience. 'Ladies and gentlemen,' he said. 'Let me present my son to you.'

'We knew.' The two tiny women said this in unison and then one of them added, 'We knew as soon as we saw him. He looks so much like you.'

My father and I glanced at each other for a moment; our eyes met, but then we looked away. 'Timothy,' he said, 'is very much his own man. He won't thank you for seeing a resemblance.'

'No.' I went up to him and shook his hand. 'I do thank them.' And, yes, there was a resemblance in the general cast of our features which even I could now discern. Or, rather, he was one version of what I might become; he was, perhaps, some ghost of the future.

He grabbed my shoulder, in the same way he had when I was a child. 'You see how the magician can even make his son appear out of thin air?' They laughed at this, but not, I suspect, without embarrassment. He sensed it, too. 'I think, my friends, that owing to exceptional circumstances this meeting must come to an end. Thank you very much.'

The two women clapped their hands while the tall men behind them slowly uncurled themselves; they could not stand upright inside the caravan but were bent over, smiling at me all the time like friendly giants in a fairy tale. The four of them then left in single file, the two women leading the way, and for a moment I thought that my father and I were alone. But almost at once I heard a female voice coming from a small alcove at the back of the caravan. 'Won't you introduce me to your progeny, Clement? What have you spawned?' A middle-aged woman, with long black hair hanging down to her waist, came out from this recess; she was stroking her hair with one hand and, as she came closer, I noticed that the violet paint on her finger-nails matched the violet of her lipstick.

'May I present the mermaid?' my father said, stepping up to her and then stepping back again as if engaged in an elaborate dance between the two of us.

Instinctively I looked down, but she seemed to possess two perfectly normal legs. She understood my glance. 'A mermaid only in the aquarium, my love. My gills are my work.' She held out her hand to me. 'Shake a fin.'

'A true professional,' my father murmured.

I took her hand with reluctance, expecting some patch of dampness; but she had a dry and almost too vigorous hand-shake. Then she smiled, sidled past us, and left the caravan without another word.

Now that we were truly alone together, my father seemed more nervous than before. I was determined not to complain about, or even to mention, his sudden disappearance from Albion Lane; after all, I was hardly without blame. I had left him in order to start a different life, and I had made no effort to trace him over these last three years. 'I saw your name,' was all I could think of saying.

'On the posters?'

'Yes. That's why I came.'

'So now you know, Tim. I *am* gainfully employed.' He laughed, but I could tell that he felt some sense of shame in front of me. 'Five pounds a week.'

'I didn't know you were a magician.'

He must have taken this as an accusation, or a criticism, because he blushed violently. 'It's my life now,' he said quietly.

'I understand that, dad.'

'You do?'

I had the strangest sensation, then, that he had become the child and I the father; it lasted only for a few seconds but, in that moment of transition, I also had a sudden consciousness of my real self. 'What kind of magic is it?'

'Just stage magic. Illusions. Tricks. Disappearances. As you know, Tim, I'm good at those.' It was the first reference he had made to his own past, and he had managed to treat it as a kind of joke; perhaps I admired him for that. 'Look.' He put a hand up to my ear and took from it a small jewel. And another.

'When did you learn to do that?' Then I had a sudden memory of similar tricks, which he had performed for my entertainment many years before. 'Didn't you do something like that in the kitchen? In the old place?'

'I learnt conjuring long, long before that. Before you were even thought of.'

'You mean before –'

'Before I met your mother.' He seemed about to say something more, but with a deliberate effort he restrained himself. He went over to the oval window in the side of the caravan and, when he turned around, he had a pile of books in his hands. 'As if by magic,' he said. 'These are the books from Hackney Square. The ones you left behind. Do you remember them?' I remembered the volume on top of the pile very well: it was the anthology of English poetry which I had always placed in the right-hand corner of my bookshelf. It occurred to me also that, since he kept the books here, he must be living with the mermaid. 'It's a tiring life, Tim, travelling like this. Moving on week after week. Poetry is my comfort, just like it used to be in the old days. I haven't changed at all,' he added, nervously. 'Not really. Come outside with me, and I'll show you our preparations.'

We left the caravan and walked among the tents and booths which were still being erected, my father greeting the people who worked busily among them. He stopped for a moment to speak to a middle-aged man whose hair came down to his waist. 'That's the strong man,' he whispered confidentially to me afterwards. 'The mermaid's cousin.' He waved to a young man in a moth-eaten fur coat. 'One of the acrobats,' he muttered. 'Comes from a very long line. And there's Bob, the principal clown . . .' He pointed to a cheerful young man, who, on spotting my father, put two fingers in his mouth and

let out a loud and prolonged whistle. 'We get along well
enough,' my father said as soon as the whistle had died away.
'We're fellow travellers.' He was looking at me curiously, as if
he were expecting me to say something. But in the end it was
he who spoke. We had come out by the coconut-shy, and my
father had just exchanged a few words with its proprietor – I
recognized him well enough, since it was the very thin young
man who had performed the cartwheels in front of me. 'That's
Dan,' he said as we walked away. 'He doubles up as the
spider man.' It was now that he went on to remark, almost
casually, 'I met your mother here. In Upper Harford.' It was
obvious to him that I did not understand what he meant. 'I
met her while I was working for Blackmore's Circus. Back in
the old days. That's how I know all the conjuring tricks, Tim.
Do you see? Now you've been told the whole story.'

I was astonished. As far as I could comprehend what he
had just said, my father was working as a circus magician at
the time he met my mother. Was that the truth of it? But
then all the work we had performed together in the old hall,
all the meetings and the conversations with spirits, had been
no more than a sequel to his circus life – or, perhaps, an
extension of it. He had been a conjuror long before he had
become a healer. I was too bewildered to feel anything. So
what had our activities in the old hall really meant to him?
At that moment I could not even make sense of my own past,
and in my confusion I simply followed him as he walked
briskly through the fairground.

'Of course I read the English poets to the mermaid, too.
She never tires of Tennyson.' He was talking in the same
cheerful way and had been able effortlessly to change the
subject; then he looked at me anxiously for a moment, before
continuing in his old enthusiastic manner. 'Some of the others
come to my readings. The strong man loves Spenser, while
the acrobats are particularly fond of Donne. And the little
ladies could listen to Pope for hours. Do you know my favourite, Tim?' Again he seemed to glance at me anxiously.

'No, dad.'

'Blake. William Blake. *Songs of Innocence. Thel. Poetical Sketches.* I love them all. Don't you remember that he was buried in the cemetery near us?' I did not reply. 'Perhaps that's why I've come back to reading him now. In my travelling life.'

I was feeling very tired. 'It's late,' I said. 'I should be getting back.'

'Back?'

'To my grandparents. Don't you remember them?' I must have sounded very harsh, because there was an expression of distress upon his face. 'I'm sorry. I didn't mean that. I'm just tired.'

'Don't be sorry, Timothy. Never be sorry. And it's no wonder you're exhausted. You've learnt a lot today.' He hesitated for a moment, but I knew what I had to say.

'I'll come back tomorrow, dad.'

'You will? I can show you my black art table. And you've never seen all my box tricks, have you?' His exuberance returned at once, and he put his hand up to my ear before removing another jewel. 'That one must have gone astray, Tim. Come around about nine. I'll have finished by then.'

We parted as casually as if we had always been in each other's company, but it was only after I had walked away that I realized he had not invited me to witness one of his circus performances. That was a relief, in one sense, and yet at the same time I felt cheated or deprived of some essential vision of my father. My grandparents were waiting for me on my return; I really did not want to talk to them, not until I had resolved my own feelings about his sudden disclosure of the past, but I could hardly avoid them. 'I found him,' I said as I joined them in the kitchen. 'He was there.' Still they said nothing, but looked at me expectantly. 'He must be a good magician. He showed me some of his tricks.'

'I've no doubt about that,' my grandfather replied. 'Your father was always very good at his work. He doesn't make mistakes.'

I realized now, for the first time, that they knew more about my father's history than I had ever done; and that, for some reason, they had kept it from me. How had my mother encountered him in Upper Harford? When did he leave the circus? And was there some connection with the time when my grandfather came to take me away? I wanted to discover the truth of all these things but, somehow, I could not bring myself to ask: I suspected too much. I kissed them both and went up to my mother's room.

I returned to my father the following evening, as I had promised, and I found him alone in the caravan. He was sitting at a small side-table, with his head bowed, gazing at the floor; he did not seem to hear me enter, and only looked up when I walked over to him and touched his shoulder. 'I was hoping you'd come back,' he said.

'Of course I came back. Why shouldn't I?'

'I don't know.' He sounded very tired. 'Not everything goes according to plan, does it? Just look at me.'

I had rarely seen him in such a weary and defeated state. 'Do you remember the old days,' I said, in an attempt to cheer him, 'when we came back from the meetings? And we were so tired we could hardly walk? I used to hold on to you, and you would just drag me along!'

'Yes, Tim. But, as I recall, it was you who helped me.' He looked up at me again, but with so sad a smile that I could hardly bear it. 'You see, Tim, I remember everything.'

He was about to say something else when the door was suddenly opened and a bald, red-faced man came striding into the caravan; he was apparently furious with my father and stood in the tiny space struggling for breath. 'If that happens again, Harcombe,' he said at last, 'you're through. Out.' My father merely nodded, weakly, and kept on staring at the floor. The bald man seemed to relent a little. 'What was the matter with you? You just can't walk out of the ring like that. Nobody was ready. Nobody was in position.'

'I know. I'm sorry.'

'It's no good being sorry. Just don't let it happen again.'

The man left quickly, but not before glancing curiously at me. Neither of us said anything for a while, until my father sighed and leaned over in his chair. 'I should be used to this life by now, Tim. I've been doing it long enough.' He had been humiliated in front of me, and I was ashamed for him. No, I was ashamed for myself. I felt that I bore some responsibility for his present state, and not just because I had left him in Albion Lane; there was some deeper and more complicated sense of failure which connected us. 'I'm glad now I told you about the past,' he said. He did not need to elaborate; his confession, that he had worked in this circus before I was born, still hung in the air between us. 'I didn't mean to tell you, Tim. It just happened. It came out.' I could feel once again the pressure of his shame and humiliation, literally keeping his head bowed in front of me. But his shame was not just of recent date; it seemed to be a reflection of one which he had harboured for many years but which he had successfully kept from me. Now, as he said, it had all 'come out'. But I could not bear to see him falling backwards into that past, as if he were being swallowed up by it.

'There's nothing to worry about, dad.' I went over to him, bent down and put my arm around his shoulder. 'What difference does it make if you worked in a circus? Think of all the people you helped. Think of the time you cured Stanley Clay. And Matthew. All of them.' Once again I was back with him in the old hall: I could smell the dust burning by the gas-jets, I could hear him playing 'Jerusalem' on the piano, I could see the pitted wooden benches in front of me, and now once more I was standing beside him as he called the people towards him.

'Don't you see, Timothy, it never really was me. It was you. You had the power.' I sat down on the floor of the caravan and said nothing. 'That was why you were always with me. That was why I used to hold you up. I kept my hand on your head. Don't you remember?'

'Yes.'

'You were the one who healed them.' He had raised his voice, almost as if he were shouting at me in defiance. 'You were the one who saw visions.' Then just as suddenly he was quiet again. 'It was the son who helped the father, Tim. Why do you think you had those dreams?'

'I don't understand what you mean, dad.'

'Because you could *see*.' He was still staring at the floor as he spoke. 'I was afraid for you. Afraid of what might become of you. It was the only life you knew, but it was such a desperate existence really. So uncertain. So confusing. That's why I was willing to send you back to your grandparents. I wanted you to lead a normal childhood, Tim, do you understand that? I wasn't sending you away. I wasn't rejecting you. I was trying to protect you.'

'But you let me work with you.'

'That was the worst thing of all. We had to live, I suppose. We had to survive. But it was your power, and I knew I was abusing it. So I stopped it. And you went down to Wiltshire.'

'But I came back.'

'You were older then. You weren't helpless any more. And you proved it. Didn't you leave me to my own devices in the end?' He tried to laugh. 'And what did I become without you? A circus performer.'

So he had known all along that my dreams were part of some larger power which I possessed, some power to heal the sick and to hear the voices of the dead. I looked down at my hands and noticed with interest that they were trembling. But if I were the one who possessed that power, how could I not have recognized it within me? And how was it that the vision had been transferred from the son to the father? He had been the one to address the spirits, after all, even when I had said nothing to him.

'I can't think of these things for too long, Tim. That's why I have my books. As I said, poetry is my comfort.'

I lay down on the floor of the caravan and closed my eyes so that I would not have to look at him. I was exhausted now and did not try to fight against the oblivion which, I knew, was coming to protect me. I could hear my father moving around, and then I was conscious of his voice reciting the poetry of William Blake:

'For I in Two Thousand Years walk up and down;
Not one Moment of Time is lost, nor one Word or Cadence
But all remain: every work of Two Thousand Years
Exists within my Vision. Awake, Albion, awakc!'

SIXTEEN

A WAKE, ALBION, TO THE ENDLESS note of English
music
Created hour to hour, day to day, and year to year:
All that has existed in the space of two thousand years
Permanent and not lost. Not forgotten nor vanished,
But living eternal within your golden fields and cities.
So, spirits of Albion, who inspire and animate poetic
song,
Guide my journey through your immortal realms
As I record the visions of those who came before me.

Awake, Caedmon, awake, Cynewulf, arise from your
long
Slumber of two thousand years. Within your ancient
words
I search out Albion in visions of woods and trackless
ways,
Unwinding the allegories you found among the
wilderness.
Unfolding time, I hear your sound and cadence gladly
As Beowulf is sung in labyrinthine halls
And the poets are led along the banks of rejoicing
With harp and drum and trumpet and clarion.
They are unknown but they lie now in the rough
basement,
For who else built the stubborn structure of language
And rose against a silent melancholy and a dumb
despair?
I call you now by your proper name, English:
The Briton, Saxon, Roman, Norman, amalgamating
Into one nation and finding their sacred home in the word.

349

The old time was finished, lamented by Geoffrey of
    Monmouth
And Nennius in their dreams of ancient decaying cities,
But gone, departed for ever. The breath divine entered
Albion and in the circle of time England awoke to life,
That awakened life preserved for ever in Chaucer's
    verses,
In permanent forms, inspired, divinely human.
He laboured for eternity, in the fury of poetic
    inspiration,
To create a new England stupendous with mortal shape:
The clerk, the physician, the monk, the reeve, the
    merchant,
All divided into just types and proportions.
For every age is a pilgrimage, and we all pass on,
Each sustaining one or other of these English
    characters,
Nor can a child be born who is not found here
Rising up from the shadowy body of Albion;
For as the pilgrim passes while the road remains,
So men pass on but the nation remains permanent for
    ever.
All things acted on this island are in Chaucer's verses
And every age renews its power from his winged words.
As one age falls another rises, different to mortal sight,
But in substance ever the same. Its substance is
    language,
Which, though it may vary in form or cadence,
In its light and life it ever remains unaltered.
So I telleth thee, ere that ye further wende,
I kan namoore, my tale is at an ende.

But there is no end, for there followed him Langland
Filled with allegoric delusions and woe.
From Kent there came Gower, turbulent, confused,
But recreating the parent tongue in one voice.

From the marshes of Norfolk came Skelton of expansive
   nerves
And from Suffolk came Lydgate of ferocious speech,
Into whose verse flowed the language unencumbered.
It was Wyatt then who taught us the softer music,
In sweet delight which he and his lute have done,
And never ended is what he begonne: Sidney, Surrey,
Loud and more loud the living music floats upon the air
With the pipe, the lute, the viol and the symbol.
All these silver sounds calm Albion upon his couch.

At this time words and notes combined, playing on
   instruments
Stringed or fluted to ameliorate the sorrows of death,
Imitating the cadences of hope and desire,
Until Spenser took their form and imbued it with
   history.
Theirs had been the cloth but Spenser wove rich
   draperies
And spread out bright flowing lines of incrusted light:
Infinitely beautiful the wondrous work arose,
Out of sorrow and care a faerie world whose porches
And pillared halls received the eternal wandering stars.
O Albion, great lord of greatest isle, whose light
Like Phoebus' lampe throughout the world doth shine,
Shed your fair beams into Spenser's bright eyen
And raise his thoughts (too modest and too humble all
   the while)
So that the one true shape of Britain might take flight
And form the argument of his exalted style.
So did a golden allegory then arise, with many a
   window,
And many a door opening out upon the vast unknown,
With books and instruments of song and pictures of
   delight.
Spenser bowed low upon Albion's rocky coast and said:

'I must create a system or be enslaved by another man's,
I will not reason and compare, my business is to create.'

Yet then was heard the low thunder of another cadence,
The march of long resounding, strong heroic verse
In Chapman, Kyd, Marlowe, coming with interlinked
     hands
And then fading in raptured trance before Shakespeare.
In this period the poet's work was truly done,
The human world of time all fathomed and conceived.
For Shakespeare kept watch, and became what he
     beheld.
He became his words: he was himself transformed
As his cadences and syllables created his passions,
Framing beauty out of the dark regions of sorrow
And order within the glorious realms of sexual bliss,
Giving to airy nothings a name and habitation.
He laboured incessant within the holy forms of speech
To give bounds to the infinite and to the indefinite,
Forging the powerful words for Albion to inhabit:
All things acted on earth are seen in his bright dwelling,
Every story from hate to wayward love,
Every sorrow and distress, every affinity of friend or
     parent,
Is carved here in works of English music.
Shakespeare arose from his dewy couch, leaving Albion
     for ever
Environed by his verse; but then others in time came
     among us
Like a stream in which the bright upturned faces can be
     seen
Passing from youth to age. So there came forth Donne;
Terrified before his own creation, he hid himself in words
Like the bright sun seen thro' a mist that magnifies
The disk into a tremendous vision of last things. Donne
     fled,

Howling, before Marvell, Herbert, Vaughan and
    Traherne,
Their cabinets ingeniously made of ideas and quiddities
But containing doubts and sorrows, melancholy and
    wretchedness.
Their weeping Spectre stands on the threshold of death
Amid tear-floods and sigh-tempests metaphysical.

Then Milton arose, awakener of Albion, whose power of
    song
Came from deep consciousness of fate. I heard him speak
    thus:
'O love and life and light, all within my words!
Prophetic dreams urge me to speak: futurity is before me
Like a bright lamp, and eternity haunts my
    imagination!'
Then I saw him not, I saw only his English verses
Like pillars of fire travelling through chaos and darkness
Until he had created Albion anew out of his strong
    words.
For such a journey none but iron pen could write, and
    adamantine
Leaves receive, as Milton brooded over his creation,
Which is the mystery of England and its long durance.
Again the voice of the bard: 'I know the truth, for I sing
According to the inspiration of the poetic genius
Which goes forward from age to age, linked music long
    drawn out,
Permanently creating, to be in time revealed and
    demolished
And renewed as the vision of England eternal.
Can that which has existed cease, and can music expire?
All that has been manifest in the space of two thousand
    years,
Every line, syllable and song that has existed, all restored
Within those works of England still waiting to be born:

Shadowy to those who dwell not in language, a mere
    possibility,
But to those who enter its life it is the only substance,
For everything exists there and not one note nor word
    nor work,
Cadence or syllable, not one can pass away.'
Thus spake Milton, brooding over Albion in his own
    generation.

But now I see the past, present and future again before
    me.
O divine spirit, sustain me on thy hovering wings
As I look upon those following the fiery steps of Milton:
Milton calling aloud to English Dryden,
But Dryden was giving his body ease
At Soho beneath the poplar trees.
Dryden, thus led by melancholy away from the fiery
    beams
Of poetic inspiration, slumbering upon the green banks
Of his fettered verse, dreaming of his books in the dismal
    shade.
Then I beheld London around him, an awful wonder of
    God,
Adamantine, dark, massive, cruel in every human epoch.
Thus London speaks: 'Awake, Dryden, awake. I give
    myself
Up to thee, for my streets are thoroughfares of
    imagination
And my towers are built with English music.' Dryden
    heard not
And the muses of Albion, dismayed, closed the gate of
    the tongue:
Forgetfulness, necessity, in darkness of the mind immured
By Pope, a prince of light bound in chains of intellect,
And the visions of Albion, by reason of narrowed
    perception,

Had become weak visions of time and space attenuated,
Dryden, Pope, Prior, shut up in narrow doleful forms!
The eye of man, a little narrow orb, closed up and dark,
Conversing with the ground, comprehending great as
    very small;
The ear, a little shell, in small volutions shutting out
True harmonies and scarce hearing the ancient music.

England groans, its poets bound to sullen contemplation
In the night: Young, Smart, Gray, Cowper, Collins,
Restlessly turn on their beds of sorrow, in their dreams
They feel the crushing wheels before they rise
To write their bitter words with tears and madness.
So Johnson walked upon the shores of stern philosophy,
    saying:
'Man must labour and sorrow, and learn and forget, and
    return
To the dark valley whence he came, to begin his labours
    anew.'
In pain he sighs, in pain he bows across his dictionary.
I behold them all, and their sad fates o'erwhelm my soul
In London's darkness, and my tears fall day and night
Upon the spectres of Albion's sons who see not Albion.

Yet now I rejoice over Chatterton, his intricate poems
Antiently inspired but now condemned as fictions;
He contemplated the past in his own bright sphere,
His imagination renewing the true history of Albion,
Until in his death, self-delivered, he became what he
    beheld.
What is the price of poetry? What is the price of English
    song?
It is bought with the price of all that a man hath
And then left in the desolate market where none come to
    buy.
Yet who shall bind the infinite or curtail the music?

All things exist within the human imagination, for now
Blake arose singing:

> 'Dear Child, I also by pleasant Streams
> Have wander'd all Night in the Land of Dreams;
> But tho' calm and warm the waters wide,
> I could not get to the other side.'

> 'Father, O Father! what do we here
> In this Land of unbelief and fear?
> The Land of Dreams is better far,
> Above the light of the Morning Star.'

Blake heard the music of the generations interlinked,
The father reaching for the son, the son calling to the
    father,
Their sighs and tears intermingled so they seem as one:
To touch each other and recede, to cross and change
    and return
In the intricate maze of the dance which is also music.
The son resting on the words of the father in eternity,
The father guided by the son throughout eternity.
Thus did Blake prepare the path for those who followed:
No, not Crabbe, writing with measured groans in books
    of brass,
But Coleridge and Wordsworth, who proclaimed the
    poetic genius
As first principle and not some element of association.
Then the divine vision like a silent sun appeared above
Albion's dark rocks, rising above the moors and valleys
Where Wordsworth walked in grandeur with that friend
Who had revealed new heavens and new earths within
    him.
For these were the words of Coleridge, astonished,
    triumphant:
'If the perceptive organs vary, objects of perception vary
    also

But in the eye of imagination all things are filled with
    light!'
Then Byron arose, abominable to the traducers of his
    time,
His wisdom remains though all his memory is stored
    with woe:
'Once man was occupied with intellectual pleasures and
    energies,
But now my soul is harrowed only with grief and fear,
For now I hate and now I love, and intellect is no more.
There is no room for any thing but torments of love and
    hatred.'
Thus Byron spoke; the plough went over him, the living
Ploughed in among the dead, as the generations mingle
    in song.
Shelley took up that music with his first steps upon the
    earth,
His infant mind acquiring that dream of beauty in which
    the world
Suspires: everything that lives within his pure prophetic
    song
Lives not alone nor for itself, but in bright words moving
At will to murmur in flowers small as the honey bee,
At will to stretch across the heavens and step from star to
    star.
Even now he is not dead but awakened from the dream
    of life
Into the radiance of time where all dwell equally, not
    forgotten.
And fearest thou, John Keats, because you must vanish
And be seen no more by mortal sight, that nothing
    remains? No,
Nothing is lost: for ever dwell those thoughts, suspended,
Which once you also formed. 'Beauty is truth, truth beauty,
The imagination is not a state, it is the shape of human
    existence.

Nature has no outline but the imagination itself,
For language is eternity, issuing from the lips of Albion.'
Keats spoke in the spirit of inspiration, awakening
    Tennyson
Into his own vision whereby he sang lulling cadences
To instill soft melancholy into his imperial countrymen,
Cadences of fainting and sleep and bright delusion,
Until this English music was given in charge to
    Swinburne,
In clouds of sweet obscurity its beauteous forms
    dissolving.
But then Browning spoke the words of eternity in human
    form,
In direful revolutions of action and individual passion.
Straight was the path of gold which is called his genius,
Leading him towards a world of men who were his own
    reflections,
Once more changing English poetry as it is always
    changed,
Moving between the living and the dead, the words and
    cadences
Combining in the transactions of eternity.
Hopkins saw and envied, creating lines of concord and
    discord
Opposed to melody, strict outlines excluding light or
    shade,
Particulars beyond the movement of imagination.
Who could come after but Thompson, Johnson,
    Dowson?
Invoking visions of the upper atmosphere, singing lulling
Cadences and playing, in religious intoxication,
Comforting sounds of love and mystery and nostalgia
For a century coming to its end in mortal chronology
But living for ever in the state of eternity called Albion.

And now this verse has come, rejoicing in English music,

For the poets have fashioned a melodic line to express
The forms of English imagination through the centuries.
All things begin and end on Albion's ancient Druid rocky
    shore.
Awake, awake Albion! O lovely emanation of music,
Awake and overspread the nation as in ancient time;
For lo! the night of death is past and the eternal day
Appears above our cities and fields. Awake, Albion!
Timothy heard these songs and voices echoing around
    him,
And he understood their name: they are named
    England.

                The End
                Of the Song
                Of Albion.

SEVENTEEN

I WAS ABOUT TO CRY out at my reflection in a swiftly running stream, when I arched awake upon my bed; the dream stayed with me for a moment, but only as an image of upturned faces staring at the sky. What was I doing in this bed? I tried to rise, but I knew, from a sick unsteady feeling eddying through my body, that I would only fall sideways. Instinctively I put my hand to my face and felt the cold sweat upon it, sticking to my palms and fingers, smelling like dead leaves. Somehow the moisture was holding me down.

'Don't worry.' It was my father's voice, and when I looked up he seemed to be floating above me, his eyes and mouth in a cloud. 'Everything is fine, Tim. The doctor came.'

I did not understand what he meant. 'Have I been travelling long?' I had the strangest sensation of having grown too large, of having been stretched out, and my limbs were now so heavy that they seemed to be tied to the bed.

'No. You've been sleeping here for a while. The mermaid is staying with her cousin.'

Mermaid? I was living under water: the pressure was keeping me down, and I could not breathe. I closed my eyes and I began rising slowly to the surface, feeling the heat of the sun upon my chest and face. But then I started turning over and over, spinning faster and faster until I fell back into the darkness from which I had risen.

I recall very little of those next days; what images I can summon are so mixed up with fevered ideas, and dreams, and hallucinations, that it is hard to distinguish between what was real and what was unreal. I do remember being held by my father and given water to drink, and I remember being carried by him into a small lavatory; the fact that I was in a caravan made no impression upon me at all, unless it emerged in the intermittent delusion that I was sleeping in the cabin of a small boat which was lost at sea. Of course I knew that I was sick; my illness was like a phantom scaring the people around me, and I could see the distress upon the faces of my grandparents. Sometimes there were other faces around me, which seemed to rise and fall in time to my laboured breathing. And yet nothing seemed real; the human beings beside me were pieces of paper, no more than pages torn from books. I could hear my grandfather's voice, coming from some point in the distance. 'You picked the right spot, Clement,' he was saying. 'There's been a fair here for a long time. And, before that, strolling players. Is it the same thing? Conjuring and acting?'

'Yes. The same thing.'

Or were these the echoes of a conversation I had heard before I was sick, still suspended in the air? Perhaps that was why I sometimes found myself listening to low voices around me, the voices of delirium.

> 'I cannot choose
> But hate to see what change his face sustains.
> My blood and kindred, doubled in his birth,
> Inspires a mixed and twice descending love.'

Father, dear father. Is this your voice? Or have I returned into a dream, in which I hear myself speak freely to you for the first time?

> 'I see my end draws on. Father, I feel my plague.
> My life doth fade, and bitter sorrows flow,
> Because your name in me is thus extinct.
> O heavy wretched lot: to be the last . . .'

> 'O son, sweet and desired son, there is no end.
> These eyes you see, these hands you touch,
> Are yours and mine both equally. Look here
> On this, your father's face, and view your image.'

'Yet there is no glass can hold us both.
O cruel fate! O doleful destiny!'

I was awake, my throat as dry and sore as if I had been
calling out in some frenzy or delirium. But had I spoken out
loud, or had these words been enclosed within another dream?
I know now what my father would have said; if he had been
talking to his friends, or disciples, he would have explained
that I was filled with the spirit of the place and was re-
enacting within myself some ancient play. This was the spot,
after all, where according to my grandfather strolling players
had once come. It is a theory, at least, and theories can do no
harm.

Such matters did not occur to me then, because I had
room only for my sickness. It was a strange time. I was concerned about myself in the way that I might be concerned
for an acquaintance since, in the course of my illness, I had
ceased fully to inhabit my own body. Or, rather, it was as if
the fever had invaded some other person while I was anxiously
looking on. Perhaps that is the true explanation of the voices
I was able to hear: I had stepped outside myself, if only
fractionally, and, in the minute space which had been opened
up, all the sounds of the world (or of the past) had poured in.
And so the fever returned. There was an interval of darkness,
and then I saw my mother. I was not alarmed; I was not
even particularly surprised, since in my weakened state all
things seemed possible. She was so much like her image in the
photographs I had seen that, instinctively, I put out my arms
and

At sight of me her colour straight she changed
And like a loving child in clasped arms
She caught me up, and friendly kissed my cheek:
'My flesh, divided in your precious shape,
Could not retain my spirit; though I am dead
I live in your dear face and breath.

My son, all humankind do live eternally
For, being dead, our seed raise us to life again.'

'Ah sweet mother, ah my beloved mother,
Alas, alas, what cause doth move you now
From death to grant me such a trembling vision?'

'Great is the love which nature doth inforce
From kin to kin, but most from son to sire.
'Tis like the love each man has for his native land,
Reverence for those generations come and gone
Like music played upon the viol in Britayne's praise.
For every one that goes, another comes,
Some born, some dead: so still the note endures.
Sweet son, farewell. In death resemble me
But in life preserve your father's excellence.'

And so she faded from my sight
Whilst I was lodged within this cave of care
Where sorrows at my elbow still attended,
To company my sickness with laments,
Fresh stirred within me by this strange exchange.

And had it been a dream? When I opened my eyes at last, I
could see the air trembling around me as if somehow it were
raining inside the room. This must be how it is to die, I
thought, to see the world flowing away. 'Cecilia,' I said.

'What was that?' My father was sitting beside me, and I
realized that he had been wiping my face with a towel.

I tried to explain to him what I had seen, but already the
vision or hallucination was eluding me and eventually I
slipped back into the darkness. There were intervals between
my fevers when I must have been lucid enough, however,
since I remember holding long conversations with my father.
There were also times when I simply listened as he talked,
and then it was as if nothing had changed – I was a child
again, in Hackney Square, as he beguiled the time with his
theories and stories. 'A guiding hand, Tim,' he was saying

one afternoon as I stared out of the window at the faint sky.
'That's what it is. A guiding hand. We will have to travel on
from here . . .'

'We?' I knew that in my present state I could go nowhere.

'The circus, Tim.' He looked away from me for a moment,
but not before I experienced a terrible sensation of abandon-
ment. Then he put his hand upon my forehead, which soothed
me at once: I was like a child in other respects, also, and my
emotions succeeded one another with extraordinary rapidity.
'But every journey has its appointed course, and I believe
we're following one even now. Do you know how the circus
travels from town to town?' I nodded. 'Well, we must be
following the tracks of the fairs and the wandering players
before us. Generation after generation of travellers. Century
after century. Look at this history I've been reading.' In his
excitement he got up and took a book from the shelf behind
him. 'I like to read while you're asleep,' he said, almost
apologetically. 'It takes my mind off . . .' He held it in front of
me, and I could see it was a copy of Mallory's *Morte d'Arthur*.
'This is about another journey. A quest. One person dies, and
another lives.' He stopped again and passed his hand across
his face. 'I'm not doing a very good job, am I? I'm supposed
to be cheering you up, and here I am talking of . . .' He got
up and began tucking in my sheets, smoothing my pillow,
and generally fussing around me. 'And there's another thing,'
he said, unable to keep the excitement from his voice. 'In the
old stories there are references to ancient cities in England,
forgotten cities, cities buried beneath the earth long ago. Do
you think that they might make up the stages of our journey,
Tim? Are they plotting the course we take? What do you
think of that theory?' I did not believe a word of it, but he
sounded so enthusiastic that I could not bear to dishearten
him. I looked up at him, and then I slept again.

Sometimes other people would join us. My grandparents
were often by my bedside, and I believe they took care of me
while my father was performing; in fact I came to expect and

appreciate the reassurance of my grandfather's presence. He would bend down over me, his bright eyes upon my face, as if he were scrutinizing the very contours and patterns of my illness. There were less frequent visitors – the mermaid came once and, when I thanked her for the use of her caravan, she asked me if I was keeping my head 'above water'. I told her I was trying my best to do so. The female dwarves were often with me, and sometimes the giants would wrap themselves around the doorway and inquire if I was still 'poorly'.

'Getting better,' my father would invariably reply. 'Always getting better.'

I had very little interest in my own condition or, rather, I had lost all connection with the self I could only dimly remember; perhaps that is why, when the fever returned, my hallucinations seemed to acquire such a strangely impersonal form. I remember one in particular, because it came as the last of all. I believed that I was asleep; in other words, I was watching some kind of dumb-show in which the image of sleep was displayed to me. I was surrounded by other shapes or shadows, no doubt refractions of the real people in the caravan, but then I heard my own voice calling out:

> 'Father, escort me now beyond the gates of horn
> Where dreams have passage in the silent night.
> Yet lend me first your book, so I may read it,
> And turn myself into what shape I wilt;
> Then, gentle sleep, where'r my body rests,
> Give charge to Morpheus that I may dream
> A golden dream of ancient cities and a quest.'

I woke up suddenly, to find the female dwarves standing at the foot of the bed with their palms turned outwards towards me. They were chanting in unison

> 'The father shall all willing heal the son,
> The son shall slay the sire and know it not.
> It is the story of the generations:

Your father reared you up, you pluck him down.
So listen to your sire's sad music
Before you make your own: his life in yours,
And in your own succession, shall for ever live.
Such singing there, such musical harmony!'

My father was kneeling on top of me, his hands around my throat, his face no more than an inch or so from mine. I knew at once that this was no fevered phantasm: this was happening to me now. I could feel his breath upon me, and I could see the sweat running down the sides of his nose and into his mouth. I was too frightened to move. He was muttering something, and then suddenly he placed the palms of his hands against the sides of my head. I knew the gesture very well. It was one he had used frequently in the old hall during those years when I believed that he healed the people who came before us. He was pressing his fingers against my temples, but I felt no discomfort, only the passage of something which set up a breeze or a vibration; and it seemed to me, as I recall, that some form of heat passed out of me and entered my father's body. Now I understood the words he was muttering: 'Look up at me and be healed. Look up at me and be healed.' Familiar words, even still, and, as I stared into my father's eyes, I glimpsed the infinite recesses of his wounded spirit. And yet there was also a brightness within them, which increased as the heat of the fever passed between us. I remember thinking, Yes, you have the power after all.

When I woke up, I sensed that the fever had gone. I was exhausted but I knew that I had regained possession of my body, and I clenched my fists in triumph. I looked across for my father but could not see him anywhere near me; it was only when I leaned over the side of the bed that I noticed him lying crouched on the floor of the caravan, asleep and breathing heavily. I did not want to disturb him, and instead I lay back in order to consider the change within me and to reflect upon the events of that strange day. I understood very little but it seemed probable that my father, growing more anxious about my condition, had decided to invoke his old skills and techniques in order to cure me. He could not have been certain of success, since he had already told me that I was the real source of any power he deployed, but no doubt he thought the chance worth taking. And this was the extraordinary thing: he had healed me. He did, after all, possess his own power. But was there also some way in which I acted as a catalyst – that this gift, whatever it was, existed only in the presence of father and son? I knew nothing for certain, and I could not even discount the possibility that I had naturally recovered from my fever.

My father was awake now; he was on his side, leaning his elbow on the carpet, and seemed to be in a kind of daze. He was looking at nothing in particular, but for some reason I closed my eyes and pretended to be still asleep. And then, curiously enough, I did sleep. A sleep without fever. A sleep without dreams.

'Timothy.' He was standing beside me, a cup of tea in his hand. 'You were breathing easier. You don't have a temperature now.' He seemed very cheerful.

'Thank you, dad.'

'What for?'

'For the tea.'

He laughed at this. 'Seriously. You are much better.'

'I know. You cured me.'

'That can't be true –'

'Yes it is. I saw you. I knew what you were doing.'

He was delighted by this and, I suspect, had been waiting for my confirmation that he had taken away my fever. 'But you know what, Tim . . .?' He suddenly became very serious.

'What?'

'I could never have done it without you.' Then he burst out laughing again.

That evening I was sitting in a chair beside the small gas-fire in the caravan, wrapped up in my father's overcoat; it was April now, the circus was about to move on, and I could hear all the sounds of departure around me. That may have been another reason why my father had decided to try his powers: it was his last chance to do so. It was a cool evening and I was huddled inside the coat, experiencing that sensation of relief not unmixed with nostalgia which comes after successfully passing through an illness. 'What caused it, dad?' Already I enjoyed talking about it.

'I don't know. Exhaustion. Stress.' For a moment he looked gravely, almost fearfully, at me; it must have occurred to him, over the days of my sickness, that his revelations about his past and his confession that (as he thought) he had merely been exploiting my powers had in some way so unnerved or depressed me that I had fallen into a fever.

I knew what I had to say. 'I hadn't been feeling well for a long time. I think that's why I left London.' He was clearly relieved by this. 'It turned out to be the right decision, too, didn't it? You were the one who cured me.'

'We can talk about all that later, Tim. Rest now, and you'll soon be your old self again.'

But what was my old self? And what was I supposed to do with it, once I had regained it?

We decided that I should return to my grandparents' house in order fully to recover my strength; my father would be leaving Upper Harford in two days but, since the circus was only moving to the outskirts of Marlborough, he would be able to visit me frequently. In truth I was happy to stay with my grandparents – I wanted to tell them that it was Clement Harcombe who had cured me – and so it was with something like excitement that I waited for my grandfather's arrival. He came the following morning, shook hands with my father and then stood quietly in front of me. 'Shall we get going?' he said. 'We can't have you catching cold.'

'Let him get his medicine first.' My father was laughing and holding out a bottle of Gilbey's Invalid Port.

'Port of good hope,' my grandfather replied. 'Now that he's sailing home.'

I parted cheerfully enough from my father, knowing that I would see him again within two or three days, and followed my grandfather to his car. 'You made a quick recovery,' he said as we drove away from the common where the circus had been held. 'We were very worried.'

'I know,' I said. 'He cured me.'

'You mean –'

'He cured me.' All my doubts about him vanished as I spoke – largely, I suspect, because I wanted to convince my grandfather that Clement Harcombe was more than simply a circus performer. 'He wasn't lying about what he could do, that time you came to see us in Hackney. He was healing people then, just like he has healed me.'

'That may be so, Tim. But don't forget your own powers.'

'My powers?'

'Your powers of recovery. You're tough. You helped yourself, too.'

I stayed silent. I did not want to talk about myself, not yet; I suppose that I did not want to get too close to my 'old self', as my father had put it, at this moment of recovery and renewal. I also felt freer than before, as if I had been carried out of some dark place, and for the first time I wanted to talk about matters which otherwise would have remained concealed. 'What was my father like?' I asked as we drove through Upper Harford.

'Like?'

'What kind of man was he when he married my mother?'

'Clement Harcombe has always been the same.' He might have been talking about a stranger. 'He thinks that he grows and develops, but he doesn't.' He gave me a bright glance, and then he added, 'I've always liked him. There's nothing deliberately harmful or unpleasant about Clement Harcombe. He can be weak sometimes and, as you know, he can talk too much. He likes the sound of his own voice. But essentially he's a kind person.'

I knew then that my grandfather was willing to talk freely

to me about the past; perhaps he had always wanted to do so, and only my reluctance or fear had held him back. 'How did they meet?' I asked him.

'Your mother went to the circus with some friends. I think they met by chance afterwards. In the town somewhere. What do they say? Love at first sight?'

So they had found each other by chance, and yet that accidental encounter had changed the pattern of their lives and had found its issue in me – in this person writing now, staring ahead and retrieving memories I would rather leave behind. Yet how could it have been chance? If that were so, then the whole world and all its generations would be established upon caprice or coincidence. What was it that my father had once said? There is no such thing as chance. Everything proceeds under a guiding hand.

'I don't really know what happened next,' my grandfather told me. 'A week later they left for London. Of course Cecilia came down to see us. She said she couldn't stay away. She was happy with your father, but she liked her old room and her dog. Do you remember the dog, Tim? Then you were born a year later.' And, at my birth, my mother had died. My grandfather looked across at me. 'Don't worry,' he said, smiling, 'she came back in you. And now, look, we're home again.'

My father often visited me at the farmhouse over the succeeding weeks. He no longer seemed so hesitant or uncertain with my grandparents, and I believe that my recovery from illness had something to do with his new self-confidence. They were also more relaxed in his company, and it was as if the suddenness of my cure had reconciled them. A month passed and, although Blackmore's Circus had moved on again, my father found the time to drive to Upper Harford two or three times a week; I can see him still, striding up and down in the parlour, talking about everything and nothing. My grandparents often left us alone together while they walked in the garden, and one afternoon he sat beside me on their green

sofa in front of the bay window. 'I've got my own caravan.'
For some reason he was whispering. 'One of the giants has
retired and sold it to me.'

'What about the mermaid?' I knew that they had been
living together in what she sometimes called her 'grotto'.

'We drifted apart, Tim,' he explained very seriously. I
started laughing, and I could not stop. But all the time I
knew what he was about to ask me. 'Being a giant's caravan,'
he said at last, 'it's big enough for two.' I had expected
something like this ever since my recovery. 'We've always
worked together well, haven't we, Tim?'

'Yes, dad.'

'So why not again? I know it's not what you're used to . . .'
He spoke very slowly, in elaborate recognition of the fact that
any new collaboration between us would be in circumstances
very different from those of Hackney Square or even Albion
Lane. 'I admit,' he went on, 'that it's not the same thing as a
religious experience. It's more of a theatrical experience,
Tim.'

'What's the difference?'

'I'm the last person to ask.' It was his turn to laugh. 'There
must *be* a difference, I suppose, because we used to help
people, didn't we? Or rather it was –'

'Perhaps you help them in the circus, dad. Perhaps you
cure them with your magic wand.' I suddenly had a vision of
my father as a child, watching the clown performing in front
of him, and at that moment I regretted my supercilious tone.
'So what would you want me to do?'

'You could assist me. You could stand beside me.' He smiled
and put his hand upon my shoulder. 'Or perhaps I should be
assisting you. It was you who possessed the power, after all –'

'No. Don't. I don't want to hear anything about that.' I
still did not want to get too close to myself; I was frightened
of this power I was supposed to possess, for to examine it
would be to examine the precise relationship between my
father and myself. It might invite a form of retribution.

'Put it this way, Tim. We could just work together like any other act.' He suddenly became excited again. 'I could teach you the illusions. I could explain all the tricks I learnt when I was young.' He hesitated. 'I never told you this before, Tim . . .'

'What now, dad?'

'My father worked in the circus. Your grandfather. He was a magician, too. But he was a great ventriloquist. The best. Who knows what you might do?' So my grandfather had been a circus performer as well. I was no longer particularly shocked, but the disclosure only served further to complicate my sense of myself. 'You're part of the family now,' my father was saying. 'Not that you ever really left it.' But how far did the line stretch back, and what was my position upon it? What had I inherited from all of these people, from previous fathers and sons? What was the nature of inheritance? Perhaps it was simply the passage of time itself, that 'guiding hand' my father loved to invoke. At this point I was certain only of one thing: as soon as my father had asked me to join his work, I knew that I had no alternative but to accept.

'Well,' I said, feigning reluctance, 'I suppose I was looking for a job.'

'Of course you were. You were looking for this job, because you were looking for me. For all of us. And there's another thing. I've been thinking, Tim —' I knew that phrase of his from before, and it always made me wary. 'Do you think there's a possibility we could include some of the old material?'

'What old material?'

'From the hall. You know, when we cured people?'

'Dad!'

'No. You're right. Pay no attention to me. I was just think-ing aloud.'

And so somehow it had been decided: I would leave my grandparents' house and accompany my father on his travels with the circus around the country. It would be a new life, certainly, but almost like some caricature of our previous one. On reflection I realize that my father and I passed through many varied styles, but at the time they seemed to issue so naturally from one another that I hardly noticed any difference. My grandparents accepted this latest change with equanimity; they were not surprised by my decision and, I believe, they had even expected it. In particular my grandfather had begun to recognize the resemblance between my father and myself; he often saw us together, and he would look from one to the other with the strangest smile.

My father started training me at once, even while I stayed at Upper Harford. He sat in the kitchen with me, holding a deck of playing-cards in one hand while with the other he made circles in the air. 'You've got to force the card,' he explained. 'Force it. Make them take it. Mrs Sinclair, may I borrow you for a moment?' My grandmother came over and sat beside him. 'Take any card,' he said. 'Go on. Any card.' She picked one. 'Now would you be so kind as to burn it for me?' She went over to the gas-stove without a word and dutifully ignited the card. 'Now, Mr Sinclair, will you take that envelope from your breast pocket. Yes, sir. That pocket.' My grandfather complied, smiling at me all the while. 'Would you please open it, sir?' He did so, and there, much to my grandmother's amazement, was the card she had just chosen. 'It's the patter as much as the trick,' my father whispered to me as he bowed low in response to our applause. On another occasion he caused a vase of flowers to appear on the kitchen table and, an hour later, had changed around all the furniture in that room even while the door was locked and he remained with us in the parlour. The kitchen had been transformed into a cave of magic, and I knew that my grandparents appreciated the spectacle as much as I did.

I thoroughly enjoyed all of these preparations and, as I learned to deploy my newly acquired skills, I seemed to be fulfilling some central aspect of myself. Nothing gave me more delight than the arts of illusion, and in performing these tricks

I was more fully alive than I had been since childhood. I describe them as tricks but, on looking back, were they not also a form of true magic? The farmhouse had been transformed, certainly, and my grandparents had themselves become more energetic, more excited, under my father's spells. Was this an illusion, too, or was there some reality comprehended within it? Perhaps there was no real division between the two, between true magic and the conjuror's artifice – which may explain why it became so natural and powerful an activity for me.

The time came to depart. One midsummer morning we left my grandparents on the doorstep, my father and I turning around at the same time to wave back to them as we passed beyond the gate; they waved and smiled in return, but I knew that, for them, something had come to an end. And then we were on our way. The giant's 'caravan' turned out to be a lorry, with living and sleeping areas in the back. My father took one bunk, which folded out to become a table, while I slept upon an ancient couch pushed against the side of the vehicle. But there was room for two; we were comfortable enough and, as my father drove from town to town with the rest of our troupe, I read or practised my tricks in the back. Sometimes I read out loud to him as he drove, and his chosen book was still *Morte d'Arthur*. He often called me 'Merlin,' and would point out various ancient sites as we carried on with our journey.

The roads were quite familiar to him, yet there were occasions even still when I experienced the peculiar sensation that we were really travelling nowhere at all. We drove from one destination to another, often through rain and mist, with the certain knowledge that we would shortly be leaving for another place until finally we arrived once more at our point of origin. And yet there was really no beginning: I was accustomed to think of ours as a linear movement across the country but, of course, all movements become circular in the end. My father believed that there were certain buried lines of force which propelled us forward; for him it was not so much a journey as a quest, a search for the past, which is perhaps the same thing as the search for one's own self. And yet there came a time when even that belief failed to excite me as much as he expected. I was sitting beside him one evening as we drove past Derby, when I suddenly became aware of my place in the dispensation of things. I was moving on to a location which had already been prepared for me; I was fitting my steps to a track which would eventually slope downward, only to rise again for someone who came after. Then would the circle be completed. I looked across at my father, who was softly singing an old song, 'I'm Going to Have to March Away', but I could say nothing. So the lorries and caravans of Blackmore's Circus migrated across the country, finding rest and then moving on again.

The months passed quickly enough, and soon I had grown proficient in my new art; there were even times when I was not sure how we managed to create all the effects of our performances. I had also been accepted by the rest of the troupe, and even the mermaid, who remained quite cool with my father, sometimes allowed me to strap on her golden fins and tail. Her trick was to be lowered into a glass tank of water, in which she seemed to talk, whistle, drink a cup of tea and smoke a cigarette. Of course it was an illusion, although curiously enough she did not like that fact mentioned even among her fellow professionals. 'I never discuss business on dry land,' she would say.

A year later we returned on our predetermined round to Upper Harford and, as soon as we had settled on the familiar site outside the town, I decided to go back to the farmhouse. I was still so delighted by the details of my new life that I wanted to tell everything to my grandparents; I was eager to show them some of the tricks I had mastered, also, and I hurried down the high street in order to catch the bus. I passed the old inn where I had often sat with Edward Campion and, on an impulse I did not try to check, I quickly entered through the dark oak doors I knew so well. He was sitting there, in a corner, bent over a glass; he did not see me at first but, when I stood beside him, he looked up at once. He seemed smaller, no, somehow indefinably changed. 'You've come back,' he said.

'I knew I'd find you here.'

'Did you? Well, you were right. I'm always here.'

I sat down beside him and, wary of the silence already gathering between us, I launched at once into an account of my travels over the past year; I told him about the performances, and the tricks, and the other members of the circus. It was the first time I had been able to discuss these things with an outsider—or 'jossers,' as we called them—and, perhaps under the influence of my own enthusiasm, Edward began to listen intently. Twice he wanted me to explain the feat of levitation and, although I could not divulge the secret of the act, I described the effect which it had upon the circus audience as I rose three or four feet into the air. Then he asked me how easy it was to vanish.

We left an hour later and, when we crossed the threshold into the high street, I realized that I had not asked him anything about his own life over the past year. It was a cool spring evening and, as we walked together, he told me quite suddenly that he had lost his job. 'What happened?'

He turned clumsily and looked back at the place we had just left. 'I like it too much in there,' he said. 'It's home.' I did not want to ask him about his family, to whom he had once been so close, but after a few seconds he stopped. 'I go down here,' he said, pointing to a narrow lane which ran off the high street. 'I've got a room now.' Then he put his hands up to his face and began to weep. I stood beside him as he cried, uncertain how to comfort him. Then he stopped, sniffed, and smiled at me: it was the smile he had had as a child. 'Shall I come tomorrow night?' he asked.

'Come?'

'To the circus. I want to see that vanishing act.'

He left me on the corner, and I watched his swaying,
shambling figure until he opened the door of a tiny house and
went inside.

I had intended to go on to my grandparents, but suddenly
I felt very tired; in any case it was growing late and, as the
dusk gathered, I made my way back to the circus site. My
father was waiting for me as I clambered into the back of
the lorry. 'How did it go?' he asked me eagerly.

'What?'

'Your grandparents. What did your grandparents think?'

'I didn't see them. I met Edward Campion. Do you remember Edward?' He nodded, but he seemed upset by my
failure to visit them; it occurred to me then that he suffered
some residual guilt about removing me from their life. And
was it some echo of the guilt he felt at having once taken their
daughter away from them? 'Don't worry,' I said. 'I'll see
them at the weekend.'

'And don't forget to tell them how well you're doing now.'

'No, dad.'

'This is a proper career, you know. Don't forget to tell
them that.'

As he spoke I was thinking of Edward, and the sorrow
or failure he must have endured when I so eagerly described
my new career to him. I recalled all the hopes he had
once had for his own life, but the true image that remained
now was of him stumbling homewards down a narrow lane.
'Do you really remember Edward?' I asked my father when
he had finished elaborating on the merits of conjuring as a
profession.

'Who?'

'My old schoolfriend, Edward Campion. You met him at
the farmhouse years ago. When we were having tea.'

'Did I?' He stared at me for a moment, and then gradually
became more intrigued. 'He was a cripple, wasn't he? Yes, I
remember him very well.' He seemed so interested now in my
old companion that I described my encounter with him in

some detail. He was smiling and nodding, as if he were already quite familiar with all the aspects of Edward's life; he scarcely seemed to be listening at all. 'You know, Tim,' he said after I had finished talking. 'As soon as I saw him, that day at the farmhouse, I thought that we might be able to help him. Do you know what I mean?'

'No, dad.' I knew precisely what he meant.

'Yes, you do. Of course you do.'

'I'm not sure . . .'

'We've done it before, Tim. Why shouldn't we help your friend? And we *can* help him, now that we're together again.'

So confident was he once more, after my restoration from illness and our own successful performances in the circus ring, that he was willing to try out the powers which we had deployed together in the old hall. But to cure Edward? I had never even considered such a possibility; he had been so close to me that it seemed almost an act of violence to change the person whom I knew so well. At once I felt anxious – anxious not only about Edward but also about myself, for had not my father said that it was really my power which was involved? Was that still his opinion, or had he come round to the belief that it was our combined presence which created the appropriate conditions? That the power belonged to neither of us separately, but resided in the very fact of inheritance itself? It seemed such an abstract category, inheritance, and yet it glowed with all the power of the world.

'And there's another thing, Tim. I've been thinking. If we did manage to help him, could we change the routine a little bit? It would be a shame to waste –'

'Dad!' So that was his purpose: to use Edward as a preliminary test before the full restoration of our old act. To try out our powers and see if they still remained. For a moment I was horrified by this calculation on my father's part. But, if we did heal Edward, it would have served a proper purpose. And why should we not then heal others? I said nothing further – which meant, I suppose, that I had acquiesced.

Edward visited the circus that following evening; I had been waiting by the entrance and, when I saw him, I ran to greet him. 'Will you come and see me afterwards? My father has something to tell you.'

He seemed disturbed, although he tried to conceal it. 'How will I find you?' was all he said.

'I'll be dressed like a magician. I'll be wearing a pair of green trousers, with a jacket of stitched blue and red sequins in the shape of eyes.' He laughed at this. 'It's true! But don't worry. I'll find you. If you get lost, just ask for Harcombe and Son.'

The routine that night was more than usually tiring, and by the time we had finished I was feeling blank and worn; there were occasions like this when the whole prolonged performance seemed to erase my personality, so that I scarcely knew who I was or what I was doing. My father remained oddly alert and excited, however, as if the idea of assisting or even curing Edward had keyed him up to a pitch higher than usual. Yet I noticed the strain and fatigue upon his face, and I was about to urge him to rest when I realized that any such advice would simply renew his determination. I left him, and found Edward waiting for me on the grass in front of the circus tent. He still had no notion of our plans, and I took his arm to guide him towards our lorry. My father greeted him warmly, almost munificently – an effect which was heightened by the fact that he was still wearing his circus costume of scarlet sequins and green trousers. I was wearing mine, too, and it was with horror I realized that neither of us had removed our stage make-up. Edward did not seem to notice any of this, but seemed ill at ease under my father's benevolent scrutiny. 'You know,' he said, removing his top-hat (from which that evening several kinds of bird had flown), 'you shake more when you're feeling a little bit anxious, don't you?'

He said this in such an affable, almost cheerful, manner that Edward readily agreed. 'It's been like that all my life.'

'All your life? Is that right?'

'Yes. I've always been a cripple.'

My father glanced at me briefly but his attention was upon Edward. 'Now tell me,' he said, 'have you ever dreamed that you could walk normally?'

'Oh yes. Of course I have. Show me a cripple, and I'll tell you what he dreams about.'

'That's right. That's good. And tell me this, Edward, have you ever thought that you might enter that dream whenever you wished?'

'That would be ridiculous.' He started to become angry with my father, as if he suspected that he was merely being whimsical at his expense. It was clear, also, that he did not want to be reminded of this dream – not, at least, in his waking moments.

'I'm serious, Edward Campion. Have you considered it?'

There was something in my father's voice which commanded his attention. 'I don't like to think about it.'

My father hardly seemed to notice his answer, but instead he beckoned me over and put an arm around my shoulder. 'Dreams are very particular things, Edward. They can be more real than anything in the ordinary world. They can even determine what happens in this world. Have you ever considered that?' Edward simply looked at him. 'And do you know why? Because a dream brings out the secret life of the world. It can reflect all the things we have forgotten we knew. It can bring out the spirit of a place or a person, like music which no one has previously been able to hear. Do you understand that, Edward Campion?' My friend nodded, while my father kept a tight grip upon my shoulder. 'And do you understand that we can help you, after all?'

Edward now seemed frightened and was about to turn away, when my father stepped forward and grabbed him; he took his head and pressed against his temples with the palms of his hands. 'Welcome to the Chemical Theatre,' he said, 'where all the spirits of your past can be removed.' I put my hand up to my mouth, overwhelmed by the gust of childhood memories, and turned my head away for a moment. Edward was trembling violently, in some kind of fit. I rushed over to help him, but my father roughly brushed me away. 'Go behind him,' he shouted. 'Go behind him and catch him when he falls!'

As I did so Edward let out a great scream, arched backwards, and then seemed to lapse into unconsciousness. My father, still with his hands on Edward's temples, very lightly pushed him against me as he fell into my arms. He was very hot and, as soon as I held him, I could feel some fearful shaking rise up within me. It was as if I were being buffeted and pummelled in all directions, the ground beneath me began to tremble, and my eyes rolled back into my head. I could not stand still; even my fingers began to quiver violently against Edward's side as I still held him, and I think that at some point I also screamed. A noise filled the air, at least, and when I looked up to see from where it had come I noticed Edward standing a little way apart from me. He was very still, his arms stiffly against his sides. I slumped on to the floor and simply watched him.

'It's gone,' he said at last. Slowly he put one foot forward, and then another; he was not trembling at all, and all signs of his disability had vanished. He started walking quickly around in circles, in his excitement picking up objects and then putting them down again. 'It's gone,' he repeated. And then, smiling wildly at me, he jumped from the lorry and began running very quickly around the open field.

Then something happened behind me. I heard a sound very much like a sigh, and when I turned around I saw my father leaning against the side of his bunk; his stage make-up had melted and was now running down his face. Then he slumped, and began to fall sideways. He was falling silently and slowly against the small bookcase, and I distinctly remember how, when he crashed against it, he dislodged the copy of Malory from which we had been reading. And he was still falling: I went towards him, arms outstretched, and he seemed about to put out his arms to me in reply. But he could not do so. He fell heavily upon the floor, his eyes still upon me.

EIGHTEEN

<hr>

I<small>T BEFELL IN THOSE DAYS</small> that the Maimed King was dying, when right so came by him Merlin who saluted the king and asked him why he was so pensive. 'I may well be pensive,' said the king, 'since I grow heavy for the earth and have many thoughts for this country I am leaving.'

'That know I well,' said Merlin, 'as well as yourself, and all your thoughts. But you are a fool to take account, for it will not amend you. Also I know what you are, and who was your father, and on whom you were begotten. Your fate is greater than yourself, and truly if you die for your son you shall get great praise and soul health, and worship to your lineage.'

Then Merlin left him, he knew not whither he had departed; then on the morn his son came to him, and the Maimed King was passing glad of his coming, so that he left his bed and knelt before him. 'Alas my own dear father, why kneel you to me? You are my sire.'

'No, no, my lord. It is not so. I am your father and of your blood, but as soon as ever you will be the king of this place.'

'Fair sweet father, I will always yield me to your will. But, I pray you, be not so saddened.'

'No, in truth I am not so sad. I will discover my heart to you, for you know well that I shall soon pass out of this world.'

'No –'

'Yes. It is so, for such pain I have endured that no man else might have suffered long. But now I trust the term is come, and my pain shall be allayed as was promised to me.' And then the Maimed King told his son all that would come to pass, just as Merlin had told him. 'For as the fruit may fall from the bough,' he said, 'yet the tree will be flourishing inwardly. So when I am put in the earth, you will rise into my estate.' Many other matters were spoken between them, and they both wept and both were passing glad. Yet before he was done, the Maimed King on a sudden sighed aloud and said to his son: 'My end draws nigh and it is time that I were gone. Make broad your shoulders to receive my weight and bear me to the margin.'

So, as it was foretold in ancient times, the son bore the father down to the water's side. And it was known as the water of Albion, from which all things on this island have come. 'Well, my son,' the king said, 'unto this have you brought me, nigh to my end. Lift up my head so that I may see the broad span of the oak near the bank yonder, for I shall it never see again.' And as the Maimed King gazed upon the ancient oak, fast by the bank hoved a barge with many folk in it, and the son saw that they had black hoods. And all they wept and shrieked when they saw the king. 'Now put me in the barge,' he said. 'And let me float into the everlasting. My time passes on fast, and I am come to my end.' So he was laid within it and his body was covered with black silk. At this time a wind arose and drove the barge far from the land, and his son beheld it till it was out of his sight. Forthwith there fell a tempest suddenly of thunder and lightning, as all the earth would have broken. The world seemed to have turned up-so-down, for the son who so lamented his father.

Then following upon these things there was such wretchedness and darkness in the land that in truth fathers knew not their sons, and the sons knew not their fathers: for it is said that on the death of a great king the son shall not love the father and the father shall not love the son, but every man shall bear his own burden. And so there befell a great pestilence, and great harm to the realm; there increased neither corn, nor grass, nor fruit, nor in the water was found no fish and in the air was heard no music. Therefore men call it the Waste Land, because of that dolorous stroke.

And the son wandered in the midst of his own darkness.

'Alas,' he cried. 'Alas that ever this misadventure befell me! Here I am in great duress and never like to escape out of this wilderness. The words of Merlin were but empty words, for the line is broken with my father's death and I have not the power, no, nor the strength, to take his place: all my hope is in vain, for the prophecies of Merlin shall never be achieved!' And so he went on, in doleful case, but a little way forward from this he came upon a tree which brought back into his memory the tree upon which his father had looked his last. Forthwith he gazed upon this tree and there suddenly he saw a passing great bird. And the old tree was wholly dry, without leaf; so the bird sat above and had younger birds around it which were dying for hunger. Yet at last he smote himself with his beak which was long and sharp, and the great bird bled so fast that he died among the boughs. And the young birds took life by the blood of the great bird.

The son pondered upon this a little, until he was disturbed by the sound of a voice behind him: 'So must it be.' He turned and beseemed a reverend old man, and he had a crown of gold upon his head, and his shoulders were naked and uncovered unto his navel. Then it was that the son espied that his body was full of great wounds, all on the shoulders, arms and visage. 'So must it be,' the old man said again. 'The old wounds heal not but give sustenance. Drink of their blood, and live.' At these words he faded. The son was sore astounded at this marvel, and fell into a swoon. Thus he lay until it was broad day but, when he heard the young fowls sing upon the tree, then somewhat was he comforted.

Thereupon he departed from this place. Then, as it fell by fortune and adventure, he came to a mountain where he found a chapel passing old and built in the great times of Albion; he found therein nobody for all was desolate. He regarded the darkness and the darkness regarded him not, but he came into a little room to the side of the chapel and there again saw the worm-eaten and feeble tree upon which the great bird had died. Then he said, 'This is a marvellous thing and an adventure, to look upon this sight!' To the left side of this tree he espied a chair set and, when he approached to it, he saw carved in dark letters upon it: NO MAN CAN SIT HERE BUT HE SHOULD LOSE HIMSELF. So he was in great thought, until he said to his own self: 'It belongeth not to me to understand all that I have seen this day, but nevertheless I must meet my destiny in patience and humility.' So he sat him down in the chair next to the withered tree: he sat down, and was heavy in thoughts of his dead father, and therewithall he fell asleep. And anon as he was in sleep, it befell him there a vision that Merlin came to him and spoke.

'Do you know whom you seekest?'

'No.'

'Well I know whom you seekest, for you seekest Merlin. Therefore seek no further, for I am he. Wherever you journey, I will not be far behind.'

'What are you?'

'I was sometime an earthly man and now I am of a strange country. But hither I come to lead you.'

'Sir, what signifieth these words that I have found? "No man can sit here but he should lose himself"?'

'Marvel not, for I understand them better than you or any man living.' So the son listened as Merlin told him the history of this island, and of his own place within it; how it began and in like wise how it might end; how its truth was written down, passing from hand to hand as it does from parent to child. Which brought him then unto this further question: 'Ah, fair boy, when heard you tidings of your mother?'

'Truly I heard none of her, but I dream of her much in my sleep, and therefore I know not whether she be dead or alive.'

'Certain, your mother is dead, for after she gave birth to you she took such agony that even as she was confessed she died.' At this the son was about to break his breast in a grief when Merlin spoke again. 'But I bring you word that she lives within you, as your own father does likewise. Now it is beholden unto you to go on a great journey, to find the writing that will save you and your line. The best men in the world will go along with you. I shall disclose them in time, and you shall see them, and only thus can the Waste Land be once again redeemed. Find the words, and all shall be well. For just as this tree can be forewithered before flourishing anew, so can your lineage. Look upon this.' And in his vision, the son saw how out of each bough came many flowers and therewithall fruit great plenty. Then as the tree flourished he found himself beside it, where his father once had stood, and the water of Albion was once again before him. Merlin held out to him a book marvellously wrought. 'This is the very emblem of your heritage,' said he. 'Take this book, and throw it into the water as far as you might.' He did as he was enjoined, and there came an arm and a hand above the water of Albion, and took it and clutched it, and shook it in the air and brandished it, and then vanished with the book into the water. 'Meseemeth your quest is now almost begun,' Merlin said to him, 'and in the passing of the book you may see the passing of your inheritance from generation unto generation. Your father may not come to you yet, but he will return when you have penetrated this mystery.'

'Sir, what mystery must it be?'

'The mystery of time, and how to journey from time into eternity.' Indeed as Merlin devised, so in the end was it done. 'Seek me when you will,' the magician said after this, 'and you shall find me. But now depart from this place, till the adventure brings you to a fair dwelling upon a plain.'

When he had said this he vanished away and the son knew not what had become of him. Yet he awoke now from his enchantment, and was much comforted. 'I will embark upon this journey mentioned in my dream,' he said, 'and, as it is written in this place, I will lose myself only to find myself and my lineage again.' So it was that the quest began in his heart.

Now turneth the tale unto his adventure: on the first day he came into a meadow filled with herbs and flowers. 'I have seen such things inscribed in blue and gold,' said he. 'For this is known as the old language of truth. I may rest here at my ease and refresh myself.' On the second day he came into a perilous forest, where he espied a well which boiled with its water. As soon as he spoke into this well, his echo seemed therewithall to make it clear so that it burnt no more and anon the heat departed away into the upper air. 'Thus may I silence troublesome voices,' he said, 'by speaking my own words until I hear their true echo.' On the third day he came to a fair tower and, when he entered into it, he saw before him a tomb of marble on which were moulded his own features. But he was not wroth at this for, as he said, 'This is an image of hereafter, when I am laid into the bosom of Time. And surely it must give me greater strength to go on with my quest, if there be a marvellous tomb to hold my corse.' Then on the fourth day he came into a deep valley and, when he saw that he might not ride up its steep sides, he there stopped under an apple tree. Then he laid him down to sleep, saying, 'I hear the waters of the crystal stream, and the flutes of the shepherds who roam with their flocks through the barren places. All these great marvels and adventures have been foretold in the old tales, so I am also at peace here.'

On the fifth day he came to a fair dwelling upon a plain, at which he stopped and wondered. 'For this is how it was foretold by Merlin in my dream, that I should come to this place at the end of my journey.' Then he came up to the gate which opened before him; and anon he came into a great hall, where befell a marvellous adventure: that the doors and windows of the hall shut by themselves, and all was greatly darkened. Yet he could hear murmurings and voices all around him, for there in the shadow were figures of which the countenances could not be seen. Then there came to him a voice, which was like unto the voice of Merlin as well as the voice of his own dead father. And it spoke thus: 'When you depart from hence I am sure you all shall never meet more together in this world, for you each shall be devoted to your own quest. But, before you shall depart from me out of this world, behold now you are in a round to signify the roundness of time. Yet which of you shall see eternity?'

Anon he heard a cracking and crying of thunder, and in the midst of the blast entered a sunbeam more clear by seven times than ever he saw day; he began to behold the others around, standing together to form a complete circle, and he looked upon every one of them as if he had been dumb. Then they began to speak, and he marvelled at their words. 'Go we to seek that we shall not find,' saith one. And then another spoke out thus, 'Look you that in our quest our hearts and mouths accord, for then we may ensure that we have the more worship.' There was a table before them upon which lay the wondrous volume which heretofore had sunk beneath the water of Albion, and on a sudden Merlin came beside him and led him forward. 'Lo, this is the old custom and usage of this land,' said he, 'and men say that we of England will not lose that custom. For in this book lies our inheritance.'

'What is this book before me?' he asked.

'You will know of it in good time.'

He heard music coming upon him, as from a distance beyond distance. Not harp, nor horn, nor aught we blow with breath or touch with hand, was like that music as it came. English music. And now the others stood plainly before him, but what tongue might tell their names? There were poets here, and story-tellers, and those who wrote all manner of English prose. Merlin was once more beside him, and spoke to him thus: 'Some men say in many parts of England that these are not dead, but have gone into another place, and some men say that they shall come again. Yet I will not say that it shall be so, but rather would I say: here in this world they gave their lives so that their vision might be seen, and all the land be healed. Their words will remain for ever.'

And then he fell on slumbering again, nor sleeping nor thoroughly waking, when it seemed that there came his father to him. So when he saw him he said, 'Welcome, I thought you had been dead. And now I see you in life!'

The father beckoned him to follow him. So he followed, and he found no gate nor door, but the hall was open. And at the last he found a chamber whereof the door was shut, and he beset his hand thereto to open it, but he might not. Then he listened and heard a voice which sang so sweetly that it seemed no earthly thing, for it was cast to the same music he had heard before. And these were the sounds that he heard:

> He may not wander from the allotted field
> Before his work be done; but, being done,
> In moments when he feels he then must die,
> This vision still remains: England's music
> In sweet notes interlinked from age to age.

And with that the chamber door opened and there came out a great clearness, so that the room was as bright as if all the torches of the world had been there. Right so entered he into the chamber and came towards a table of silver, and when he came near to it he saw a great marvel: for the body of his father was lying upon it. He was stark dead but with many flowers and flourishing boughs around his corse; and he lay as he had smiled, and there was the sweetest savour about him that Timothy ever he felt. 'That was my father which lieth here in this chamber,' he said. 'Far from hence will I never go, by my will.' Yet as he looked upon the face of his father he saw it changing in wondrous wise, and taking on the lineaments of other faces which he knew. For he thought he saw his grandparents thereupon, and other yet more ancient faces. 'So does my lineage stretch back to the beginning,' he said. 'And on my own face I have the pattern of the old times.' Whereupon he felt a breath that he thought it was entrammelled with fire, which smote him so sore in the visage that it might have burnt upon him. And therewithall he fell to earth and had no strength to arise, as he that had lost the power of his body and his hearing and his sight. Then he saw his father rising up before him, and he felt that his father's hands took him up and bore him out of the chamber door.

Then he heard his voice once more: 'In you I will come again to my kingdom, and dwell with the Britons with much joy. The old order changes, yielding place to the new, but I am eternal for I am Albion.'

NINETEEN

Y FATHER WAS DEAD. HE had suffered a sudden cere-
bral haemorrhage, according to the doctors, just after
Edward's cure. That is one explanation. But, on looking back
at the events of that evening, it seems clear to me that he
expended too much power; he had ignited a flame which
could only destroy him. Perhaps it was necessary for my
father to die in order that Edward might be healed: but of
this I am not so certain. The funeral was held in Upper
Harford a few days later, after the coroner's inquest and the
usual local inquiries. My grandparents sat on either side of
me in the front pew of the church, while behind us the circus
artistes solemnly followed the funeral service – the mermaid
was there, and the female midgets, and the strong man. Even
the giant came out of retirement and, as we left after the
service, my father's coffin was carried by the six members of
the flying-trapeze act.

It was then that I saw Gloria Patterson; she was sitting at
the back of the church, looking very fiercely at a carved
cornice as my grandparents and I walked past. I glanced
again and then, to my surprise, saw Stanley Clay sitting
beside her. He put one hand in the air and smiled rather
sheepishly at me. They followed the procession into the cemetery, and we all stood awkwardly together as my father's
body was laid in the earth.

'I'm glad you came,' I whispered to her.

'I have a right to, haven't I?' It was her old self, flaring up,
but now she bit her lip as she stared down at the open grave.
'He wasn't all bad,' she said. 'Not as bad as I made him out.'

Stanley had taken her arm; he seemed more confident than
I had ever seen him before. 'You wanted to apologize to Tim,
didn't you, Gloria?'

She gave me another fierce look for a moment, but at once it was subdued. 'Yes,' she said. 'Some of the things I said . . .'

She broke off, as my father's coffin was covered with soil. The giant had turned away, but I watched everything: I wanted to be able to recall every detail, since only then would I be at peace. The headstone had the inscription, CLEMENT HARCOMBE, 1889–1936, and as I gazed upon it I remembered the time he had cried beside my mother's grave.

Everyone came back to the farmhouse – everyone, that is, except for Gloria and Stanley. They were uneasy with my father's friends and, I suspect, also with me. But I was pleased to have seen them: they appeared to have found some kind of life with each other, which was more than either of them could have expected. 'Gloria was very lonely all that time,' Stanley told me in a low voice as I accompanied him out of the churchyard. 'She told lies because she didn't know how to talk to people. I couldn't bear it no longer, so I went round to see her. That's when she explained it all.'

I looked back at Gloria, who was walking with my grand-parents. 'It's the best thing that could have happened, Stanley. I'm delighted for you. For both of you.'

'She always had a soft spot for you, Tim.'

'Oh, did I?' She had come up to us suddenly, as arch as ever, but then she kissed me on the cheek. 'Goodbye, Tim,' she said. 'We wish you luck with the rest of your life.' And they were gone.

It is not usual for circus people to get drunk (their work is too painstaking and relentless for that), but the giant, in his retirement, felt able to take what he called 'the long view, from the bottom of a glass'. Eventually he had to be helped back to the circus site by the strong man and two jugglers, but not before he had paid a tribute to my father. 'Now you've got to carry on the tradition,' he said, turning awk-wardly towards me. 'Didn't our parents and grandparents teach us the patter? Didn't they take us through every move-ment and gesture? Didn't the jugglers teach their children?

Of course they did. So we have to carry on – all of us.' At this point he lurched forward and upset a sideboard of fruit and cake which my grandmother had carefully laid.

'Don't worry,' she said, rushing forward. 'He means well.'

It was at this point I realized that Edward had not attended the service.

I stayed with the circus and, as the giant had insisted, I took on my father's act; it really never occurred to me to do otherwise. I continued his work, not out of homage or gratitude, but out of instinct. Yet over the months, and years, it did become my act. I had my own special costume: a black three-piece suit, with bowler and red bow-tie; I wore white make-up and there was always a large false flower in my buttonhole. My blank white face made me seem mournful and was of great assistance to me in my illusions: the audience, which sat on row upon row of wooden benches behind the ring fence, were so curious about my demeanour that I was, by sleight of hand, able to pull off more spectacular surprises. I could make a rope rise fifteen feet and then climb it; I could vanish from the centre of the ring and then be discovered among the people watching me; I could make any number of objects appear and disappear at will. I particularly enjoyed ventriloquism. I soon discovered that I had an ability to 'throw' my voice in any direction I pleased, and I so refined that skill during my performances that it became an integral part of the act: I would sit quietly in the middle of the ring, and my voice would come from the region of the high wire, or from a certain row in the audience, or even from a particular person. Sometimes there were many voices, and the ring would come alive with sounds and echoes. This always amazed the audience, who were as bewildered as if they had heard various spirits haunting the circus. But my speciality lay in 'thought-reading'; my eyes would be bandaged by one of the ring boys (I could never bring myself to employ an assistant), and then I would be able to name the card which someone had chosen at random from a pack or read a message which had been scrawled on a piece of paper and then sealed in an envelope. It was one of the first tricks I ever performed on my own and, as it turned out, it was also to be my final one.

It was a stormy autumn evening, I remember, when I went into the ring for the last time. I had already recognized with some alarm that over the previous few weeks I had been losing some of my confidence or energy – it was hard to say which – but for some reason I entered that evening in a heightened state of expectancy. I went through my usual repertoire, my effects given additional power by the sound of the wind roaring around the canvas, until the time came for my reading of thoughts. I went to the ring fence, nonchalantly jumped over it, and started wandering in front of the first rows of the audience. My attention was drawn almost at once to a young woman who sat two rows back: she had dark hair, and there was something about her attitude, as well as the serious expression upon her face, which was indefinably familiar to me. So I decided to employ her: I asked her to write a phrase or saying on some paper, while I kept my back turned, and then I asked her to place the paper in an envelope before sealing it. She then passed this to another member of the audience while the ring boy put the bandage over my eyes. The envelope was then handed to me. I will not dwell upon the details of this particular trick – it has to do with the switching of envelopes – but on this occasion I knew as soon as it was given to me that something was wrong. Something was different. I had an extraordinary feeling of loss or emptiness, and I sensed at once what was written there. I said the words out loud, as I always did, but this time without any subterfuge: '*Go home now. They are dead.*' There was a silence in the audience and I tore off my bandage; but the young woman who had written those words had gone. I could not carry on with the act. All the power seemed to have left me and I ran from the ring in bewilderment.

I realized what these words signified. My grandparents had

died. I did not need to consider anything: I simply knew it, and immediately I set off for Upper Harford. I travelled through the night in a hired taxi, but the doctor was already there when I arrived. A neighbour had just found them, lying together in the kitchen; my grandfather had suffered some kind of stroke, as it turned out, and my grandmother had died soon after. At the time I simply noticed how peaceful they seemed, as peaceful together as they had been in life. I fed the dog, who had remained with them throughout the night, and then I went up to my mother's room. It was exactly as it always was: the old-fashioned gramophone was beside the bed, and I put on some music; as I listened to it, and looked out at the unchanging landscape, I knew that they were all together at last. My grandparents, with my mother and father, and others besides.

A few days later, after their funeral, I was working in the garden when I noticed someone coming up the white lane towards me; it was Edward Campion, but he was walking so freely and so easily that for a moment I did not recognize him. 'I thought I might find you,' he said. 'I heard. I'm sorry.'

I was so pleased to see him permanently healed that I clapped him on the back. 'But you are well,' I said.

'Yes. I'm well. I don't really know what happened that day –'

'My father had been very ill, Edward.' I lied, in order to protect him from any fear that he had somehow been responsible for his death.

He looked at me for a moment, and then kicked his shoes in the dust. 'They left you everything?' I nodded. 'Now that's what I call an inheritance.'

We both laughed at this. 'Come on,' I said. 'I'll show you around my new estate.'

And so we walked together, the dog running ahead of us, across the lawn towards the pine forest on the other side of the muddy track. 'Do you think you'll stay here for long?' he asked me.

I told him that I was settled in the farmhouse but, as it turned out, I was wrong. My grandparents had died in the autumn of 1938, and in the following year all prospects of peace and safety disappeared. I was called up, and did not come back to Upper Harford for another seven years. By the time I returned Edward had married, and soon I looked upon his children as part of my own family. I had no other now. I told them all about my mother and father, and about the circus, but to them it seemed from so distant a time that there were occasions when I preferred to say nothing and keep my memories to myself.

I am an old man now, and I live alone in the farmhouse. I no longer read the books which my father left me, but I keep them in the room which once belonged to my mother. They are always present in my mind, just as my friends are still present: I feel as if I have only to turn my head to see Margaret Collins or Stanley Clay again. Or my parents. But, for the moment, I am happy to stare out through the window at the familiar landscape. What was it Edward Campion told me once – that in the prospect of the unchanging hills and streams there is some inkling of eternity? Yet I feel the same about the old buildings and streets of Hackney; if I stared at them long enough, no doubt I would see eternity there. I might even see myself as a child again, rushing from our lodgings to the pie-and-mash shop with a silver sixpence in my hand. And then, excited and happy, hurrying back to my father through the gas-lit streets . . .

Yes, I have inherited the past because I have acknowledged it at last. It belongs with my father, and with his books, but it also belongs with me. And, now that I have come to understand it, I no longer need to look back. Edward was wrong when he described the recurring cycles of history: they disappear as soon as you recognize them for what they are. Perhaps that is why I have written all this down, in a final act of recognition. I do not know what is left for me now, but I feel able to rise to my feet in expectation and walk steadily forward without any burden.

I was sitting by my window the other morning, having turned off the television news. I was looking out at the sunflowers which were growing up once more against the old stone wall, when I noticed Edward's granddaughter kneeling down by the side of the lawn; she had come into the garden without my seeing her, and she appeared to be reciting some kind of prayer or poem. I was curious enough to leave the house and walk over to her. 'Cecilia,' I said, 'what are you doing?'

She turned around, and she was in tears. 'Can't you see?'

She had dug a small hole in the earth and had placed inside it a small dead bird. 'No need to cry,' I said. 'It's safe now. Its soul has flown away.' I knelt down beside her with some difficulty, and helped her to scoop out some more soil. Then we covered the body and smoothed down the earth with the palms of our hands.

'I've already said a prayer for it,' she told me. 'But you can, too, if you like.'

So we knelt together as I prayed for the spirit of the dead bird. I don't know why I tell you such a simple story, in conclusion, but perhaps that is what I do best now – simple things, like this burial. And then another bird flew down from a tree in front of us, perched upon the gate and, after a short time, filled the white lane with its song. So you see, as I explained to you before, I no longer need to open the old books. I have heard the music.

A NOTE ON THE TYPE

This book was set in a typeface called Baskerville, a modern recutting of a type originally designed by John Baskerville (1706–1775). Baskerville, a writing master in Birmingham, England, began experimenting in about 1750 with type design and punch cutting. His first book, published in 1757 and set throughout in his new types, was a Virgil in royal quarto. It was followed by other famous editions from his press. Baskerville's types, which are distinctive and elegant in design, were a forerunner of what we know today as the "modern" group of typefaces.

Composed in Great Britain
Printed and bound by Arcata Graphics,
Martinsburg, West Virginia